DARK HORSE

DARK HORSE

DARK HORSE

Marilyn Todd

Severn House Large Print
London & New York

This first large print edition published in Great Britain 2005 by
SEVERN HOUSE LARGE PRINT BOOKS LTD of
9-15 High Street, Sutton, Surrey, SM1 1DF.
First world regular print edition published 2002 by
Severn House Publishers, London and New York.
This first large print edition published in the USA 2006 by
SEVERN HOUSE PUBLISHERS INC., of
595 Madison Avenue, New York, NY 10022.

British Library Cataloguing in Publication Data

Todd, Marilyn
    Dark horse - Large print ed.
    1.   Claudia Seferius (Fictitious character) - Fiction
    2.   Rome - History - Empire, 30 B.C. – 284 A.D. - Fiction
    3.   Detective and mystery stories
    4.   Large type books
    I.   Title
    823.9'14 [F]

    ISBN-10:   0-7278-7450-0

Printed and bound in Great Britain by
MPG Books Ltd, Bodmin, Cornwall.

To Teresa Chris, agent extraordinaire

One

Rome was hot.

So hot, that one flimsy shift was one too many.

So hot, that if the Tiber began to steam, no one would blink.

Biting flies moved in, little black things with long proboscises and big brown brutes with even longer ones. The overwhelming stench of sewage was everywhere. There were no festivals to compensate for the sweltering heat. No Games, no processions, no theatres, no nothing.

But for Claudia Seferius, the Tiber could boil and it would be cool compared to her current predicament. Bastards! Thought they could drive her out of business, did they? Over her dead body! The vegetable market was packing up as she cut a diagonal path across the cobbles. No shade in the market place at this time of day. Shadows would not fall from the Palatine Hill for another four hours and those cast by the Capitol had already passed over.

'Nice sprig of fragrant mint, lady,' an enterprising trader offered, 'to counteract the river pong?'

Sweat poured down his face to drip off his chin but not, Juno be praised, on to his herbs.

'How kind,' she said, sweeping the bouquet out of his hand as she passed.

Ordinarily, Claudia would have had her litter take her to the Field of Mars, but for the job she had to do today, the less attention drawn to her presence the better. Slip in, slip out, don't get noticed. Impossible in a litter draped in turquoise and silver, shouldered by eight hunks in matching tunics!

Skirting mushy cucumbers and mouldy marrows, limp lettuce leaves and slimy beans, she made her way to the river. No chance of getting noticed down here. The wharves were busier than a wasps' nest being smoked out. Barrels and amphorae rumbled over the flagstones, sacks were tossed down from the gangplanks. Lions in crates, camels in ropes, great blocks of marble were swung on to the dock; ungreased pulleys whined out their protest. Stevedores shouted up to workers in the towering warehouses in an air thick with everything from spices to hemp, cedar to salt fish. The mint came in jolly handy down by the bridge. A dead dog had got stuck under one of the piers, where its bloated corpse was happily being prodded by a group of boys with a stick.

From the tumult of the quayside, Claudia merged with the crowd heading for the Field of Mars. Official festivities might be thin on the ground, but Rome's entrepreneurial spark was alive and well in the form of privately organized horse races on the flat belt of grassland in the bend of the Tiber. Nothing like the chariot races in the Circus Maximus, of course, but they were no less serious a business. Already rival supporters, their legs and faces painted in their team colours, were goading each other. Fists were only an insult away.

In the officials' enclosure, vets inspected hooves and ears as grooms plaited the horses' manes and tails and wove in the team ribbons, and flustered clerks shored up last-minute changes to the programme. Who, among the jockeys flexing their joints and pulling on rawhide gloves and the harness-men adjusting the reins, paid attention to a young woman in a simple pale-grey linen gown? Claudia slipped through to where the horses for the third race were tethered. Easy to pretend you're studying the thoroughbreds as you feed one a handful of grain...

'Now there's a sight I never thought I'd see,' a rich baritone murmured in her ear. 'Claudia Seferius looking a gift horse in the mouth.'

Above the acid tang of the dung, she smelt sandalwood overlaid with a faint hint of the rosemary in which his long patrician tunic had been rinsed. A.k.a. the scent of the hunter.

'Beats looking at the other end,' she said airily. 'Still, as I've always said, Orbilio, one good nag deserves another. Here you go.'

She stuffed the little blue cotton sack of grain into his hands and turned on her heel.

9

'Don't leave on my account.' His tone was mild. Particularly for someone who'd stepped in front of her and blocked her exit. 'The second race is barely under starter's orders. Or are you telling me you've given up gambling in favour of opening a stud farm?'

'Tut, tut, Orbilio. I would have thought that the Security Police know gambling's illegal.'

His gaze skimmed the betting tables, where coins and bronze vouchers were changing hands like the cards in find the lady. 'Obviously, were I to see evidence of such nefarious activities, I would be duty bound to report it,' he said, and was it the sunshine or was there a twinkle in his eye? 'Oh, look, they're leading the horses out for the third race.'

'*So soon?*' Bugger.

'A group of supporters rushed on to the track during the second race, so the steward's had to abandon it. Why don't we see if this one is as exciting?'

There was no arguing with the hand which had slipped under her elbow and was steering her firmly towards the course, a euphemism for the rather rough and ready arrangement of two wooden posts driven into the grass six hundred paces apart. A dozen four-year-old mares were already jostling against the starting rope, fresh, skittish, eager to run.

'No cheating, no holding back,' the course steward announced through his speaking trumpet. 'Any hint of match fixing results in instant disqualification. Anyone who runs on to the track this time or throws missiles to put

10

the horses off gets an automatic one-hund-red-sesterces fine.'

'Booo!' the crowd yelled, although Claudia noticed that several stones plopped surreptitiously to the ground.

'White Star to win,' Orbilio said, folding his arms confidently across his chest.

'Didn't I hear someone say she was the favourite?'

'Your bookie, probably.'

Damn right. Owned by Hylas the Greek, White Star would knock spots off the rest. These weren't the top runners you saw in the Circus Maximus, but horses for courses, as they say. Today's entrants were trained especially to compete on rough grass rather than a smooth running track, and when it came to breeding winners for these provincial derbies, Hylas the Greek was second to none.

'What's a bookie?' she asked.

Up went the rope. Up went the cheers. Up went a cloud of divots and dust.

'Come on, White Star!' cried the crowd.

'Come on, White Star!' cried Marcus Cornelius.

Claudia yawned and pretended to study her nails. Come on, come on, you stupid nag. From under lowered lashes, she followed White Star as the mare thundered up the track, turning at the post neck and neck with her rival, Calypso. Back they thundered, then another tight turn and back up. Faster, you clot, she urged the jockey, what do you think spurs are for? The rest of the field started to

11

trail. Five times they'd turned now. Still Calypso and White Star kept pace. Six laps. Seven ... Her knuckles clenched white. Only the final length left.

'Calypso!' the race judge called. 'Calypso by a head!'

Across the enclosure, she noticed Hylas's thickly greased curls jerk up fast. He muttered something to one of his flunkies. The flunky's eyes scanned the crowd. A finger pointed. To a woman in a pale-grey linen gown.

'Well, this has been absolutely fascinating,' she said, as Hylas beckoned over a couple of heavies. 'But I really must be off now, Marcus. Things to do, you know, places to go—'

'People to annoy?' Beside her, the tall, dark patrician with the wavy hair grinned. 'And to think you haven't even asked me what I'm working on.'

'The usual Security Police heroics, I imagine.' Unmasking killers, rooting out assassins, keeping the Empire stable.

'Those, too,' he said, falling into step as she pushed her way through the crowd. 'But I'm keeping my eye on a couple of other things at the moment.'

Me too. They're about six feet five, weigh three hundred pounds each and have muscles where most people have brains. Juno be praised, they had reached the road at last.

'*Litter!*'

A shabby green arrangement came running, but it was already taken and trotted

12

straight past.

'Burglary, for one,' Orbilio said amiably. 'A large number of wealthy patricians have been steadily relieved of their gold and precious jewels in the eight months since Saturnalia, and since ordinary investigations were getting nowhere, my boss thought my blue blood might help shed insight into the matter.'

'How riveting. *Litter!*' Oh, thank you, Jupiter. 'The Forum,' she told the head bearer, 'and I'll double your fare if you run.' To Orbilio, she said, 'We really must do this again some time.'

'I'm free on Monday.'

'I was thinking of some time in the next life.' Claudia clambered inside and pulled the drapes shut. She would send her scribe to collect her winnings later.

'I'm working on another case, too,' Orbilio said, as the bearers picked up the litter.

'Really?'

'Something which I think might interest you.'

'I doubt that.' Claudia's sole concern was the two oafs who had been making such singularly fast progress through the crowd.

'Not even,' he asked, as the bearers adjusted the weight on their shoulders, 'if I tell you I'm investigating race fixing through the doping of horses?'

A small blue cotton bag appeared between the curtains and dangled in mid-air for a second before landing gently in her lap.

'Yours, I believe,' he said smugly.

13

Two

Two days later, and Claudia Seferius was in no mood for visitors.

'My cousin said *rhubarb rhubarb rhubarb...*'

How could Hylas the Greek have found out where she lived?

'*...blah blah* divorced and marrying again *blah blah blah...*'

It was that bloody bookie, wasn't it? She'd kill him. By thunder, she'd bloody kill him. Rip his heart out, feed it to the cat, chop his children into pieces and make meatballs out of them.

'*...rhubarb rhubarb rhubarb* this magnificent embossed betrothal medallion...'

Once she was free of Hylas's clutches, of course. Dammit, couldn't the man see she was perfectly prepared to apologize? Explain that she hadn't realized the grain she'd fed his horse was doped/a rival breeder put her up to it/pure coincidence Calypso won the race. Oh, all right, twelve pure coincidences if he wants to be pedantic, but the point is, don't these Greeks negotiate? Like a stoat negotiates with a rabbit, according to the scribe who tried to collect her winnings. Adding that in his opinion Hylas was in a less conciliatory, more a break-both-her-legs kind of mood.

14

Shit, there were only so many ways a girl can sneak out of the house when his bullies come calling...

'...*blah blah* these are very difficult times for...'

Then there was the Security Police. Was it coincidence that Marcus Cornelius Orbilio just happened to be hanging around on the off-chance that someone would drug the top runners? The hell it was. Someone tipped him off and suddenly it's Saturnalia and his birthday all rolled into one, because some stupid bitch actually hands him the bag of doped grain! What a mess.

'...*rhubarb rhubarb* I quite understand if you—'

'Wait!' Hold it right there, chum. Claudia suddenly began to pay closer attention to her visitor. Mid-thirties, tall, dark haired, well-built with a slight cleft in his chin, Leo was a patrician to boot. 'Say that again.'

'I said I was so, so sorry to hear about your husband's demise. I met him several times over the course of the—'

'No, the bit after that.'

'Uh ...You mean, when I said how courageous I thought it was of you to take on his business, because it can't be easy, you being so young and a woman as well?'

'Not that bit either.'

That was the reason she was in this shit – taking on the bloody business. Dammit, if those bastard fellow wine merchants hadn't banded together to try and drive her to the

15

brink of ruin, she wouldn't be doping horses to raise capital, which meant Hylas the Greek would have no axe to grind and she wouldn't be facing several years in penniless exile because the Security Police had been handed the incriminating evidence in a little blue cotton bag. Which Orbilio had returned, true. But only after conscientiously removing the contents.

'Didn't you mention something about inviting me to visit your estate in the Liburnian archipelago?' she prompted Leo.

Orbilio can build up as compelling a dossier as he likes, but if the chief suspect is nowhere to be found, such was Rome's magnetism for criminal activity that it only needed a couple of juicy murders or a really good conspiracy and race fixing would drop right off the end of his scale of priorities.

Oh come on, it was only a gentle narcotic! A few seeds from a species of chervil given to her by an Armenian for whom she had once done a favour. Not enough to give the horse colic, merely sufficient to render White Star a little unsteady on her hooves and induce a pleasant feeling of equine apathy. (Provided the damn drug had time to work, which is touch and go if the second race ends up being abandoned!)

'I thought it might take your mind off your grief,' Leo said, 'if you saw my revolutionary method of training the vines.'

For all she cared, Leo could use whips and a three-legged stool to train his damn vines.

16

Claudia was packed almost before she'd said yes. Unfortunately, there just didn't seem to be the right moment to confess that the grieving widow wasn't exactly grieving. Not unless it was on account of the inheritance coming in vineyards, bricks and mortar instead of the luscious gold pieces she'd envisaged. I ask you. Who can buy a new gown with half a coppersmith's on the Via Latina? Or take home that delightful little brooch shaped like an owl with a stubby old vine bush or two? But even before her husband's pyre was cold, the sharks had moved in.

First they'd tried to buy her out, at a price far below the market value.

Then they'd tried to squeeze her out.

That did it.

Her husband, may he rest in peace (and she really must visit his grave along the Via Whatever sometime), had worked hard to build up the outlets for his prestigious Etruscan wines. Goddammit, these sons of bitches couldn't just barge in and take what they wanted for nothing. By hell or high water, or Hylas the Greek, Claudia would not let it go. Not, of course, that she knew the first thing about viticulture. That was what she employed experts for: to save her the bother of having to learn which of those twiddly bits needed pruning, whether it was better to line the vats with pitch or with resin. All she cared about was how it tasted. Because that made the difference between 7 and 10 per cent profit.

17

* * *

'I promise you,' Leo said, as the sails of the little merchantman bellied in the warm summer breeze, 'you won't regret coming to Cressia.'

Four hundred miles from Rome, Claudia had no doubts whatsoever on that score. She'd have taken up his offer had it meant spending the summer in the middle of the Libyan desert, providing that certain Greek nationals and the Security Police didn't get to hear about it. But the instant she set eyes on the island rising vertically out of the water, its wooded cliffs plunging hundreds of feet into the sparkling Adriatic, Claudia knew Leo was right.

Through adversity comes opportunity – and it didn't need to knock twice at Claudia's front door. Talk about landing on her feet! The Island of the Dawn, according to one legend. Paradise for Claudia Seferius. Set amid hills redolent with a thousand aromatic herbs, Leo's estate was an idyll of orchid-strewn pastures, oakwoods, pines, olive groves and vineyards, peppered with caves and freshwater ponds.

All of it eclipsed by the Villa Arcadia.

Shaded by figs and pomegranates and ancient gnarled olives, and affording breath-taking views over the Liburnian Gulf, luxury oozed from every pore. Over the past few months (as Leo had explained at numbing length during the journey), a veritable army of builders, sculptors, painters and mosaic-makers had been brought in, no expense spared, to turn the house into a palace. Extensions had been added, gardens landscaped, every surface covered with marble or gold, and the work was not finished yet. A squad of Rome's finest artists were still beavering away, covering the walls with frescoes and such like, in preparation for Leo's forthcoming marriage.

'I know you're eager to see my vines,' he said, as the ship docked in the only deep harbour on the island.

Claudia flashed him her eager-to-see-vines smile as she checked out the beaches.

'And I know you'll be equally keen to get back to supervise your own estate.'

Claudia flashed him her keen-to-supervise-estates smile as she checked out the delightful rocky coves.

'But I'm rather hoping I can persuade you to stay on until after my marriage festivities.'

'We-ell. I suppose I *could* stretch a week or two more.' Even then you'd need a chisel to winkle me out. 'After all,' she added happily. 'Rome *is* rather hot at the moment.'

So there you have it. While Rome sweltered under a vile and viscous heat, and Greeks chased shadows and the Security Police chased their own tails, Claudia Seferius would be sunning herself amid a harmonious unity of rocks, sea and fragrant pinewoods enrobed by sapphire seas in a sumptuous villa at the courtesy of a tall, dark, handsome aristocrat for the summer.

A dirty job, but hey – someone has to do it.

And besides. What's the point of having double standards, if you don't live up to both?

Three

The demon stirred. Its sleep had been long, but in its sleep it had grown restless. The pull of the island was strong.

The island of Cressia was part of Illyria, a great land stretching from the Alps in the north across the mountains to the east, as far as the border with Thrace. A thousand years ago, the Greeks believed Istria, the heart-shaped peninsula which separated Italy from the arid shores of Dalmatia, to be the edge of the world. It was there, they thought, that the Daughters of the Evening Star dwelt in the walled Gardens of the Hesperides, protected by the hundred-headed serpent who guarded a tree of golden apples.

A gentle legend, for a gentle country teeming with lush valleys and forests bursting with game. But the living on Istria was easy. On Cressia, as with the twelve hundred other islands in the Adriatic, life was a constant struggle for survival and there was no room for myth. Only fact.

Cressia's history ran heavy with blood. Every inch of her soil was steeped in treachery and drenched in betrayal, chronicling stories of murder, trickery and revenge...

The demon stirred and licked its lips. The pull of the island was strong. Too strong to resist any longer. It had smelled the blood of her past in its dreams. Now it wanted to taste it.

Four

Paradise is all very well, with its forests of laurel, cypress and beech, its wild ginger, sandy beaches and bottomless freshwater lakes, but paradise is also prone to serpents.

'Touch me up once more, you odious little pusboil,' Claudia said, 'and I don't care how old you are, you'll be chewing your own chitterlings for supper.'

Beside her on the dining couch, Volcar's rheumy eyes shone like twin beacons. 'Now, now, gel. Surely you wouldn't begrudge an old man one final walk down mammary lane?'

'Remind me again how you spell "yes".'

'Trouble with you, young lady,' he chortled, 'is that you have no sense of indecency.'

'Trouble with you, old man, is that now you've discovered where the grass is greener, you're too old to climb the bloody fence. This lawn's private property.'

Volcar had heard about the notion of a man's four score years and ten – and had promptly spat in its eye. Shrivelled, bent and with a face like a pickled walnut, his appetite for life was undiminished. Rumour had it, the furthest he had ever been from a drink in his life was twenty paces.

'Can't blame a fellow for trying,' he said, smacking gums as hard as mussel shells as liveried slaves filed in with the first course of baked eggs, cheeses, asparagus and truffles. 'They say a man's only as old as the woman he feels, and at my age so long as I can feel something, I know I'm still alive.'

'You'd feel something, if you try to scale my fence again.'

'Y'know, I like you,' Volcar said. 'You've fire in your belly, gel, and I've always had a hankering for women with spunk. Not like that frosty faced fossil over there.'

He used an asparagus spear to point to Leo's sister-in-law, the exquisite, immaculate, glacial Silvia, whose age was the same as Claudia's – twenty-five – whose plucked eyebrows arched in perfect symmetry. And whose honey-coloured ringlets wouldn't dare to droop, no matter what the circumstances.

'Wouldn't think, would you, seeing them tiny tits, that Silvia was a mother of three? Here's another thing I'll bet you didn't know.' Volcar lowered his voice to a conspiratorial whisper. 'For all her airs and graces, madam there daren't show her pretty face in Rome.'

Didn't show it much round here, either. In the week that Claudia had been on the island, she'd barely exchanged a dozen words with

22

the only other female in the villa. 'Because...?' she asked.

'Don't know, and to tell the honest truth, gel, don't care to know more about the prissy bitch. To listen to her, though, you'd think she owned the bloody place. Huh. Gets right up my nozzholes, does Silvia.' He chewed on a succulent white truffle. 'Mind, if I were to hazard a guess, I'd say, wouldn't you, that abandoning her children might have a bearing on the scandal.'

'You, Volcar, are a wicked old man.'

'One who's too old for flattery, gel. Why don't you just let me feel your bum instead?'

The small man sitting next to Silvia leaned over to his host's couch, tapped him lightly on his forearm and mumbled something Claudia couldn't hear.

'Oh, not again!' Leo muttered. He turned to Volcar. 'Llagos tells me you're up to your old tricks again, Uncle.'

'Me, lad? Never laid a finger on the lassie.'

Scepticism expressed itself in a twist of the lips. 'Sorry I've left you to the randy old sod's mercy,' Leo told Claudia, as the dishes for the first course were cleared away. 'Only as the wedding draws ever closer, conversation tends to be more progress report than witty repartee.'

Looking round the couches, Claudia tried to imagine any of the assembled party being remotely amusing. Silvia? Too self-absorbed to waste her energies on exploring the philosophies of the meaning of life. Saunio?

23

The fat, pretentious but brilliant artist reserved his animation for his work, while Nikias, the famous Corinthian portrait painter, would never use one word when none would do. Llagos the priest *might* be capable of levity, but his accent was invariably too heavy to follow and in any case, when he laughed, his protruding front teeth had a tendency to spit. Which just left Shamshi, Leo's personal astrologer-cum-augur. And the less that man said the better!

Persian by birth, Shamshi retained the traditional garb of knee-length baggy trousers and shoes which tied in a bow. Like most of his people, he wore thick bands of gold in each ear, though Shamshi went one stage further and drew attention to his earrings by shaving the whole of his head apart from a small cap of black hair right on the top. What really made the hairs of Claudia's neck stand on end, though, was the way his soft, sibilant, girlie voice seemed to caress every inch of her skin. With Volcar, you knew where you were: he was forthright, outrageous and funny. Whereas Leo's human channel to the future was as slimy as you can get without leaving a trail.

'So if I'm neglecting you, I apologize,' Leo told Claudia as the main courses were ferried in on steaming silver salvers. 'But I'm concerned the building work won't be completed in time for the wedding. Any idea when the atrium will be finished, Saunio?'

'Tomorrow,' Rome's most illustrious artist

announced pompously. 'Tomorrow you may go in and have a look at the finished artistry, if you wish.'

'Very kind, I'm sure.' Leo chuckled, darting an amused glance at Claudia. 'My own atrium,' he mouthed, 'and I'm not allowed to see it!'

'It's why you commissioned the great Saunio,' the artist replied, running a podgy finger over the little curled beard that encircled his chin. 'To create magic.'

'Modest with it,' Leo murmured.

'Modesty is for the mediocre.' The great man sniffed. 'Saunio is anything but mediocre. Note, ladies and gentlemen, how in this dining hall I have designed the painted shadows to fall away from the light entering through the double doors behind. This is because when the sun...'

Volcar nudged Claudia in the ribs and nodded at Saunio. 'I'll wager the old sod's got goat's legs and cloven hoofs under his tunic,' he muttered, slithering an oyster down his stringy throat. 'You've heard the gossip, I suppose?'

Hadn't everyone? The maestro and his BYMs. Beautiful Young Men. Travelling around the Empire with a team of thirty junior artists, labourers and apprentices as he sold his services to anyone wealthy enough to afford his exorbitant charges, rumours were bound to spring up. Typically Saunio, the gossip could never be less than ostentatious: tales of orgies, unnatural practices, blood-

25

thirsty rituals, the list was endless. Volcar wouldn't be the first person to liken the maestro to a satyr, not when Saunio got his barber to shave his upper and lower lips, leaving just that preposterous narrow band of dyed hair round his chin. But how much of the gossip was fiction? Claudia wondered. How much lies, put about by jealous rivals? While Saunio lectured the assembly on the principles of perspectives, his curls adhering themselves to his forehead with a mixture of perspiration and their own dye, Claudia thought, love him or loathe him, you had to hand it to the little chap, he'd built himself a monumental reputation as an artist, a reputation well deserved.

'You don't believe those rumours?' she said.

'Believing's got nowt to do with it, gel. What's the point of having gossip unless it's to pass on?'

'You, old man, are incorrigible.'

'At my time of life, I can't afford to wait for discretion to come calling.' He let out a wheezy chuckle. 'These days when I bend down to pat old Ajax here –' he ruffled the ears of the ancient hunting dog chomping on a chop bone – 'I try to find other things to do while I'm down there.'

'Exactly how old are you?'

'Put it this way, gel –' Volcar winkled a snail out of its shell with a loud plop – 'when I was a boy, the Dead Sea was only sick.'

'Something funny over there?' Leo called across.

26

'Do share it,' Silvia drawled, dabbling her long slender fingers in the scented water bowl. 'We could use a laugh.'

Laugh? In six days, Claudia had not seen the Ice Queen so much as smile.

'Silvia's right,' Leo said. 'We've had enough shop talk for tonight, let's change the subject. Any suggestions?'

'Pirates,' Volcar said, spearing a prawn on his knife.

Apart from Nikias, who didn't look up, the others all exchanged glances.

'Oh, come on, Uncle,' Leo said. 'Surely we can think of a better topic to entertain our guest—'

'Why?' the old man cut in. 'Seen 'em, haven't we? Prowling the waters out there. Heard 'em, too. That weird wailing's enough to send shivers down a dead man's spine. Like a banshee, it is, howling for blood.'

Claudia ran her finger round the rim of her wine glass. 'Is piracy a threat?'

'No,' Leo said, glowering at Volcar. 'We're as solidly defended as any place in the Empire. Take no notice.'

' 'Course it is, gel,' Volcar said, pulling a crab claw out of its cracked shell. 'Sure, the mainland which encircles this archipelago is defended, but Rome can't do much to protect the coastline. Too deeply indented, see?'

'You're scaring her, Uncle. Cressia's a large island and—'

'Size don't mean diddly, lad, and you know

27

it. In fact, I'm not sure it don't make matters worse, us being right at the head of the Adriatic as we are.' He eased another claw out of its casing. 'We're just one of twelve hundred islands, you see, gel. Them fast pirate ships can dart through the channels, in and out the inlets, and what can the Imperial Navy do? Bugger all.'

'That's not true, Uncle, and you know it. The navy's on patrol—'

'Sod all use that is to the poor sods who've had their crops raided, their livestock stolen, their women and children raped and carried off to be sold. Whole bloody settlements have been torched, the marauders long gone before the first imperial trireme hoves into sight.'

The mainland. So near and yet so far...

'Ignore the old buzzard,' Leo said firmly. 'Volcar, you should have been a cook, you're that good at stirring. And on the subject of cooking, Claudia, I insist you try our local mutton. The salty grass combined with a diet of wild herbs gives it a magnificent flavour and—What? Not leaving already, Llagos?'

'Sorry, yess.' The little priest was shaking his robes as he slipped into his sandals. 'I hef to be up early,' he explained. 'Temple busyness.' He shot an apologetic smile at Claudia. 'Much complicated on Cressia. Because we are island, we worship the Sea God above all the others. Me, I say, Bindus, Neptune, Poseidon, what does it matter in what name we invoke his protection? For Bindus we had

28

only humble stone altar. For Neptune we have magnificent temple now, with gold and marble and a splendiferous statue three times the height of a man. But some –' his small shoulders shrugged eloquently – 'some peoples here cannot forget the old ways. So tomorrow –' he made a salute of farewell – 'tomorrow iss one time when I must also serve the old ways, keep everyones happy. But!' He lowered his voice to a comical whisper. 'You must not tell the Romans, heh?'

'Talking of mutton reminds me,' Leo said, barely troubling to wave the priest off. 'Tomorrow, Claudia, I *must* show you the vineyards. They'll knock your eyes out,' he insisted. 'I got the idea from apple trees, originally. I thought, hell, if you can espalier fruit trees along ropes for good cropping, why not vines?'

'Excuse me?'

'Told you it was a revolutionary technique.'

'You don't seriously grow them *sideways*?' Even the slowest dunce knows grapes aren't grown laterally. Ask any vintner. They're trained horizontally on a trellis of overhead poles between elm trees.

'Why not?' Leo laughed. 'The soil's pretty poor on Cressia, this way we can manure that more often, the goodness reaches the plants that much faster and it makes it easier to hoe round the roots to keep the soil open. I admit the grapes aren't yielding as well as I'd hoped, in fact they're twenty per cent down on what I was expecting, but still high. It's early days yet and in any case, my wine's pitched at the – well, let's say lower end of the market.'

Produce more, sell for less, and still make a bloody good profit? Funny how the idea of growing them laterally didn't seem quite so stupid all of a sudden...

Looking at Leo, tall, lean, with thick, dark, wavy hair and that attractive dimple in his chin, she wondered why he'd left it so long before finding a wife. Most patricians married in their early to mid-teens. Leo was thirty-six. Scooping up a juicy scallop in rich garlic sauce, she thought, you know catching him at certain angles – say, in profile, when the light is right – he looked a lot like someone else she knew. Someone she'd seen recently, in fact. Except Orbilio's hair was darker, with subtle highlights which glistened in the light. It was thicker and wavier, too, with a fringe that flopped over his face when he was angry. Also, now she thought about it, Orbilio had a funny way of spiking his hair with his fingers when he got annoyed—

Not that she thought about it, and dammit, that bloody scallop had gone down the wrong way, too. Claudia took a long draught of chilled wine. From now on, she really must check the shellfish. It would not do to find she'd eaten a bad one.

'Nikias,' Leo said, 'how's my painting of the Banquet of the Gods coming on?'

Silvia let out a pointed sigh.

'Fine,' Nikias replied, not raising his eyes from his plate.

Although theoretically a member of Saunio's team, since he was on sub-contract to the maestro on this job, Claudia disqualified the Corinthian from the BYM category on technical grounds. At thirty-eight, he was too old to be young. With an intensity of expression bordering on the hostile, he was far from pretty. Also, she did not think he was homosexual, either.

'Still scheduled for completion next week?' Leo persisted.

'Yep.'

'And you don't foresee any problems with the deadline on the portrait of my bride and myself above the bed of the new marriage chamber?'

'Nope.'

Well, that settled that, then. As silence descended on the group, Claudia took to admiring the dining hall's splendid white marble columns garlanded with deep-blue delphiniums, white oleander and sulphur-yellow hibiscus. Aromatic resins crackled in wall-mounted braziers and fragrant oils burned in the dozens of lamps which hung on the walls and from tall silver stands. In this brilliant artificial light, the bronze dining couches gleamed like gold.

Shamshi took advantage of the lull in conversation. 'Bees,' he announced, in his soft sibilant voice.

'*Bees?*' everyone echoed in puzzled unison.

'I noticed a swarm,' he said, 'travelling east. Coupled with the flight of three pigeons

31

across the sun at midday and the fall of the bones, there is only one conclusion to be drawn.' His dark eyes fixed on Claudia. 'Before a new light is born in the sky, bad news will come over the water.'

'Ah,' Leo said thoughtfully. 'Will it, indeed?'

This time a longer silence descended on the diners, and Claudia wondered how much notice Leo paid to the Persian's prophecies. From what she'd seen of him, he seemed a level-headed enough chap. But then he had been resident on Cressia for several years, and on an island where dark deeds figured heavily in its past, superstition found a perfect breeding ground in a race of people isolated by the sea. How much of this hocus pocus had Leo absorbed? And how much of an influence did Shamshi exert on his patron? Leo did not strike Claudia as the imaginative type, so was it the Persian who had planted the idea of training vines in rows like soldiers? To espalier them sideways, instead of dangling them from overhead trellises? Ditto the Villa Arcadia. Architecturally, the mould had been broken here, too.

Abandoning the traditional concept of four wings round a central courtyard, Leo had expanded the accommodation to cover three wings of the original building and demolished the fourth in favour of a fabulous marble portico lined with friezes and statuary. The trades which used to be contained within the original villa now lay outside in a cluster of sheds, mills, stores and workshops, and he'd built a brand new self-contained bath house, complete with domed roof and gymnasium.

Volcar's acerbic quote came to mind. 'All he needs now is a smattering of beggars and the odd painted whore, gel, and he's created a whole bloody town. Don't know why he just doesn't call the place "Leoville" and be done with it.'

An old man's bitterness at his nephew's success, while he was reduced to living on handouts? Or sharp insight into a side to Leo's character Claudia had yet to discover?

'Of course I'm going to bloody well kill it,' Leo said.

What? She had been so busy daydreaming, Claudia had missed the start of this new conversation. What was he going to kill? A rumour? Volcar had nodded off on the far side of the couch, his breathing in rhythm with his ancient hunting dog, Ajax, snoring at his feet.

She glanced at Silvia for clues, but the Immaculate One was torn between selecting a roast hazel hen and the squid in coriander. Claudia suspected this was about the toughest decision the woman had ever had to make. Unless, of course, it was deciding which frock went with which emeralds. On the couch opposite, Shamshi was busy picking his hooked Arab nose, no help there, and Saunio sat stroking the pretentious beard that encircled his chin, while Nikias's face was, if that were possible, even more of a blank. He seemed more intent on pushing a sardine round his plate with the point of his knife, as though teaching it how to swim in the thick mustard sauce.

'I'm right, aren't I, Claudia?' Leo asked.

'Absolutely –' she began, then noticed that the sardine had stopped moving – 'not,' she finished firmly. The sardine continued smoothly on its course.

'You disappoint me, Claudia, really you do. I'd thought better of a fellow wine merchant and estate owner.' Leo snorted. 'It's only a bloody fish, for gods' sake.'

'A dolphin is not a fish,' Nikias pointed out, steering his sardine east to west now and avoiding an anchovy amidships. 'It's an animal, and a very intelligent creature at that. It's harmless, gentle, the children adore it—'

'That's the whole point.' Leo's fist thumped the arm of his couch. 'The entire town loves that – *fish*. Ooh let's swim with it, ooh let's play with it, ooh let's sit on its back,' he mimicked. 'Thanks to that *fish*, half the island's tramped over my land. The point's one of the few places round here with easy access to a beach and you ought to see it, Claudia. So much ground's been churned up, it looks like a bloody battlefield. They're scum, that's what they are. Thoughtless, ill-mannered scum, and the mess they've left is disgusting.'

'It's only scrubland that's been disturbed,' Nikias murmured. 'Try asking them to take their litter home.'

'I don't need to ask a bloody thing,' Leo

34

snapped. 'This is my property and these people, goddammit, are trespassing.'

The Corinthian ran his tongue slowly under his upper lip. 'You've heard the stories of invalids being healed after swimming with dolphins? That crippled boy in the town? The cobbler's son?'

'Cobblers is right.' Leo waved his chicken bone in emphasis. 'It's all in the mind. If they think they'll be cured, then the superstitious sods will be. Good luck to them, I say. Just don't expect me to put up with their blasted mess a moment longer, and since it's my bloody land they're trampling—'

'Actually, it's my bloody land they're trampling,' slurred a voice from behind. 'And *I've* given them permission.'

The woman swaying in the great double doorway was in her early thirties, no great beauty, but striking. With clothes well cut and hair well styled, she exhibited all the grooming and bloom of her class. As all eyes turned on the newcomer, Claudia noticed Saunio slipping quietly out through a side door.

Volcar suddenly snorted awake. 'This'll liven up the evening,' he murmured, smacking his gums with relish.

'Who is she?'

'Don't y'know?' the old man sniggered. 'That's the wife!'

Volcar wasn't with it. He'd woken up too soon, was still dreaming, poor old duffer. 'Leo hasn't actually *got* married yet,' Claudia

35

pointed out gently. That was the whole point of these costly renovations. 'He's fetching a bride over from Rome in a couple of weeks, a rose-grower's daughter or something.'

Volcar's chuckle was positively ribald. 'He didn't tell you, then, the crafty bugger? Not surprised, frankly. Should be ashamed of himself.' He leaned closer, but this time it wasn't to touch her up. 'All of a sudden, just like that, he upped and divorced her. Said Lydia wasn't giving him children, so –' he made a scything motion with his hand – 'end of marriage.'

No. Not Leo. Surely not?

'Tossed the poor cow out on her ear,' Volcar whispered. 'Built her a crummy little house on the point and – oh, sssh, sssh. I want to hear this.'

'Lydia, you're drunk,' Leo said. The word 'again' all but hung in the air. 'Go home. Please.'

'But this *is* my home, Leo. Or at least the improvements are mine.'

'You're talking gibberish, woman. Go back. Sleep it off.'

'Gibberish is better than bullshit, which is what you gave me, Leo. Bullshit – *and* no baby.' She suppressed a small burp. 'Now you're using my money to pay for a few pretty pictures, a new bath – and for what? To impress a man who grows *roses*, for gods' sake. Oh, those drapes are new.' She staggered over to finger the elaborate tapestries which graced the arches. 'At least you're putting my

36

dowry to good taste.'

Leo's face coloured dangerously. 'This is neither the time nor the place to discuss the financial settlement, Lydia. I'll get someone to escort you ho— back.'

'Who says I'm going "back"?' Lydia retorted. 'Who says I might not decide to spend the night here? In one of the— how many bedrooms are we up to now, Leo? Ten?' She leaned over and helped herself to Claudia's wine. 'Ooh, you're new, too,' she purred. 'But you're out of luck, darling. If it's his money you're after, there is none. He lost it in those bloody vines, despite what he tells everyone, and he lost in half a dozen other hare-brained ventures, as well. Now the bastard's spent my divorce settlement on his wonderful refurbishments, so I'm in debt, too. God, I hate you, Leo. How I didn't see through you years ago I don't know!'

'Lydia, please,' Leo cajoled. 'You're embarrassing yourself.'

She turned her wine-laden breath upon Claudia once again. 'You're too old for him, sweetie. You're young and you're beautiful, but darling, you've got *breasts*. Has he told you how old she is, his little prepubescent bride? Thirteen. Can you believe that, sweetie?' Her laugh was bitter. 'Now if we'd had children, how do you think Leo would have felt about some middle-aged pervert taking *his* thirteen-year-old daughter to bed?'

'Enough!' Leo jumped to his feet. 'I will not have you inferring I'm some kind of depraved

37

monster, simply for wanting an heir. It's a man's right, dammit, to continue the bloodline, and the girl hails from good breeding stock.'

'Stock. Yes. How sensitive you are, Leo, seeing her in terms of a prolific foaler.' Lydia staggered between the dining couches until she was eyeball to eyeball with Leo. 'Eighteen years,' she hissed. 'Eighteen years I put up with your boorish behaviour, your insufferable arrogance, and how am I repaid? I'm put out to pasture, while you fuck a child in my bed.'

Teetering, she knocked the table sideways, sending a salver of honeyed peaches slithering over the mosaic floor. The smell of split fruit exploded into the air. No one moved. All eyes were riveted on Lydia.

'Well, fuck you, and fuck the rose-grower's daughter. You're not my concern any more. I came here tonight to talk about Magnus.'

'Who's Magnus?' Claudia whispered, but Volcar flapped a hand to silence her.

'What did you tell him, Leo? What did you say to frighten him off? Or did you bribe my little marble man away?'

When she tried to laugh, it came out a throaty, unstable rumble. As though Lydia's tenuous hold on her emotions would give way any second to a stream of unstoppable tears.

'That would be the ultimate insult, wouldn't it? You buying off my suitor with my own money?' She waved her hand in weary dismissal as he opened his mouth. 'Oh, spare me

38

more of your lies, Leo. I don't care what you told Magnus, it doesn't matter, really it doesn't. I don't want a man who can be bought off or bullied.' She paused for breath. 'But you went too far, Leo. Now it's my turn.'

'I'm trembling.'

'Mock all you like, but I'm still putting a stop to your marriage.'

'Impossible. I'm already wearing her betrothal medallion. We exchange wedding rings on the girl's fourteenth birthday. Even *you* can't break the contract.'

'*I* don't intend to,' Lydia said, and there was a glint of triumph in her glazed eyes. 'You'll be the one doing the breaking.'

'That contract's sealed in law. No one and nothing can break it.'

'What if I say, "life and death", my dear darling husband? Life and death cut straight through signatures and seals.'

'Bollocks.'

Lydia let out a soft snort of contempt. 'Don't say I didn't warn you, Leo. Didn't I tell you I wasn't prepared to stand by while you wrote me out of your life like some cheap playwright editing a character out of his script?' She pounded his chest with two feeble fists. 'Dammit, I'm entitled to *something*, you bastard.'

'This isn't the—' he began, but at that point, Lydia's heel caught on a peach and, skirts flapping wildly, she tumbled backwards in an inelegant heap, landing on the low dining table and sending everything flying.

Nikias gallantly lent a hand hauling her upright.

'*Lydia!*'

This was the first time Silvia had spoken since the visitor had burst in, and her voice was imperiously cold. She made no attempt to disguise her revulsion at the combination of bad language, bad behaviour and the food mashed into Lydia's clothes.

'Lydia, you're tired, you're obviously overwrought and ... and it doesn't appear you've been eating properly,' she added in venomous euphemism.

'And since when have you been interested in my welfare, you self-centred cow?' Lydia snarled, ungraciously shaking off Nikias's arm. 'You bugger off without a word, you don't write, the family have no idea whether you're dead or alive, and suddenly wham! Up you turn, four years later, out of the blue. And where do you set up camp, you snobby bitch? With me, your darling long-lost sister? Or with Leo, because his house is grand and comfy?'

Claudia wondered whether anyone, above this furious interchange, had heard her gasp of astonishment. Silvia and Lydia were *sisters*? She knew, of course, that Leo was Silvia's brother-in-law, but she had blithely assumed the connection was on Leo's side. But yes, now you looked closer, you could see the family resemblance. Even though Lydia was ten years older and a brunette, the nose and high forehead were the same, as were

40

the hands.

'Well, you've made your bed, baby sister, you can bloody well lie in it,' Lydia sneered. 'I just hope what you're giving him in it is worth it.'

'Right!'

Leo's tolerance finally snapped and grabbing Lydia roughly by the upper arm, he dragged her through the wide double doors on to the terrace.

'Qus!' he bawled, and his tall Ethiopian bailiff came running. 'Qus, will you please escort my lady wife home.' He closed the double doors firmly on Lydia's profanities. 'Messy things, family feuds,' he said to Claudia. 'I'm really sorry you had to be party to that ugly scene.'

'What did she mean,' she asked innocently, 'about only life and death being able to break a contract?'

That Leo had behaved so abominably was bad enough. That Claudia hadn't realized he was capable of such callous behaviour was unforgivable.

Silvia, her lips white, patted her immaculate ringlets and ran a finger over each elegantly plucked eyebrow. 'Vitriol always flows when my sister takes to the wineskin,' she said. 'Take no notice of Lydia.'

That, thought Claudia, wasn't the question. And you weren't the one I was asking. She glanced at Leo, his head tilted on one side, and wondered why Silvia had answered for him. *And why he had let her*. There was an

41

undercurrent running between them. She had noticed it several times since her arrival. An undercurrent which was anything but sexual.

'For heaven's sake,' Leo snapped, 'let's have some music in here!'

Flautists and harpists launched into a cheerful tune, and an Indian girl clacked castanets as she danced.

'Come on, Shamshi, Nikias. Clap along,' Leo said, but his voice was strained, his jaw clenched. Why? Because be was embarrassed that his ex-wife had aired the dirty laundry in public? Or had it got to him that Lydia might, just *might*, be in a position to queer his forth-coming marital pitch?

Having dropped one stone into the pool and created a few ripples, Claudia tried another wee pebble for size. 'Who was this Magnus character Lydia mentioned?' she asked, adopting just the right air of dis-interest. 'A marble merchant, didn't she say?'

'Sculptor,' Nikias corrected.

'Not,' Claudia's jaw fell to the floor and bounced twice, 'not *the* Magnus?'

'I only hire the best,' Leo said.

'Magnus doesn't simply recreate a super-ficial likeness,' Nikias said. 'Next time you stroll through the garden, read the expres-sions on the figures he's sculpted, see how his subjects carry themselves, the way they look back at *you*, and you'll find yourself looking at their hopes and aspirations, their virtues and their faults, their energies and frailties. Take a

42

long hard look at them, Claudia. Get to know the people Magnus captured. Because by looking at his sculptures, you're staring straight into these people's souls.'

The stunned silence which followed was broken only by the clack-clack-clack of the dancer's castanets. No one had ever heard Nikias speak for so long. Or with such passion.

Leo cleared his throat. 'Yes. Well. If you kiddies will excuse me, I'm for an early night.'

He made a circuitous loop round the central table, as though by avoiding the piles of overturned seafood, the mangled poultry and splattered peaches he could somehow pretend Lydia's visit had not taken place.

'Given that I have to spear a fish in the morning,' he added.

'You're making a mistake, Leo.'

Leo faltered. Perhaps having thought the taciturn artist had shot his bolt, he was surprised to find himself mistaken. Or perhaps he was just not used to people standing up to him in this way.

'Are you threatening me, Nikias?' He chuckled.

'Nope.' Nikias leaned back on his couch and stared at a point on the ceiling. 'But I'm not prepared to let you butcher a tame dolphin, either. Not when it means so much to the children.'

'They'll forget soon enough,' Leo said, dismissing the notion with a wave of his hand. 'Isn't that right, Shamshi, old man?'

The Persian laced his bony hands together and locked his dark eyes on Claudia's. 'I've said everything I have to say,' he lisped quietly. 'Before a new light is born in the sky, bad news will come over the water.'

The last click of the castanets died away in an echo.

'When the gods speak,' Shamshi whispered, 'only a fool covers his ears.'

Five

Drifting on her swansdown mattress beneath a damask coverlet scented with rose petals, Claudia dreamed. She dreamed of thumping great lobsters, of crayfish and, of course, those succulent white truffles from the forests on the Istrian mainland, and there was nothing to interrupt her aromatic slumber. In Rome, darkness signalled the opening of the city gates to traffic, and thus there was a rowdy cacophony of rumbling wagons, cracking bullwhips, shouts from the drivers, tavern brawls, the whinnies and neighs of the dray animals and the constant clatter, clack and bang of loading and unloading. In Arcadia there was only silence, broken, perhaps, by the odd creak of settlement, the muffled sound of a door closing, the faint too-woo of an owl in the pinewoods behind the villa.

Nestled into the dip at the base of Claudia's spine, Drusilla, her blue-eyed, cross-eyed, dark Egyptian cat twitched her whiskers and dreamed, too. She dreamed about big fat spiders, crunchy moths and the mice she would torment in the morning.

Peace. Perfect peace. The night was warm, the air pleasant and, together as always, mistress and cat slept, and the three-quarters moon rose in the sky. Far away, a fox barked, and a nightjar churred on the wing.

Fire!

A sixth sense alerted her, even before her throat prickled with the distinctive tang of burning. Claudia swung her legs over the side of the bed, stubbing her heel in the dark on its bronze foot. Like every room of this single-storey villa, hers had double doors opening outwards. Throwing open the shutters, she saw that, less than a hundred paces from the house, flames were licking through the roof of a small building raised on vermin-thwarting stilts.

Leo's grain store.

With a low howl from the back of her throat, Drusilla shot behind the chair.

'FIRE!' Claudia shouted.

Croesus! Nobody heard! She cupped her hands round her mouth.

'Fire in the grain store!'

No good. People were in too deep a sleep. She drew a deep breath to yell her lungs out when something caught her eye in the moon-light. There, on the steps. Squinting through

45

the swirling smoke, she tried to make out the twisting shape. Wrong. Not one shape. Those were two separate figures, writhing together on the narrow stone stairs. Bugger. That's all we need. A private war while an inferno rages!

Decisions, decisions.

Raise the alarm? Or stop the fight before the fire spreads?

Racing across the flagstones in her bare feet, Claudia covered her mouth against the choking fumes and questioned the intelligence which made two grown men scuffle on the steps while the whole damn corn supply went up in flames behind them.

'Hey!'

They couldn't hear for the crackle of the flames.

'Hey!' she called, louder. 'Stop that!'

From the corner of her eye she saw movement in the bushes. Praise be to Juno, the cavalry was here!

'Come on,' she called, 'we've got to stop those two and prevent the fire spreading.'

What was this clot waiting for? A bloody medal?

'Well, hurry, then!'

The figure in the bushes backed away. Oh, suit yourself. Spinning round, she raced on down the path. Two seconds later, she heard heavy footsteps thumping behind her. About bloody time! The footsteps were gaining. Even better. Stronger muscles to break up the fight.

'What the hell?'

46

Shit! The muscles were strong, all right. They'd clamped round her in a bear hug.

'Not me, you idiot. *Them.*'

But the vice was tightening. Breathing, heavy in her ear. She tried to wriggle her arms free, but the lock was tight.

'Let me go, you bastard!' Squirming, kicking, Claudia tried to wrestle herself out of his grasp. 'Let go of me!'

The air was being squeezed out from her lungs. She couldn't scream. Could hardly breathe. She tried to dig her elbows back, but there was no room for manoeuvre. What the hell was going on? Was he trying to prevent her breaking up the fight? Or was the motive more personal? Rape?

'I'll kill you for this,' she hissed, kicking backwards with her heels. 'Your life won't be worth a—'

The alarm horn blew then – long, low and piercing – and instantly every dog on the estate began barking. As though this was a signal, the grip broke and she found herself tipping forwards through thin air. She put out her hands to break the fall, yelped as her knee grazed the flagstone. Then a shadow fell across the path. Glancing up, she heard a whooshing sound, caught a faint scent of cinnamon, saw something dark scything towards her.

Suddenly a thousand stars exploded in her head.

And this time, when Claudia Seferius toppled forward, she didn't get up.

Six

'Ooh, fank gawd!' The anxious face of one of the maidservants pushed its way into focus. 'When I couldn't wake you, I fought somefing terrible 'ad happened!'

Hadn't it? Through a thick haze, Claudia tried to piece back the memory. Vaguely she saw two figures. Wrestling on the granary steps. Felt two strong arms round her chest. Huh. Bad dream! She was here, wasn't she? Tucked up in bed. In her room. With one of the maids Leo had hired for his new bride bending over her.

'Ouch.' Except dreams don't leave lumps the size of onions. Or clash cymbals against your brain. Or smell of – 'Fire!'

'That's why I was trying to wake you,' the girl said, hauling Claudia up by her shoulders. 'Do 'urry, mistress. Please, mum.'

What was that dreadful noise? Was that inside her head, too? Then she realized. It was the sound made by feet stampeding down the villa's cool marble floors mingled with screams and shouts, with whimpering sobs and the slamming of doors in a mad clamour for open air. Through the windows, a ghostly grey light was pushing its way through the heavy blanket of sky to the east.

This, Claudia thought, is one hell of a way to greet a new dawn.

Holding her head with both hands to prevent it from rolling into a corner, she fumbled her way to the window. How long had she been unconscious? Weeks? Months? It could only have been minutes, she thought. Just a few minutes. Thick plumes of smoke smothered the courtyard and panic was spreading. Fieldworkers from the dormitories knocked one another aside in the rush. Slaves huddled in terrified knots. Children wailed.

'We're going to die! We're all going to die!' someone shouted.

'Run for your lives,' cried another.

Four rooms along, Silvia's imperious tones drowned the rumpus. Any frantic activity on her part had taken on a distinctly more pragmatic note.

'The jewels,' Silvia ordered her servants. 'Save the jewels.'

'Please, mistress,' Claudia's maid pleaded. 'You've gotta get out.'

'Go away.'

'What?' The girl blenched. 'An' leave you when you're ill?'

That was the trouble with hired help. Claudia could have brought her own entourage, but the fewer who knew where she was, the safer for all concerned, so she'd only brought the head of her bodyguard.

'I'm not ill.' If only those castanets inside her head would stop trying to compete with the cymbals...

The maid flung her single heavy plait over her shoulder as a gesture that she was standing her ground. 'You've picked up one of them fevers, that's what you 'ave. If I wrap you up nice and warm, you'll feel better.'

'You'll feel the back of my hand, if you don't stop fussing.'

'Now where the devil did I put your long fick woollen wrap? It's bin so 'ot, I honestly didn't fink you'd need anyfing that warm.' The girl scratched her head. 'Perhaps it's in that chest over there...'

She lifted the lid. Claudia slammed it down hard. *'Out.'*

Bundling the girl unceremoniously out of the room, she explored the lump on the side of her head, the bruises round her upper arms where she'd been clamped. She swallowed. Lifted her shift. All right. She swallowed again. Let's see what other violations had taken place...

Juno be praised, she hadn't been raped.

Across the narrow pathway, orange flames crackled and spat, and shattered the terracotta roof tiles. What the hell kind of twisted mind knocks a girl unconscious then takes the trouble to carry her back to her bed? The burning stung her eyes. As she watched, one of the interior timbers let out an ominous crack. Hysteria swept through the crowd like a flash flood. As one, they surged towards the cliff path.

'Stop.'

Leo's cultured tones cut straight through

50

the shrieks of the slaves, the screams of the women, even the terrified yelps of the dogs.

'Everyone remain where they are.'

This was a voice which was calm, controlled, and brooked no disobedience. Even when a large section of the roof collapsed with an ear-splitting crash, no one dared move.

'Qus.' He addressed his tall, Ethiopian steward, who had come running. 'Organize buckets, use the water from the bath house. The rest of you, form a chain, each man one arm's span apart – and that includes you, Saunio.'

'Me?' The maestro threw back his head in a theatrical gesture. 'I am an artiste,' he protested. 'I cannot risk damaging my hands. These hands are my work. My life. My art.'

'I am told that, over time and given plenty of nursing –' Leo shot a withering glance at the coven of pretty young men clustered around him – 'blisters *eventually* recover.'

Saunio looked for another way out. His contract was to design, not to act as a skivvy. 'But your beautiful frescoes,' he wheedled. 'I am barely halfway through the project. If the famous Saunio's hands burn, who will complete his magnificent masterpieces?'

'The next painter I hire,' Leo barked, 'now jump to it. Listen up, everyone. It only needs one small spark to cross this courtyard and the house goes up with it, so put your backs into it. You too, Silvia. Grab a bucket.'

Straightening the wrap which covered her

51

embroidered linen nightshift, Silvia tilted her patrician chin and was about to give a sharp rejoinder when she realized that Leo was no longer beside her. With a militant sniff, she stalked across the cobbles in the direction of the herb garden. If he wanted to get himself burned to a crisp, that was fine by her. He was only her brother-in-law, after all. She had no intention of so much as singeing an eyebrow herself. Good heavens, what did the man think slaves were for?

'Where the bloody hell are you sloping off to?' Leo snarled, spinning Saunio round by his arm. 'I told you. We need every man we can get, which means you and your nancy boys. Everyone pulls their weight in a crisis like this. *Everyone*, do you understand?'

'It's Bulis,' the artist whined. 'I'm worried about the poor boy.'

'In your shoes, I'd be more worried about me.'

'You don't understand. I can't find him anywhere—'

'Bugger Bulis. Just join the sodding chain, before the whole bloody place goes up.'

Watching the furious activity from the shadows of her bedroom, Claudia wished she'd seen the combatants more clearly. They had been of a same size and build, that much she could tell, but any further detail had been lost in the dark, in the smoke, in the fact that they were locked together. And before she'd got close enough to identify either party, someone had thoughtfully smashed a flower-

52

pot over her head.

Was that why? To stop her identifying the brawlers? Or to prevent her from breaking up the fight?

Round her ankles, hackles raised and tail swishing like a scythe through hay, Drusilla yowled obscenities from the back of her throat.

'I know, poppet,' Claudia whispered, bending down to stroke the spiky fur flat. 'It's too slick, isn't it?'

Far too slick. Watching Leo striding back and forth across the courtyard, issuing orders in his calm, patrician voice, was like watching rehearsals for some theatrical drama. The slaves and fieldworkers might be terrified, and justifiably so, but not Leo. A fire breaks out, despite the vigilance of a whole corps of nightwatchmen. It catches hold. Becomes an inferno. Not for Leo, though, to be outdoors in his nightshift! There he was, striding around in long, patrician tunic, neatly belted, and he'd even taken the trouble to comb his hair and lace up his boots.

Drusilla's back arched, her tail stiffened.

'Exactly, poppet. Think how little time passed before the alarm was raised. Yet here's Leo, immaculately groomed, establishing authority on chaos.'

It was as though every scene which unfolded had been carefully – if badly – choreographed. In fact, so methodical were her host's actions, a girl could have been forgiven for thinking infernos were a weekly occur-

53

rence here at the villa.

'Leo was prepared for this,' Claudia said. Or at least, something *like* this, she quickly qualified. The drill was good, but it was far from practised. As though this was the first rehearsal in a play suddenly sprung upon the actors by the theatrical director.

'If proof were needed, just look how uninterested he is in his nightwatchmen.'

'Hrrrrr,' Drusilla growled.

'My sentiments entirely. All those big burly men staggering about holding their heads?'

Any normal master would have assumed they were drunk and beaten them for falling asleep at their posts. Not Leo. He *knew* their sleep had been induced by something more sinister. But make no mistake, Leo was angry. Very angry. Witness the stiff back, clenched fists – body language which suggested that, although he hadn't been caught on the hop, this Leo was not a happy lion.

As dawn began to throw her pink veil across the hills to the east, Claudia's eyes narrowed to slits.

Just what the hell kind of game was Leo playing here?

And what was the *real* reason he'd invited her to the Villa Arcadia?

Seven

Bucket by leather bucket, water from Leo's newly constructed bath house subdued the flames and, with it, quickly quenched the danger. Now only a single plume of black oily smoke punched its way through the hole in the roof. Testimony, just like the empty oil jar which lay beneath the stilts, that the fire had not started accidentally.

'For gods' sake, someone silence those bloody dogs!' Leo yelled. 'And you lot in the chain. Stop slacking, the fire isn't doused yet.'

Maybe not, but the crisis had undoubtedly passed and the sooty fire fighters, coughing from the smoke, saw no reason to keep up the back-breaking pace. The line of buckets settled into an easy, more manageable rhythm and gradually the barking of the estate dogs subsided, until all that could be heard was the twitterings of Saunio's coven of pretty boys bemoaning the state of their hair, their hands, the damage to their delicate skin.

In a pale-lemon-yellow gown, Claudia joined the throng in the courtyard. 'Good gracious, what on earth have I slept through?' she trilled.

A dash of white face powder, a judicious grouping of curls and the lump was almost invisible. To one side of the path, a pot of deep-pink spotted lilies lay in shards, the blooms trampled to mush. An unlikely weapon, Claudia thought. But effective.

'Are you all right?'

Under the grime she just about made out the earnest features of Corinth's famous son peering deep into her eyes. For what, though? Genuine concern for her welfare? Or to see whether she recognized him from earlier?

'I'm managing to keep a lid on the panic.'

Trust no one. It was a good rule to live by. One which had served her right the way through from the slums. Nikias didn't look the sort to swan around clonking women over the head, much less the type to go brawling. But if still waters ran deep, then Nikias was an ocean, and who knows what secrets the ocean holds?

Taciturn as ever, the Corinthian gave a tight-lipped nod before slipping back to take his place in the chain.

'Dear child, you could have *died*,' whispered a soft, sibilant voice in her ear.

Claudia jumped. That was the second time in the early hours of this morning someone had crept up on her. A habit she was keen to break. But soot or no soot, nothing could disguise Shamshi's features. The hooked Arab nose. The distinctive circular mop of hair on top of a head otherwise shaved from temple to nape. That weird, lisping voice.

'Our host has been *most* irresponsible,' he murmured, 'not checking your room had been evacuated.' He sniffed. 'In his place, *I* would have posted servants to make *sure* your slaves wouldn't ignore any alarm.'

Claudia imagined the alarm would have had skeletons banging their heads on their gravestones, such was the startle factor of that particular blast.

'Had I been in any danger, Shamshi, you would have been the first to know.' She declined to take the bait about her bodyguard failing in his duties. 'After all,' she smiled, 'you're the one who sees the future, remember?'

The Persian did not return her smile. 'I am an augur, not an astrologer,' he lisped. 'I study entrails, observe birds, watch for portents, interpret dreams. The signs I have been shown don't foretell death, dear child. Only –' he paused for effect – *'disaster.'*

Must be a hoot at children's parties, Claudia thought, as he turned away, his trousers flapping round his bony knees. Was Shamshi one of the men tussling on the steps? Thanks to the smoke, she couldn't tell, but there was a man she could well imagine wielding pots of lilies. It was the thought of those skeletal fingers touching her comatose body that didn't bear thinking about!

Extricating himself from the working party at last, Saunio, strutting like a plump pigeon, despatched a squad of BYMs to locate Bulis.

'If I find out that wretched boy has buggered off to town again, I'm adding three months to his apprenticeship,' he spluttered.

'I won't tolerate slackness in my team. Not from any one of you, you hear?' The remainder of the BYMs nodded grimly.

Dawn had turned the Adriatic rosy red, giving definition to what the islanders called Sorcerer's Mountain. This was the high peak on the Istrian mainland, where snow clung to the crevices even in summer. More sinisterly, in superstitious Cressian eyes, was the cap of white cloud which engulfed the peak most of the year. What other explanation than a smokescreen for the sorcerer to work his evil magic? Thus every morning, when they arose, the islanders made the ritual gesture against enchantment. Which was precisely what they were doing now. Slaves from the household, slaves from the fields, slaves who toiled in the outhouses and the workshops, all held up their right hands, the two middle fingers held down by their thumbs, and made the sign of the horns to protect them.

'Quick, sir,' Qus called out, 'look at this!'

Alerted by his tone, all notions of ritual gestures were abandoned in favour of looking at Leo's muscle-bound bailiff standing in the blackened grain house door. Necks craned forward as Leo bounded up the stone steps two at a time in response. Avidly the crowd watched as Qus passed his master a moistened linen handkerchief to cover his mouth and nose against the smoke. Both men had to duck to pass beneath the smouldering lintel. Where the ground sloped away behind the building, the soil was scarred by runnels of oily black sludge, the after-effects of extinguishing the inferno. The timbers resembled crocodile hide.

As the crowd waited for the men to emerge, the first bubble of birdsong began to rise. Within seconds, wheatears, whinchats and whitethroats were singing their hearts out from spiky perches out in the scrub, tits and redstarts warbled from the pines and a hoopoe crooned in the distance. Undeterred by the acrid air, swallows twittered under the eaves of the villa, dipping and diving as they fetched flies for their ravenous young. Several minutes passed before Leo finally reappeared from the grain store. His expression was grim.

'I'm telling you this,' he announced in a low voice, 'because I don't want any false rumours bandied about. Qus has...' He paused, swallowed, started again. 'Qus has discovered the charred remains of a body inside the granary.'

A collective gasp rose from the crowd.

Oh, no, Claudia prayed. Not Volcar. Oh, please, not old Uncle Volcar.

'Bulis!' cried Saunio. 'I knew it, I knew it. It's my boy Bulis, isn't it?'

Leo didn't reply for a moment, then slowly he opened his fist. In his palm lay a blackened signet ring. 'It is,' he said, 'if your apprentice wore this.'

It went without saying that there would be no other way of identifying the remains.

Saunio's voice cracked. 'Gold?' he asked.

'Set with one single pearl?'

Leo rubbed the ring on his tunic. For a brief second, his eye held Saunio's, then he gave a bleak nod. The artist covered his face with his hands. The BYMs fluttered round once more to comfort their patron as well as each other.

'That's not all,' Leo said. 'The corpse – I, mean, Bulis –' he paused, and Claudia felt something cold slither around in her stomach. 'Bulis,' he said, 'was found chained to a pillar.'

Eight

Cooled by white marble and shaded by honeycomb screens, the great soaring atrium oozed peace and tranquillity. Fresh flowers scented the Senator's hall – roses, lilies and pinks. A fountain splashed prettily, birds with bright plumage trilled from their cage in the corner and servants glided silently in and out, while the strumming of a lyre filtered through from a room at the back.

Working for the Security Police, Orbilio had almost forgotten, until recently, what it was like, the indolent lifestyle into which he had been born. A lifestyle of seaside villas like this, where families could just up sticks and retreat for the summer, while his own time was passed scouring crime scenes and meeting informers in strange, secret places or trawling drinking dens and whorehouses in search of those creatures of the night who could help him unravel his latest investigation and bring the perpetrator to book.

'Marcus? Marcus, can it really be you?'

He spun round, his eyes widening in surprise and delight. 'Margarita!' He had forgotten the Senator had remarried.

'There was a time,' she said, linking her arm through his and drawing him towards the back of the house, 'when you were less formal. Called me Darling, Lover, Cherub—'

'That was a long time ago,' he reminded her as sternly as he could muster. 'You're a respectable wife and mother now, Margarita.'

'I was a wife and mother then, too,' she flipped back, 'and I'll kindly thank you not to call me respectable. Give me a kiss.'

He leaned down to plant a chaste kiss on her cheek, but Margarita clasped his face in her bejewelled hands and drew him down hard on her lips. He wondered how long it would be before he'd be allowed up for air.

'I'm investigating a series of burglaries which has been targeting wealthy establishments since Saturnalia,' he explained, once she'd finally released him. 'I gather your own house was a recent victim?'

Robbery was hardly his usual line of enquiry, but after eight months of getting nowhere and with the upper classes growing restless, Orbilio's boss had begun to feel the

61

wind of change blowing underneath his high-backed office chair. Sort it out fast, the breeze was telling him, or there'll be someone else's butt on this cushioned upholstery. Orbilio didn't resent the routine enquiry. It made a change from rapes and murder, allowed him to investigate the horse doping business himself instead of delegating to others, and also, thanks to the intricacies of aristocratic lineage, many of the families involved happened to be his own relatives. Which gave him a perfect opportunity to catch up.

'The bastards took all my lovely jewels, darling. Come in here, and I'll tell you all about it over a jug of chilled wine. It's vintage Ligean, of course. You'll adore it.'

Margarita led him into a small chamber overlooking the sea, where shutters offered shade, coolness, silence – and total privacy. Lavender oil burned in a brazier, heroic scenes plastered the walls and a large, white cat snoozed in a basket. Orbilio noted that the wine and glasses were already in place on the table. Not for him. For anyone, he realized sadly.

In the three, maybe four years since he had last seen her, Margarita had lost weight. Gone was the voluptuous bosom, the dimpled cheeks, the unforced laugh which had attracted him so deeply when he was at a low ebb after his wife had walked out. Now, seeing the lines scoring her eyes, the dyed hair, the increased reliance on cosmetic aids, Marcus felt a pang of something he

62

couldn't identify.

'Absolutely scrummy,' she said, pouring the wine. 'Colour of honeydew with just a hint of freshly mown hay and greengages in the bouquet.' She linked her arm through his and chinked glasses.

'When you say "all" your jewellery...?' Orbilio said, smiling, as his gaze took in the rich array of gold pendants, emerald earrings, silver tiara and bracelets, as well as pearl-studded hair combs.

'These little gewgaws are what I was wearing at the banquet the night we were robbed. They're all I'm left with, unless –' with one deft movement, she unclipped her left shoulder brooch – 'you want to search the premises more thoroughly?'

'Margarita, please.' His voice was hoarse. 'Cover yourself up, before someone comes in.'

'No one will come in,' she assured him, but his eyes told her that fear of disturbance wasn't the reason for the rebuff.

Marcus drained his wine in one swallow. Some things never change, he reflected, although he had forgotten, until now, how Margarita had favoured quick-release clothing. How she'd never bothered with under-wear.

'Sex should always be spelt with three Fs,' was her motto. 'Frequent, fast and frivolous, darling.'

Now he understood the lines round her mouth, the hollows under what had, not so long ago, been bright eyes. He had hoped that remarriage to the Senator would have made her happy, let her find whatever she'd been seeking from life, and he watched impassively as she drew the fine embroidered linen over her naked breast and pinned back the brooch without a flicker of embarrassment in her hazel brown eyes.

'You don't know what you're missing,' she said, but he knew exactly. Casual sex, as Margarita was finding to her cost, is not the answer. It leaves a person aching and incomplete, wanting more from life than a succession of bleak hydraulic manoeuvres.

'I'm sorry,' he said, and he meant it. 'My philandering days are behind me.'

Dalliances where the soul plays no part were no longer the answer. As time passed, Marcus Cornelius Orbilio found he needed more. Much, much more.

'You're in love, darling.'

'I most certainly am not,' he protested.

'Who is she? Do tell. Do I know her?'

'Margarita, I'm here to talk about last month's robbery.'

'If you say so, darling.'

As she settled herself provocatively on a couch richly upholstered in a deep shade of scarlet, Orbilio let the wall take his weight. In the basket, the white cat began to snore softly. 'Tell me about the banquet.'

Her cherry-red mouth turned down at the corners. 'One party's much the same as another, darling. Nothing stands out.'

That was the problem, of course. In the twenty-eight robberies since Saturnalia, the overlap between guests and jugglers, dancers and musicians, caterers and slaves was enormous. No one and nothing stood out.

'These are sophisticated thefts,' he explained. 'Each job netted a tidy haul, but no one's tried to fence any of it. Where's the stuff going?'

'Perhaps you're chasing a thrill-seeker, who steals for the sheer hell of it?' Margarita ran her fingertip round the top of the glass until it let out a soft hum.

'A thrill-seeker with a warehouse to store the stuff in.' Marcus laughed, topping up both their glasses with the chilled wine. 'No, this has to be for pure profit.'

'I don't see how the scam could work without an outlet,' she said, letting her fingers brush his as he handed the glass back.

'Sooner or later I'd expect things to resurface,' he said, pretending not to notice. 'Then someone somewhere would recognize their own necklace in a shop in the Forum or see their rings on someone else's fair hand. Yet in eight months, nothing. Not one single lead.'

'Marcus, dear, this is all very interesting, and it's a real shame I won't see my lovely baubles again – there was a cameo I was particularly fond of, the one you bought me, remember? – but darling, at twenty-six don't you think you should consider adopting a more appropriate career?'

'Margarita,' he said, laughing, 'you are

65

impossible.'

She stuck out her pretty pink tongue and he watched the light dance on the emeralds round her neck as she stood up and walked towards him.

'I'm serious, darling,' she whispered, coiling one arm round his waist. 'Your father was a highly respected advocate, both your brothers are in the law and, if you really want that seat in the Senate, that's where you should be, too. In court.'

'I often am,' he insisted softly, uncoiling the arm. 'Giving evidence for the prosecution.'

Hazel eyes rolled in mock exasperation. 'You know damn well what I mean,' she said, and somehow the arm was back. 'You want to swap your lowlifes for the high life again, settle down, raise a family.'

'I was married.'

'I know you were, darling, I helped you get over the bitch. But the Senate won't take you unless you're married, and funnily enough, I know just the girl. Sweet little thing, she'll give you boatloads of babies and I promise she won't run off with a sea captain from Lusitania and leave you broken-hearted like that other cow.'

'Since our hearts were never joined, there was nothing to break,' he said carefully. 'Humiliated is the word, I believe. Not broken-hearted.'

'Whatever,' Margarita murmured, entwining her other arm round his neck. 'But I know this girl, she's my niece—'

66

'Hold it right there.' He laughed. 'You, of all people, know I'll be buggered if I'll kow-tow to family convention with a second bloody marriage of convenience. Not when the first one caused such grief.' Past tense? Orbilio could tell Margarita as many lies as he liked, but the bottom line was, that marriage was causing grief still. 'When – *if* – I remarry,' he said, 'social class won't come into it. Love's all that matters. Without it, there are no foundations to build on.'

'Love!' she scoffed gently. 'When your foolish plebeian infatuation wears off, what will you be left with? I can tell you in one short word, Marcus. Isolation. Your peers won't respect you, the lower orders will see it as weakness, you'll be despised and ostracized on all sides. Duty, darling. Duty is what counts, because at the end of the day, duty is all there is.'

'Bullshit. I joined the Security Police because that's one place where I *can* make a difference. By rooting out vermin who undermine our society, I help make Rome a safer city to sleep in, which in turn stabilizes the whole Empire.'

'And this business you're engaged in at the moment? How exactly does investigating common burglary buttress the Empire, darling?'

'You're incorrigible,' he said, disentangling his curls. 'I'd have thought you, of all people, would be pleased that I'm assigned to this case, considering many of the targets are your

67

own relatives.'

'*Our* own relatives,' she corrected. 'And I am, darling. If anyone can catch the culprit, it will be you. The Senator and I are well aware of your record. One hundred per cent success rate, so I'm told.'

'Ninety-nine,' he corrected, thinking of a certain young widow with vineyards in Etruria and principles nowhere to be seen.

'Your trouble,' Margarita breathed, 'is that you need a woman, Marcus.'

Goddammit, she was right, he *did* need a woman, but it was not Margarita he longed for. Whenever his loins stirred, it was at the thought of a girl with thick, dark curls streaked with the colours of an autumnal sunset which tumbled over her shoulders. A wild, unpredictable creature, who raged like a forest fire out of control, scorching everything within range. He pictured her long legs scissoring up the Forum, her laugh filling the whole room, her eyes blazing with passion, her magnificent breasts heaving like the ocean in winter. And there was only one woman like that. Claudia Seferius.

But he needed a wife, too.

Not, as Margarita suggested, as a good career move. It was true that the Senate would not accept him without one, but his reasons for wanting a wife was more for a soft, warm embrace to come home to at night than for ambition. He longed for someone to laugh with, to share his triumphs and his tribulations, as well as his bed. He wanted a

68

wife, a best friend, a lover, someone to grow old and wrinkly with. But, most of all, Marcus Cornelius Orbilio longed to hear his house ring with the laughter of children. His children. And therein lay the problem.

For all his passionate arguments, he was a patrician whose family traced their ancestors back to Apollo himself. Could he really, when all was said and done, deny his children their birthright by marrying a woman from a lower social order?

Sadly, he knew the answer to his own question.

And the knowledge made him feel sick.

Outside, seagulls screamed as he ripped off the gold shoulder brooch. A tumble of embroidered linen cascaded on to the floor, and suddenly Orbilio was glad Margarita wore nothing but perfume under her gown.

Nine

Two people fight. Now one man is dead. Was Bulis one of the tussling pair? He couldn't have been, Claudia thought. No one could have entered that inferno to tie someone up without succumbing themselves.

Besides, Bulis wasn't just tied. He was *chained*.

Was that what the fight was about? One

person trying to prevent another from entering? Was Bulis alive while they struggled? Sweet Juno, was he screaming? Begging for help as Claudia ran across the path in the early hours? She hadn't been able to hear anything over the crackle of timbers. But no one on the steps could have missed his cries of agony...

A grim-faced working party mounted the stone steps and disappeared inside. Knowing the grisly task they had to undertake, the sound of sawing put her teeth on edge, and her mouth was drier than the Sahara as they carried the body out on a stretcher. Impossible to believe those charred remains had once been a living, laughing human being. What terror filled your heart, Bulis, as the first of the flames began to take hold? Which gods did you pray to for mercy? Which gods closed their ears to your prayers?

In silence, the stretcher-bearers manoeuvred the body down the steps. A path cleaved through the horrified crowd. By the bakehouse, several of Bulis's beautiful colleagues were sobbing openly.

'How could this have happened?' one of them spluttered through his tears. 'How could this have happened to Bulis?'

And Claudia thought, how indeed? How did a young apprentice come to be chained up like a hay rake? Did the arsonist know the boy was inside? Or, god forbid, had burning Bulis alive been his objective? The night-watchmen had been drugged, the grain store flooded with oil and set alight, but who was fighting on the steps while the inferno raged, and who had clamped her tight in a bear hug then knocked her out? She could understand it if he'd left her where she had fallen, but instead he'd taken the trouble of carrying her back to bed. Later, she thought, she would go through a few rooms, see who scented their clothes with sweet cinnamon. Because some-one—

A woman's scream cut through her conjecture.

So jarring was the sound, so utterly obscene in this moment of reverence as Bulis's remains were carried indoors, that at first no one understood what was happening. Then people saw where the woman was pointing.

And more screams filled the air.

Sails brailed, oars shipped, a galley lay at anchor in the calm, rose-red waters. Slim and symmetrical with her high carved posts fore and aft and her single bank of oars, there was no mistaking her for a merchantman. But the galley formed no part of the Imperial Navy. The colours she flew were of Mars, God of War. And the painted eyes were right at the front, on her bow. All the better to see her prey.

So much for the threat of piracy not being substantive.

'Jason!' Leo hissed through his teeth. 'Qus, arm the men! Everyone, man your stations! Prepare to defend to the death.'

Out on her prow, its bronze ram glinting in

71

the rising sun, one man stood alone. His arms were folded over his chest. Like the Dacian tribes over the hills to the east, he was tall and wore black pantaloons tucked into red leather boots. He wasn't a Dacian, though. Dacian warriors wore a beard as their badge of identity. This man was clean shaven. And unlike the Dacians, his swordbelt tied under the crotch. Other tribes did that, of course, including Shamshi's fellow Persians. What gave him away were the blue tattoos on his forearms. Those tattoos pronounced the captain a Scythian. That savage race of warriors who sacrificed horses – and occasionally humans – to the sun god they worshipped.

Suddenly a lot of things fell into place.

'*Bastards!*' Leo ran to the cliff edge and waved his fists. 'Murdering bloody bastards,' he yelled.

The lone figure performed a long, insolent bow before resuming his original pose. Gold glittered in the sunlight when he leaned forward. At his neck and also at his belt.

'Qus!' Leo roared. 'Is the *Medea* ready?'

'Naturally,' the bailiff replied. 'You gave strict orders to keep her primed to sail at a moment's notice.'

'Well, this is the moment, Qus! Muster the crew. I'm going after that murdering bastard.'

'But that's what he's waiting for,' the Ethiopian protested. 'He's trying to goad you into giving chase.'

'I'll give that sonofabitch chase all right, Qus. When I catch him, he'll wish he'd never been born!'

'You can't hope to outstrip him with the *Medea*.'

'Who bloody can't? Leo turned to his head slave and glowered. 'You just make sure that ship's ready to sail in ten minutes or you'll find yourself turned into cash come the next auction.'

Ten

In the field behind her simple cottage in the hills, the woman called Clio unhooked her robe and slipped naked into the freshwater pond. Sensuously, she splashed her face, her neck, her arms, paying particular attention to her magnificent breasts. She drizzled the soft, clear springwater over her thighs, her buttocks, the soft curve of her belly then lay back in the water, eyes closed against the sun, her dark hair streaming on the surface like a veil, her breasts bobbing.

There was no food in the cottage. She had eaten the last of the bread with her breakfast. The fish and the fruit had run out two days before. Even the cheese was gone now: it had comprised her meagre dinner last night. At least after her bath, she'd be able to go into town to stock up.

If you could call that hole a town!

Anywhere else in the Empire and the place would be awash with marble temples and airy basilicas, with triumphal arches and statues covered with gold. Day and night it would be thronging with spice sellers, money changers, perfumers, astrologers, the air ringing with the whine of self-blinded beggars, the crack of the wagoner's whip. All cities these days seemed to be a league of nations, with one group wearing gaudy turbans, others in fringed pantaloons and, everywhere, strange, exotic animals.

Clio sighed, and made circles with her wrists in the water, sending out a series of seductive ripples.

Alas, no giraffes here. No fast chariots. Nor pavements for them to rattle over, had there been any to start with! Cressian philosophy, like its inhabitants, was quite simple. Dump a few flagstones, call it a wharf. Erect a poky little building, call it a shrine. (Erect a bigger one and you get to call it a temple!) Clio rolled over on to her stomach, butterfly-crawled a few strokes. Where were the hotels, the fountains, the landscaped parks and gardens? Where were the public latrines? Croesus, there weren't even *shops* on this primitive island! Not even a single shoe-maker.

She changed her swimming to the breast-stroke. Merchandise, such as it was, was bought and sold in the open air around the harbour, everything traded and bartered and haggled for. You want a barber? The price is

74

three candles or a cheese or half a flagon of beer. You need dry goods? A bolt of cotton, maybe? Lead? Timber? Pitch? No problem. The trade ship's due in a month – or two, depending. Never get sick. A bow-legged, one-eyed caulker doubled as Cressia's dentist, there wasn't a surgeon, and if you need the island's one and only physician, you'll find him passed out on the floor stinking of booze.

Fine. Clio could work round that. She wasn't planning to be here for long. *Just however long it took.* But she so missed the *life.* The vitality. Some small indication that Cressia wasn't populated by living corpses. Croesus, all you ever saw were human statues! Fishermen sitting round mending their nets. Basket makers weaving the willows. Slowly. Very, very slowly. So slowly they never seemed to move. Zombies.

What she wouldn't give to see fire-eaters capering over the quayside! She swam to the edge of the pond and perched herself on a rock, like a mermaid. Jugglers would do. Or gaily dressed acrobats, accompanied by musicians cheered on by the masses. She let out a short laugh. Masses? *What* bloody masses! Dabbling her toes in the water, Clio reckoned you could round up every man, woman and child on this island and still never fill a barrel.

Mind you. If anybody ever got round to it, Clio would be the first to roll the barrel off a cliff. Good riddance. She despised these filthy islanders. They were impoverished, ill-educated, stank of stale fish and stale sweat and bad teeth.

Moreover, she was aware of their opinion of her.

Suspicious and superstitious, their skins wrinkled and leathery from working outdoors in the sun, the islanders could not imagine how a woman past thirty could – by natural methods – retain a complexion like milk and hair which shone like damascene. Especially long black hair which fell to her waist, with not a single strand of white to be seen.

Rumours spread like heath fire. The newcomer was one of the *Lamiae*. Women who took men to their beds then feasted off their living flesh to keep themselves young. Clio's contemptuous snort startled a small herd of goats grazing in the distance. *Lamiae* indeed! She waded back to the shore, each leg slowly, sensuously, parting the water. Some young boy decides he's had enough of this island, hitches a ride on the first available ship, and suddenly the dark-haired woman on the hill is accused of eating the poor bugger alive! Were their lives really that narrow?

Picking up a towel, she blotted off the excess water, spending longer than necessary on her beautiful breasts and the soft insides of her thighs. When she was finished, she knelt on a soft patch of grass and bent over the water, washing her hair with a mixture she'd concocted herself to bring out the shine.

Combing her dripping black mane through

to the ends, Clio knew what had started tongues wagging. She'd arrived out of nowhere, taking over this abandoned stone house on the hilltop without explanation. No servants, no husband, no children. Such a solitary existence was not natural in the islanders' view. And on Cressia, if something's not natural, then it has to be ... unnatural.

Sure, the locals took her money in the market, but they made no effort to disguise the sign they made to avert the evil eye. Beauty came at a price, they believed, openly chanting spells and incantations to make sure *they* weren't the ones to be paying it. Behind her back they called her witch, enchantress, sorceress – and worse. Fine. Let them make the sign of the horns. What did she care? It was only superstition, at the end of the day. And superstition doesn't put food on the table.

Getting back into her robe to signal that the show was over, Clio heard the two silver coins clink on the hard ground. No trading for her. Strictly cash. There was a rustle in the bushes behind the drystone wall which grew fainter and fainter until only silence remained.

She scooped up the coins, bit them to test the metal and smiled.

Sprats tonight!

Eleven

'Sir –' Qus's voice was a strained whisper – 'a word before we sail?'

Behind a pillar in the colonnade, Claudia froze. Her pale lemon-yellow gown was the same colour as the marble, rendering her all but invisible in the early morning light. She held her breath.

'What now, Qus?' Leo asked tetchily.

'I found this when I unlocked the bath house this morning.'

The Ethiopian was holding a wooden spear adorned with carvings, ribbons, feathers and what appeared to be a dozen clumps of hair. When he shifted position the spear rattled, and halfway up the lance a sheet of parchment was impaled.

'Embedded in the door,' he said, 'like last time and the time before.'

'Not quite,' Leo said. 'The previous delivery was lodged in the stables, the first we found impaled in the boat shed.'

'Same thing.' The Ethiopian shrugged.

'No, there's a pattern, don't you see? Jason,' Leo said, 'has been creeping that little bit closer to the house every time. Now the bastard's turned his terror tactics to arson and murder.'

78

'Surely you don't think *Jason* killed Bulis?'

'Who else?' Leo said. 'Dammit, Qus, his flames have been terrorizing the archipelago for weeks. Sooner or later he was bound to cross the line.'

Not just these islands, either, Claudia thought. Everywhere, villagers were fleeing in droves from attacks which Rome, their so-called protector, was powerless to prevent. Small wonder the natives were getting restless.

'Same bloody message,' Leo sneered, pulling the note off the lance. *'Give back what is mine.'*

'I suppose you could always give it to him?' the Ethiopian ventured.

'I don't have anything belonging to Jason. It's just a ploy to provoke me.'

But there was a depressing lack of conviction in Leo's denial and a few more pieces of the puzzle started to slot into place. The arson attack, for one. Upping the stakes in whatever game was being played out on this paradise island. It explained the pirate's cool demeanour in the bay – that low insolent bow. It explained why he hadn't simply stormed the place, too. The Villa Arcadia might boast strong defences, but if Jason gathered a small pirate navy, they'd be no match for Leo's resistance and heaven knows there were enough spoils on this site to go round. Whatever it was Leo had and Jason wanted back, it was something Jason couldn't simply come in and take.

79

So why didn't Leo simply ignore the ship in the bay? Why bother to go after the Scythian?

'This remains strictly between ourselves,' he warned Qus. 'No one else is to know about these spears, understood?'

There was a slight pause. 'Of course.'

Leo leaned into his face. 'Cross me, boy, and I'll have you demoted to labouring before you can even say "sorry". Do I make myself clear on that?'

'Absolutely.' Pause. 'Sir.'

'Good man. Now let's go strip the hide off some pirates!' Flexing his shoulder muscles, Leo grinned and slapped his bailiff on the back. 'Show 'em what fibre we Romans are made of.'

Maybe it was a trick of the light, but Claudia could have sworn she saw the big Ethiopian flinch.

Three speared warnings, each creeping that little bit closer than the last, was the classic hallmark of the psychopath as he piled on the psychological pressure. Arson had probably been his original intention last night. So close to the villa, it had been meant as a warning. But then he'd found Bulis wandering about – and Jason didn't strike Claudia as the type to kiss an opportunity goodbye. Wrong man in the wrong place at the wrong time, poor sod, Bulis had been a matter of simple expediency. By killing the young apprentice, Jason's warning could not possibly be ignored.

And Leo, the blockhead, had taken the bait. Every piece of ornamentation on that

80

Scythian lance was a symbol of the warrior's courage and skill. The rattles represented the swiftness of his horse's hooves. The carvings reflected the tattoos on the warrior's skin: totems to protect him. The feathers were the feathers on his arrows, those deadly instruments of death that even Rome's finest bowmen couldn't match. The yellow ribbons exemplified the rays of the sun god. And the clumps of hair? Actually, they symbolized nothing. These were trophies pure and simple.

Scalps of the men the warrior had killed.

Sweet Janus, who did Leo think he was tangling with here? Hadn't he learned any lessons from history? You just do not mess with these people!

Scythia was the vast and rugged country to the north and west of the Black Sea. No matter what Rome had thrown at her over the years, Scythia had withstood every attack, had repulsed every advance, not an inch of territory had been conceded. Pity. Because Scythia controlled trade and shipping; a nice little earner for Imperial coffers if the country had fallen. But the point was, if the whole might of the Roman Empire couldn't defeat these superlative warriors, what hope had Leo in the *Medea*?

This, remember, is the race who scalp their enemies and use their flayed skins to cover their quivers. The race who gild the skulls of their enemies and use them as ceremonial goblets. *The race where human sacrifice is*

81

still practised...

Leo, dammit, had not only chosen to go head to head with one of these barbarians but to hell with anyone caught in the crossfire.

Claudia slipped quietly through the gate which led to the herb garden, where the the apple fragrance of camomile mingled with the scents of mint, coriander, thyme and spicy basil. Sun, shining through the feathery fennel, dappled the lemon balm, and bees buzzed around the hyssop and the lavender. Same old Silvia, she thought. Immaculate and unruffled, regardless of the crisis, be it fire, pirates or – hefting pots of lilies? Her fair hair gleaming in the early morning light, she was sitting on a bench while an oriental slave girl sang about unrequited love as she gave her mistress a pedicure.

'You do know there's a pirate ship in the cove?' Claudia asked.

'The captain's a Scythian and his name is Jason.' Silvia indicated to the girl to continue singing. 'Apparently his mother's an Amazon and he gets his looks from her.'

Claudia imagined Jason would get looks from hundreds of women.

'Aren't you worried about a galley full of barbarian thugs on your doorstep?' she asked. Dammit, this woman was a mother of three. She couldn't always be this detached, could she?

'He's just taunting us,' Silvia said, holding out her other slender foot for attention.

'Maybe so, but your brother-in-law has taken the bait.'

'Then he's a fool.' Silvia picked up the tortoiseshell lyre on the bench next to her. 'Water is Jason's element and Leo should know better than to charge off making a fool of himself.'

She wasn't serious? 'A boy's dead, Silvia. He's bound to feel passionate about exacting revenge.'

'Revenge!' Silvia began to strum softly. 'No individual can possibly take on Jason single handed and win.'

'You're not suggesting Leo lets him get away with this outrage?'

'Don't be silly, dear.' She might have been talking to a small child. 'We're merely saying it's high time our brother-in-law used his head for a change. Or more pertinently, his family connections.'

'Trust Leo to have a naval commander in the family.'

'No, no. His cousin Marcus is attached to the Security Police—'

'*What?*' Some spiteful Cressian god is playing tricks with my ears. 'Orbilio is Leo's cousin?'

'Know him, do you?'

'We may have met.'

Silvia adjusted the tension on the second string. 'Well, then, you'll know that with Marcus's clout, we could get troops, boats, artillery, whatever is necessary to rid the Gulf of these desperadoes.'

Dammit, Claudia should have paid more attention that day Leo came calling! Vaguely (now!) she recalled him mentioning that his cousin Marcus had suggested he pay her a visit, but come on – there are an awful lot of Marcuses in Rome and besides she'd been too busy wondering how Hylas the Greek had traced her so fast and worrying what size of dossier the Security Police had been compiling on her doping activities to venture into family histories. Stupid cow! Claudia ground her heel into the camomile. Croesus, she'd even remarked on the family resemblance. Same tall build, same lean physique, same thick, dark, wavy hair. No dimple on the chin, of course, but instead of putting a simple two and two together, she'd been too busy digging an escape tunnel from Rome. *Shit!* Orbilio had counted on that, dammit. That's how he'd sprung his trap.

'Younger than Leo by a decade,' Silvia drawled, 'but twice as handsome and ten times as ambitious. Has his sights on the Senate, you know.'

'Actually I do know.'

And guess who's his fast track? Given that the more results a man can clock up, the closer it takes him to the Senate, think how much faster his travel when the perpetrators conveniently hand over the incriminating evidence themselves!

'If only Leo were not so obstinate on the issue of assistance.' Silvia laid the lyre on her lap and fixed her big blue eyes on Claudia.

'Given the laurels he'd win for ridding the Liburnian Gulf of marauders, Marcus would not be able to resist the challenge.'

Much less if his cousin got himself killed out there this morning! Dear Diana, a snapping turtle could sink that pathetic little crate, never mind a seasoned warship. What on earth was Leo thinking of? The only good thing that could possibly come out of it was that the death of his cousin at the hands of a bunch of pirate rebels would fire a crusade so strong, so fierce in his proud patrician breast, that Orbilio would comb every inch of this secretive landscape until he had the Scythian at bay. What's more, he would have the backing of the whole damn Roman Empire behind him, there would be nowhere for them to hide.

But for heaven's sake, there had to be a better way of making the seas safe than through Leo's martyrdom! Which, of course, there was. Provided Claudia could think up a way to prevent Leo from sailing.

Twelve

The demon yawned, stretched and, had it been a cat, it would have purred. Like a leech, it had grown fat on the blood upon which it had feasted last night, but blood was this island's birthright.

Why should it not be the demon's, also?

Of all the islands in the Adriatic, Cressia's history was the darkest. Inextricably linked with one of the most famous exploits of all time, that of Jason and the Golden Fleece, it was here, at the head of the Adriatic, that the Argo had dropped her anchor all those years ago.

Opinion on the Fleece itself was divided. One school of thought had Jason sailing through the Hellespont and round the Black Sea until he reached the land of Colchis on its south-west shores. The hypothesis was sound. Alluvial gold washed down from the Caucasus was still collected today by laying fleeces along the river bed in spring. Therefore to scholars in this camp, the Golden Fleece was exactly what it purported to be. A fleece of pure gold.

Colchis, others claimed, was Greek for Kolikis, a stronghold of the Liburnian tribes on the mainland north of Cressia and once an important station along the amber route which, in those days, ran pretty much in a straight line from the Baltic to the Aegean. This suggested Jason was more trader than raider, and that the Golden Fleece was that ultimate status symbol of wealth: a sheepskin cloak studded with thousands of tiny beads of amber.

But whether Jason was a gold-digger or an amber merchant was irrelevant to the demon. Cressia's dark history wasn't about Jason. It revolved round a woman.

Medea.

Voluptuous, beautiful, she was a princess of Colchis. She seduced Jason, stole from her people, double-crossed her own father, murdered her brother, dismembered his corpse and threw his body parts into these very waters.

Perhaps the old Greek historians were right in that the goddess Athena refused to allow Medea to leave with her brother's blood on her hands. Then again, perhaps the Argo's crew simply refused to take her on board without her repenting. Either way, before Medea could sail with Jason, she was forced to seek purification on this island, the Island of the Dawn, where Circe the enchantress dwelt in a sumptuous palace.

Except Medea did not repent. Her wickedness was never expunged. History records how she went on first to kill King Pelias, before butchering the king of Corinth and then how, when Jason wanted to divorce her, Medea burned her love rival alive and later went on to poison her own children. What made this story particularly interesting was the poison she'd used. Colchicum. The bulb of Colchis. From whom could she have learned such a skill? The demon knew the answer full well. Circe was the King of Colchis's sister, whose powers as a sorceress were well documented. She could tame wild beasts, turn men into hogs, conjure up the winds with her spells. And the bulb of Colchis flourishes all over this island.

The demon saw a very different scenario to the theory about Medea needing repentence. It saw this as a smokescreen, whereby she could engineer a call on the aunt who had been exiled by her father, the king. It saw two like minds, plotting and scheming far into the night. Medea, we know, sailed away with new skills, but Circe? What *became of the king's sister?*

The demon knew the answer to that conundrum, as well.

After Medea sailed away with her Jason, the Trojan hero Odysseus had been so captivated by the enchantress's beauty that he stayed seven years as her consort. She had borne him three sons and with each generation, that knowledge had been passed down. Fresh. Undiluted. Pure in its wickedness and guile.

For much of the time, the evil remained dormant. But every now and again the dark demon stirred.

Bulis had been a good start.

Thirteen

'Psst!'

Claudia beckoned her bodyguard round the side of the weaving shed, and that was another thing she'd picked up about the Villa Arcadia. So many perfect places for someone to lurk with pots of lilies.

'Here's what I want you to do,' she told Junius. 'I want you to go and pick a fight with Leo.'

'You ... you aren't serious, madam?'

'Any pretext you can think of. Only make sure you knock him out cold, there's a good boy.'

'You're asking *me*, a slave, to knock out a *patrician*?' The young Gaul had received many outrageous instructions since being promoted to the head of Claudia's bodyguard, but this, surely, took the honey cake. 'Madam, with respect, he'll have me fed to the lions a limb at a time.'

'Junius, you were asked to pick a fight with Leo, not with me. Now I don't wish to remind you that I could have been chargrilled in my bed last night because you were negligent in your duties—'

'*Negligent?* But it was you who insisted I spend the night in town to find out what I could about—'

'Spare me the grovelling apologies, Junius. The *Medea* sails in less than five minutes.'

'And I'm supposed to stop him?' The young Gaul's Adam's apple was working overtime. 'Would you mind telling me how exactly?'

'With a strong right hook, you dumb ox.'

Funny chap, that Gaul. Tall, tanned and muscular, his most attractive trait as far as Claudia was concerned was his ability to keep his eyes wide open and his lips tight shut. Oh, yes, and the fact that he always did what he was told. Eventually.

Claudia moved across to the steep-sided rock face to see how her bodyguard would handle this particular task. Although she had no idea what was going on concerning those messages impaled on the spears, she had a strong gut feeling about Jason. Like a cat, he enjoyed taunting his prey. Had he wanted to kill Leo outright, wouldn't he have set fire to the house? Done his dirty deeds at night and by stealth, the same way he'd delivered his notes? No, no. That slow bow said it all. The sick bastard was milking the situation for all it was worth, inciting Leo to give chase by taunting him with a warship that wasn't even primed to take flight. Leo has something Jason wants and so, in another turn of the psychological screw, Jason intends to humiliate him in the most public way possible.

Now, if Claudia could see this as plain as the nose on her face, then surely so could a highly educated scion of society like Leo. Yet he was walking straight into the trap, and why? Because Leo, the arrogant sonofabitch, thought he could win.

The scrubland on the cliff where she was standing had been laid to flagstones, affording a perfect view. Down on the jetty, a preposterously small and ill-armed boat was being made ready for sail. Leo, who had changed out of his patrician robes into serviceable boots and a short green working tunic, was galvanizing the *Medea*'s crew into action. Further out, on the warship whose oars still remained firmly shipped, Jason mimed a slow sarcastic handclap.

Since taking over the Imperial reins, Augustus had waged war on every bandit, footpad, robber and pirate in the Empire. It was his belief that, day or night, winter or summer, every traveller on any main road or shipping highway had the right to make his journey in safety. Note the key words there. *Main* road. Shipping *highway*. With the best will in the world, no army could patrol every square mile of an Empire which stretched from Iberia in the west to Syria in the east, and from Egypt to the North Sea. What hope a stretch of coastland so indented, so wooded, there were hidey-holes everywhere and islands too numerous to count? None! The only hope of making these waters safe was to set a trap and bait it, and then for someone to inform Rome of the situation in order for reinforcements to be sent. A policy Leo was staunchly set against, suggesting only one explanation: Leo wanted the glory! Why else would he keep quiet about Jason's speared messages? If word spread that Jason wasn't half the threat he appeared to be, then his heroics would be seriously diluted, his authority undermined. Can't have that. In any case, he probably saw this as the perfect solution. Eliminate Jason, eliminate problem. Talk about tunnel vision!

Ah! There, at last, was Junius, trotting along the jetty. Claudia couldn't hear the actual exchanges from the clifftop, but judging by the hopping up and down and flailing arms and wild gesticulations down below, that was some row he had instigated. Leo might well be older than his cousin by a decade. But you wouldn't know it from the acrobatics.

Concerned that his verbal assault wasn't having the desired effect, Junius raised the stakes by jabbing Leo firmly in the chest with his index finger. In response, Leo leaned forward and snarled something nasty back. Junius bunched his fists. Terrific. Claudia clapped her hands in relief. I *knew* I could rely on that boy! All we need now is one good punch to lay him out – and that's precisely what happened.

Right on cue.

Wallop.

Unfortunately, it was Leo who swung it.

Fourteen

Violet-blue coral glimmered in the crystal-clear sea a hundred feet below and, when the sun caught a wave, its crest reflected the light like a mirror. Sea ravens croaked from precarious clifftop perches and, to the north, white-headed griffon vultures with wingspans greater than the height of a man soared over Cressia's peaks. The mid-morning heat turned the gravelly paths into a shimmering haze. Claudia had decided to take this walk on the basis that if at first you don't succeed, quit worrying. She'd done her damnedest to stop Leo setting off after a warship in a wooden hip bath. All she could do now was chew her nails and hope to glory that Jason's humiliating dance would lead the *Medea* away from the rocks and into open water where even Leo wouldn't be able to sink himself!

Strolling beneath the dappled grey canopy of the olive groves, her skirts released waves of fragrant pinewood scent as they brushed the yellow blooms of the pine-ajuga. Animal bells played a soft and melancholy tune as black-faced sheep and horned goats chomped noisily on the sparse clover patches. Bees droned round the tall spikes of the poisonous sea squills and explored the delphiniums, while crickets rasped in the coarse, dry grass.

Nowhere on the island had Claudia felt more isolated. More disconnected from civilization.

Settling down with her back against a gnarled trunk, she drew her knees up to her chest and stared across the sparkling Gulf, where the densely wooded slopes of the mainland slid like a wanton woman into the warm cobalt waters. Fishing boats like ink spots spattered the ocean, hauling home baskets teeming with lobster, crayfish and crab. How easy to picture the *Argo* out there...

Fifty oars. A hundred oarsmen. Rich men's sons for the most part. There were famous boxers, wrestlers, swimmers on the expedition, though a few brought rather less obvious skills. The bee-master, for instance. What use had he been? Never mind. Luckily for the crew, the ship carried a shape-shifter on board, two winged men (obviously), a seer and a poet (naturally), one virgin huntress (who wouldn't?) and, of course, for those little everyday emergencies, a transvestite.

Gazing up at the heavy clusters of green olives swelling beneath their leathery, silver-grey leaves, the past and the present fused.

Jason and the Argonauts.

Jason and the brigands.

It could, of course, be coincidence that Leo's ship was called the *Medea*, but co-incidences were stacking up fast. First we have a pirate called Jason, then we have the *Medea*, and let's not forget Colchis is a Scythian trading post on the Black Sea. The past and the present. Coiling together like snakes.

But one thing at a time.

'Here's the deal,' Claudia told Neptune. Sure he had an enormous territory to patrol and couldn't hope to be everywhere at once, but it was high time he swept the cobwebs out of this particular corner of his watery domain. 'You sink that galley flying the red flag of your brother' – Mars wouldn't miss one skitchy little trouble-maker, would he? – 'plus you dispose of any ships bringing tall, dark, aristocratic members of the Security Police to these parts, and in return I'll give you a beautiful white bull as a sacrifice. Not a black hair on its body, I promise.'

'Who are you talking to?'

Claudia had heard of woodland nymphs, dryads they were called, and nut-nymphs, caryatids. But she'd never actually believed in them. Much less olive-grove nymphs!

94

'Neptune,' she said, leaning her palms on the thick drystone wall where, on the other side, a pair of eyes as big and as bright as a rabbit's peered out of a filthy little wedge-shaped face. 'I was asking him to protect Leo and the *Medea*.'

'Can Neptune hear you?' Somewhere beneath all those ingrained layers of grime was a girl of nine, maybe ten, on her scrawny knees pulling up roots.

'Why shouldn't he? You did.'

'Personally, I don't bother with that praying lark,' the girl said, with a sad shake of her matted curls. 'What's the point? The gods only answer the prayers of the grown-ups.'

Claudia was not about to disillusion her by disclosing that the gods don't always bother with that. 'Should you be out on your own?'

'I much prefer my own company,' the child said. 'It's so noisy at home.' She pulled up another plant and shook the soil off its roots. 'Kids,' she muttered. 'Who'd have 'em?'

Claudia blinked.

'If they're not squabbling, they're bossing each other around.' The girl clucked. 'Sometimes I don't know how I manage to cope.'

'Lots of you, are there?' Claudia sucked her cheeks in hard.

'Thirteen or fourteen, I suppose.' The girl shrugged. 'You lose count after a while.'

Maybe that explains the rabbit eyes, Claudia thought, debating whether perhaps the child was also concealing a powder-puff tail underneath her cheap cotton shift. 'What are

95

you picking?' she asked. The stonework was searingly hot through her skin, and a green lizard darted into a gap in the wall near her foot.

'Alkanet.' Little hands tugged up another root and examined it carefully. 'Nanaï wants to dye blankets for winter, only she won't let us pick them while they're in flower, she says it's a waste of a pretty blue life.' Her small dusty faced tipped to one side. 'We'll still be here, you know. In the winter.'

'Yes. I'm sure you will be.' And now it was becoming impossible for Claudia to stifle her laugh.

'No, I mean it. I heard Nanaï tell Lydia. "He can't throw us to the wolves," she said. "It's not fair, turfing us off like we were ticks on a sheep", but Lydia said there was no contract, nothing in law, and Nanaï said, "That doesn't matter because Leo swore on his oath".'

Ah, so that was it. The poor child's absurdly large family was a pawn in some tradesman's dispute. Connected no doubt to Leo's massive renovation programme, for reasons unknown (bad workmanship probably) Leo had served the family notice to quit. At her feet, the girl was still chirruping on in her world-weary voice as she stuffed more alkanet roots into her tightly clenched fist.

'Lydia told Nanaï to be careful. Leo's word couldn't be trusted, she said, he was a bastard down to his core. But Nanaï laughed, and said she was used to handling bastards.'

96

Claudia wondered what the odds were that other people had conversations with ten-year-old minnows who gossiped like fishwives? But then, moving house would be a subject very dear to little hearts. Stability is everything to children and by relating the conversation between Nanaï and Lydia, this dusty bag of bones could convince herself that nothing was going to change in her tiny world. That they *would* all still be here, come the winter.

'Do you know what "having no leverage" means?' she asked Claudia, screwing her grubby face into a frown.

'You lose your bargaining power.'

The little face relaxed. 'Ah, so that's what Lydia meant when she told Nanaï that if Leo tossed us out, she wouldn't have any leverage. Not that Nanaï was worried. She told Lydia she had no intention of waiting until we got thrown out. In a few days, she said, there wouldn't be a problem, we'd be safe.'

Claudia felt a chill of alarm prickle her skin. Was that a threat she'd just heard repeated from those tiny lips? And if so, just how substantive was Nanaï's warning? Then she looked at the bony-kneed scrap, burrowing around the dusty stone wall, and decided this was getting too fanciful. Her nerves were upside-down-inside-out thanks to the fire, the charred body, the scalp-mongering pirate – and (admit it) because she was scared stiff Leo would not come home. Rattled nerves do not make for rational thought!

'Does Lydia often visit your mother?' she asked, changing the subject.

'They've been friends for ever,' the little girl said. 'Only now Lydia comes more often because she hates that little white house Leo built for her on the point and she hates Leo and she hates having no money and hardly any servants, but I don't see what all the fuss is about. If Leo wants a baby so badly, he can have one of ours, we've got loads and Nanaï won't miss one, I'm sure. Oh, and you've got it back to front about Nanaï, but if you want to know more, I'm afraid you'll have to come home with me. You see, I haven't got time to hang about nattering. My bread's ready to come out of the oven.'

Fifteen

The tavern was a typical harbourside tavern, filled with fishermen, BO, tall stories and splinters. Orbilio, in a knee-length linen tunic tied with a woollen belt, had to raise his voice for his call for a second jug of wine to be heard. The wine was coarse, like the people who drank it, but at least in these rough drinking dens where he searched out information, the darkly lit bearpits, the rowdy bordellos, people were honest about who and what they were. He spiked his hands through

98

his fringe. It was more than he could say for himself.

Croesus, what made him take Margarita like that? A pain shot through his body, violent and searing. The cheap truth of it was, he had made love to her (if that was the term) because the woman he wanted was out of his reach and, in one rash moment, he had consumed his yearnings in animal lust. He shuddered with the shame of the memory. Mother of Tarquin, what devils had possessed him to take a woman who was shallow, uncaring and whose looks had all but faded simply to assuage a different hunger?

'Ooh, darling,' Margarita had purred afterwards. 'I shall settle for nothing less than sex spelled with four Fs from now on. Frequent, fast, frivolous and *frenetic!* You tiger, you!'

What terrible depths had he sunk to?

Around him, men talking in the local cadence laughed, threw darts or moved bone counters over an oakwood table marked into squares. Heavy-set wenches swapped badinage and gossip while they served food on square wooden trenchers and the landlord, the florid-faced husband of a small, prune-faced shrew, turned a blind eye to a flea-bitten tomcat stealing a pilchard. Through the doorway, Orbilio watched a weary black donkey grinding wheat on a treadmill as fishermen stropped the points of their harpoons.

Margarita had seen nothing sordid in that

99

bleak exchange of body fluids. What had once
been a succession of dazzling affairs for her
had congealed into casual sex as a substitute
for affection, and as much as he would like to
attribute her depressing transformation to
remarriage to the Senator, that was wishful
thinking. Marcus Cornelius Orbilio had been
as instrumental in her downward slide as
Margarita had been herself. As a wife and
mother, she'd represented fun without judgement, sex without commitment when he'd
been at a low ebb. He'd simply accepted the
affair as it came, on a plate, without considering how it might affect Margarita, being loved
then discarded as a matter of course. Today,
she was one step short of becoming an old
bag. An old bag whom he'd laid in a rabid
desire for somebody else!

Still. He drowned another goblet of wine.
The school of hard knocks had taught him
yet one more bitter lesson in this sorry
episode. At least he knew this craving he had
for Claudia Seferius wasn't love. If nothing
else, yesterday's sordid session had shown
him how to recognize lust when he saw it.
That pain, that tearing passion, that burning
need for fulfilment which ripped him apart
might have many names, he reflected bitterly.
But love wasn't one of them.

Croesus almighty, though. Doping thor-
oughbred racehorses! He knew why she was
doing it. She'd climbed out of the gutter,
inveigled herself into marriage with a rich
wine merchant who'd then died and left the

young widow the lot. Clearly, if a girl was to continue living in the manner to which she's grown accustomed, then adjustments had to be made – and since she wasn't able to off-load the business assets, it stood to reason that, with Claudia, not all of those adjustments would be legal. Typical of the woman to mix business with pleasure. She never could resist a gamble! Even though betting was against the law. At least in theory.

Augustus was a wise old owl when it came to his people. Although most of Rome's wealthier citizens had absconded to the hills or (like the Senator and Margarita) to their seaside villas to escape the torrid summer, nearly a million souls had not. Worse, while they were effectively incarcerated in the city, irritable from the heat and bored to the nines, their incomes had plummeted from loss of trade.

'A people that yawns is ripe for revolt,' the Emperor had been heard to murmur on more than one occasion.

He had decreed that it might not hurt if the controls on gambling were eased during the hot summer months. Augustus, bless his campaign boots, understood that the poorer the individual, the more money they bet, simply because they had the most to gain. So he introduced the idea of bronze raffle tickets with food prizes for the winners. What pittance they earned might disappear on liquid pleasures or a horse's hoof, but a shoulder of mutton and a brace of hare stops them from crossing the line into stealing.

Orbilio tuned in to the local chatter in the tavern. Already he had picked up a good deal, either from conversation or from eavesdropping, information he would never have acquired in patrician garb. Across the room, he nodded acknowledgement to a man in his mid to late forties, greying at the temples, a fish out of water if ever there was one in this flyblown harbourside dive. Fish out of water always made his instincts twitch. The fellow wasn't high born, but he wasn't poor, either, and one of the first things Orbilio had noticed were the long, spatulate fingers. The type of fingers which could tell gold from gold plating and recognize fine works of art in rich men's houses when they felt them.

The man smiled, a warm and uncomplicated smile, his eyes meeting Orbilio's full on before he turned into the town square where children sang and played hopscotch and dogs dozed in the shade. Hmm. The stolen items had been carefully targeted. Jewellery, silverware, carved ivory statuettes. And with none of the fences buckling under the strain of a sudden influx of precious goods, Marcus had a suspicion that, instead of being sold, the ivory was sent for recarving, the metals melted down for recasting, the gems prised out of their settings and recut. This wasn't a simple case of smash and grab and pocket the loot. A lot of money would be changing hands in a sophisticated organization planned like a military campaign involving people who wouldn't blink twice at eliminating nosy investigators.

Perhaps Margarita had the right idea after all, he thought wearily. Toe the family line. Settle down, practise law, sire sons. Not wait for a knife to slip between his ribs in some dreary back alley.

Marcus gulped down the last of his wine, wiped his mouth with the back of his hand and slipped out of the tavern's side entrance which, as it happened, opened into one such dreary back alley. He spiked his hands through his fringe. Croesus, what a choice. Running down cut-throats, thieves and assassins in the stinking stews and the ghettos; or making policy and laws in the Senate? He squinted along the dark passage, straining for sounds in the shadows.

No contest, old chap.

No contest at all.

Sixteen

Claudia must have fallen asleep, because when she opened her eyes, dusk was casting its soft cloak over the Villa Arcadia.

As much as a spot of light relief would have gone down rather well after the trauma and tragedy earlier, she had decided against accompanying the olive-grove nymph back to her over-populated home. If her theory was wrong – and Jason's intention was indeed to kill Leo out on the water – then the villa would be wide open to attack and Claudia had no intention of straying far from her escape route.

Thanks to plunging cliffs, much of Cressia's indented coastline was inaccessible. But not all. A great sweeping bay to the east sheltered the island's principal town and only deep harbour, though rocky coves and pretty sandy beaches proliferated. Plenty of places for a determined warship to put in. Plenty of places for a small rowing boat to be secreted, ready for a strapping bodyguard to row his mistress across to the mainland.

The pearl in a necklace of interconnected islands, Cressia was a long, narrow tongue of land forty miles long but rarely more than three miles wide. Craggy limestone mountains rose almost vertically out of the sea to the north, attracting squalls in winter and a pall of grey cloud even in summer. It was a place for only the brave, the foolish and the vultures, and much of the central hills were equally intractable, an untamed wilderness of oak, sweet chestnut and scrub. But where the landscape softened, so the climate changed, also. Here, rich pasturelands, olive groves and vineyards flourished. Warm in winter, but without the searing summer heat that bleached the Dalmatian coast to the west, deer and rabbits were hunted for game, trees coppiced for firewood, hives set up for the yellow bees which feasted off the nectar of wild herbs and produced such incomparable honey.

Heading homewards along the ridge of a hill, Claudia understood what attracted Leo to this extraordinary Island of the Dawn. The soil might be too thin, too dry, too starved of nutrients to make a fortune out of the estate, but who could blame anyone for settling here? What a bloody shame Lydia had not been able to give him the heir he so desperately wanted.

She had seen, from a distance, the small house of white island stone way out on the flat land of the point that Leo had built for his jettisoned wife. Odd. His behaviour didn't square with the man Claudia knew. Divorcing Lydia after eighteen years was one thing. He was blinkered about sustaining the bloodline and, whilst it was far from noble, he wouldn't be the first chap to set a wife aside. But to do it without notice was callous. Worse, for Lydia to find out by chance that the dowry to which she was legally entitled to have returned had been squandered on his costly renovations – well, that was simply unconscionable. How *could* he?

Back at the villa, Claudia had paused in the forecourt, absorbing the clang from the metalwork shop, the sparks from the blacksmith's, the dull thuds from the carpenter's shed overlaid with that distinctive sawdusty smell. Volcar's acerbic description of 'Leoville' wasn't so very wide of the mark. Legions

105

of slaves fetched and carried, sweat making damp ropes of their hair and sticking their cheap cotton tunics to their bodies. Sacks on backs went past. Barrels. Baskets. Jars, rumbling over the flagstones. From the kitchens came the clamour of pans being scraped, skillets washed, skivvies being clipped round the ear. The pitchy tang of charcoals tingled in her nostrils, along with the smell of the goose which had been roasted for lunch. Fish hung like washing on a line as they were cured in the sun, and water was ferried in buckets to the spanking new bath house.

Leoville.

Complete with the eagle, that ultimate emblem of Roman supremacy, emblazoned upon the entablature over the stone gateway. Leo, Leo, what a mess you've created in your stupid obsession for heirs!

Shamshi had just been leaving the bath house, his baggy trousers flapping like fish gills round his stick-like legs. 'I say, Claudia.' His wet hair clung to his skull like a black cap. Oh. It *was* a black cap, worn to protect his head against the fierce rays of the sun. Creepier and creepier. This guy wears a cap over the only part of his head that isn't shaved!

'Yes, yes, I know. Before the new light was born in the sky, bad news came over the water.'

The Persian nodded. 'Truly, the prediction was accurate. But, dear child, this morning I cast the bones and looked into the fresh
106

entrails of a goat—'

'My, my, some chaps have all the fun.' And before he could draw a second breath, Claudia's long legs had put as much distance between her and the gut-gazer as they could possibly manage.

Who can trust a man who claims to do everything? Inspect entrails, interpret dreams, observe birds, watch for portents, my armpit! With sixteen colleges in Rome devoted to an individual discipline, each requiring years and years of training, how does one lone Persian pretend to cover the lot? Creepy bastard. His boasts during the fire of how *he* would have handled her welfare, had *he* been in Leo's place, still made the hairs stand up on the back of her neck. Just let it be you who left this lump on my head. Oh, please, let it be you. But no matter how many times she'd encountered him in Arcadia, not once had Shamshi smelled of cinnamon. Bugger.

Claudia took a plate of food to her room, and that's when her exertions must have caught up with her. Because now Hesperus was settling down to join his daughters in the Garden on the mainland. The type of sunset that the islanders interpreted as the blood of Medea's murdered brother turning the sea red. She yawned, stretched, swung her legs over the bed. Four doors along, Silvia's glacial tones lashed one slave girl after another.

'For pity's sake, you stupid lump, are you colour blind? We are wearing the green robe tonight. Gre-e-e-en, do you hear? And you!

Careful with that hairpin, you clumsy girl, you've drawn blood!'

Juno save us from royal we's.

'Not that necklace, you fool. How many times do you have to be told, we want to make this a victory feast for the master. Nothing but our best emeralds will suffice for tonight.'

Whoa. Leo was *back*? And *victorious*?

Hurriedly, Claudia pulled on a gown of the finest Egyptian linen, midnight blue and trimmed with gold, and ran an ivory comb through the tangles of her hair. There might be issues to sort out with Leo tonight, but no way was she going to let that little cat Silvia outdo her in the looks department. With a quick drizzle of Judaean perfume in the hollows of her collarbone, she set off round the path outside her bedroom, adjusting her golden girdle as she went.

Looking even smaller in the red glare of the sunset, sure enough, the *Medea* was safely moored against the jetty. No holes in her side from where she'd been rammed. No mast missing. No keening of widows and orphans.

'Everything comes to those who wait, whether they want it or not,' a cracked voice said.

Volcar? 'What are you doing hiding behind trees?'

'Thinking,' the old man said.

'Drinking more like.' She could smell it from here.

'Thinking, drinking, same thing at my age.

108

A man drinks to think and thinks to drink, sod all else to do in this dreary backwater.'

We have murder, vendettas, eviction orders on children and execution orders on dolphins. We have sisters at war, a bitter ex-wife, scandal, financial betrayal, the clash of artistic egos and the dark influence of a Persian astrologer. What kind of a life had Volcar led that he considers *this* dreary?

'Why don't you go back to Rome?'

The old boy spat in the dust. 'Ask Leo. See what answer you get from him.' He pointed his stick at the *Medea*. 'What d'you make of that business, then, gel?'

What indeed. She ought to have been relieved; everyone home safe and well. Instead, anger flared in Claudia's breast. Damn you, Leo. Damn you to hell. You are reckless, feckless and utterly irresponsible. You callously risked the lives of dozens of men in the name of your own naked pride. Then she remembered the body of a young apprentice chained to the pillar. And maybe, just maybe, Leo's impetuosity didn't seem quite so misdirected after all.

'What happened?' she asked.

'You tell me.' Rheumy eyes flashed a surprisingly shrewd sideways glance. 'First I know of it is Leo, standing with his hands on his hips, and smug wasn't the half of it. "Take my word, uncle, the murdering bastard will think twice about tangling with Rome from now on".'

Claudia's eyes stood on stalks. 'He actually

sank the pirate ship?'

'Sink the *Soskia*?' Volcar's wheezy chuckle drowned the rasping of the cicadas. 'That'll be the day, when someone scuppers Jason! But to hear Leo go on, gel, you'd think he'd won the Battle of Actium.

' "Did that headless chicken run!" he laughed. "First, he ducked round the point and when he saw I was still on his tail, he put out across the Gulf to outrun me, but he was no match for my *Medea*. Realizing his tactics weren't working, he tried to lose me round the islands, but that warship hasn't a fraction of the manoeuvring power you might think, Uncle, and in the end I sent him scurrying away across the open water, tail between his legs." ' Volcar smacked his gums loudly and with relish. 'You're an intelligent woman. What's your verdict on that little episode?'

Trust no one, the little voice whispered again. Trust no one.

Age had not diminished the old man's senses, they were every bit as sharp as a man half his age. He'd been able to recount Leo's triumph word for word, and in doing so had revealed how Jason had indeed mocked Leo with a humiliating chase round the Gulf, just as Claudia had anticipated. But Volcar had not stopped there. The old man had deliberately gone on to expose Leo's arrogance in believing he'd won the encounter. The smell of rodent tickled her nostrils. Why would Volcar confide his kin's shortcomings to a

110

virtual stranger?

'What's my verdict?' Claudia tucked a wayward curl back under its ivory hairpin. 'What I say, Volcar, is that if a man can smile when things have gone arse over tip, then he's found someone to blame it on. Tell me what you know about Jason.'

'There's others here better qualified to answer that question, gel.'

'Leo?'

One skinny shoulder shrugged slightly. 'Could be.'

Strange time to start acting coy. 'Where is he?'

'Search me, gel. And just think of the pleasure you'd give a lonely old man while you do it.'

Still laughing, Claudia swept along the portico towards Leo's private quarters. This was where the sculptor Magnus – correction, *the* sculptor Magnus – had depicted scenes from the Odyssey on a magnificent marble frieze and Claudia was following the hero's adventures as he faced everything from the wrath of the man-eating Cyclops to the twin sea monsters, Scylla and Charybdis, when she heard a soft whistling.

Leo's Ethiopian bailiff was striding across the courtyard with a bolt of bright-blue cloth slung across one naked shoulder, his dagger tucked into his belt. His skin had been oiled, and in the fiery sunset, it glistened red, like blood, and the tendons on his arms and neck stood out like ropes.

'You don't know where Leo is, do you, Qus?'

He paused in his stride. 'No, my lady.'

Hm. 'Qus.'

'My lady?'

'What made you think Jason didn't kill Bulis?'

Dark eyes stared unblinkingly down at her. 'Jason killed Bulis.'

'When you showed Leo the third spear this morning, you sounded distinctly surprised that Jason had turned his tactics to murder.'

'I was not thinking straight then, my lady,' Qus said politely, and suddenly his loping gait was eating up the flagstones once again and he was gone.

Fine-looking man. Broad of shoulder. Chest like a hammered bronze breastplate. Five parallel lines running horizontally across his forehead that did nothing to lessen his attraction. Claudia wondered how much it hurt, having tribal marks scored that deeply into the flesh. How old he had been at the time. And why the devil the bailiff had lied. *On both counts.*

Just below the part on the frieze where Odysseus stuffs candlewax in his ear to resist the song of the Sirens, she collided with a small, fat swarthy body.

'Ah, Claudia. What a delightful surprise,' Saunio said.

Might be for you, chum. 'Have you seen Leo?' she asked.

'Pfft.' The maestro waved a lazy hand. 'He

promised to inspect the atrium at sunset, but where is he, that's anyone's guess. Come, my lovely. *You* can be the first to observe Saunio's finished artistry.' Hot fingers closed round her arm as he drew her into the room. 'There now, give Saunio your honest opinion.'

'Of your work?' she asked. 'Or the fact that you were waiting for me in ambush out there?'

'I fear you are mistaken,' he said with a small laugh, but the light which had hardened in his little beady eyes gave the game away. 'It was Leo I was waiting for, although it is perhaps ungallant of Saunio to admit it.'

No point in arguing. If he was the type to hang around in the shadows hefting pots of lilies, he'd regret it soon enough. Claudia saw herself tying the maestro to a chair while she shaved off his trademark curly beard and washed the dye out of his hair. See what the BYMs thought of their precious mentor then!

'Ta-da!' Saunio spread his fat arms wide. 'Looks twice the size, doesn't it?' The illusion was amazing. False rooms led off everywhere. 'Deceive the eye and art will triumph,' he said. 'Take that triptych, for instance.'

Quite. A visitor would be hard pushed to say it wasn't a real shrine opening off from the atrium, because such was Saunio's genius with perspective that, no matter where you stood, the impression didn't waver. The left- and right-hand panels depicted long marble tables adorned with four-handled vases narrowing inwards to the centre panel, a

113

shrine to the goddess Minerva. This kind of thing had been done before, of course (although not quite with such skill). What made Saunio's work breathtakingly original was that he'd added to the illusion by incorporating a scaled-down marble altar on which equally scaled-down offerings could be made. A miniature torch also burned in Minerva's honour as though this was an actual shrine, not a one-dimensional painted image.

But one thing was missing in this glorious room. True, there was enough gold leaf round the capitals of the columns to make even Midas turn green with envy. Rare eastern woods. Ivory carvings. Fine marble busts. The place was awash with onyx boxes, silver mirrors, and gleaming copper waterspouts funnelled the rain from the roof into a central pool where a fountain splashed out a soft tune, and small birds the colours of Arabian jewels sang their hearts out from an aviary at the end of the hall. But something was missing in this sumptuous room.

And that something, unfortunately, was Bulis.

The pitiful remains that had once been a laughing, living apprentice had been laid on a wooden bier and garlanded with laurel earlier in the day, but the steward hadn't been sure what to do with it. Place it in the atrium, as though the boy was a guest or a family member? Or leave him in the servants' quarters, as though he were a common slave?

Until Leo returned, poor Bulis had been stuck in the woodshed in a spiritual no-man's-land. But Leo was home now, and clearly a decision had been made. Bulis might well have been caught up in Leo's vendetta and paid the ultimate sacrifice. But when it came to social status, the young apprentice didn't make the grade.

While Saunio lectured her on drama and fusion, movement and light, Claudia observed the grey hue of his face, his hollow, red-rimmed eyes, the waxy, stippled texture his skin had taken on during the course of the day. Unmistakably, the physical manifestations of grief. But Saunio was a professional through to the marrow. One of his beautiful young apprentices had met an agonizing end, but Bulis's death would not alter the agenda.

'Schedules cannot mourn,' he'd pronounced, refusing his crew so much as one hour off. 'Timetables cannot grieve and neither can we until the contract is finished.'

Grief and shock, he added, tolerated no margins of error, it was business as usual on the frescoes. So, with Saunio standing over them, the labourers laboured to ensure the plaster was mixed to the exact level of dampness required to take a brush. The apprentices ground pigments to the exact mix of colour. An exact amount of outline was drawn for the artists to fill in.

'...the future,' he was saying, 'lies in illusionistic art, my lovely. Art is truth and truth is art, but therein the question lies.

115

What constitutes *truth*?'

'What indeed.'

'Take the meander in the banqueting hall. At first glance, it looks like a maze, but follow any of the lines with your eye – any one of them, Claudia – and you realize it is nothing but illusion. Misinformation. Created by shadows and spaces and geometrical trickery.'

His hollow gaze fixed itself on the pool, where he stared through the sparkling water to the green veined marble which lined it. So deep was his gaze, that he might have been staring straight into Hades itself.

'If the eye can be led, so can the mind,' he said slowly. 'For we can all be made to believe things which are not there.'

It was probably the light from the oil lamps flickering on the water, but Saunio's reflection made him appear even more squat and reptilian than usual tonight. Almost an allegory of depravity to fit the rumours.

'Illusion,' he said. 'That is the path for the artist to follow.'

'Wrong.' With a jerk of her thumb, Claudia indicated the exit. 'That is the path for the artist to follow. Goodbye.'

Shamshi was waiting, hands folded, outside the entrance to the dining hall. He was no longer wearing his baggy green trousers, but an ankle-length kaftan with a deep and richly embroidered hem. The brilliant artificial lights glinted off the thick hoops in his ears.

'Claudia.'

'Well, if it isn't Uncle Happy, the kiddies' pet.'

His mouth stretched a fraction sideways, the closest it came to a smile. 'Dear child, I need to speak with you,' he began, but at that point, Nikias turned the corner.

'Imparting your latest prediction?' he asked, and Claudia wondered whether she'd caught a flash of mischief in his eyes, or whether it was a trick of the flickering lamplight.

'I *tried* to tell her, Nik,' Shamshi said, his sibilant voice treacly with smugness. 'Earlier this afternoon, I tried to tell Claudia what I'd read in the entrails of my goat.'

The portrait painter grimaced. 'Stick to books, old man. Not so messy.' To Claudia, he said, 'Coming?'

'*We* will join you in a minute,' Shamshi said, indicating in no uncertain terms that the conversation was private. Nikias responded with an as-you-wish nod, but Claudia had a different idea on how to spend her evening. It did not include Persian gut-gazers. But as she swept past, a bony hand clamped over her shoulder and stopped her dead in her tracks.

'Listen,' he whispered, and his mouth was so close that his breath wafted her hair and the scent of it was as sweet as an overripe melon. 'I bring you a warning.'

Even though she shook his grip free, the memory of his fingers lingered on her skin like a burn. And he *still* didn't smell of cinnamon, dammit.

'This morning at dawn,' he said, 'I cast the bones, inspected the entrails, searched the skies for the signs until finally the gods spoke.'

'Until finally the goats spoke, you mean.'

'Do not mock what you do not understand,' he snapped. 'Heed my warning. Before the sun stands thrice more over our heads, a woman shall die.'

Did her heart miss a beat there? 'I thought your omens couldn't foretell death? Only "disaster"?' Funny how the rules change to suit the occasion.

'Vivid portents can *never* be ignored,' Shamshi said. 'The signs are as clear as though they were written in stone. Before the sun stands thrice more over our heads, it is decreed that a woman shall die.' He leaned towards her, his dark eyes searching her face. 'Take care, Claudia. Take very good care. Danger lurks among us tonight.'

Seventeen

Tall as a Dacian, lean as an athlete, bronzed as Apollo himself, Jason stood on the deck of his warship the *Soskia*, gazing up at the stars. Overhead was Draco, the Dragon, snaking its way between the Great Bear and the Little Bear in the way dragons do, its fiery mouth snarling at Vega, brilliantly defiant in the zenith above. Draco was the hundred-headed serpent who had guarded the golden apples in the Gardens of the Hesperides. It was said that each mouth of the dragon spoke a different tongue.

Jason turned his gaze past the black brailed sails towards the eastern horizon, but the heat haze prevented even a glimpse of Pegasus galloping through the night sky. There would be no rumble of celestial hooves tonight, Jason thought. No thunder, no lightning, the weather was settled. No rain would fall in these parts for some weeks.

The fires which flared along the Liburnian waterfront would have to be doused with seawater.

The *Soskia*, Greek for '*moth*', was anchored too far out to discern any of the frantic activity or hear the shouts and the screams.

Moths do well to keep clear of flames.

'Ale?' rumbled a gruff voice in his ear.

Jason turned to see Geta, his stocky, red-headed helmsman, holding out a horn beaker of foaming black beer. Until the first swig hit his tongue, he hadn't realized he'd been thirsty. Raucous laughter bellowed up from the closed deck below, the clink of mugs, the tang of fermented grain. Guards patrolled the upper deck and sentries kept watch from the wales.

As Jason gulped down his ale, the helmsman studied his captain.

Unlike other Scythians, Geta included,

119

there was no Asiatic slant to Jason's eye. Aye, but then Jason were warrior caste, Geta thought, an expert swordsman, at home with scimitar, lance and battleaxe. Depending on who you listened to, he were either the by-blow of a prince or the bastard of a Trebizond merchant. Jason never let on, but then he wouldn't. Men from the Caucasus don't talk much.

But Jason's history were common knowledge on account of his ma being a priestess, like. One of fifty who served the moon goddess Acca. Foreigners called 'em Amazons, since Acca's priestesses bore arms for certain rituals, and that were how Jason came to be a warrior. Through the temple.

Like Geta's, the captain's body was also covered top to toe in tattoos. They were Scythians. Weren't given no choice. But every man's brands were unique. Up Jason's arms flew Tabiti's sacred crane and Acca's sacred wryneck bird. On his thighs galloped the horse sacred to Targitaos the sun god, while his totem clan, the bull, shielded Jason's chest from evil. Dzoulemes, the sharp-sighted lynx, kept watch on his back.

Geta were from the Danube delta, so it were natural that his totem were the water serpent. His father were a boatman, aye, and his father before him, and Geta had absorbed the complexities of the Danube's watery labyrinth with his mother's milk. Before he were ten, he could navigate its tortuous channels. At fifteen he'd progressed to working the trade ships round the Black, Aegean and Ionian seas. By eighteen, he could read clouds and the behaviour of seabirds, were able to predict when storms would whip up, and where, and knew the best refuges to run to.

Piracy were the obvious step. Blindfold, he could circumnavigate them blue ice floes cast adrift from Russian rivers – what some called the clashing rocks. Likewise, that strange cluster of islands in the Sea of Marmora, round whose cliffs the winds turned without warning. Geta had had many a rich picking off the wrecks around them! Only then that bloody Roman Emperor started interfering, didn't he? Aye, and buggered up a smashing little earner. Armed bloody escorts to protect the merchant fleet. What kind of life's that, when a man's not even given chance to plunder the wrecks? When Geta heard the *Soskia* was recruiting, he jumped. Plunder, he reckoned, might not be so hard to come by under a fellow Scythian!

Precisely *what* a fellow Scythian were doing here, Geta neither knew nor cared, but he knew a shrewd move when he saw one. For all their highfalutin ideas, the Romans understood bugger all about the nations they'd conquered. Just cos an eagle flies in the sky, it don't follow that every creature on the ground is a mouse! They might pay lip service to this Roman legislature, but beneath the surface, the people round the Adriatic resented subjugation. Bitterly. Which, Geta reflected, tipping back the last of his ale, added up to an awful lot of bitter people.

Illyria was a bloody big place. Hundreds of tribes, stretching from Liburnia in the north to Dalmatia in the south, as well as twelve hundred sodding islands in between. And when you start totting 'em up, that's an awful lot of people paying taxes to an Emperor they've never seen, sending sons to wars they'd never heard of. The problem had always been how to shake off the yoke. How could these disgruntled souls, too widely scattered to muster a co-ordinated attack, ever rid themselves of their oppressors?

All the while they passed sesterces in place of their old coins and bent their knee to Neptune instead of Bindus, resentment seethed. It seethed and simmered, simmered and seethed, the pressure building up, up, up like a volcano. Who did these foreigners think they were, storming in and dividing up the land among themselves? What right had bloody Romans to strip it from the people who owned it? How come the very people who'd worked this land for generations suddenly become enslaved to strangers overnight?

Aye, Geta weren't half glad he were Scythian, not part of the Empire. Them what resisted were executed, else they became chattels to the very men who'd seized their own farms from them in the first place. Slaves! Geta spat over the side of the rail. Bought and sold like bloody sheep, without

122

rights, without respect, without a say in their own fucking destiny! Troublemakers were castrated or put to work on the treadmill cranes, six at a time, so what could the ordinary man do? Not one damn thing.

Until one man – Azan – began to move among his people.

Always wary of the dark ways of the informer, Azan listened to their grievances, reassured the dissatisfied that they were not alone, that others baulked at the same injustice. Above all, he gave the buggers hope. They did not have to suffer, he told them, freedom *was* within their grasp. The same freedom their Dacian neighbours enjoyed to the east, and the Scythians beyond, and the Cappadocians and Armenians beyond that.

Hearts began to stir. Could freedom truly be more than a dream?

Oh yes, my brothers, Azan assured them. What's more, he would be the one to deliver it. He would drive the settlers from every inch of Illyrian soil, make it a kingdom once more. And he would start with the coast and the islands! Once those territories were liberated, the inland colonies would be isolated. Helpless and unprotected, they could choose: fight, surrender, or flee. Soon, Azan promised, the land would belong to the Illyrian people once more.

Quite how the rebel leader had joined forces with a Scythian warrior, Geta didn't know. The warship was Jason's, but the crew were Azan's men, whose drunken laughter echoed louder into the night with every pitcher of beer. Geta wasn't Azan's man, of course. He was no man's bar his own.

Out along the coast, he watched the fires burn, yellow, red and orange. Flickering tongues that spat and hissed in the black void in supplication to the fire god, Agni.

'Reckon it'll take two days to put out that shipyard.' He chuckled. 'Aye, and two more before it stops smoking.' He planted his callused hands on his hips. 'For an easterner, you're pretty handy with a burning arrow, lad.'

A corner of Jason's mouth twitched. 'You're no slouch yourself,' he said, 'for a navigator.'

Geta aimed a mock punch at his captain, their cross-cultural jokes hiding a Scythian truth: in order to remain outside the Empire, every Scythian must be able to defend himself with cutting-edge skill. Regardless of their different backgrounds, even as small boys both would have had to practise with dagger and short sword until their little arms ached, and afterwards they'd have been sent straight to the butts for more. Warriors in particular were required to be expert in every conceivable weapon, including the scimitar, the battleaxe, the spear and the double-handed sword that sliced through metal helmets like a fist through parchment. It was a known fact that you weren't granted warrior status unless you could take an eye out at three hundred paces with the slingshot.

'Where to tomorrow?' Geta asked, his eyes

fixed on their crackling handiwork. Darting here, flitting there, no hit was ever predictable and he wondered how soon they could start to plunder.

Jason ran his finger slowly round the chain from which hung the purple amulet which all sailors wore as protection against shipwreck. 'You know, Geta, I rather fancy paying the Villa Arcadia another visit.'

'Ain't that a bit risky, son?'

'Not a bit of it. Who would expect us to return to a strike scene the very next day?'

'Crafty bugger, you are.' The redheaded helmsman tipped back his head and roared with laughter. 'Keeping them bastards on their manicured toes!'

But Jason didn't hear. He was gazing into the water, talking to himself as much as to his valued helmsman.

'The thing is, Geta, I don't think my message is getting through.'

He drummed his fingers gently on the ship's painted wooden rail.

'High time I sent another one, which will.'

From her vantage point on the hill, the woman called Clio could not see the shipyard ablaze, nor the warehouse beside it, nor any of the other buildings which burned along the Liburnian coast. There was too much of a heat haze this evening, blurring the horizons and softening the contours of the island.

But she knew there would be fires burning somewhere tonight. There always were. No matter how many the precautions, or how careful, Jason slipped through.

Superstitious types believed that the darkness rendered his warship invisible. In practice, the Scythian was simply intelligent, inventive, resourceful. And Clio knew all about intelligent, inventive, resourceful...

Below her, the lights of the little harbour town twinkled softly in the dusky night. She wondered what the dullards down there did for entertainment. Was there music and dancing in the taverns? Men fighting each other with feet and fists over a woman? Did they gamble, throw dice, bait bears or stage cock fights? Croesus, had they ever *heard* of those things?

They didn't think she understood their language. Just because she spoke to them in Latin, they didn't stop to question that she might actually speak their tongue. But Clio had been born in Liburnia. Understood everything those smelly sons of bitches were saying about her. Her rich ripple of laughter was mellowed by the sultry air. Didn't that latest rumour beat everything? Having abandoned the idea of a flesh-eating monster on their own doorstep, the silly sods had now labelled her one of the *Striges*. Vampires, who sucked the blood out of virgins. Virgins, indeed! Croesus, did any woman look less like a lesbian than Clio? She rolled her eyes, but accepted that the gossip was to her advantage.

Fear and superstition kept the nosy buggers away.

Clio had come to Cressia for a purpose, and privacy was its key – and of all people, the priest was her best ally in this. Llagos walked a religious tightrope. Cressian by birth, he was astute enough to have adopted Roman practices and pocket Roman coins while at the same time pacifying the islanders who followed the old ways by pandering to their pagan superstitions. The best of both worlds, she thought sneeringly. Like the peep show she staged for the horrid little runt.

Hooves crunched on the path below. The moon, two-thirds full, was rendered fuzzy from the heat and she could see no more than the rider was tall and well built. Pushing back her long, dark, heavy tresses, Clio watched the man dismount and tether his horse to a bush. The climb to her cottage was steep. She heard his breath, ragged from exertion. Behind her, the door to her cottage stood wide, sending out wafts of oregano oil burning in the single lamp which hung in the window. The horse snickered softly.

'Clio?'

He could not see her. Standing in the shadows, her black hair and dark-purple robe rendered her all but invisible. It was a quality she traded on, invisibility. The ability to move, yet not be seen.

'Clio, it's me.'

She counted to ten, then jangled the bracelets on her left wrist. When he jumped, she smiled to herself. He still had no idea she was

127

only four feet away.

Silhouetted in the pale moonlight, Leo moved towards the place where he imagined she was standing. 'I can't stop,' he said. 'They're waiting for me at dinner.'

Clio let him approach. He was close now, his nose almost touching hers, and she smelled woodsmoke in his hair and wine on his breath, and could see that the torque he wore round his neck was of solid gold.

This time she only counted as far as five. Then slapped his face so hard, her ring slashed his cheek.

Eighteen

Large or small, every event in life has a consequence which colours our future from that point on. We are who we are because of the choices we make. We endure or fail from those decisions. In the light of last night's revelations, it was a very different Claudia who made her way the following morning along the garden path which ran behind the villa.

What had started out as sanctuary from Hylas the Greek was no longer that simple. Escape from the law was not that easy. A young man had died – fried in paradise – and Saunio's words drifted back. If the eye can be led, so can the mind. It can be made to believe things which are not there.

He had been talking about the use of illusion in art, but the same sentiments applied to Bulis. Providing Leo didn't have to confront the issue of the boy's death – which he undoubtedly would, were the garlanded corpse lying in state in his sumptuous hall – then Leo could pretend nothing had happened. Whatever motives had inspired him to go swanning off after Jason in that glorified fishing boat, endangering not only his ship and her crew but the hundreds of men, women and children left vulnerable on the estate, Claudia could have forgiven him had one of those motives included anger. Pride and humiliation make fools of us all and Leo wouldn't have been the first idiot to charge off, blinded by grief or by passion. Sure, he'd been provoked. But such was the measure of Leo's ego that he'd believed himself capable of seeing off a pack of vicious sea wolves. *And still did*.

Try explaining that to Bulis's mother.

Slipping into Leo's office through the open double doors from the garden, Claudia stopped to listen. Only a slave whistling as his heather broom swept the interior courtyard competed with the sound of birdsong. Deft fingers searched his scrolls, ledgers and tablets. First rule of combat, know your enemy. Come on! Something. Anything! Just a tiny hint as to why Orbilio should have got his cousin to invite her here—

129

'You can't do this!' a female voice shrieked. 'You promised me, Leo, you swore an oath.'

The woman was in the garden, heading this way down the path. Leo, approaching from the opposite direction, was on a head-on collision course, destination: office. Claudia ran to the other door to escape through the courtyard, but hell, the damn thing wouldn't budge.

Leo's response to the shrieking female was indistinct. Nevertheless, as Claudia fumbled with the handle, she was hard pushed to find an apology in it.

'You bastard,' the woman screeched. 'You dirty rotten bastard! You won't get away with it.'

Leo's growled reply suggested he already had, and that he wasn't losing his beauty sleep over it, either.

Key. Key. Where's the bloody key?

'You told me that cottage was mine.' So. Nanaï. 'You've no right to kick us out. Where will we go?'

The answering mumble suggested Leo didn't particularly care.

'But the children. Think of the children, Leo!'

The gist of his reply this time seemed to be along the lines that it was her fault, she should not have had so many.

Claudia had her hand on the door key when, with a distinct lack of tact considering the room was already occupied by one irritated female, Nanaï reversed into the doorway. Bugger. Claudia dived beneath the maplewood desk and hugged herself tight into a ball. With luck, the two outside would pass like angry ships.

Luck wasn't listening.

Leo barged straight past Nanaï into his office.

'Sorry, but it's settled. I told you time and again that place wasn't to be used permanently, yet you continued to bring brat after brat in, and now you try to tell me they're my responsibility. Well, Nanaï, they're not.'

'Yes, they are, dammit. You represent Rome on this island—'

'And Rome didn't mind helping out with free accommodation, food, firewood, clothes, but it's sick of giving you continuous handouts while you make no effort to curb the numbers. You brought this situation upon yourself, Nanaï. I gave you fair warning to quit, and now there's a new order coming which starts with my marriage. From now on, I have my own children to look to, and I'll not risk them picking up disease from your lazy brood.'

'You're a cruel man,' Nanaï said, her voice dropping to freezing point.

In the light of the morning sun streaming through the windows, her eyes shone the green of the first leaves of spring and her hair was the colour of malt. But her borage-blue gown was faded and going to holes, and there were deep scuffs in her patched leather sandals.

'In place of a heart, you have only a dark empty space. But know this,' she said, wagging a finger of warning, 'I make a dangerous enemy.'

'Then, Nanaï, you should know how I deal with my enemies.'

'Ach, so you threaten helpless women now, do you?'

Eyes blazing, Nanaï stared at him for several seconds. She opened her mouth, changed her mind, and had there been skid marks on the flagstones outside, Claudia would not have been remotely surprised. What did surprise her was that you'd think, wouldn't you, that producing a litter year in, year out would leave Nanaï with a figure like a sack of mouldy turnips, not straight of back and clear of skin. And that she'd be too exhausted to scream like a banshee.

Leo swore as he rattled a bunch of keys, and while he searched for the right key for the lock, Claudia wondered whether Nanaï might also have been Leo's lover. She was also a good-looking woman – cultivated, intelligent and a Roman to boot, who had raised her children to speak Latin without the trace of a Cressian accent. But oaths given by men in the grip of passion might not seem quite so important to them once the novelty had worn off, whereas discarded mistresses tend not to see things in the same accommodating light...

Whatever the rights and wrongs of the issue, though, and however high-handed Leo's actions appeared on the surface, when all's said and done this was his land. No contract had been signed and whatever their relationship, Nanaï ought not to make promises she couldn't keep. Children need trust every bit as much as they need security—

'Qus!' Leo's bellow made her jump. 'QUS!'

'Sir?'

'I don't care what tactics you have to resort to, but I want Nanaï off my land and now. What are you waiting for, man?'

'I can't do it, sir, and to be blunt, neither should you. The children have nowhere to go –'

'Qus, you're my bailiff, not my bloody social conscience. Turf the rabble out, or I'll find myself a bailiff who will.'

There was a pause of perhaps five beats. 'Very good, sir.'

'With the mood she's in now, you might find her a mite stubborn and while I'd rather you didn't use force...'

'Sir?'

'Well, if you have to, I quite understand,' Leo finished in a rush.

'I will not use force on a woman!'

'You will if I bloody tell you to. And once they're out, get the men to demolish the building and plough up the ground, because I'm not having her sneak back only to go through this rigmarole twice. When my bride and her family arrive, there will be no trace of that place. Understood?'

This time the silence seemed to stretch for

133

infinity. 'Whatever you say, sir, but I can't do it today. Every hand is working flat out on repairs to the *Medea*.'

'What are you blathering on about, man? There's not a scratch on her.' Leo's fist thumped the desk above Claudia's head, making the inkpots rattle. 'Janus, Croesus, Qus, do you think I'm bloody stupid? Everything I do lately you defy me and I won't tolerate insolence—'

'She's listing badly, sir.' Pause. 'Didn't you know?'

'*Medea*? How the bloody hell did that come about?'

'It would appear that someone holed her below the water line during the night,' Qus said.

'Fuck!' Leo slumped into his chair, and Claudia wriggled tighter into a ball. 'Fuck, fuck, fuck, that's all I bloody need.' He wiped his hands over his face. 'Much damage?'

'The shipwright says three days, maybe four on the stocks. He's hauling her out of the water right now.'

'That bloody Nikias,' Leo muttered. 'He knew I was going after the dolphin this morning.'

He stood up and Claudia's internal organs rearranged themselves more comfortably.

'Well, while he's about it,' Leo said wearily, 'tell the shipwright to change the boat's name back again. *Medea* doesn't suit her, I don't know how I got talked into altering it, really.'

'It's bad luck to change a boat's name.'

134

'Croesus, man, don't you ever just obey a bloody order? Anyway, she's been changed once and we're still alive and kicking, so I see no harm in reverting to the original. *Medea*'s too ... too...'

'Dark?'

'Precisely.' Leo scooped up some coins and briskly dropped them into a purse. 'Right then, I'll have a word with Llagos,' he said, chinking the purse. 'See if I can't get him to bless her the new name. And tomorrow you sort out that business with Nanaï, but no later, do you hear?'

'Oh, I hear you. Sir.'

Claudia watched the Ethiopian's thonged sandals stride across the hunting-scene mosaic, heard his hand lift the latch.

'There's still one other matter, Qus. That ... *thing* in your quarters. It's still there, I notice.'

The latch dropped back into place. 'I've explained about that, sir,' the Ethiopian said quietly, and this time the tone was one hundred per cent deference. 'I have to keep the crystal for nine more months according to the custom.'

'Custom be buggered, man, I've been patient enough. Now either that thing goes, or you do and this time I mean it. Think carefully before you make your decision, boy. Think what job you'd be doing if I sold you on, and it won't be a cushy bailiff's number, I can assure you.'

'Oh, sir, please. I must keep the crystal for a year, it's my duty. Three months have

135

already passed, I'm only asking for another nine.'

'If it wasn't for the rose-grower's daughter, Qus, you could have ninety. But look at it from my point of view. This girl is going to give me the children my wife couldn't and I can't afford to have anything go wrong. No miscarriages because of ... *things* that she's seen.'

'It's in my own private quarters, your bride would never see it, I swear.'

'Nothing is private, Qus, that's the first point. I own every inch of this land, every inch of your skin for that matter, and the same rule applies to my bride. Nothing is forbidden to her, no place is off limits, and if she does stumble into your rooms ... Look, there's little point in discussing the consequences, because I'm not prepared to take the risk in the first place. Either the crystal goes, Qus, or it and you leave together. Your call.'

A head appeared upside down under the desk where Claudia was curled. The head had a small cleft in its chin. 'You can come out now,' it said.

Apologies were pointless, dignity impossible, she simply commiserated with him on the *Medea*.

'If I could prove it was Nik, I'd nail his hide to a pole,' Leo said, 'but he's not even man enough to own up to it. Janus, I despise cowards, I really do.'

'Maybe it wasn't Nikias?'

The rumble deep in the back of Leo's throat suggested he wasn't particularly enamoured with Claudia's theory. 'I won't be beaten, not by him or anyone, dammit. If it means commandeering a fleet of bloody fishing boats, I'll net that dolphin and so help me, I'll skewer it right under his nose.'

'No you won't,' a calm voice announced from the hallway.

Nikias, his face and tunic spattered with paint like a rainbow, walked into the room wiping his hands on a rag. Across the corridor, the door to Leo's new marital chamber stood wide and Claudia could see the scaffolding Nikias had been standing on to finish the portraits of the happy couple.

'I've warned you, Leo, let the animal be,' he said. 'It's not harming you, it lifts the islanders' spirits and it helps the children heal and recuperate.' He turned to Claudia and once again, she was struck by the inscrutability of the Corinthian's expression. 'A lone dolphin won't stay long,' he said. 'Another few days and it will take off on its own accord, no harm done.'

'None at all,' Leo growled, 'because tomorrow it's dolphin for dinner.'

Nikias looked at him long and hard before turning away. 'Don't bank on it, Leo.'

'Janus! I'd fire the surly bastard,' Leo rumbled, 'if he wasn't the best portrait painter in the whole damn Empire.' Leo kicked the leg of his maplewood desk, carved

137

in the shape of an antelope's leg. 'Damn you, Nik!' he shouted. 'Damn you to hell!'

In response, the door across the corridor closed softly on its oiled hinges.

Claudia sat herself down on a high-backed upholstered chair as though she'd been invited. 'The rose-grower's daughter must be quite a catch.'

Leo filled two goblets with ruby red wine. 'She is,' he said. 'For three generations, the women have averaged five children apiece, with boys outnumbering girls three to one.'

'A gambler would call that good odds.'

Leo smiled, perched himself on the edge of the desk. 'You don't approve of my actions, do you?'

'Which actions in particular, Leo? I mean, are we talking about risking the lives of your crew in that ridiculous attempt at heroics? Butchering a harmless dolphin? Forcibly evicting women and children? Dumping your wife? Using her divorce settlement to revamp the house? Scuppering her chances of love with a sculptor?'

'Him!' Leo was quite unabashed at the tirade. 'Magnus wasn't worthy of my wife, Claudia. He's the son of a *barrel-maker*, for gods' sake.'

Claudia rolled the glass between her hands. 'Which puts the rose-grower's daughter where, exactly, in the social pecking order?'

Leo shot her an amused glance. 'I know how it looks,' he said, 'but things aren't all they seem, trust me. Lydia's angry with me right now and she has every right, but I'm not a fool, Claudia, and I'm not quite the bastard you think. Magnus was out of her class – and I mean that in more ways than one.'

'Isn't that for Lydia to decide?'

'My wife's hurting, which makes her vulnerable to the first man who makes sheep's eyes at her, but she's patrician stock and ... and...' He stared into the bottom of his glass. 'I'll square things with Lydia, you can bet your sweet life on that,' he said, adding solemnly, 'and Magnus, take my word, isn't the man for my wife.'

Claudia wondered who was. She waited a few seconds, then said, 'That's a nasty gash on your cheek.'

'What?' His fingertips flew to the line where Clio's ring had slashed his face the night before. 'Oh, that. Yes, I – slipped in the dark.' He swallowed his wine as though it was beer quenching a thirst. 'Embarrassing really. Caught my cheek on the edge of a flagstone.'

'And I can turn myself into Pegasus and fly.'

Leo stared at her for what seemed like hours. 'My cousin Marcus said you were sharp,' he said slowly. Suddenly, grabbing both arms of her chair, he leaned right into Claudia's face. 'If I tell you my plan,' he whispered, and there was pain in his eyes, 'you must promise it will remain strictly confidential, no one else—'

'Might we have a word, Leo?' Exquisitely groomed, immaculately coifed, Silvia was elegance personified in a pale-pink gown and red slippers with a white feather fan in her hand. But her eyes were as hard as the pearls which hung round her neck. '*When* you've finished.'

'Silvia!' Like a scalded cat, Leo jerked away from the chair. 'It's – This is not what you think.'

So. The Ice Queen thought he was kissing her, did she? Use your eyes, girl. There was no sexual chemistry between Leo and Claudia.

'Don't mind me, I'm just leaving,' Claudia said airily. There just happened to be a nice big bay tree just outside the window that offered endless possibilities.

Retreating through the double doors, Claudia clip-clopped down the garden path, humming loudly as she went. Once round the corner, though, she kicked off her sandals and belted barefoot behind the aromatic laurel.

'Please, Leo, don't think we're not grateful for what you did yesterday,' Silvia was saying. 'In fact, we wanted to thank you in person, only no one seemed to know where you were last night.'

'Estate business.' He tried to sound off-hand.

'At *that* hour?'

'You know how it is. Things crop up.'

'I suppose they do, but the thing is, Leo, while you have our undying gratitude for running Jason out of town, so to speak –' she paused '– it doesn't affect the principal issue.'

'You already have my answer on that. No.'

'Leo, it's your only option.'

Claudia sensed a gritting of lovely white teeth.

'Go to hell.'

'Thanks to you, brother-in-law, I'm already there.'

'Look, you'll get your damned money back. I told you. Once the grapes are pressed and the olives harvested—'

'Bullshit,' Silvia snapped. 'You tricked us into lending you every copper quadran we owned, then you skinned us out the same way you did Lydia and countless others—'

'For gods' sake, cut with the royal "we" crap, you sound ridiculous.'

'Don't shift the subject, Leo. On account of you, we – *I* am penniless, but *I* am not my sister.'

'You don't know the full story.'

'Who cares? It's been tough luck for Lydia, but in times such as this, it's every girl for herself.'

'Jupiter's thunderbolts, you're a cold bitch! Don't you care *anything* for your sister?'

'I was six years old when Lydia married you,' Silvia said flatly. 'That hardly made us close and, as you know, there's been no love lost between us since. Now, then. When we came to Cressia, we told you it was to start a new life. I'll be honest with you, Leo, this wasn't exactly what we had in mind and it's not our first choice frankly, but by Croesus, it'll be enough to launch us back into society.'

'The answer's still no, Silvia, whether I'm

141

first, second or last choice.'

'I repeat, Leo. You have no option *other* than to marry me.'

Claudia nearly fell into the bay tree. MARRY?

'Options be buggered! No one is going to overturn my wedding to the rose-grower's daughter,' Leo snapped. 'Least of all you, you blackmailing bitch.'

'Name-calling is as pointless as it is childish,' the Ice Queen said levelly. 'You owe me, Leo, and debts have to be settled one way or another. I've borne three sons already, I'm more than prepared to do the same again for you, where's the problem? You'll still have your precious heirs, I'll be reinstated in society—'

'Enough! Get out of this room, Silvia. Get out of this house. In fact, get the fuck out of my life.'

'How *dare* you!'

'I mean it.' Leo's dismissal was as cold as the Arctic. 'I'll pay back every sesterces I borrowed, you have my word. But set so much as one toenail on my land, you contemptible backstabbing harpy, and I'll have Qus throw you in jail as a trespasser.'

In the tense silence which followed, Claudia could almost see Silvia drawing herself up to her full height, her lips pursed white with the effort, as she tilted her strong patrician chin high in the air. She imagined the haughty flick of the white feather fan, the toss of the honey-coloured ringlets.

142

'So that's how the wind blows, is it? In that case, and I regret we've had to come down to this, but it appears we have no choice, other than to tell the rose-grower about you and Clio.'

'Wrong,' he snarled. 'I'm putting you on the first boat to Istria, where your tongue can cause no more damage.'

'You daren't throw us out,' Silvia hissed. 'Not with what we have on you.'

'Watch me.'

'Think it over, Leo, when your head is cooler.' Silvia's red slippers tip-tapped across the hunting-scene mosaic in anything but a defeated rhythm. 'Marry me – or by all that is holy, you *will* regret it.'

On the beach down by the point, Lydia watched the children strip off their clothes and swim like eels to the deeper waters where a lone dolphin waited to play. The children were brown as conkers, uninhibited in their nakedness and their joy, and at the sound of their splashing and squeals, her heart contracted in pain.

Eighteen years. Eighteen years she had longed to hold a babe of her own to her breast. Feel its tiny fist clasp round her fingers, sing lullabies to it at night. Eighteen years of waiting, hoping, weeping, praying.

To Diana, to Flora, to Fortune, to Juno, all the goddesses who could influence her fertility, and especially to Luna, who govern-ed her monthly cycles. She had hung votive offerings in the trees, drunk midsummer dew, buried garlands in the earth, strewn nuts in a circle and still Lydia hadn't given up. Last summer, she had even made a pilgrimage to the shrine of Carmenta at the foot of the Capitol, to hear the priestess sing the fate of her womb. But the priestess was sorry. She could only sing the fate of the new-born, she had said sadly.

Eighteen years Lydia had been waiting. Cursing the flow that ran so regularly each month. Cursing the womb that betrayed her...

'Iss it all right for uss to still come 'ere, miss?' a small, heavily accented voice piped up.

'Only some says Master Leo will have uss for trespassing.'

Lydia looked down at the brown, limpid eyes of the farrier's stocky twin daughters and smiled. 'This is my land,' she said, helping them out of their coarse linen tunics. 'And as long as I'm here, you are free to come and go whenever you please.'

'Whoopee!' Hand in hand, the two little girls scampered off to join the others splashing in the warm, translucent waters with the dolphin. She was still watching them when a shadow fell over the hot sand.

'But how long, Lydia,' a voice whispered in her ear, 'will you be here? That's the question you need to be asking.'

Nineteen

Blood had stirred the demon from its slumber, blood had given it fuel. But blood alone wasn't enough.

From Circe it had inherited the knowledge of centuries, and for a long time it believed the answer to its destiny lay in interpreting the messages jumbled inside its head. How wrong it had been! How much time wasted! Instead of trying to decipher the signals in terms of spells and incantations, the demon should have listened to its heart. To the real message pulsing through it.

In taking Bulis, it had believed it had followed its instinct, but when it came to the kill, the demon had discovered, to its great surprise, that it was still very much a novice in these matters. Wisely, it stopped, pulled back, and listened to the whisperings of the past.

Circe had been an enchantress. But Medea's blood also ran in the demon's veins. Don't forget that! Individually, the women were powerful – but together they were omnipotent, and this was the wisdom which had been passed down as it travelled the world and which now thrived in its place of origin. Circe had shown her niece how to create disguises, illusions, how to use the bulb of Colchis to deadly effect, and in return Medea had taught her aunt the black art of calculation. The demon saw them huddled over a cauldron in which perfidy, cunning and betrayal bubbled, waiting to be distilled into ruthlessness.

At which point it realized that blood was not its life source at all.

Power was the driving energy.

Destruction the foundation stone of its strength.

Once it grasped that basic principle, the demon's potency swelled. To have a human being at your mercy was the greatest power of all. To kill or to spare. To terminate life swiftly – or absorb the victim's vitality slowly.

Control.

To have total authority over the situation. To dominate the human spirit as well as the flesh.

That *was the demon's inheritance.* That *was its destiny. Now it had to set about fulfilling it further.*

Twenty

In her cottage on the hilltop, Clio lay on her bed, her hands folded underneath her head, and watched a spider make its spindly progress across her ceiling. She had been a fool. A bloody fool to think she could trust the word of a patrician. She rubbed at the throbbing in her temple and wondered what the hell she was going to do now. She had no money. Not so much as a copper quadran to her name. No possessions. Any food she'd needed up till now she had earned by staging peep shows for that buck-toothed runt of a priest from the Temple of Neptune.

Goddammit, Leo! How could you have reduced me to this?

Blistering tears welled up behind her closed eyelids, but Clio was not prone to self-pity. She had come here for a purpose, had gambled everything on Leo's assurances and discovered, belatedly, that they were as worthless as marzipan coins. But she wasn't beaten yet.

There was no breeze inside the cottage and the late afternoon air was sticky and cloying. Her cheeses were starting to smell. The bread would go hard in this heat, the fruit would be rotten by morning. This was no way to live. She rose, pulled on a fresh linen gown, belted it. Defeat did not figure in Clio's vocabulary. There would be a way out of this mess. She just had to find it.

Following a dusty goat track over the brow of the hill, she set her mind to thinking. And as her feet ate up the ground beneath her, so the sun dipped below the soft rolling Istrian hills across the water, the signal for a million cicadas to start rasping in the rough, dry, spiteful Cressian grass.

Leo had betrayed her.

(As men do.)

But there had to be something Clio could salvage.

After an hour the track led her back to the

147

cliff path overlooking the island's single wide sweeping bay, where sunset had turned the waters a flat, matt, dusky pink. She settled herself on a rocky outcrop and gazed down at the jumble of stone houses and the wharf populated by human statues. Today, the townspeople's lethargy and uncouth manners were no longer a source of amusement for Clio. Things were turning nasty down there, too.

What had started out as hilarious entertainment – that she was a witch, a sorceress, an eater of human flesh – was no longer funny. A girl, the wife of a fisherman, had died in the night. Her illness began, so the wagging tongues claimed, the day Clio arrived on the island. Now her spirit was gone from her body – and guess who they blamed?

Yesterday, Clio would have laughed in their faces. Told the townspeople straight out that their kinswoman had died from a wasting disease, any half-wit could tell she must have been ill for some time. But today the eight-year-old son of a carpenter had taken to his bed, and instead of admitting the disease might be catching, a scapegoat was sought. When she had returned from the market this morning, sprigs of whitethorn had been scattered close to her cottage. The bloodied guts of a piglet lay on the path. The message was unequivocal: VAMPIRE KEEP OUT. Call it primitive, call it superstition, call it a straightforward knee-jerk reaction, but if they seriously believed whitethorn warded off

148

those dark birds of the night and that intestines could propitiate bloodlust, then Clio knew it would only need one more victim to fall to the contagion and we'd be talking lynch mob mentality here.

There was no seeking protection from Leo on this. He'd made his position quite clear when he had called at the cottage shortly after midday.

'You'll have to leave the island,' he'd told her.

Commendably, under the circumstances, Clio had held on to her temper. She'd lost it last night. Big mistake. Power comes through control, not through the loss of it.

'And go where?' she'd asked.

'Istria,' he'd said, and with a cold thrill of horror she realized he'd been planning something along these lines all the time. The suggestion had tripped too easily off his tongue. He'd been looking to get rid of her from the moment she landed on Cressia. 'I have relatives in Pula,' he'd told her. 'That's less than a day's sail from here. I could easily call on you under pretext of visiting them.'

'Alternatively, you could send your estate physician to treat the carpenter's child. That would quash the vampire rumours.'

'Oh, that.' He'd dismissed the accusations with a wave of his hand. 'Ignore the wagging tongues, that'll pass. It's Silvia who bothers me. She knows about us, Clio. She's threatening to blab.'

'Let her. No one will take a blind bit of

notice, not after the names I've been called here.'

'Clio, you don't understand my position here. I am effectively Governor of Cressia and if Silvia starts talking, it will spell total disaster. I'll be recalled to Rome – I suppose you know my cousin Marcus is attached to the Security Police?'

'What of it?'

'Don't play stupid,' Leo had snapped. 'You know damn well what the consequences will be. He's smart, too bloody smart for his own good sometimes, and I can't afford to have him sniffing under stones.'

She'd slapped his face so hard she'd opened the wound she'd made last night. 'I am not something under a stone.'

'You know what I mean,' Leo had said irritably, holding a pad to his cheek to staunch the blood. 'Look, the only sensible solution is for you to leave Cressia. Go to Pula. It's a lively city, you'll be happier there, trust me.'

'Trust you? I don't trust you further than I could throw you,' she'd said.

'A deal is a deal, Clio. I won't renege. It's just that I've—'

'Spent my share on that bloody villa of yours.'

'I've apologized about that. I didn't realize how much it was going to cost. Saunio, Nikias, Magnus, these guys don't come cheap. But the rose grower's coughing up a hefty dowry, and once the olives are harvested and the grapes pressed—'

'I'll still be left with nothing.'

'You're over-reacting,' Leo had said. 'You'll get your half, it's just going to take longer than I thought. Three – well, all right, maybe six months, but if you can hold on that long and be patient, you'll get your money. With interest.'

Six months. Yes, she could cope with that. Just about.

'I'll need something to live on in the meantime,' she'd said, and he would never know what it cost her to ask him – a man – for money. 'Call it an advance on my share, if you like.'

'Agreed. I'll bring thirty gold pieces after nightfall, and you can leave it with me to arrange passage to Pula.'

'Who said I was leaving?'

'Clio!'

'I'm serious. If I have to wait six months for my money, then it will be in a place where I can keep my eye on you.'

'Croesus!' he'd shouted. 'If Lydia gets to hear about us, or the parents of my new bride! Think about the consequences, woman!'

'Considering so much hinges on Silvia's loose mouth, why don't you pack *her* off to Pula instead?'

Leo had run his hands wearily over his face and suddenly he'd looked ten years older. 'Look, I'm dealing with Silvia,' he'd said heavily. 'She won't be a problem after

151

tomorrow, you have my word on that. But it would still be better all round if you left Cressia.'

'Better for you.'

He'd studied her for a moment or two, then cast a caustic glance round the comfortless cottage. 'I know how you earn your food, Clio.'

'That bastard runt of a priest's been bragging, has he?'

'You imagine Llagos would own up about his cheap thrills? You're forgetting whose land this is. Clio, I know every damn thing that goes on on this estate. If a bird poops, I know about it.'

He'd drawn a deep breath.

'But it doesn't have to be like this. You're not stupid. You know Llagos will start wanting more and more for his money. How low are you prepared to stoop in the name of your goddamned feminine pride? Thirty gold pieces to leave Cressia tomorrow. Nothing if you remain.'

'You bastard.'

'I'm sorry,' he'd said, and shit, for a moment she'd almost believed him. 'I'll bring the money two hours before midnight—'

'Screw you,' she'd spat. 'Keep your bloody money, I'm staying put.'

Even though it left her with no food, no money and worst of all, no hope for the future.

Sitting in the gathering dusk, Clio prayed to Nemesis, goddess of vengeance, to strike that loose-mouthed society bitch, Silvia, dead!

Were it not for her, there'd *be* no bloody problem. Through the priest, Leo could silence those preposterous vampire rumours, allowing Clio to continue living here, quietly and unobtrusively, until Leo paid her and then ... And then she would return to her home town in Liburnia a wealthy woman! (See what the mealy-mouthed bastards had to say about that!)

All those 'ifs', though. All those bloody 'ifs'. Fine for Leo to say he was sorting out the Silvia problem. Clio had a future to consider, and the old proverb drifted back to her: to get a good job done, do it yourself. Dammit, she should never have trusted Leo in the first place. Who knows what else he might cock up on?

Her clifftop musings were diverted by a sudden burst of activity in the town below. Along the wharf, fishermen had been galvan-ized into life, abandoning their mending of nets, the checking of lines and lobster pots. Arms were waving about. People jumped up and down. The entire damn community was running here, scurrying there, spilling out of the taverns, shuttering their windows and doors. Children were being scooped up, rounded up, told to shut up or else. Barking dogs reared and strained on the leashes which kept them chained to the houses. Chickens scattered. Craftsmen hustled their wares and equipment inside and battened their shop-fronts.

All except one man. The stranger.

Clio had seen him this morning, when she was doing her shopping. A head taller than the average islander, there was a presence about this man. She couldn't put her finger on it, but like a panther who'd just eaten its fill, the stranger exuded that same sense of understated menace. He might walk around seemingly uninterested in what went on, but he was poised to react at a moment's notice.

Some said the rebel leader Azan was bearded, others claimed he was clean-shaven. According to who you spoke to, he was Libumian or Dalmatian, some even said he was Roman, and that was Azan's skill: to move unrecognized as he whipped up insurrection. Was the stranger Azan? Clio wouldn't be surprised, and had felt a thrill of superiority that the islanders didn't even realize who it was staying in their fleapit tavern.

Hugging her knees, she watched the cause of the town's pandemonium approach without interest.

Black sails brailed up for lack of wind and powered instead by threescore strapping oarsmen seated two abreast, the *Soskia* cleaved a persuasive path through the water. Swoosh. Swoosh. Swoosh. Swoosh. You could almost hear the flute which beat time for the oars.

Out here on Cressia, folk didn't need to damp down their houses, the buildings were, almost without exception, built of stone. Stone didn't catch fire, but it could be looted, smashed and destroyed. But the town was safe enough tonight, Clio noted. The pace of the warship did not so much as dip when she hove into view. Swoosh. Swoosh. The galley cruised passed the wide bay and rounded the headland.

Only when she'd reached the cliffs below the Villa Arcadia, did the *Moth*'s wingbeats start to slacken.

By which time Clio knew exactly what she must do to eradicate her problem once and for all.

Twenty-One

The islanders watched the sea turn red. Red, like the blood of the sorceress Medea's brother, whose body she'd so heartlessly dismembered. Red, like the flag of war the pirate warship flew. Red, like the pirate captain's leather boots. They had heard the prediction of Shamshi the Persian, and they feared the worst.

Men barricaded their families indoors and fell to their knees in prayer. Beseeching Mars, god of war, to preserve them in safety and bestow peace and prosperity upon them. Calling upon the goddess Ceres, who protected this gentle month of August, to use all her powers of persuasion to bring concord.

155

Placating Eris, goddess of strife, with offerings of wine that she might turn her attentions elsewhere.

Right around the town, all across the island, the power of prayer was strong. The question is, was it strong enough?

Watching the *Soskia* drop her anchor stone and ship her oars, Claudia experienced a chilling sense of disquiet. Not because of a possible raid. This was not Jason's intention. He had lit torches the entire length of her deck until the little *Moth* was lit up as brightly as a midsummer noon. Jason was here to show menace. That he could come and go as he pleased and that Rome couldn't stop him. I, he was saying, am all powerful. Fear me.

The people had every right.

'What are you waiting for?' Leo yelled to the lone figure standing, arms crossed, on the prow. 'Too scared to take me on again?'

'Leave it,' Silvia urged. 'You're only provoking him further.'

'Let's see what you're like pitched against armed men, you bunch of fucking cowards!' Leo shouted down. He had outfitted every man on the estate with a weapon and then lined them up along the cliff in a massive display of strength.

'For heaven's sake, ignore him,' Silvia hissed, but she was wasting her breath. Leo's tail was up, his blood hot. It made no difference at this time of night that the *Medea* was out of action, he could not have followed

156

in the dark anyway. Instead, he was daring the brigands to come ashore and prove who was the strongest.

'Brinkmanship,' Volcar muttered in Claudia's ear. She swatted his hand away from her waist and thought, he knows. The old man knows it's a performance. He knows, as Leo does, that Jason would not fight head to head.

For two long hours Leo's men stood in silence, gripping their clubs, their swords, their axes, as the lights along the *Soskia*'s deck glittered on the metal shields which lined the rail and her bronze ram glinted double in the placid sea. By torchlight, the torsion-sprung ballista that she carried amidships oozed menace. Capable of shooting a flaming fireball right into the heart of Arcadia, it could equally loose off a volley of lethal iron bolts. But the most menacing weapon of all was the figure who stood motionless out on the prow. What game was he playing down there?

Claudia's nerves stretched to infinity and then beyond, and when a screech-owl screamed from a pine, her heart almost stopped. Was it really only a few hours earlier that she had stood on this same spot, watching a pair of blue butterflies chase one another round the hollyhocks as a flycatcher trilled from its perch in the almond? Then, heliotrope and pinks, yarrow and vervain had scented the late afternoon air like a welcome breeze. Now their heavy perfume pulsed through the heat like a drum. Cloying,

157

nauseating, clinging tighter than ivy.

Before the sun stands thrice more over our heads, a woman shall die.

Garbage. No woman was going to die, get a grip!

Except that before the new light was born in the sky, bad news had come over the water.

Stop it. That creepy, hook-nosed fraud makes it up as he goes along. Cressia's an island, for gods' sake. *All* news comes over the water. Fifty-fifty chance whether it's good or bad. Shamshi was aware of the passions brewing here in the villa, knew something had to blow soon. Isolation breeds oppression and, just like this throbbing, interminable heat, there's no escape. The tendrils wrap round you, tighter, tighter, drawing you in, drawing you down. A slow, treacly whirlpool, sucking you deeper where no one can hear you scream, because the scream is only inside your head. And the old fraud capitalized on that incestuous whirl of emotions. He'd been present at dinner when Lydia had threatened to blow Leo's marriage plans out of the water, and he'd know all about Nanaï's refusal to leave, the landlord's patience running out, Nanaï's threats once she could no longer get her own way.

'I make a dangerous enemy,' she had warned Leo, inciting him to retaliate with threats of his own by reminding her how he dealt with his enemies.

Shamshi would know about Silvia, too. How she was trying to blackmail her brother-

158

in-law into marriage, and the threats she had made if he did not play ball. And it was more than likely the Persian knew about the mysterious Clio, as well. Part intelligence gathering, part mumbo-jumbo, but with women at the centre of each of these blazing rows, why not chance your arm with a sinister prediction? Accidents happen. When emotions are heated, people become careless, it's easy to lose concentration. One slip on the clifftop, for instance, and hey presto it's a coin for the ferryman.

Two hours passed that seemed like twenty.

The moon had surely stuck in the sky.

Then – *boom*. A single drumbeat sounded out across the water. As one, the lights along the deck were extinguished, strong arms hauled up the anchor rope and swoosh, swoosh, swoosh, as the flautist played time for the oars, the little *Moth* fluttered away. As suddenly as she'd arrived.

'Cowards,' Leo called after her. 'Snivelling cowards, the lot of you!'

He turned to his bailiff.

'Qus,' he said, 'post armed guards along the shore and station lookouts there, there and there. Also, the *Medea*'s vulnerable up on the stocks, so have a contingent keep a close watch on her and, one last thing, I'm taking no chances, post six men round my wife's house.'

'The mistress won't like it.'

'There you go again! Defying me! By Croesus, I don't give a toss what the mistress likes or doesn't like, and you can remind her highness, if she starts yelling, that it's my bloody land and I'll protect it how I please. Those men stay until I give the all-clear, understood? I said, *do you understand?*'

'Yes, sir. I understand exactly what you mean.'

Leo turned to the rest of the men.

'Tonight,' he announced, 'we celebrate a second victory over the pirates. They're nothing but bullies and thugs, and now we've shown them we're prepared to stand and fight, that we won't be run off this island like rats, they'll find weaker targets to pick on. That's unfortunate for the victims concerned, I realize, but that's an issue which will have to be addressed through the appropriate channels in Rome. Tonight, though, it's wine all round, men! Let us toast that glorious goddess, Victory, until our throats are too hoarse to shout!'

The answering cheers would have deafened the dead.

It was late evening. Bats twittered under the eaves. Moths were drawn to the flames of the torches which burned in the formal gardens, illuminating the paths and the statuary. The tall spikes of angelica glowed like robust parasols and, now that the *Soskia* had slipped away, the air was no longer cloying, but pleasantly redolent with the scent of late-summer flowers. Laughter rang out as the wine flowed like floodwater in the courtyard beyond, but for Claudia, inside the cocoon of tall cypress hedge, the pale-green heads of the hops seemed to nod as though in penitence as they twined up the pillars, night crickets rasped like a saw and she could not shake off a sense of impending doom. It hung like a canopy over the villa.

Before the sun stands thrice more over our heads, a woman shall die.

A tawny owl hooted, and she reassured herself with the touch of hard steel hidden in the folds of her gown and the stiletto strapped to her calf. She could not see him, but Claudia felt the presence of her bodyguard close at hand. Whoever attacked her two nights before wouldn't find her such a soft target next time.

As she strolled the paths, the statuary drew her attention. Despite Nikias's hyperbole, she had expected to find Magnus's work every bit as lacking as the man who had courted a vulnerable woman then allowed himself to be warned off by the ex. Instead, the symmetry and balance of the statues took her breath away. Take the old man reaching up to pluck a ripe peach from the tree in the corner. Not only had Magnus captured the essence of Volcar, but the angle of his outstretched arm mirrored the spurt of the fountain on the opposite side of the path. Any moment, that young mother and her daughters would finish their frozen dance among the alliums and the vervain which grew round their podium, and the tears from the kneeling stone virgin

161

would drip silently on to the grass. All they needed was the warm breath of Jupiter upon their lips and suddenly marble nymphs would giggle aloud—

'The knack is to manipulate height and texture in harmony with their surroundings.'

Claudia spun round. So much for vigilance! But sitting on a marble bench beneath the plum tree, one leg crossed over his knee as he leaned comfortably against its corrugated bark, the stranger posed no immediate threat. Mid, maybe even late forties, with dark hair greying at the temples there was only one person this man could be.

'Magnus?' *The* Magnus? 'You're the man who looks into souls?' And toys with vulnerable female emotions?

'At your service, ma'am.' Grey eyes twinkled as he gave a faint nod.

'I thought you'd left Cressia.' Did Lydia know?

A long, artistic finger traced a line along the crisp pleat of his tunic. 'Let's call it unfinished business.'

Oh-oh. Lydia's dowry. Silvia's savings. Claudia began to get the strangest feeling that Magnus's bill might not actually have been settled yet. 'Leo owes you, doesn't he?'

'Leo owes everyone.'

Claudia's gaze took in the statuary, the way he had reflected back every nuance of this fabulous island. The blue of the sky, the turquoise of the sea, the perfect gold of the sands. Magnus had taken the seasons one by

162

one and made them prostrate themselves before his chisel and paintbrush, and it was no coincidence that the statue of the Emperor Augustus, resplendent in purple, stood on a podium under which cyclamen and columbine flourished, and where the blaze of gold leaves in the autumn would match the Emperor's crown. Nikias had it wrong. Magnus didn't create lifelike images of his subjects, he bestowed immortality upon them.

'You're wasted on Cressia,' she said bluntly. 'Talent like yours should be in Rome, for everyone to feast their eyes on.'

'We all sell our skills to the highest bidder in the end,' Magnus murmured. 'It's the nature of the beast.'

'Bollocks. You've created a spiritual paradise here.' Any second now, the father would heed the tug of his son's marble hand on the hem of his tunic and bend down to scoop him up. 'That frieze along the portico depicting the adventures of Odysseus—'

But Claudia was talking to thin air. When she turned back, the bench beneath the plum tree was empty and only the swinging of a bramble along the path testified that Magnus had ever been in the garden tonight. That, plus the physical manifestation of his prodigious talent. She blinked. That rearing stallion by the fountain? Did its mane really flicker? She half expected it to snort and gallop off down the path, its hooves kicking up clouds of dust in its wake. She smiled. Trick of the light. Spluttering torches were all that made these figures dance beneath the waning moon. A dozen or so bitumen-soaked reeds set alight. Nothing more.

Then one of them moved.

Slowly, stealthily, silent as death, it backed out of the shadows and was swallowed up by the night. Claudia pushed a strand of hair out of her eyes. How long had the Persian been here, she wondered. How long had he been watching and listening – and waiting?

Before the sun stands thrice more over our heads, a woman shall die.

A cold shiver ran down her back and, not for the first time, she asked herself how much Shamshi manipulated events at the Villa Arcadia.

How far would he go to ensure his prophecies were fulfilled?

Another hour must have passed, maybe more, before Claudia became aware of a man singing and footsteps weaving down the colonnade.

> *'I once had a girlfriend called Vera,*
> *She would not let me near 'er.*
> *I courted a girl called Amanda,*
> *Her father made me unhand 'er.'*

The tune was interrupted by a stumble followed by a muffled curse as the singer disengaged himself from a pillar.

'But then I met Alis,
Who liked my big phallus,
We worshipped sweet Venus,
So I—'

'Thank you, Leo, but the dawn chorus doesn't start for another few hours.'

'Claudia.' He lurched over, his eyes dancing with wine and something she couldn't identify. 'What do you say tomorrow, at first light, I take you on a tour of my vineyards?'

'First light?'

'Uh...' He made a deprecating gesture. 'Maybe a little later then, eh?'

She patted the bench for him to join her. A man in his cups and with his defences down? Show me a better time to take a prod.

'Was that the real reason you invited me to Cressia? To look at your wines?'

He tutted as he hitched up his long patrician tunic and sat down. 'Take no notice of my wife. I apologize if she offended you by implying things about you and me, but...' He hesitated. 'My wife says a lot of things she doesn't mean when she's drun— emotional.'

'I'm sure.'

'And Silvia jumps to conclusions, too.'

Never mind them. 'I didn't think you'd invited me here to seduce me,' she said. 'I was asking whether you brought me over to look at your wines ... or,' she paused, 'to invest in them.'

Leo roared with laughter. 'My, you don't mince your words, do you? Marcus told me

165

you were one shrewd cookie. I didn't appreciate quite how shrewd.'

That's it. Spoil a perfectly good evening by bringing Mr Let's-hear-it-for-the-Security-Police into it.

'I have to come clean, Claudia, I did have something along those lines in mind, but not an investment as such. I was thinking more of a partnership. Proper contracts, drawn up in law, all legal and binding.'

'Do tell me more,' she said softly.

'Well, first off let me confess it wasn't actually my idea,' he said. 'My cousin suggested you might be amenable—'

'*Marcus* suggested it?' The same Marcus Cornelius Orbilio who'd caught her fixing races by doping the hot favourite and knew she was broke?

'Smart lad, my cousin. He's going places, that boy. Of course, he needs a wife before he can think about a seat in the Senate, they wouldn't take him otherwise. Divorced man with no heirs? Jupiter would turn celibate first, especially after the scandal attached to his marriage.'

'Caused a rumpus, did it, the wife turning the household slaves into cash and using the money to run off with a sea captain from Lusitania?'

Leo shot her a strange look. 'I – er, didn't realize you knew.'

Know your enemy, Leo. And Orbilio, make no mistake, was a dangerous, dangerous adversary. 'Talking of our proposed partner-

166

ship contract,' she said, 'what do you suppose Lydia meant about life and death breaking yours with the rose-grower's daughter?'

'Can't imagine.'

'Aren't you curious?'

'Not remotely.'

'Strange. Because half an hour ago I could have sworn I saw you talking to your ex-wife over by the cliff edge.' Felt sure I heard you telling her that this was only a temporary arrangement and asking her to bear with you, you'd see her right, on your mother's eyes, I think you swore. 'And didn't I also hear Lydia telling you to go fork yourself – that *was* the word, wasn't it?'

Leo found a sudden urge to adjust his belt buckle. 'No,' he said. 'Wasn't me.'

Claudia allowed the resulting silence to stretch. 'I met a woman called Clio while I was out walking today,' she said idly. Why should Leo have the monopoly on lies? 'She mentioned you.'

'Clio? Clio?' Leo stuck out his lower lip as though thinking. 'No. Doesn't ring any bells, I'm afraid. Look. Um.' He made a clumsy gesture towards his bladder. 'Need to empty the old wineskin, getting urgent. We'll, er, thrash out those partnership proposals tomorrow, when I show you the pressing house and the vats...'

'Can't wait,' Claudia said, as her host lurched off in the opposite direction to the latrines.

And it was turning into quite a night for dropping eaves, because another familiar figure hove into view. Beads of sweat dotted his forehead and from time to time one trickled down his neck to nestle in the folds of fat. His eyes had been reduced to small black hollows all but lost in a face waxy in texture, grey in colour, and which still bore the porridgey etchings of grief. This man needs to lose weight, Claudia thought. He needs to take time out to sleep. But most of all, Saunio needs to mourn properly the death of his eighteen-year-old apprentice.

'Leo's gone to one helluva lot of trouble,' Saunio murmured, nodding towards the retreating figure, 'for a fourteen-year-old who'll be far too homesick to care.'

Interesting that it was the maestro, of all people, who should be concerned with the bride's welfare. Even Leo only saw the girl in terms of a vessel for siring sons.

'It's one of the reasons he wants the renovations complete before she gets here,' Claudia said. 'To minimize the disruption.'

Actually, it was to minimize the risk of miscarriage, which reminded her. She really *must* check out that mysterious crystal in Qus's quarters!

Saunio smiled, but the smile did not reach his eyes. 'At least one can't accuse Leo of not being driven by a strong sense of conviction.' He laced his fingers and stared at the waning three-quarter moon through the trees. 'Even if that sense of conviction is distorted.'

'I prefer to see him as a man driven by passion.'

'Saunio hates to contradict a beautiful woman, but that's a load of bollocks, my lovely. He's controlling, stubborn, blinkered, obsessive—'

'Are you always this loyal to those who commission you?'

Saunio let out a soft snort which might have been laughter, or then again might have been undiluted derision. 'Loyalty is worth socks to a man who won't listen.'

So that was it. Stags locking horns. The clash of two brawny egos. 'Leo's problem,' she said, 'is not that he won't listen. It's that he makes snap decisions without thinking things through, and once that course is set, failure isn't an option.'

He'd implemented a revolutionary new method for training his vines, and even though yield was a staggering twenty per cent down with this new method, reverting to traditional ways would smack of failure, so he steadfastly stuck to his guns. Likewise with Jason, Leo believed himself capable of beating the Scythian both in and out of the water, but that wasn't enough. Even though he knew damn well Jason would not set one red leather boot on Arcadia tonight, he'd armed the men in a public demonstration of his superiority over the pirates. Ditto Nanaï. He'd served her notice to quit, and quit she would have to, once the cottage was demolished and the ground ploughed up afterwards. Leo had to be *seen* to be successful. The same with Silvia. He had taken so much,

169

but once he'd made up his mind, that was it. The Ice Queen was history. Perhaps that was why Qus walked the fine line that he did? He knew just how far he could push an issue before his master became intractable.

'Do you also justify his obsession for heirs?' Saunio asked.

'The concept of wanting sons isn't new,' she said carefully.

'Don't you feel it's a rather dangerous concept, sidelining a wife of eighteen years then building her a house on the edge of the very estate where you've installed the new wife?'

Something was twisting the air here tonight. Stifling, oppressive, it braided the atmosphere, made things appear to move when they hadn't, cleverly concealed those things which did. And that hand that did the braiding was evil. A dark demon hypnotizing them with its spell. Claudia did not wish to be drawn into discussions about Leo and his ex-wife, and yet ... and yet ... The demon was sucking her in.

'Dangerous in what way?' she asked.

Before the sun stands thrice more over our heads, a woman shall die.

'Emotions are not an architect's plans on a page, my lovely, where a line can be rubbed out here, redrawn over there,' Saunio said. 'Trample hearts into pulp and the backlash is stormforce.'

Around them, bats squeaked, the watercourse babbled and emperor moths spun

170

silent cocoons in the heather. The night air was pitchy from the spluttering torches and voles scuttled beneath a protective umbrella of cranesbills. There was something compelling about this fat little creature with the ring of curled hair round his chin. On the one hand, he was so earnest, so professional, every bit as obsessive as the patron he railed against, and yet every bit as blind. He could not fail to be aware of the rumours. Orgies, unnatural practices, bloodthirsty rituals – how could these have passed him by? Yet Saunio had never once refuted the gossip. Why? *Because it was not without foundation?*

He'd excused himself from dinner tonight on the grounds that Helen of Troy took priority. He'd barely outlined madame, he'd announced pompously, merely sketched in the landscape, and apparently Paris was a blur, Agamemnon a cipher and the plaster poised at a particularly delicate juncture of dampness. He could not – nay, would not – compromise his art for the sake of his belly and when Claudia saw him later, he was beavering away on Helen of Troy like there was no tomorrow.

Which, of course, for his apprentice there wasn't.

But that wasn't to say he needed to dig himself a grave next to Bulis. And why would a man who lived for his art fritter away precious spare time on the emotional issues of a chap he despised?

171

'You haven't answered the question, my lovely. Do you, as a woman, agree that a man is entitled to take whatever action he deems necessary, no matter how drastic, when it comes to the question of sons?'

'You're quite right, Saunio. I haven't answered the question.'

His thick Pan-like lips stretched themselves into something resembling a smile. Claudia leaned over and sniffed. No cinnamon. Only a weak metallic odour of malachite pigment.

The small boar-like eyes fixed on a point over her shoulder and for a moment he paused, as though debating within himself. Then the moment was gone. 'You must excuse me,' he said. 'The brushes call, and Saunio must not keep them waiting.'

Alone at last in the garden, Claudia had the strangest feeling the maestro had been trying to impart a coded message and, now she thought about it more carefully, she believed that had also been his intention in the atrium yesterday.

For the life of her, though, she didn't know what that message might be.

Twenty-Two

When Apollo reined his fiery chariot over the eastern horizon the following morning, the air over Cressia was calm and warm, heavy with the scent of the oregano which grew wild on the hillsides. Birds sang, but their arias were brief. Territories had long since been established and there was little energy to spare with fast-growing chicks demanding so much food.

In the hills, foxes slunk home to their dens, stone martens suckled their second litter and rabbits sniffed warily as they emerged from their burrows.

Out on the water, still pink from the dawn, fishermen dropped polished pebbles into the sea – offerings to Neptune, for protecting them from the pirate. Garlands of campion and storksbills bobbed from where their womenfolk had already cast their thanks-givings earlier.

Further out still, the cascades of water caused by a lone dolphin arcing in and out of the limpid sea were turned to silver in the burgeoning sunshine.

The fruit on the pomegranate trees which shaded the Villa Arcadia swelled and ripened in the summer heat. The figs grew luscious and sweet.

Wings warmed by the sun, brown argus butterflies, painted ladies, commas and graylings formed a mobile chequerboard as they danced over blooms in search of nectar. Bees droned. Lizards crawled out of their cracks in the wall.

After the celebrations which had lasted until the wee small hours, Leo's slaves had permission to sleep in. A cockerel crowed in the distance. Horses in the stable block shuffled and snickered, and one stamped its hooves. Scorpions scuttled beneath stones.

Floating on her mattress of swansdown beneath a counterpane scented with camomile as the eye of the day slowly opened, Claudia Seferius dreamed. She dreamed of epic sea voyages in search of adventure, of golden fleeces and giant one-eyed cannibals, encounters with sorceresses, sea monsters and the deadly song of the Sirens, and beside her, in the crook of her arm, the ribcage of her blue-eyed, cross-eyed, dark Egyptian cat rose and fell in unison with her breathing.

Another hour passed, and no one and nothing in Arcadia stirred.

In fact, another hour would drift by before the first slave shuffled bleary-eyed along the portico and noticed the Scythian spear embedded in the aromatic cedarwood of the atrium door. But in that hour, fieldworkers and artisans, household slaves and children, even the dogs, slumbered on. In good time, they would wake, stretch, clean their teeth.

Some would turn and make love to their wives. They knew nothing about the spate of messages which had been delivered, three times in total, courtesy of a Scythian spear, so they weren't afraid. The pirates had gone, and in any case what was the spear but a harmless piece of polished cypress with a few ribbons and rattles and barbaric carvings?

And since only Qus knew about the spears, they would not know that on previous occasions there had been a message attached, saying: *Give back what is mine.*

There was no piece of lettered parchment on the lance when it was discovered on this beautiful, calm summer's morning.

What was impaled in its place was a body.

Shamshi the Persian had made a prediction. Before the sun stands thrice more over our heads, a woman shall die. Shamshi the Persian was wrong. It wasn't a woman who'd been speared through the gut and left to die on the atrium door.

It was Leo.

Twenty-Three

Words could not describe the effect on the island.

It was like the aftershock of an earthquake. So terrible, so devastating, that it could only

175

find expression in silence. People were paralysed physically as well as emotionally. Incapable of moving. Of speaking. Even of thinking.

If Jason could sneak back under the noses of a score of armed guards and slaughter the most powerful man on a hundred and twenty square miles of island, what hope for the rest of them?

They had always been on their guard against pirates, but the barbarism of the killing stunned everyone. That Leo had been murdered was horrendous. That he had been impaled made the crime as horrific as anything they had ever heard of.

In the past, the people of Cressia made no secret of their dislike of their overlord. They'd resented his high-handed Roman ways, the way he strutted around as though he owned every inch of the island, dispensing justice when a crime had been committed, ensuring taxes were paid to the Collector once a year. Every time they saw one of his slaves in their bright-yellow livery and watched how many sacks were unloaded from the trade ships for just one villa, and every time they counted the timbers shipped to him from the mainland, the bales of bright cloth, amphorae of wine, the barrels full of lemons from Africa, Damascan plums, Egyptian melons or ridiculously priced spices from India, the islanders' resentment grew fiercer. It reinforced their own poverty, the usurping of traditional Cressian ways. In Leo's wealth and ostentatiousness, their noses were rubbed into the footprint of Rome.

Oh, but what would they give to have Leo throwing his weight around once again! To return to the safety and security of Rome at their back. The islanders were too shocked to weep at their misfortune, but already they realized they'd taken Leo for granted, and without his protection, their chickens had come home to roost.

At the Villa Arcadia, the end result was the same, even if the process was different. Here, spunk from the slaves had drained away slowly, like water from a cracked bowl. A slave is a chattel, an object to be bought and sold at the auction block, at least, that's the theory. In practice, most rich men's slaves lived better than freemen. They were guaranteed food in their bellies, good food at that. They were housed and clothed well, their children educated and taught a trade. They earned money from the work that they did, and this bought them fancy clothes, jewels, concubines and, best of all, they did not have to pay tax. Even the lowliest labourer lived well. Prudent slaves put their salaries aside to save for businesses of their own – usually a shop – and they often owned slaves of their own. It wasn't a bad life, considering, and many chose to remain enslaved rather than purchase their freedom. They lived better that way. Got fat quicker.

Providing their master was alive to look after them.

Now Leo was dead, brutally murdered, who would protect them when the pirates came back? Even in the unlikely event that Rome came to their aid in time, families would surely be broken up as the estate was sold off. Where would they go? Who would buy them? Would their new masters beat them?

In killing Leo, hundreds of other lives had also been wrecked.

And still the birds sang and the butterflies danced, and a lone dolphin made silvery arcs in the water.

Twenty-Four

The heart of the demon rejoiced. It could feel it physically swelling with happiness, pulsating with energy against its chest wall.

A tide of destruction had been unleashed.

Let there be more.

Let there be no end to the carnage.

Twenty-Five

In a bedroom darkened to near blackness by closed shutters for privacy, Claudia sniffed back the tears. Leo had his faults – more than most – but no man deserved to die in such a manner. Whatever score Jason wanted to settle, that was simply too high a price.

You bastard! You cold-blooded, calculating, evil-minded bastard. She saw Jason standing in that rosy-pink dawn three days ago on the prow of his warship. That insolent bow. The slow mime of the handclap. The gold which had glinted at his neck and his belt in the sun. You didn't even have the decency to kill Leo quickly, you callous son-of-a-bitch.

But he'd made a mistake, killing a high-ranking Roman. Leo's barbaric murder would bring the whole damn Roman Navy up here – there would be no place for Jason to hide. Informers would be richly rewarded, retribution on those who backed Azan would be grim, and reprisals for those who sheltered the *Moth* did not bear thinking about. There would be no port or cove left for the rebels to put in to, and Claudia had no pity for Jason once they'd been run to ground. Captured alive (the Emperor would make sure of that), he'd be dragged back to Rome, paraded in chains round the streets and sentenced to a humiliating, protracted death in the arena.

'And I shall be in the front row, cheering for Leo,' she said aloud.

'Hrrrow,' Drusilla agreed.

It was so unfair. She scrubbed away the tears that streamed down her face with her sleeve. 'The only way Leo gets to see his beautifully refurbished atrium is with a coin under his tongue for the ferryman.'

'Mrrrr.'

Pity his family, too. He'd be in his urn long before the news reached halfway to Rome. His sisters and brothers, his cousins and nephews, friends and colleagues would gather instead in the Forum to hear a sombre ovation in his honour. Like the families of soldiers killed in war, they would have to hold the feast without holding the funeral. Grieving would be harder because of it.

Fumbling in the drear darkness, Claudia stuffed a protesting Drusilla into her cage.

'Meeee-out!'

'Sorry, poppet.' She rammed the latch home to make her point and hurriedly tossed underclothes into her trunk. 'We need to get clear of the risk zone. Pronto.'

'Worried Jason'll come back?' a voice asked from the doorway.

Thank Jupiter for bodyguards! Hardly his job, but with the maids poleaxed from shock, Junius would just have to pitch in with the packing. Claudia wedged a pair of sandals down the side of the chest and said,

'Not Jason, you clod. Orbilio.' Get in there, dammit. She pressed down on her gowns, stuffed the last two on top, but would the wretched lid close?

'Would that be so much of a problem?'

'Junius, I am not in the mood for stupid questions.' How the hell were her cosmetic jars supposed to fit into *that* tiny space? 'Supersnoop will win enough glory bringing Jason and the rebels to book, they'll erect a statue to him in the Forum.' May the pigeons have a field day with it. 'He doesn't need to add my little dodge to his heroic collection.'

'Which little dodge might that be exactly?'

How come I've got a blue slipper left over? 'Junius, come and sit on the lid of this trunk, will you?'

Damn. The doorway was devoid of bodyguards. Claudia sat on the lid herself and bounced up and down until it closed.

'No, really.' Now the voice came from the corner. 'Are we talking about the tax dodge on your wine exports to Spain? That spot of smuggling earlier this year? Or slipping narcotics to the hot favourites in provincial derbies?'

When she stood up, the lid sprang up too. 'For goodness' sake, Junius, stop buggering about and put your Gaulish butt where it matters. On this trunk.'

But Junius wasn't in the corner, either. Squinting in the blackness, she could just about make out his shadow by the windows, then suddenly she was blinded as the shutters were flung open and sunlight dazzled her eyes. And now, of course, she realized her mistake. The hair was too dark, far too wavy, and the figure wore a long patrician tunic.

'Sorry, Leo, I thought you were my bodygu—'

Leo? Oh. Shit. His ghost was still walking.

'Father Mars, protect me from the undead.'

Beans. I need beans. Beans are used to drive away ghosts. There was fruit in the silver bowl – cherries and apricots, peaches and figs – but what calibre of servants forget to include black beans in the arrangement?

'Deliver me from the vengeance of this poor wretched soul in torment.'

The words tumbled into one, but still the ferryman didn't row Leo away. Had someone forgotten to slip him the down payment?

'Mighty Pluto, god of the underworld, take this stubborn shade to his ancestors. Quickly, if you don't mind.'

What was this, another aristocratic perk, that noble spirits were allowed to remain earthbound longer than anyone else's? Exorcism! That's it, I'll exorcise the bloody thing. Claudia made the sign she'd seen a priest use during an exorcism in Rome, thumb and first two fingers raised stiff, the fourth and little finger turned down. Unfortunately, it had been a Phrygian priest making the blessing for a Phrygian ghost; clearly there was a language barrier here. She tried making the sign with both hands, which set the spirit's shoulders heaving, as though it found

182

something amusing.

'Beans!' she told it.

'Beans yourself,' it said.

'Help me,' she implored Pluto. 'How do you drive ghosts back to Hades?'

'In a one-hearse chariot?' the apparition suggested.

One-hearse? Oh, terrific. Not a ghost. Ghosts you can deal with, of course. All you need is a handful of beans, the right words and *pfft*, off they trot. Hauntings by the Security Police, on the other hand, are much harder to exorcise. Far from being four hundred harmless miles away, Marcus Cornelius, that ace champion of the truth, was here on the island of Cressia.

'Just what the hell game are you playing, Orbilio?'

'It's lovely to see you again, too.' He helped himself to an apricot from the fruit bowl. 'I brought you a present.' He tossed across a cheap clay mug, the type sold by the hundred the day after the races, engraved with the names of the winners. The name on the mug was Calypso. Very droll.

'Answer the question.'

'My cousin's been murdered, remember?'

'You could not possibly have known that when you left Rome.'

'True.' With the toe of his boot, he flipped open the latch of Drusilla's cage. A dark blur shot out of the room without so much as a thank you. 'But it doesn't alter the fact that Leo was killed. Slowly and very unpleasantly.

183

Or that, if I'd been at the villa instead of in town, I would have prevented his murder.'

Claudia doubted Jupiter himself could have prevented the killing. More likely Orbilio would have got himself butchered, too. Aloud, she said, 'You were in town?'

'Gossip,' he said, 'is best picked up locally.' He carefully deposited the apricot stone in the middle of the window still then flicked it with his thumb and forefinger as hard as he could. There was a ping as it connected with a flowerpot in the yard. 'You'd be surprised what I picked up in that tavern.'

'The clap?'

He laughed. 'For the life of me, I don't know why you don't marry me and be done with, Claudia Seferius.'

'You think so little of me that you'd have me chained to a pompous, self-opinionated bore?'

'A pompous, self-opinionated, *good-looking* bore.' He let the wall take his weight. She'd almost forgotten those green flecks that danced in his eyes.

'When did you land?' she asked, because a nasty feeling was starting to congeal in the pit of her stomach.

'Day before yesterday.'

The feeling solidified into a ball. *Before a new light is born in the sky, bad news will come over the water.* Of course. Shamshi had been looking at her – her! – when he made his pronouncement at dinner. He'd been as surprised as the rest of them when he saw that

184

pirate ship in the bay.

'Then you'll know about Jason?'

'Oh, yes.' Orbilio prodded Claudia's mattress. 'I know *all* about our strapping son of an Amazon.'

'Son of a something, anyway.'

As he bounced up and down testing the feathers, she caught a whiff of sandalwood, with just the faintest hint of a rosemary rinse in his clothes. She recognized the combination. It was the indisputable scent of the trapper. But he smelled, too, of rough tavern wine, of salt spray from the air, and there were smuts on his fine linen tunic. Make no mistake. The death of his cousin had hit Orbilio hard. Grief was etched deep in the lines of his face, his eyes were red-rimmed and puffy. But even through his raw emotional state, danger pulsed through him.

He leaned across and extracted the stopper of her alabaster perfume pot on the table next to the bed. 'Nice,' he said, sniffing.

She snatched the phial out of his hand and replaced the bung. In her haste to pack, she'd almost left it behind. Now she stuffed it in her leather travelling bag, already full to overflowing, and thought about the ship making ready to sail in the harbour. This was the freighter Leo had intended to put his sister-in-law on. Only a puny fifty-footer, but the point was, it had a vacancy for a female passenger, plus luggage.

Marcus flopped back on the mattress, stretched out his long legs and folded his

185

hands under his head. 'Don't you think it's odd, these fires along the Liburnian coast?'

What is odd, my friend, is thinking about burned-out warehouses when Leo's just been skewered like a scallop. *Odd* is staying in a tavern incognito, instead of announcing your arrival to your cousin. *Odd* is appearing on the scene within a few hours of the tragedy. And *odd* is not seeing the Roman Navy lined up in the Gulf when you obviously know all about Azan's rebellion.

'Define odd,' she said.

His eyes traced the painted rose garlands which scrambled over the cornice. 'Leo's domestic situation, for a start,' he replied. 'Wife shoved out, sister moves in, husband set to marry a girl who's little more than a child. A little on the unusual side, don't you think?'

'Isn't that par for the course for your lot?'

Whether, engrossed as he was in testing the softness of the pillows, Orbilio missed the jibe against his class or whether he deliberately chose to ignore it Claudia wasn't sure. His eyes closed, and for a count of thirty his chest rose and fell. She did not fall into the trap of believing he'd fallen asleep.

Her hand closed over the strap of her trunk.

'What do you make of the fair Silvia?' he asked.

Damn. 'Charming girl. Love her to bits.'

A muscle twitched at the side of his mouth. 'And Nikias?'

Safer ground here. 'Nikias does with portraits what a Greek musician can do with a lyre.' Makes you weep with the depth of emotion.

'What about the dolphin?'

'Sorry, never met it. Can't give an objective opinion.'

'So you wouldn't know how the *Medea* came to be listing in the water?'

'Woodworm?'

The twitch broadened to reveal a row of white, even teeth. 'The trouble with casting Nikias in the role as saboteur,' he said, eyes still closed, 'is that the Corinthian can't swim. Whereas your bodyguard, apparently, cleaves the sea like an otter.'

'Good heavens. All this time, and I never knew.'

'Well, maybe you knew he was hanging round the saws in the carpenters' shed the night before the *Medea* was holed?'

'His spare time is his own business, Orbilio. I don't like to pry.'

'Good,' he said, opening one lazy eye. 'Glad we cleared that one up.'

All right, so with hindsight she wouldn't have sabotaged the ship and thus eliminated in a stroke any chance of mass rescue, should Jason raid Arcadia tonight. But — 'We don't all have crystal balls, Orbilio.'

'You've been peeking.'

His eyes shut, so he missed the volley of fireballs which bombarded the bed. What *did* he mean about those fires along the Liburnian coast being odd? Then she looked at his

187

face, understood the performance he was putting on, the act of forced joviality over what must have come as a thunderbolt from the blue: the discovery that even the Security Police aren't exempt from the effects of grief! Here, she realized, was a man juggling anger with guilt, anguish with sorrow, while trying to retain a grip on reality by doing his job. Behind those closed eyelids Orbilio was battling to control a whole host of undisciplined emotions – so was there ever a better time to sneak away and catch that fifty-foot freighter to Rome?

Unfortunately, Claudia would never know.

The scream four doors down made sure of that.

Twenty-Six

Short but shrill, surprise mixed with panic. Marcus sprang. In three paces he was off the bed, through the door and racing along the portico. In Silvia's doorway, the little oriental pedicurist slammed into him, her eyes bulging with panic. Her breath was drawn, ready to scream a second time, but at the sight of Orbilio, leadership personified, she gulped it back.

'Sir, sir, it's the mistress—'

He had already pushed the girl to one side.

188

'Fetch the physician,' he ordered.

A fine example of patrician tact, Claudia thought, racing behind. Anyone else would have called for the undertaker. Shamshi's soft, girlie voice floated somewhere above her.

Before the sun rises thrice more over our heads, a woman shall die.

Silvia lay on the bed, arms by her side, as though she was sleeping and had thrown back the covers in the night. She wore a nightshift of the palest buttermilk linen, so fine it was transparent, emphasizing the swell of her tiny breasts. Her head was turned sideways, facing the wall, and her honey-coloured hair streamed across the bolster, soft and shining and longer than one might imagine from seeing it curled. Around her throat, like some hideous necklace, hung a string of purple bruises.

'Pass me a mirror,' Marcus said, leaning over. 'Quickly.'

Claudia grabbed a polished bronze mirror from Silvia's table and thrust it into his hand. She watched as he turned Silvia's head towards him and held the mirror close to her lips.

So young, she thought. Death had stripped ten years from the Ice Queen. Impossible to believe Silvia had borne three small children. Who, she wondered, would break the news that their mother was dead? Indeed, who would know where to find them?

Three murders on top of an uprising and piracy, Orbilio would have enough on his

189

plate here. Right about now, the freighter would be weighing anchor, hoisting her red and white striped mainsail as she set off back for Rome, but no matter. There was still Plan B in reserve. Namely, Junius rowing his mistress across to the mainland just as quickly as she could give Supersnoop here the slip.

'Mother of Tarquin,' Marcus breathed. 'She's alive!'

The mirror clattered to the floor as he pressed his mouth to Silvia's, forcing life from his lips into hers. Claudia wondered why the sight of it should bring such a sharp pain to her chest. Five, six, seven times the needle jabbed before Silvia's eyelids fluttered open.

'M-Marcus!'

'Don't try to speak,' he said, trickling water a few drops at a time down Silvia's throat.

A colourless hand closed over his wrist. 'You – saved my life.'

'I can't take the credit for that,' he said gently. 'I merely speeded up the recovery process.' He pulled up the bedsheet to cover the transparent nightshift, smoothed the crumples on the counterpane, brushed a strand of hair from her eyes.

'Thank you.'

'Hey!' He wagged a finger in mock anger. 'Doctor Orbilio expressly ordered his patient not to talk, remember? And when she does, he confidently expects her first words to be the name of the man who did this.'

With trembling fingers, Silvia explored the bruising on her throat. 'Don't – know,' she

190

rasped. 'Dark. I was asleep.' Tears filled her big blue eyes. 'Thought I was – going to – die.'

Orbilio said nothing, but then what could he say?

That was what her attacker had expected, too.

Twenty-Seven

The demon did not need to look in any polished bronze mirror to know that its reflection was perfect. In any case, it had transcended the physical plane, the body was merely a vessel. One to be cherished and admired, admittedly. But a vessel nonetheless. A receptacle for the knowledge which had been handed down through the centuries and which had travelled the world as Medea had travelled the world, and Circe's sons by Odysseus had travelled the world, spreading their seed across all the lands and the islands.

And now the knowledge had come home. Back to where it belonged, in Illyria, on this magnificent Island of the Dawn.

The demon sighed with contentment. Its ancestors had been two beautiful, clever, manipulative women whose power lay in their ability to make people trust them. Only too late did their victims realize Medea and her aunt were capable of treachery, betrayal, murder – and much worse.

The demon toasted their memory with wine.

Twenty-Eight

'With thiss libation, I pray and beseech thee that thou mayest look propitiously upon thiss house.'

Dressed in flowing white robes, Llagos dribbled wine over the threshold to appease the gods who guarded the entrance. The whole estate staff, even the children, were congregated in the yard outside the atrium, but only Marcus, as chief mourner and next of kin, and Llagos stood on the portico.

'That thou preserveth those who enter here' – the priest sprinkled salt on the stone still darkly ingrained with Leo's blood – 'and those who leave.'

Claudia thought back to the moment when, in her haste and panic, she mistook Marcus for his cousin. Was it any wonder, seeing the place where Leo's life had oozed into oblivion, that she'd mistaken him for one of the *Lemures*? Those lost, lonely spirits left wandering the earth unable to comprehend their untimely deaths? Now, as the priest wafted incense over the cedar-wood doors, a rock lodged in the base of her throat. Was any death more untimely than Leo's? To die young is bad enough. To die alone and in unspeakable agony – she swallowed, but the rock would not budge. Such hate, she thought. Such unimaginable spite. Standing on the spot where he died, she could feel its malevolence. The hairs prickled on the back of her scalp. Gooseflesh covered her skin. She shuddered, but the cold hand of evil could not be shrugged off.

'Ye gods of the threshold, accept thee thiss sacrifice for the outrage that hass been committed.' Llagos beckoned forward one of the temple acolytes holding a white sheep by one of its gilded and beribboned horns. 'Take the life of thiss animal –' he paused while the acolyte stunned it with a hammer '– let its strength be thy strength' – a sharp knife slit its comatose throat – 'and mayest thou receive the power from the sacrifice to protect thiss house once again.'

Without trumpets on hand to drive away evil spirits, Cressia's squint-eyed miller blew into a pair of pipes fashioned from ash wood, coaxing unearthly shrieks from a sheepskin bag as he pumped. A stranger could be forgiven for thinking the sheep wasn't dead and the miller was intent on strangling it slowly to death, but when it came to dispelling spirits, the bagpipes shred them to pieces. Good and bad.

As the screeching died away, the butchered joints were roasted upon the open fire in the courtyard. Shamshi had taken away the soft internal organs, muttering to himself in Persian as he pored over heart, lungs and liver while Saunio's BYMs hugged one another and wailed like cats in a mincer.

Claudia's gaze swivelled to her left. To Lydia and Silvia, standing together, one as fair and petite as the other was dark and tall. Neither had spoken. Neither had shed a tear. Silvia had pinned a scarf across her neck to hide the bruises and when, on the odd occasion, she glanced at her sister, it was to flash her a look straight from the Arctic. Watching the Ice Queen, fists clenched, shoulders rigid, one might almost think Silvia hated her sister.

Lydia's spine was equally determined, her fists equally tight, but not out of grief, and not out of animosity or spite either. Indeed, pride seemed to be the overriding impression. There was a bloom to her skin, a glow to her face and for a woman discarded by her husband, abandoned by her lover and then left widowed without a penny, Lydia looked pretty damn radiant.

'Let us eat,' Llagos said, descending the steps to hand round platters of crisp roasted lamb.

Leo's voice echoed back. *You must try our local mutton. The salty grass and diet of wild herbs gives it a magnificent flavour.* Maybe. But Claudia could not force a single mouthful of lamb past her lips.

'What's that?' she asked Llagos, pointing to a thick white slime on the doorpost. Already the salt was starting to bleach out the bloodstains on the white stone step below.

'Wolf's fat,' the priest said proudly. 'For

Roman ways, iss used in marriages, yess? But on Cressia, iss protection against sorcery. We hef no wolfs left on the island so iss very precious commodity, but iss much needed right now.'

'In what way?'

'Because although there iss always much superstition on island, when things go bad, peoples revert to the old ways to see them through crisis.'

'To which the priest of Neptune turns a blind eye?'

'No, no,' he said. 'I *help* them. To ask peoples to change when they are suffering iss not good. So I work with them, alongside them, let them see we are brothers shouldering our burdens together. But at the same time I show them the new ways, let them decide for themselves which is best. Also,' he winked, 'thiss way, I always know what iss going on this island!'

Cunning old bugger.

'But now cerymony is finished, you muss please excuse me. There iss problem in town. Iss escalating, and though I am not sure how to deal with it yet, I muss go with the peoples this afternoon to the hills.' He pulled a face. 'The old ways hef a lot to answer for, sometimes!'

Orbilio was still standing on the portico, staring unblinkingly up at the frieze of Odysseus, deep furrows etched in his forehead. Saunio and Nikias were engrossed in discussing the merits of haematite crystals versus

Spanish cinnabar, Volcar was whispering something into the ear of a kitchenmaid, making her blush to the roots of her hair, and she could be mistaken, but Claudia thought she caught sight of Magnus hovering at the edge of the crowd talking to Qus. Beside her, Silvia and Lydia remained stiff and unspeaking. A sisterly show of solidarity, but that's all. A show.

When she glanced back, the portico was deserted, and now Qus and whoever he'd been talking to had disappeared. She edged her way through the tremulous crowd, who were alternately sobbing and praying, scared of what might happen next. So far, though, Orbilio had made no move to address them and allay their fears.

What the hell was going on here?

Twenty-Nine

Alone in her isolated cottage on the hilltop, Clio strained to listen.

'Come out, I know you're there.'

The heat throbbed like a pulse, creating mirages on the stone path and shimmering the far horizon. Cicadas rasped in the harsh, dry grass, vultures wheeled and a snake slithered under a boulder.

'You don't scare me,' she shouted.

196

Maybe she was over-reacting. Suppose it was just that runt of a priest, hoping for a free peep show? Children, perhaps? She listened for sniggers, for Llagos's ragged, aroused breathing. Despite the searing heat, Clio's teeth were chattering.

There was only one door to the cottage.

'Don't think I don't know what you're trying to do,' she called to the shrubs beyond the clearing.

Legends linger. Like precious date palms, they were nourished and fed, giving every attention to make sure they stayed alive here on Cressia. Centuries back she suspected some recluse had settled up here, perhaps a healing woman, and perhaps this woman had a daughter, and so on. Gradually, with the passage of time, generations of solitary dwellers had rolled into one creating a legend of immortality endowed with all kinds of mystical powers. Circe!

A goat bleated far in the distance, and four or five small birds twittered over her roof and were gone. Clio shivered and hugged her arms to her body. Why, oh, why couldn't the islanders have seen her as a reincarnation of the enchantress? Embraced her as Circe, four maybe five hundred years old, to be left offerings to win her favour and left in peace to work her magic powers. Instead, they interpreted Clio's long black hair as a cloak of evil. Her clear, unwrinkled skin as the result of a bloodlust. Made her a scapegoat for the island's misfortunes. Drought last year?

Blame the witch. Olive blight three seasons ago? Plague of thistles? Bad harvest? Even though she could not see them, she felt the islanders' malevolence outside her cottage.

'How many of you cowards does it take to frighten a woman? Four? Five? Twenty-five?'

Her worst fears had been realized in the night.

The carpenter's eight-year-old son had succumbed to the same wasting disease that had claimed the fisherman's wife. Leo's murder was the final straw the ultimate affliction on the islanders' fortunes, having the security of Rome whisked from under their feet. Someone must pay.

And once the witch was dead, the evil spell would be broken.

From the single window, she could see higher piles of whitethorn, more heaps of intestines, rotting, stinking in the midday heat. But the islanders' hex had proved ineffective. The 'vampire' had still managed to carry off two more victims. And all the while, the crickets rasped.

'You iss alone now, pretty one.'

The disembodied voice made Clio jump. *'Who's there?'*

'No ones to protect you, iss there?' called another.

'Becoss Leo is dead,' a third piped up.

'Dead as your wicked black soul,' the first voice sneered.

Enough! Clio slammed the door, bolting it loudly behind her. That second voice! That

198

was Llagos the priest! With shaking hands she slammed the shutters closed, plunging the cottage into Stygian blackness. Now even the temple was beyond refuge! If only she'd taken Leo's thirty gold pieces. She'd be on that little freighter sailing to Pula.

The prediction of Leo's astrologer was common knowledge across the island. *Before the sun stands thrice more over our heads, a woman shall die.*

Her breath was ragged, her body wracked with convulsions she could not control. Sweet Janus. She was alone up here in this isolated cottage. Alone. And trapped. With no one to turn to – and a prophecy that needed fulfilling.

Tonight, she thought. That's when they'll come for me.

Tonight.

Clio sank to her knees. She had never prayed before in her life, but this was as good a time as any to start.

Thirty

Silvia made her move immediately after the purification ceremony had been disbanded and the last of the sacrificial roast thrown to the dogs. Claudia wasn't surprised. Any woman who had managed to curl her hair,

199

disguise the bruises and adorn her elegant frame in a soft peach-coloured cotton robe within an hour of nearly drowning in the River Styx wasn't going to let the grass grow beneath her finely tooled purple sandals.

'Marcus.' Her voice was still low and croaky as she caught him in the courtyard. 'Might we have a word? In private?'

Waste of time, kid. Orbilio's defences may have hit rock bottom, but he's way too sharp to fall for the old big-blue-eyes-and-the-toss-of-the-ringlet routine. He knows your history, sweetheart. Nevertheless, there was no chance of sneaking away from the Security Police in broad daylight, and even though she had another call to make before she left, Claudia was curious. She gave them ten minutes before taking a nonchalant stroll which, surprise surprise, just happened to be via Silvia's bedroom. Because you can bet your bottom denarius that any social pariah worth her salt intent on snaring a wealthy, successful, good-looking meal ticket will kick-start her campaign in a place brimming with pillows and a soft double mattress! First it would be the scarf dropping to the floor to reveal the bruises, poor me. Then I feel faint, I must lie down. And finally it would be the my poor throat, I can't speak, come and lie here beside me while I whisper what I have to say.

In your dreams, girlie.

The door was a quarter open and, by bending down to adjust the thong on her sandal,

200

Claudia had a clear view of the Ice Queen, if not her quarry. Sure enough, the scarf was already a soft pool of peach on the tail of a mosaic lion. She heard the gentle glug-glug-glug of pouring wine. The murmur of two people conversing in undertones.

Undertones?

Silvia she could understand. Never mind play-acting, her throat really *would* be painful after that ordeal. But why should Orbilio whisper? Then she remembered how delighted Silvia had been to see him when she came to. The tenderness with which he had brushed that wayward strand of hair from her face and covered her revealing nightgown with the counterpane. Surely...? Nah. Not Orbilio. What would he see in that icy fish? She contrasted her own unruly dark curls with Silvia's obedient ringlets. The way Silvia glided under her pleats like a swan, while Claudia's gown billowed behind like a sail and her hands flapped when she talked, whereas the dainty patrician kept hers folded in front of her, and—

And—

And let's face it. Lots of men find flat chests appealing.

But come on. He couldn't. He wouldn't. Not *Silvia*.

Could he?

Silvia was only six when Lydia had married his cousin, but despite limited family contact, these two would still have known one another from childhood. Who knows what went

201

through his mind, seeing her again out of the blue? Claudia became aware of a nasty taste in her mouth. Marcus was no longer a set product of his class. Convention didn't matter to him and he wouldn't give a tinker's damn that disgrace clung to her like a second skin. *If she was the woman he wanted.* Claudia felt the return of the needle which had jabbed when his lips closed over the Ice Queen's.

'...there was a child,' Silvia's sexy damaged voice was saying.

'There was *what*?' The baritone ceased being a rumble.

'A boy,' she began, but at that moment, Orbilio turned and saw Claudia on her knees at the open door. She knew what he'd do. He'd shoot her a glance which was both admonishing and amused. She'd indicate her sandal as though to say look, stone in my shoe. His left eyebrow would say like hell there was and, then, with a twinkle in his eye and a twitch at the side of his mouth, he'd close the door ever so gently in Claudia's face.

Which he did. Closed it, that is. But there was no amusement on his face, only a look like thunder, and he did not shut the door gently, either. He slammed it so hard, the hinges feared for their lives.

'You sent for me, madam?'

In daylight, Junius's injuries looked even worse. His left cheek was up like a puffball, the eye half closed and purple. My, my. That

202

was some punch Leo had packed.

'It's just as well you don't work here,' she told him, clicking her fingers for him to follow her into the herb garden. 'Leo would have had you sold at the auction block for clashing with the estate livery.'

Was that a smile which flickered at the corner of his lips, or a grimace of pain from the place where Leo's punch had connected? You couldn't tell with the Gaul, enigmatic wasn't the word. High, wide and handsome, the bodyguard did a bloody good job, keeping tight to his mistress as though expecting an assault on her life any moment. Yet you couldn't accuse him of being *over* zealous. Conscientious, but in an intense, absorbed sort of way. Any other chap, of course, and Claudia might have suspected him of carrying a torch, the way his blue eyes fixed on her with an expression of solemnity bordering on pain. But good heavens, Junius must be four years younger than her – and what boy of that age lusts after mares, when there's a whole paddock of fillies out there?

'Now then.' Stripping leaves from a hyssop, she mashed them with water from the fountain and rubbed it into his bruises. 'Your honest opinion, Junius. Do you think you can row us to the mainland in the dark?'

The Gaul puffed out his cheeks. 'It's got to be at least fifteen miles,' he said, 'and after this latest attack, there's no guarantee the villages will be lit at night to act as a guide. So, no, madam. It's far too dangerous and I really wouldn't care to risk it.'

Clearly, if a girl wants an honest opinion she's going to have to give it to him herself!

'Moonrise at the cove it is, then. Be there, or I'll row off without you.'

How hard can it be, pulling on two lumps of wood for fifteen miles?

'In the meantime, I have another little job for you. Er, did I just see your shoulders slump?'

'Me? No, madam. Certainly not.'

'Then why are you frowning?'

'Squinting, madam. Against the sun.'

'You're standing in the shade, but it doesn't matter, Junius. You are still going to do it.'

'Do what?' he whispered hoarsely, and look how fast the hyssop poultice worked, because even the swelling had turned pale. 'With respect, madam, I've already picked a fight with an aristocrat and sawn a hole in his ship.'

'Yes, and now you're going to search Orbilio's room.'

'*Why*?' he rasped.

Leaning her hip against the white marble sundial as a scramble of white roses offered up their fragrance in a perfumed libation to Apollo, Claudia thought that was pretty obvious. 'Because I want to know how much he's got on me, of course.'

'No, madam, I meant why me?' Through the gate, the young Gaul glanced nervously across to the portico, where Marcus Cornelius had returned to stare at the marble frieze of the Odyssey. 'If he catches me, a common slave, searching not only a patrician's belongings, but Security Police papers as well—'

'He's too busy thawing icicles to bother about that,' Claudia assured him, 'and excuse me, I won't have it bandied abroad that any of *my* slaves are common! Now chop, chop, Junius. I'd do it myself, only I have to check something out before we go.'

'Dawn would be less chancy, madam.'

'No wonder Rome conquered Gaul. The place is teeming with wimps. Now, if you could just take my trunk down to the cove? Plus my leather travelling satchel, a couple of blankets in case it turns cool, some cushions to sit on, don't forget Drusilla – she'll be hard to round up if you wait until vole time – and that golden statuette in the atrium.'

Which ought to sort out four, if not five, angry creditors.

'Statuette, madam?'

'Next to the left-hand pillar as you go in, the one with Persephone holding a pomegranate in her outstretched hand, but you're right. Bring that gold unicorn with you, as well.'

That should keep another three sweet.

'Unicorn...'

'Leo specifically wanted me to have it. He said, and I quote, if anything happened to him ... Anyway, while you're about it, you might pack a light picnic for the journey. Half a dozen meat pies would be nice. Two or three cheeses. A chicken. Ham. One of those big smoked liver sausages I saw hanging from

205

a hook in the kitchens. Some wine and honey cakes would go down well, one of those big crusty olive loaves, and I saw them stuffing dates with almond paste yesterday, so you can pick up a jar of those as well. Yes, and don't forget we'll need a jug of wine. Oh, and Junius?'

'M-madam?'

'Close your mouth, please. You look like a goldfish.'

Thirty-One

On the grassy shores of a small island many leagues south of Cressia, Jason lay on his back, his shirt open to the waist, one knee raised, the other ankle resting on it. His hands were laced across his eyes to shield them from the fierce rays of the sun, and a wolfhound snoozed at his side. Music and laughter floated out from a tavern in the village beyond, but not so loud that they drowned the splash of terns diving into the shallow lagoon or the snoring of the taverner's dog.

He lay there, chewing on a leaf of the mint which rampaged across the island, and considered the tall and graceful woman who had given birth to him thirty-three years before. Nearly five years had passed since he'd seen her, and although the High Priestess had insisted the cough had been curable, his mind would not be at rest until he saw for himself. Sixteen hundred miles away, all he could do was pray to the moon goddess, Acca, to keep her devoted priestess safe and well – and make sacrifices to Targitaos, the sun god, that her warrior son would acquit himself well in her name.

Targitaos had listened to his entreaties. Thanks to his offerings, the sun god had kept the warrior in the peak of good health, made his muscles strong, his mind a powerhouse and, had he not been cheated out of what was rightfully his, Jason would be back home in Colchis already.

Boots crunching over the gravel set the wolfhound growling.

'Easy boy,' Jason said. 'It's only Geta.' He'd know that rolling gait anywhere.

'Since you ain't coming in to join the revels,' the big helmsman said, 'I brung you some food. Oh, and this.'

He tossed a wineskin next to the cloth in which sausage, pastries and a whole ham had been wrapped.

'Dunno about you,' he said, sitting beside his captain and ripping off a chunk of spicy red sausage, 'but I were getting mighty sick of fish.'

As his eyes scanned the lagoon, as blue as the turquoise for which his homeland was so famous, a heron glided effortlessly across the water margins. Geta's trained eye evaluated the small puffs of white clouds which had appeared on the horizon, but they were no threat and he took a long draught of the wine.

'Y'know,' he said thoughtfully, 'if that Roman Emperor ever do send his warships after us, them villagers back there'll squeal like virgins in an Arabian whorehouse. I ain't so sure we shouldn't slit their throats before we leave.'

'If Augustus sends in the navy,' Jason said, cutting into the ham with his dagger, 'I can't see the locals being too keen on telling Rome they took rebel money in return for food, wine and the favours of their womenfolk.'

'Ah.' Geta chomped on the sausage, feeding titbits to the dog to stop it from drooling on to his trousers. 'So what was you so deep in thought about, then, when I come up? Raiding Dalmatia, like what I suggested?'

'Actually no,' Jason said. 'I was thinking about my mother.'

When the redheaded helmsman laughed, sausage spluttered over the grass. 'Take it from a bloke whose clan totem is the emblem of the love goddess herself,' he said, tapping the serpent tattooed on his chest, 'you need a woman, son. In fact, I'd go so far as to say that if you're thinking about your old momma when there's a dozen bare-breasted scrubbers gagging for it just a few feet away, you need a woman bad!'

The captain sat up and sorted out a warm pastry stuffed with honey, raisins, apples and cinnamon. 'I wouldn't argue with that diagnosis.'

'The fat one with the ring through her nose ain't much to look at,' Geta said, scratching his armpit, 'but she ain't half a goer. Wears yer bloody dick out, her.'

'Isn't that a good reason to avoid her?' Jason laughed. 'But no.' Out in the shallow lagoon, the *Soskia* looked strangely top heavy. It was because the land was flat here, he decided, no hills. Made things look smaller and out of perspective. 'That's not the kind of woman I meant.'

The helmsman picked a bit of gristle out of his teeth and frowned. 'What other kind is there?'

Jason stared down at the blue tattoo being warmed by the rays of Targitaos, the sun god, on his own chest. The tattoo of the bull. His clan totem.

'The kind of woman,' he said slowly, 'one finds at the Villa Arcadia.'

Thirty-Two

'Hop in, gel.' A wizened face peered round the damascene curtains of the litter. 'Need to talk to you.'

The litter bearers exchanged glances. Half-way up the precarious cliff face wasn't their first choice for unbalancing the load and it damn well wouldn't be Claudia's, either. One slip, and she and Volcar would end up as fish bait. Not such a disaster at his age, but personally, she was rather looking forward to fifty more glorious years.

She was on her way back from the stocks. Junius had done a good job on the *Medea*. Several planks had to be cut out and replaced and the shipwrights wouldn't even be able to start caulking for another two days. Oh, yes, a wonderful job. Thanks to his mistress, hundreds of people were now stranded on Cressia at the mercy of Azan's thugs until reinforcements arrived from the garrison at Pula, two maybe three days down the line. Claudia hoped the dolphin was grateful.

'Whatever you want to discuss, old man, it doesn't need your hand resting *there* when you say it.'

'Sorry.'

'Or there.'

Volcar let out a wheezy chuckle. 'Can't blame a fellow for wanting to recapture his youth.'

'Tell me when and where he escaped, and I'll send out a search party for you.' Claudia wedged three large cushions between herself and him, and sat back to enjoy the ride. She had a feeling it was going to be bumpy in more ways than one. 'What did you want to talk about?' she asked.

'The will, of course.' He smacked his gums in derision. 'Only two things matter when you get to my age, gel, health and the future. Well,

I'm as robust as I was when I was fifty, but I need to know what's going to happen to me now Leo's dead.'

'If it's your fortune you're wanting told, try asking Shamshi.'

Volcar snorted. 'Don't trust that smarmy git any further than I trust that other bunch of poofs. Something rum about the lot of them, if you ask me, but that ain't the point. You have the ear of that young whippersnapper from Rome. What's he found in Leo's will?'

'Let me see if I've got this right? Your nephew was discovered less than six hours ago skewered like a scallop on the atrium door ... and all you're worried about is what he's left you?'

'Who said he was my nephew?'

'Silly me. I assumed that when he called you "uncle", it was because you were his uncle.'

'Clan breeds like swamp flies,' the old man retorted. 'Find me an aristocrat who isn't related to another and I'll find you laughter in Hades. Leo? I think I was his great-uncle by a second marriage or something, but the boy had no blood of mine, I assure you.' He spat out the side of the litter. 'None of my kin would swindle an old man out of his life savings.'

Janus, Croesus, Leo. How many other people have you 'borrowed' from in your obsession for heirs? And what the hell did it *matter* whether the atrium had pillars of marble – or stone?

211

'Leo would have paid you back,' she told Volcar.

Damn you, Jason, damn you to hell, for leaving so much business unfinished.

'Bollocks,' Volcar said. 'D'you really think that with just a few paltry sacks of olives and a couple of barrels of rough wine, this was enough to repay Lydia, Silvia, me, everyone else he'd diddled out of whatever money he could?'

'You're forgetting the rose-grower's dowry.' But niggles were starting to multiply.

'Still don't get it, do you, gel?' Volcar said, scratching at the parchment-thin skin of his cheek. 'Unless Leo made provision for me, which I doubt, I have nowhere to go and no money to pay my way if I did. The bastard's thrown me to the wolves and now you know why I don't give a bugger about him or how he died. I have my own future to look to.'

Malice twisted the air inside the drapes. So much bitterness from such a small, shrivelled shell, so much venom and self-centred spite. Or was it? For a man like Volcar, for whom life is no less precious despite his advanced age, fear for the future could easily become magnified out of proportion.

Besides, Leo wasn't the type to coolly swindle an old man out of his last days of comfort, any more than he intended to cheat his sister-in-law and Claudia was certain that he'd been equally determined to do right by Lydia, too. *I'm not quite the bastard you think. Magnus isn't the man for my wife, he's out of her class and in more ways than one. I'm taking no chances, Qus, post six men round my wife's house.* Did that sound like a man who threw old men and ex-wives to the wolves?

He'd made no bones that if Lydia had given him a child, divorce would not have entered his mind. The house he'd built for her out on the point, small and stone-built, had an air of impermanence about it, suggesting that the instant funds were in Lydia's dowry she would be repaid, allowing her to return to Rome where, still a handsome woman in her thirties, she would have no trouble hooking a second husband for herself. Wasn't it more likely that Leo had brought Volcar to the Villa Arcadia so that the old boy could wallow in luxury until he was able to repay the debt?

Which was when?

And with what?

Hot-headed as he was, Leo wasn't stupid. He knew damn well he'd been living beyond his means, fully understood the implications that his estate income was insufficient to repay his creditors.

'You're talking to the wrong woman,' Claudia said, tapping on the frame for the bearers to set the litter down. 'It's Silvia whose cosy with your young whippersnapper from Rome, not me.'

Rheumy eyes shot her a sharp glance. 'Think that's a love match, d'you, gel?'

'Volcar, their fate is written in the stars.'

He's Scorpio. She's desperate.

'Y'know, I like having you around. You liven

213

things up, make me feel young again.'

'That wasn't young, you randy old sod, that was my thigh.'

Volcar roared with laughter until his thin chest was wracked with coughs. 'Can't blame the old boy for trying,' he puffed.

'No one is more trying than you, you randy old bugger.'

Claudia alighted from the litter and shook her skirts. 'Don't worry about the future, Volcar. Everyone knows you'll die at the age of a hundred and twenty in bed. Run through by a jealous lover.'

Claudia was just debating whether to get Junius to include one or two of the smaller items of Leo's silver plate in her luggage as well, when a tall shadow fell over the grass where she was sitting. Bugger. She'd rather hoped to have seen the last of the Security Police on this particular island.

'Come with me to the bath house,' the shadow said.

'What kind of a girl do you take me for?' she asked. 'I always insist on at least dinner first.'

'I'll make a note of that,' the shadow said, grinning. 'But for now, perhaps you'd just humour me?'

'Why? Isn't it funny enough, suckering me into coming out here?'

'Mildly,' he said. 'But I knew you'd forgive me once you arrived.'

'Sorry to disappoint you, Orbilio, but Cressia's far too quiet for my exotic tastes.

214

Nothing ever happens – or hadn't you noticed?'

'You could always try doping a donkey to
liven things up.'

Claudia had almost forgotten. The more
urbane, the more dangerous...

'I'd only make an ass of myself,' she said.
'What's so special about this place, anyway?'

Outside the domed bath house, its white
stucco walls blinding in the sunshine and the
heat shimmering its red-tiled roof, Orbilio
began pacing back and forth. One-two-three-
four-five paces back, one-two-three-four-five
paces forward, repeat. It took a moment
before Claudia realized he wasn't hallucinat-
ing on the fresh paint. He was working out
where Jason had been standing when he
threw his spears. So he knew about them as
well, did he? Even in grief, he functioned on
a different level, that man.

Excepting the bits in his loin cloth.

'In itself, there's nothing remarkable about
the bath house,' he said, passing into the
vestibule. 'Like the rest of the villa, it's been
built to the highest of standards.'

A steam room, a hot pool, a plunge pool,
dressing rooms plus a room to house the hot
and cold water cisterns had been built around
an open-air gymnasium which, on any other
day, would be filled with slaves playing hand-
ball in their break, wrestling, boxing, or working out with the dumb-bells. Inside, soaring
arches were covered in opulent frescoes.
Statues of the gods, twice the height of a

man, stood in niches. The mosaics boasted some of the most complex designs Claudia had ever seen.

'I've always maintained that men are like floors,' she said, tapping her toe on Cupid's mosaic arrow. 'Lay 'em right and you can walk all over them.' She smiled sweetly up at Orbilio. 'But of course, you'd know that, wouldn't you, having spent the afternoon in Silvia's bedroom.'

His neck coloured. 'Don't start,' he growled. 'Just don't start, all right. What you heard back there—'

'Wasn't remotely of interest, Orbilio. I don't give a toss who you marry.'

'Mother of Tarquin! You heard that, too?'

Indigestion. That wretched lamb had given her indigestion. Claudia rubbed at the pain in her chest, but obstinately the pain wouldn't budge.

Orbilio exhaled slowly. 'Look, I'm really sorry—'

You will be, stuck with that icy bitch.

'—that you found out this way.'

They say eavesdroppers never hear anything to their own good.

'I ought to have told you right from the beginning—'

'Sorry, Orbilio, but you're mistaking me for someone who's interested.'

Marching back across the paved yard, Claudia rubbed harder at the pain in her chest and thought, strange. She hadn't touched the sacrificial roast. Pleurisy, then, not indigestion.

216

'Claudia, please.' Strong hands closed round her wrists, she could feel his warm breath on her cheek. As she inhaled, it tasted of mint on the back of her tongue. 'We've known each other a long time, shared so many adventures.' His voice was barely a rasp. 'I'm not a fool, Claudia; neither are you. Don't insult either of us by pretending there's nothing between us, because there is. God knows there is.'

Someone had squeezed the breath from her body. Taken the bones from her legs. Pleurisy, right?

'You're right, Marcus, I can't deny it.' Was that pathetic croak hers? 'There is something between us.' Shaking her wrists free, she saw that his pupils were black and that a pulse beat at the side of his temple.

'Say it,' he whispered.

The earth seemed to spin, suck her down, she wanted to cry, to laugh, to be somewhere – anywhere – else. She wanted to die. Die in a sandalwood heaven.

'For gods' sake, Claudia, say it.'

'Very well.' She closed her eyes. Dredged up every ounce of her strength. 'I'll tell you exactly what's between us, Marcus. It's...'

'Yes?'

Claudia swallowed. 'It's a dumb-bell. Someone left it behind after they'd worked out in this yard, and now if you'll excuse me.' She stepped over the weight. 'I have some vine-yards to visit.'

Thirty-Three

The demon watched a ray glide through the water. The sea was so clear, every rippling movement of the ray's wings was cleanly visible, even the cloud of small silver fish spiralling alongside, and for a moment the demon envied the sinuous adventurer the freedom to come and go as he pleased.

Other adventurers had come and gone from this island – Jason in his fifty-oared **Argo***, Odysseus in his black ship from Troy – but nothing had really changed. Should the shades of the heroes return to these thyme-scented hills, they would still recognize the vultures, the snake hawks, the violet-blue coral, the twisted oaks, fragrant pines, the same sandy beaches and white rocky coves on which they had idled their time all those generations before.*

Centuries peeled back.

To the day the **Argo** *became trapped in this very gulf by a flotilla under the command of Medea's brother, Apsyrtus. Thanks to the connivance of his treacherous lover, Jason had been able to steal the Golden Fleece from under the nose of her father, but he had not bargained on the ferocity with which the family wanted it back. Nor the revenge they sought on the perfidious bitch who'd enabled him to take it from them.*

In its mind, the demon saw the blockade close in. The trap tighten. There is nowhere for the Argo *to run.*

A plan forms in Medea's mind. Under cover of night she rows ashore. Sends word to her brother that she's been abducted, held captive, raped even. Remorseful (how could he have misjudged her?) Apsyrtus charges in to rescue his sister. Betrayal. She kills him. Dismembers his corpse and throws the body parts into the sea. Medea's plan is successful.

First the fleet must collect the mangled remains, since Illyrian custom decrees that bodies must be complete to make their journey into the afterlife and there was no way they could let the son of the king down.

Then, leaderless, the flotilla quickly falls into disarray, allowing Jason to sail off with the Fleece, making Medea his wife.

The demon had always been a sucker for happy endings.

Thirty-Four

The heat was moulding the pale-blue cotton of Claudia's gown to her flesh like a second skin as she stormed up the vertiginous hillside. Bristly coats clipped short for the summer, goats nibbled noisily among the sea of small blue thistles as the young goatherd, no more than twelve, played a haunting tune on the pan pipes.

Earthquakes and tidal waves, volcanoes and hurricanes couldn't stop Claudia Seferius leaving this wretched island. She sent a stone winging into oblivion down the slope. Dammit, Mercury riding Pegasus wouldn't be fast enough for her tonight. Crunching on the strewing balm, yellowed and crisped from months without rain, Claudia's sandals released waves of lemon scent into the air as from time to time she stumbled over a boulder on the dusty path until, at last, a sun which had seemed particularly pig-headed about dipping today, began to fulfil its obligations. Two hours, she calculated, before the moon rose, then it was Junius down in the cove, the Istrian mainland by midnight. Even so! Good as that sounded, any technique which produces more, sells for less and still makes a bloody good profit has to be worth checking out. And now here they were. Leo's famous vineyards, where established practice had been thrown out of the window and trampled into the ground. Jupiter, Juno and Mars! If the climb hadn't already done it, the sight of his leafy green soldiers standing in rigid phalanxes would have taken Claudia's breath right away.

Slowly, she walked down the aisles.

Carefully, she inspected the ranks.

Noting the way roots were kept moist with piles of manure, fertilizing the plants at the same time. Memorizing the angle of lean to maximize exposure of the grapes to the sun. Imagine the look on her bailiff's face when she ordered him to rip up the existing overhead trellises, pull out the elms which gave the old poles their anchorage, then plant new vines like espaliered apples! Imagine the look on the faces of those bastard merchants who'd driven her to the brink of ruin! They'd be laughing on the other sides of their faces, once they realized her profits were soaring. Let's see who's driving who then!

'Only mad people laugh to themselves,' a world-weary voice said.

Claudia found herself looking down at the olive-grove nymph, who had now miraculously transformed herself into a dryad of the vineyards. (Although the dryad was still no closer to having a wet towel rubbed over her face.)

'Who's laughing?' she said. 'The dust up here makes me sneeze.'

'It's not dusty,' the girl pointed out, a fat bunch of marigolds in her fist.

'Oh dear, it looks like my secret's out.' Claudia unclipped her brooch, the one shaped like a monkey and inlaid with carnelians and Baltic amber. 'But if you keep my secret, this is yours.'

'Wow!' A grimy finger traced the monkey's outline. 'Really, *really* mine?'

'Really, *really* yours,' she assured the rabbit-eyed scrap.

'Have you ever seen a real monkey? I haven't. I don't suppose this is real amber, do you? Someone said monkeys have tails like a cat, but I think they'd be more like a squirrel's, and anyway they're as big as bears, although I've never seen a squirrel that size. Can you help me pin this to my tunic?'

As Claudia knelt to attach the brooch to the filthy rag the child called a tunic, it occurred to her that she'd done a 'Leo' herself, charging headfirst without stopping to think. Because of its value, Nanaï was more likely to confiscate the brooch to buy food for her massive brood.

'What's your name?' she asked.

'Snowdrop.'

'Because you keep your clothes so white?'

The grubby little face scowled. 'Snowdrop *isn't* a nickname.'

'Well, Snowdrop.' Claudia slipped off a ring of Gaulish silver and pressed it into the girl's free hand. 'You can give this to your mother.'

'You mean Nanaï?' Rabbit eyes rolled in exasperation. 'Good heavens! Nanaï's not our mother! We're orphans. Didn't you know?'

Er. No. Actually, I didn't – and that put an entirely different slant on Leo and Nanaï's conversation. No tradesmen's dispute. No continuous gestation. These were strays she'd picked up. Strays which Leo had been sub-sidizing over the years.

'Come with me,' Snowdrop ordered. 'There is something I want to show you.'

She led the way along a winding goat track through the scrub, all the time cautioning Claudia to mind her arms on the brambles,

222

watch out for rabbit holes, this bit was slippery, careful she didn't snag her gown on the roses, mind this fallen tree branch.

'Thinking about it,' she said, 'I'm not so sure you *are* mad. You were laughing at Leo's vines, weren't you, but you shouldn't.'

'So sorry, milady.' Claudia pulled a solemn face. 'Very remiss of me to speak ill of the dead.'

'Is it? Then you'd better tell Nanaï, because she's been saying all sorts of horrible things about Leo this morning, but that's not what I meant. Nanaï says that when someone tries really, really hard to do something, you should never laugh at them, because it's always better to have tried and failed, than not have tried at all. Anyway, there's nothing to laugh at. Leo's method might be odd, but it does ever so well. He got much bigger grapes than when the vines ran the other way, dangling down, only – promise you won't tell?'

Claudia sucked in her cheeks. 'Vestal virgins' honour.'

'Well, the thing is, we've been taking a quarter of the crop. For Nanaï, of course. We wouldn't dream of taking them otherwise. That would be stealing.'

'But it's all right to do it for Nanaï?'

'Yes, because it's not as if we were eating them, is it? They still go to make wine.'

Claudia's mind suddenly found itself making rapid calculations. If Leo believed his yield to be twenty per cent down and was still content with the margin, whereas in reality they were twenty-five per cent up.

Oh, mamma, I'm home!

'Nanaï sells the grapes to someone in the town, and he ships them to Istria, and that's where they're made into wine.'

'Well, that's all right, then. As long as it isn't stealing.'

Snowdrop flashed her an old-fashioned look. 'Are you making fun of me?'

'Perish the thought.'

After a sharp descent through yet more gorse and more prickly juniper, the girl suddenly stopped. 'There,' she said, pointing. 'That's what I wanted to show you. That's where we live.'

Swarming over the yard (it had long since ceased to be a garden) was a storm of small children, every one of them younger than Snowdrop. In their brilliantly coloured rags, it was like watching a prism fracturing then remoulding, then splintering again in the twilight. At a rough count, Claudia made it thirteen – give or take a toddler or two – although, like Snowdrop's estimation, it was hard to be specific given that the whole gang were either tumbling over an assortment of dogs, goats and poultry or else skipping, hop-scotching or swinging from a rope looped over a branch. One, she noticed, was simply asleep where he had fallen.

Grime was the only common denominator. Some of the children were chunky, others like twigs, some had flat noses, others snub. At least two of the tots had black skin with wild frizzy mops, while others had fine hair like dark silken caps, wild matted curls just like Snowdrop's, or heads of brilliant red spikes. The closer she approached, the more ear-splitting the racket.

'Nanaï! Nanaï, look who's come to visit!' Snowdrop shrieked over the noise. To Claudia she said, 'Go on in.'

Fat chance. There were far too many folds in Claudia's gown for fleas to disappear without trace. Until small, dry, filthy fingers closed over her own, popping Claudia's resolve like a bubble.

Once, in the time before Leo moved all the workshops on the estate close to the Villa Arcadia, this had been a forge. Long, low and narrow, daylight penetrated the single room at its peril, but there was little trace of the blacksmith today. A giant cauldron hung suspended from chains above the hearth, wafting out the smell of a stew which rarely saw meat. Stinking tallows provided the light, but today, and despite the sinking sun, only one small, solitary flame flickered in a distant corner.

'She's not here,' Snowdrop announced unnecessarily. 'Sit down.' With a wave of her arm, she indicated the only high-backed chair in the place. 'I'll go and fetch her.'

Laying her bunch of marigolds beside a stack of wooden plates in the manner of a matronly housewife, Snowdrop gave the cauldron a quick stir with the paddle, checked the bread oven and inspected the level of the water butt before setting off to find Nanaï.

It was just as well, Claudia decided, that she hadn't sat down. The bundle of rags on the chair turned out to be a sleeping infant.

Adjusting her eyes to the gloom, she wandered around. Heaps of mattresses had been piled higgledy-piggledy against the back wall. Stools criss-crossed this way and that. A mass of small, patched clothes burst out of a wooden chest in the corner, cooking implements littered the table and toys littered the floor. A tornado would have left far less mess. The infant stirred, gurgled a bit, blew a few bubbles, then sucked its thumb back to sleep. It would not have seen more than one birthday, and it was anyone's guess what sex it was. Claudia picked up the little straw doll which had fallen to the floor and replaced it on the tiny chest.

Herbs hung from the overhead beam in thick bunches. Thyme, lavender, rosemary, oregano which could be used as rinses, disinfectants, in cooking, for strewing, for medicine, added to wax to make sweet-scented polish. Horsetails lay beside pots on the table, ready to scour them spotless. The large round loaf in the charcoal oven sent out tantalizing aromas to combat the herbs, along with the smell of cloves, porridge, and clean wool piled high next to a loom. More wool steeped in buckets of plant dye. Bright yellow juniper; soft pink sorrel; creamy parsley.

At the far end, a moth-eaten tapestry

curtained off part of the building. Claudia nudged it aside. Among the tangle of unmade bedclothes lay one black cat with half a tail and one mustard-coloured cat with exceptional whiskers. Wedged between the cats, infant twin boys lay entwined in each other's arms deep in sleep. Their faces hadn't seen water for weeks.

With no sign of Snowdrop returning, Claudia followed the path behind the back of the forge. As she did so, a three-year-old with grey eyes came barrelling round the corner. 'Ya!' he shouted, whipping an imaginary horse from his imaginary chariot. 'Ya, ya!' With no regard to pedestrians, the boy veered his chariot in a tight about-turn, knocking Claudia flying and trampling her foot in the process. 'Yeeha!'

The melee in the yard drowned her cursing, but in any case the woman swinging languidly back and forth in the hammock would have missed a meteor falling. She was crooning to a tiny bundle wrapped in her arms.

'My dear, I'm so sorry,' Nanaï said, turning a radiant smile upon Claudia. 'Snowdrop said we had a visitor, but as you can see, the baby's asleep and I really did not want to wake her.'

You take Leo's handouts, live here rent free, the children are in rags, the house is a shack and you steal his grapes to sell on, so where's the money been going?

'What do you think I should call my little sweetheart?' Nanaï asked.

227

'How about Adoor?'

'What kind of a name is that?'

'The kind that's short for Another Drain On Overstretched Resources.'

Nanaï's laugh was fresh, like a mountain stream over rocks. 'The boys I've named after birds,' she said. 'There's Raven, Jay, Merlin. Young Sparrowhawk up the tree there.'

'Don't forget the Little Bustard,' Claudia muttered, rubbing her bruises. Across the yard, the grey-eyed monster whipped his chariot into the chickens.

Nanaï brushed back wisps of white baby hair with her little finger. 'Mostly they're girls who are abandoned, and to them I bestow flower names. Tulip. Angelica. Lupin. Camomile. There's usually a trait I can home in on.'

'What was the inspiration for Snowdrop?' Claudia asked, settling herself on a fallen log.

'As her namesake blossoms through the snow, so my little Snowdrop blooms.' Nanaï smiled. 'To look at her, scrawny little mite, you'd think she'd keel over in a strong wind, wouldn't you? But don't be fooled. She's a survivor, my Snowdrop. I found her on my doorstep, three years old and almost dead of pneumonia, covered in ulcers, poor love. To be truthful, I didn't think she'd survive that first night.'

A fat tear of remembrance dribbled down Nanaï's cheek and splashed unnoticed on to the baby in her arms.

'I don't know why the gods chose me to care for her,' she said, 'but I do know I nursed

228

that child for six weeks and that if her natural mother had come back to claim her after the journey we'd made together, Snowdrop and I, I truly don't know what I would have done.'

Claudia felt a cold hand pass over her skin. There it was again. Bubbling under the surface, the raw passion which drove Nanaï to protect children who weren't even hers like a tigress would protect her cubs. *To the death.*

'But praise Cunina, who watches over babes in the cradle, the occasion didn't arise,' Nanaï said cheerfully. 'Once news spread that I'd taken on a child no one else wanted, other women started to sneak up in the dead of night to leave their babes on my doorstep.'

Just like the burbling little bundle in her arms now, Claudia thought, moved by the tenderness with which Nanaï wiped her fallen tears from the baby's cheek with her thumb. (The same thumb on which her own ring of Gaulish silver now glistened!)

A stone marten scampered home across the clearing as the baby suckled on Nanaï's finger. Was its colouring the reason her mother gave it away? Better to pretend the child was stillborn and give it to someone who would love and take care of her, than let her olive-skinned islander husband discover the fair-haired creature was not his? Claudia put herself in the distraught mother's shoes and knew that, in her place, the husband would have to go before the child.

'With hair that blonde, it's unlikely the baby's eyes will change colour,' she said.

'How about calling her Flax?'

'Flax!' Nanaï's green eyes closed in rapture. 'Yes, of course. *Flax.*' She began to croon softly to the bundle, a lullaby about sweet dreams and candied cherries, no doubt the same song she sang when she sat at her loom inside the tumbledown cottage.

'What will happen to you all now Leo's dead?' Claudia asked.

Even if the eviction order still stood, she didn't see Qus thundering up here with his band of henchmen, razing the old forge to the ground and ploughing up the soil while the children remained in residence. This had been another bone of contention between him and his master, but why? Because Qus found the prospect of making children homeless distasteful? Or because one of those ebony-skinned children was his?

Nanaï's malt-brown hair shone with red and copper streaks in the sunset. 'Don't worry about our future, my dear. The gods have blessed us and I know we shall be provided for. Already they have punished Leo for his wickedness, as I told him they would.'

The earth quaked, but no buildings fell. The temperature plummeted, but no icebergs appeared. Claudia swallowed the lump in her throat. 'Aren't you the tiniest bit sorry your benefactor is dead?'

'Nemesis is the goddess of retribution, dear. Once her powers have been invoked, they cannot be stopped.'

Claudia stood up. The sun had disappeared

behind the hills to the west. But that was not why she had to leave. Whether Nanaï believed that crap about Nemesis she neither knew nor cared. All she knew was that Leo had indulged this woman for seven years – yet the minute she can't get her own way, she turns and woe betide anyone who stands in her way. 'I make a dangerous enemy,' she had said.

Now Claudia understood Nanaï had meant every word. As she felt her way along the track in the dark, stubbing her toes on the boulders, snagging her robe on the prickles, she wished she could find something to like about the woman who cared for her orphans so deeply. Thank Jupiter for rowing boats. No royal barge was ever more sumptuous, no imperial chariot ever more splendid!

Not that everyone would be keen to leave paradise. Drusilla, for one, would be howling her head off down there in the cove, calling Junius all sorts of names that no cat of her aristocratic pedigree should know, much less use, and his arms would be scratched to ribbons. But then Drusilla had no qualms about reminding people that being crammed in a crate wasn't top of her list of pleasures. Tough. In the eight years they'd been together, Claudia and the cat, bitter pills had become part of their joint daily diet. This was simply one more in a long line that she'd have to swallow where the end results outweighed discomfort.

With a pang of affection, Claudia's mind

cast back to the days when they were both skinny bags of bones starving in the gutter of a rough northern dockyard. Young and alone, robbed and raped, Claudia would not have cared if she died. Then a small mewing sound pricked at her awareness, and from then on, neither she nor the cat had looked back. Now look at her. From the days of dancing for sailors in boisterous taverns, she was mistress of a town house in Rome, a sprawl of Etruscan vineyards, had slaves at her beck and call, food in her belly. She was answerable to no one and nothing.

Squinting as she picked her way along the stony path in the dark, Claudia smiled. Of the three problems hanging over her head, one at least was secure. Thanks to Leo's revolutionary techniques, Seferius vineyards were set to make their first decent profit since her husband had died. (Listen, she never said she was good at the business. Only that she was not prepared to let it go cheap.)

Which only left Hylas the Greek to contend with, and the Security Police who had compiled such a persuasive case for the prosecution. Goddammit, if she couldn't kill these two birds with one stone, then her name wasn't Claudia Seferius! There had to be some way she could win Hylas over that didn't entail two broken legs, and once she'd found it – bribes, blackmail, she wasn't proud – Orbilio would have no case to present. Now then. Let's start with the bribes. What kind of present would appeal to a successful Greek

232

horse breeder?

The hand that clamped round her waist came out of nowhere.

Before the sun stands thrice more over our heads, a woman shall die.

As she opened her mouth to scream for her bodyguard, a gag was stuffed into her mouth.

'Mmmf! Mm-mm-mmf.' (LET ME GO, YOU BASTARD.)

She kicked backwards, wriggled, squirmed in a bear hug that was terrifyingly familiar.

Before the sun stands thrice more over our heads, a woman shall die – and the sun had risen two times already.

'Mm-mmf! Mm-mm-mmf.' (LET ME GO, YOU FAT BASTARD.) 'Mm-mm-mmf!'

The bear hug relaxed. Strong arms released her. Claudia started to run. But her attacker hadn't intended to let his victim go free. Just long enough to throw a cloak over her head. A cloak which smelled of cinnamon.

Thirty-Five

Control.

Power lay in control, and power was absolute.

To have a creature helpless and at your mercy, to toy with it, play with it, hold its life in your hands, the knowledge that you have its destiny in your dominion – this was the ultimate validation of power.

Human souls.

Not blood. Not death. Not destruction. Not even authority over life.

The ability to manipulate a person's soul. Subdue it. Tame it. Force it to bow before the almighty presence. The more souls it could vanquish, the more it could subjugate and make quiescent, the faster omnipotence was attained.

The demon licked its lips and relished the slow hours ahead of it.

Thirty-Six

'Marcus!' Even through her badly bruised tonsils, Silvia's censorious tones echoed across the library. 'Marcus, good heavens, man, you're drunk!'

'Thassa coincidence.' He grinned up at all three of her. 'So am I.'

He lifted the jug to his lips and drank deeply. Under a footstool upholstered in scarlet, a long-stemmed glass lay on its side where he'd rolled it away long ago. Too small. Too bloody small. Needed to do the job faster.

'Absholutely bloody steaming.'

All this time. All this time, he and Claudia...

He upended the jug and finished off even the dregs. That easy familiarity. The jokes. The looks. The *passion*...

'Poor darling.' The triple haze that was Silvia glided across the floor towards him, her rigidity softening with each dainty step. 'We had no idea you were so deeply attached to your cousin.'

'Snot Leo.' When he shook his head there were six of her. 'Snot why I'm drunk.' He tried to stand up, but his foot kept slipping on the polished mosaic. 'Class, Silvia. Issa problem, see, being patrician. Can't just run away. Patricians have – whassa word? Obligations. That's what patricians have. Obli-sodding-gations.'

'Marcus, please.' Tragic blue eyes turned downwards. 'I've been totally honest with you about my past mistakes and it's terribly unfair of you to drag them up in this way.'

'Wasn't,' he said, belching softly. 'Never crossed his mind, frankly.'

'Then what on earth has driven you to drink your brains out, you poor love?'

'Marriage.'

'Ah.' She crouched down beside him and, as she wiped his fringe out of his eyes, a drift of honey-coloured hair floated gently in and out of focus in front of him. The drift smelled of white lavender. 'I do understand, you know, darling. It's an awfully big step—'

'Can't take steps,' he said sadly. 'Can't even stand up.'

She smiled. 'With me by your side, you can do anything.' Silvia drew a deep breath and ran a crisp pleat slowly up and down between her fingers. 'You were badly burned last time,

235

but you won't regret marrying me—'

'Birthright,' he pronounced grandly. 'Denying children their birthright issanother big problem.'

'Don't let's go into that now. It's late. Let's get you to bed instead.'

'You, Silvia, are a very beautiful woman.' In fact, all three of them were exquisite. Wasp waist, pert breasts, a carnality that belied her glacial exterior. 'But sex is outta the question.' He held the wine jug to his left eye, closed the right and stared into the blackness. 'Seferius,' he announced.

'Sadly, dear, it's only that cheap stuff from over the water in Istria that you've been knocking back. Not Seferius vintage.'

'Want her.'

'I really don't think you should drink any more tonight.' Silvia prised his fingers away from the jug's handles.

'Can't have her.'

'Absolutely not, darling. More wine will only make you throw up, and then you'll be in no condition to conduct Leo's funeral tomorrow.'

'Funeral. Hell. I forgot.' Orbilio rolled on to all fours. 'How's Lydia coping?'

Silvia sniffed. 'We would prefer it if you didn't mention that bitch, if you don't mind. Now let's call for a slave to help you to bed.'

'Claudia.'

'Common she might be, but Claudia isn't a slave, you silly goose. Can you manage there?' she asked, as his hands closed over a cypress-

236

wood chest filled with the works of Homer and Plato.

'Need to talk to her,' he said, testing the grip before hauling himself upright. 'Have to explain.'

'Well, it will have to wait, I'm afraid.'

He lurched from chest to chest round the library until he reached the door. 'Morning will do, I susuppose.'

'It'll have to wait a lot longer than that,' Silvia said. 'She's gone. Cat, luggage, the lot, just like that,' she added, snapping her fingers. 'Didn't even have the courtesy to kiss us goodbye.'

'Uh-uh.' The room started spinning. 'She wouldn't leave without the Gaul.'

'The rumours are true, then? It's what we suspected, of course, her and the boy, and who can blame her. Attractive young widow, all that sexual energy has to go somewhere.'

Orbilio tasted regurgitated wine in the back of his throat. Claudia and the Gaul? Entwined between the sheets, naked, buffered in sweat, groaning in mutual pleasure ... He put his hand on the door jamb to stop himself falling.

'But to put your mind at rest, Marcus, the boy has gone, too.' Silvia ruffled his hair like a child's. 'So whatever it was you needed to explain to the lovely young widow, you're either going to have to keep it until we return to Rome or else put it down in a letter.'

'You don't understand.' A vice clamped round his ribcage.

237

'Letter, definitely, seeing how it worries you that much. Now it's two hours past midnight and you need your sleep, you poor darling. Come along.'

'No.' He couldn't breathe. 'I knew she'd try something, so I – Silvia, you don't understand.'

'Understand what, dear?'

'I locked the Gaul in the woodshed.' Justified on the grounds that he'd caught the bastard sneaking round his papers. 'Shut the cat in there, too.' Serves him right if she scratches his lecherous eyes out.

'Marcus, darling, two men have been brutally murdered and the *Medea*'s on the stocks. That makes Cressia an extremely hazardous place to be at the moment, and whatever else one might say about the woman, Claudia Seferius doesn't strike one as the type who'd wait for her toyboy when pirate ships are on the rampage.'

'Agreed.' Suddenly he was sober again. 'But there's one thing she'd never go without.'

Claudia would never leave her beloved Drusilla behind.

'Meaning?' Silvia asked, linking her arm through Orbilio's.

'Meaning,' he growled, shaking the arm off, 'the silly bitch is in danger.'

238

Thirty-Seven

The silly bitch certainly was. With all that had happened, she had completely forgotten that incident outside the grain store. Now, bundled under the cloak, everything came flooding back. The same grip. The same bear hug. The same sweet smell of cinnamon. Only tonight there was no question of him carrying her back to her bed.

Time passed, or then again, maybe it didn't.

Trussed and helpless, all Claudia could do was to wait. Wait and remember...

If only she'd thought to pull out the gag once he'd released her! At least she'd have been able to breathe, call for help. But her instinct had been to run. To pitch headlong away from her attacker. She hadn't banked on him netting her like a hare.

Cinnamon.

If she never smelled it again, it would be too soon.

Once the cloak was thrown over her, a rope had been looped round her waist to pinion her arms, but there were still two cards hidden up Claudia's sleeve: the knife she carried in the folds of her gown; and the thin stiletto strapped to her calf.

While she fumbled for the knife on the

239

clifftop, she'd lashed out at her attacker with her feet to distract him. But before she could get a firm grip round the handle, she was tossed over his shoulder like a sack of old turnips. Surefooted as any mountain goat, he trotted down the hillside, dumped his squirming bundle into a boat then quietly relieved it of the knife hidden in the folds of her gown and the stiletto strapped to her calf. Obviously the moon had started to rise; its light had betrayed her steel defences. Acca must be laughing her bloody socks off.

An eternity later, dizzy and dazed, Claudia felt the boat grate to a halt. Heard the scrape of wood against sand, the slap of water against rocks. Defenceless as a kitten, she was once more bundled over his shoulder and then it was another climb, up another cliff, and she had no idea whether this was still Cressia or whether he'd brought his victim to a different island completely.

They'd reached the top and dammit he was barely panting with the effort. Throwing her over his other shoulder, hardly a minute had passed before her abductor slowed to a halt. She heard him kick open a door. Inside, his footsteps echoed, but the echo was not stone or marble. Solid. Dull. More like tamped earth. He lowered her down. Not softly, but not roughly either. Claudia didn't move. She would not give him the satisfaction of struggling again. Whatever he did, she would not flinch. She'd deprive him of the pleasure of watching her suffer.

But the bastard was biding his time.

Whistling softly under his breath, the footsteps retreated across the room. She heard the squeak of rusty hinges. The graunch of the bar as it was rammed home to lock the door from the outside.

With the sound, all hope died in her breast.

Bound and gagged, blindfolded and trapped, Claudia could only wait for her attacker to return. She had no weapons with which to fight. No one knew where she was. She couldn't break free, much less break out of this prison.

Whoever it was had planned it well.

In her soft, cinnamon tomb Claudia waited.

Darkness had barely covered the hills before Clio heard the first of the rustlings. Her heart was pounding, her mouth dry. Straining, she heard further shuffles. A rock dislodged here, a scrape of foot there. Through a crack in the shutters she saw torchlights, which were quickly extinguished. How many of them had gathered? Were they armed? Did they intend to kill her now? Or take her alive and do it slowly?

She imagined Llagos the priest denouncing the whore who had tried to seduce him, faithful husband and father of four that he was. No mention of the silver he left, or who approached who.

Then the cobbler would probably tell how Clio cast the evil eye over him as she passed his stall. His valiant fight to resist the lethal pull. How the effort made him sick. Forget that the bastard was a habitual drunk.

The widower fisherman would be one of the group. Grief finding an outlet in vengeance, his own inadequacies drowned in her innocent blood. With the witch out of the way, he could bury his conscience along with his wife. Never having to question whether he should have noticed how ill she was, and that maybe he shouldn't have worked her so hard to the end.

And the father of the boy who had died. The carpenter. He had seemed a reasonable enough man, even though Clio had never actually exchanged more than a nod or two with him. Did he know she had never even clapped eyes on his son? Did he care as he swelled the mob's numbers?

Bigotry plus helplessness equals explosive combination.

All it needs is one little spark...

Leo, Leo, what a price we are paying. All because we wanted riches! She put a hand over her lips to stop them from trembling. Her hand was colder than ice.

If the men rushed the cottage, they would probably kill her. Clubs, knives, something quick. But if the women were outside, huddled in groups further down the hillside, she was facing a very different scenario. Witch. Vampire. Flesh-eater. It didn't matter what names they called her. The bitches would want her alive.

Once more, Clio dropped to her knees. She

hadn't known where to start, who to call on, when she began praying earlier. In the end she had chosen the great falcon god of her Liburnian ancestors, whose vision was sharp and whose flight was swift. The god whose vengeance was deadly.

'Come to me now,' she murmured. 'Bestow upon me your wisdom and courage, oh lord.'

The heat in the cottage threatened to engulf her, crushing her chest like a millstone, and the blackness was the blackness of hell.

'Make my ears deaf to the footfalls which shuffle closer each minute.'

And the soft whispers which called for her blood...

In the blackness of her cottage, Clio felt something brush her cheek. It could have been a moth, of course. Then again, who was to say it wasn't the wings of the falcon god? The one whose vengeance was deadly.

Thirty-Eight

The whistling was light. Jaunty even. The whistling of a man looking forward to what he was about to do.

At first, Claudia thought the whistling was part of the birdsong. The dawn chorus had just started up, led by a blackbird solo before the rest of the choir joined in. This whistling was different. It had a tune. A rush of weakness enveloped her. Was that the last sound she'd hear? Not even the liquid trill of a warbler, the harsh chatter of a magpie, but the tune of her killer? *Or would the last sound she heard be her own scream?*

The whistling grew louder. Closer. Unbearable. Hands closed round the bar across the door. She shuffled backwards on her bottom against the stone wall. Pressed her backbone hard against it. Willed the stone to absorb her flesh.

'Zlat.'

The bar didn't shift. With a grunt, he heaved again. Blood thundered in her ears, her heartbeat jumped out of its rhythm. She felt sick. There was a dull thud from where the bar landed on the ground. A squeal of ungreased hinges. I'm going to die. Oh, god, I'm going to die. Instinctively, Claudia curled herself into a ball.

'Sorry about this,' he said, and although the accent was mild, it was Latin he spoke. 'It was the only way I could – *vlodor zlat!*'

Even under the cloak, she squeezed her eyes shut. Footsteps covered the room in three strides, but miraculously Claudia's arms were sprung free from the rope. Rescue! She heard a primeval whimper and realized it came from her.

'Da vlodor stapo injio!'

For a moment, she couldn't believe it. I'm safe, I'm safe, I'm not going to die. Trembling hands pulled the gag out of her own mouth, but when she tried to push the cloak off, it weighed more than lead-covered ivory and it was left to other hands to pull it off. As the curtain rose, she saw the grey light of dawn streaming in through the rough wooden doorway of what looked like an abandoned shepherd's hut. Stank like it, too. Her eyes picked out the crude tamped earth floor. Rat droppings. Patches of mildew. A pair of boots – oh, shit. A pair of red leather boots.

The cloak was finally clear of her face. Her gaze locked with that of the pirate.

'Oh, no,' Jason groaned. 'Not you again.'

The expression out of the frying skillet into the fire drifted into her head. Here she was, being helped to her feet by the same son of an Amazon who'd chained Bulis in the grain store before generously setting it alight. The same Scythian warrior who doesn't bother employing heralds to deliver his letters, he sends them spear-post instead. The pirate who spitted Leo like a sardine and left him to die in unspeakable agony.

'Here.'

The perfect gentleman, he unhooked the goatskin at his belt and pulled out the stopper. Who'd think he drank wine – this wine, probably – out of the gilded skulls of his enemies and used their flayed skins to cover his quiver? Claudia hesitated, and discovered the uncomfortable truth that the need to rehydrate far outweighed pride. The wine was fruity and dry. More importantly, it was

245

strong. With every gulp, her strength returned.

'This is Geta's fault,' Jason was saying. 'When I told him I wanted a woman from the Villa Ar— Ach, it's a long story. Just accept my apologies.'

'Absolutely.' I mean, who's to say it wasn't purely men that he butchered? Perhaps, underneath it all, a heart of gold beat inside that white shirt tucked into his pantaloons? *Perhaps I'm the Queen of Bloody Sheba.* When his people sacrifice to their sun god, they don't do it in the swift humane manner of Roman priests, stunning the animal before cutting its throat cleanly. Scythian sacrifice was as cruel as it was protracted. First they tie the horse's front feet together, then they pull on the rope. As the horse stumbles, so a noose is flung round its neck, with a short stick to act as a garrotte. The rope is then twisted, slowly, choking the poor beast to death. *Choking.* Claudia shivered. And pictured the bruises round Silvia's throat, darker than dragon's blood...

Suddenly Claudia understood why Bulis had been killed in the way that he had. It was a ritual in the Scythian practice of human sacrifice to tie the victim to a tree or ceremonial pole to garrotte them. She handed back the wineskin and hoped he didn't see her hand shake. 'We'll say no more about this little misunderstanding, then.' She edged her way to the door. 'After all, everyone makes mistakes.'

'If it's any consolation, I'll have Geta's *dokion* – blood, for this.'

Claudia didn't doubt it. He'd probably drink it out of the helmsman's skull, too. While the helmsman was still alive.

Outside, it was pretty obvious that the strapping Geta, he with the stamina of a bear and the life expectancy of a butterfly in frost, hadn't delivered his package to a different region of Cressia. Peaks which had previously been little more than jagged shadows on the horizon suddenly loomed stark and uncompromising before her. Her heart jumped. Only a narrow channel of crystal clear water separated her from the pitted, white karst. Ducking under the lintel, Jason looped his thumb in his cloak and hooked it over his shoulder and Claudia realized that the gold she'd seen glinting at his neck from the cliffs of the villa was in fact a torque engraved to resemble overlaid leaves of willow, while the gold at his waist proved to be links of chain forming a belt. The buckle comprised two interlocking gold serpents. Well, they would be, wouldn't they. There are always serpents in paradise.

She was just debating which way to saunter nonchalantly off, no hard feelings what, when, from the corner of her eye, she saw him stiffen.

'*Zlat!*'

Now Claudia's Scythian might be on a par with her Cappadocian, but she was getting the gist of the lingo. *Zlat*, for instance. Not one for the kiddies. Nor, probably, was:

'*Litja ba kula!*'

Shielding her eyes with her hand, she followed his gaze to the three ships streaking up the Dalmatian coast. Her heart skipped again, only louder. The navy! The Imperial Navy had rooted him out! Then she realized the ships were much smaller than Augustus's triremes. In fact, they were identical in almost every respect to the *Soskia*. Including the red flag of war.

'*Mijela da navo Azan.*' He frowned. 'That means, those are the ships of Azan.'

It's Minerva. She hates me, that goddess. She's got it in for me, the bitch.

'That way.' His fingers clamped round her upper arm. 'Run.'

'You run.' Claudia dug her heels into the dry, dusty soil. 'I'm staying.'

'Don't be stupid. The island's uninhabited, no one'll know you're here.'

'Fishermen pass. I can signal.'

'This island is *sladni*. Cursed. Last summer, the shepherd and his flock died of some kind of *smicu* – what do you call it? Pulmonary infection.' He grimaced. 'Not a pleasant way to go, bleeding from every orifice.'

Claudia tried not to think about Leo.

'After that, the inhabitants abandoned the place, so even if someone sees you, they'll take you for the spirit of the plague calling them to their deaths. Now hurry. Please. We're wasting precious time.'

'*You're* wasting it.' This is a civilized world

we're living in. 'No one believes in shape-shifters and ghouls any more.'

'On Cressia, the islanders think Clio's a vampire.'

Clio. Clio. Where had she heard that name before? 'I'm still taking my chances.'

'Vlodor plut! Don't you understand? If I leave you behind and Azan's men see you, there's no telling what will happen. They're animals, believe me.'

That's rich, coming from you. 'I can hide,' she said. 'In the hut. And it's not far to the mainland. I can swim it.'

'Dammit, woman, there's no telling Azan's men won't find you anyway. And you might swim like a mermaid, but you'd never beat that coastal current.'

Which, when you put it that way, really only left Claudia one option.

She belted behind him down the cliff path to his ship.

It would not be an exaggeration to say that Claudia had never set foot on a pirate ship before and that if she never, ever repeated the experience it would still be way too soon. But you had to hand it to the crew for the speed they got a hundred and twenty feet of wood shifting.

At the captain's first yell, they were halfway to the galley before their eyelids had even opened from where they'd been sleeping out on the sand. Every man to his station, the operation to weigh anchor was as smooth as a greased bolt. While sixty oarsmen slithered below the covered deck and the bow officer took up his station, the rest of the crew cast off and made ready for battle, protecting the wales with overlapped shields and checking the ammunition for the ballista amidships.

'Why did you tell them they're Roman warships?' she asked. You didn't need to be a linguist to know that 'da navo Augusto' wasn't the same as 'da navo Azan'.

'Inside the cabin,' Jason growled.

'But—'

'And stay there,' he ordered, pushing her into a small wickerwork structure at the stern. (Cabin? Pig pens were cosier.)

From below, the rowing officer set the beat, first for the drummer, then, once the *Soskia* was underway, for the flautist. Above, on the pig pen's reinforced roof, the boots of the steersman clumped up and down as he barked orders to the men who worked the galley's giant steering oars. For whatever reason Jason was running from Azan, he was making a bloody good job of it. The *Moth* flew through the water.

And Leo thought he could outstrip this sleek, bleak killing machine! The *Medea* was only a third of the size, only a third of the power. What on earth was going through his mind when he set off after the galley?

'*Tosc!*' Jason cried. Faster.

Could the *Moth* fly any faster? Claudia ventured out on to the bucking deck, grabbing on to the red painted rail to steady

250

herself as she leaned out. The speed was exhilarating and as she put her face to the wind, her hair was swept like a pennant behind her. She forgot about Leo, about scalps and war spears, about Bulis and odd fires along the Liburnian coast. She luxuriated in the tang of pitched timbers, the taste of salt on her lips, the sound of timbers creaking as the *Soskia* scythed through the sea.

'I told you to stay inside,' a voice growled.

'I'm not in anyone's way.'

'Look around. Can't you see?'

Ah. Those rumbles among the crew, the glowers, the dark mutterings to their captain were about her, were they?

'The fleet's gaining and the men think you're the cause of their bad luck,' Jason rasped. 'In fact, the general consensus seems to be that if lead weights were attached to your feet and tossed over the side, that luck would change.'

He didn't need to shove her this time. Claudia was back in the pig pen before you could say oink.

'I've told them you're our hostage, more valuable than the treasures inside all the temples of Pula, but right now, the crew's skins mean more to them than booty. Step outside again, and I can't answer for someone taking the law into their own hands.'

What next with this man? There was no logic Claudia could employ, no rational argument. He'd tried to kidnap her once, on the night of the fire, but when the alarm horn sounded, he'd knocked her out, the quicker to make his escape. By then he had already killed one poor sod, then it was Leo's turn a little later, with an attempt on Silvia's life the same night. Yet, when he saw Claudia trussed up and gagged in the shepherd's hut this morning, he seemed surprised. So much so, he practically tripped over himself to apologize, and now he was cosseting her like a newborn babe. During trials in the basilica in Rome, Claudia had listened to killers claiming not to have remembered committing their crimes, but then they would say that, wouldn't they, when they'd been caught red-handed? They had no other defence. But now, seeing Jason, Claudia wondered whether there wasn't substance behind the concept after all. A genuine blanking out of things too horrible to contemplate on a conscious level?

In which case, it made him even more dangerous. You'd never know what triggered the change, only that it would be swift. Next time, stuff the pros and cons of staying on *sladni* sodding islands. Eat my dust, you sick Scythian bastard.

'Geta,' he called. '*Var te stluja da Soskia dur mileja kanal dara?*' Can you take the *Soskia* through that channel over there?

The shock of red hair shook violently, the general gist of his reply seeming to be along the lines of 'not at this speed, I can't'.

'*Zlat.*' Jason walked over and clapped a hand round Geta's shoulders. '*Plu Azan mjbelo,*' he said under his breath. Azan's gaining.

252

'Azan?' Geta hissed.

'*Mijela da navo Azan,*' Jason replied softly. '*Bo Augusto.*'

'*Zlat!*' The helmsman cast a worried glance round the ship, and for the first time, Claudia realized that the others couldn't make head nor tail of the exchanges between the captain and his second-in-command. Interesting. The crew weren't Scythian, then. Inside the pig pen, she stared up at the mast and asked herself, was this a good thing or a bad thing? And did it matter? After all, she only had the one scalp. This way Jason and Geta would at least get half each.

Then the copper quadran dropped. The crew might not be Scythian, but they were no less Azan's men. The same Azan, who was steaming up behind them, gaining fast. How long before some sharp-eyed sailor noticed those streaming red pennants were not Roman?

It was *zlat* right enough.

Claudia was in it up to her neck.

Thirty-Nine

Inside the cabin, Claudia lifted the lid of the carved wooden trunk.

'Looking for something?' Jason asked.

If they're gilded, I won't mind so much, but

253

if they're ... well, *fresh* ... 'I want my knives back,' she said.

'Can you use them?'

One in each hand, pal. 'I can try.'

The grin was pure wolf. 'Remind me not to stand within six feet when you're wielding them,' he said. 'Or do you throw them, as well?'

Perhaps he genuinely *didn't* remember what he had done. Perhaps he just flipped open the lid of his chest and thought, my goodness, where did all those pretty severed heads come from?

'I suppose they come in useful at banquets when you've run out of glasses?'

'You found my cannabis, then.'

'Cannabis?'

'It's what you Romans call hemp. You burn the seeds, inhale the smoke and, in your case, hallucinate.'

This was no time to explain she'd been referring to skulls. 'Why haven't you loosened the sails?' she asked brightly. 'I mean that's what they're for, isn't it? Speed?'

'There's insufficient wind for canvas,' he said, extracting her knives from the side of his trunk, 'and even if there was, the *Soskia* would most likely capsize at this speed – *Litja ba kula!*'

Claudia was definitely getting the hang of this lingo. *Litja ba kula*. Son of a bitch. 'You certainly are,' she murmured sweetly.

'Sails.' He looked down at her, and for the first time she noticed that his eyes were grey.

Grey and shining with excitement. The way a wolf's shines, when it sees a new-born lamb alone on the hillside. 'Sails, yes of course. Thank you.'

Wacko, sicko, thicko, psycho, think of him what you will, but your life's in this maniac's hands. 'You're very welcome.'

Out on deck Jason began yelling instructions to the crew in their own language. The sail master protested, but he was overridden. Within seconds men were swarming up the rigging like monkeys, unhooking ropes at the top, hauling on ratlines at the bottom. To Geta, though, Jason muttered something else. Quietly. And Claudia didn't much care for the helmsman's grim answering nod.

They were hugging the coast so tightly, any minute it seemed one of those white tongues would lash out and engulf the ship. Not like Cressia. There the cliffs plunged steeply, but they were wooded and gentle. No less comforting to a ship's ribs, of course, but at least there was something to grab hold of. The *Soskia* is *not* going to crash! Repeat after me, this ship is not going to crash.

The foresail came down with a thud, bellying out over the vicious bronze ram and blasting the ship forward like a horse at full gallop. The change brought the rowing master scurrying up the ladder from the oar deck, waving his hands at the jib and shouting protests, egged on by the sail master. The captain turned his back on them both. As they rushed round to confront him, the

255

mainsail exploded with a roar louder than thunder, hurling Claudia against the wall of the cabin. She was picking herself up when Jason ducked inside.

'Now is when it starts to get dangerous,' he said.

And here's me thinking it was a picnic. 'You mean oars and canvas will only work providing Azan doesn't follow suit?'

'I'm not looking to outrun him,' the Scythian said quietly. 'The *Soskia*'s fast, but Azan's ships appear to have the edge.'

'Then what's the point of the sail?'

'These are your knives,' he said. 'Don't baulk at using them.'

'Oh, I won't.'

'I mean on yourself.' He pursed his lips. 'The only reason the crew haven't realized they're being chased by their own comrades is because I've kept them too busy to check. Since I told them they're Roman ships, they accept that they're Roman ships, but any second, someone is going to take a longer, closer look.'

'And?'

'Then I'm dead, so's Geta and, if you have any sense between those beautiful dark eyes of yours, so will you be.' He pressed the stiletto into her hand. 'May your gods give you the strength not to hesitate.'

There was a clattering sound in the cabin. Claudia had a suspicion it was her teeth. 'What's with the sails, then? Another distraction?'

256

'Sort of,' he said. 'Canvas with oars will destabilize the ship, certainly. More than sufficiently to keep the crew's minds off their pursuers. But also,' he jerked his thumb in the direction of the cliffs, 'there are those.'

She glanced at the pitiless white rocks flitting past in a blur. 'I can see why that might sustain a person's interest.'

'Geta's a crack helmsman,' Jason said. 'He won't hit any rocks before he's supposed to.'

Her blood ran cold. 'You—' Oh, come on. Even Jason wasn't insane enough to— 'You're not seriously going to wreck this ship?'

'Geta knows where to aim for, and with Targitaos to protect us there's a slim chance that you, me and Geta can make it out of this alive. When the time comes, do exactly what I tell you – and *tosc*.'

'How slim a chance?'

'Look at this coast. Hospitable it is not. But you said you can swim and that's an advantage these men don't have.'

The ship bucked again, pitching her straight into his chest. It was solid, like cannoning into a wall, and his white shirt smelled faintly of cinnamon. Like Roman men, Jason shaved off the hairs on his chest, but not out of fashion or vanity. He shaved to display every nuance of the curved horns, flaring nostrils and thick muscular haunches of his clan totem, the bull. Man and bull. Man and bull. The Minotaur. Half man, half beast, all bad. As Claudia disengaged herself from the solid warm wall, the ship slewed sideways,

257

generating a collective groan from the oar deck. There were sixty men on the benches down there. Sixty rats trapped in a cage. And the rat catcher was locking the door.

'You have beautiful hair,' he said, hooking his little finger in one of her curls before letting it spring slowly back.

'Thank you.' But it's mine and you're not having it, chum.

'Beautiful skin, too.'

All the better to cover your quivers. And you're not having that, either.

'Remember what I said about the knife,' he murmured. 'If the time comes, hold on to your resolve, because I promise you, that time is fast approaching. *Zlat.* I almost forgot.' He crossed the cabin and hefted a sack out of the corner. The sack rattled. 'I shall be needing this.'

'Loot?'

'Better,' he said with a wink. 'Heads.'

There is a time to faint and a time not to faint, and the time not to faint is when the ship you're on hits the rocks running. Claudia had barely managed to dig out a shirt and pantaloons and a pair of black leather boots when the first screams rang out.

'Grab the mast line,' Jason yelled. 'Don't let go until I tell you!'

Her hands had no sooner clamped round the rope than fifteen starboard oars shattered to splinters. The suddenness of the impact gave the oarsmen on the port side no time to

258

adjust. Flying at speed and with only one wing, the *Moth* spun a hundred and eighty degrees on her axis, her port oars splintering like firewood before being flung against a jagged white spur. Screams turned to moans as water rushed in. The scramble for the hatches turned the oar deck into a holocaust, as the rowers trampled their injured colleagues in a desperate bid for safety.

'Jump!' Jason told her, swinging a quiver of arrows over his shoulder. 'Make for that star-shaped rock.' He repeated the instructions in Scythian for Geta.

Pointless to protest that the star-shaped rock was due south. The same direction from which Azan's ships were fast approaching. The water was warm as Claudia dived. No longer calm, but swirling with anger, it was no less turquoise, no less clear, and shields which had been ripped off the ship by the impact gleamed like underwater torches on the seabed. The surface had become a dangerous labyrinth. Clothes, timbers, ratlines and casks threatened to entangle, suck under or render her unconscious, but Claudia could not resist looking back.

She wished she hadn't.

Men with no arms, men spurting blood, men holding their guts in with both hands were surging over the rails, their screams hideous in the glorious calm of midsummer as turquoise slowly turned to crimson. Several deck hands had climbed the mainmast in a bid to escape by leaping on to the headland, but the black sails were full. With a sickening rip, the mast cracked. Faltered. Then slowly, elegantly, toppled into the water causing a surge which sent the flotsam spiralling in dangerous, unpredictable swirls.

Five minutes. Five minutes was all it had taken to kill a fully manned warship.

The cries from the drowning crew grew fainter and more pitiful, but there was no time to dwell on their fate. As Geta's great paw hauled her out of the water, shouts from Azan's lead ship could be heard bearing down on them. It was only to be expected, she supposed. A head taller than his men, Jason was easy to spot. Easier still against a white backdrop and flanked by an ox of a helmsman and a girl with dripping wet curls!

'We don't have much time,' Jason said. 'He'll open fire any second. Head for cover.'

'That's not cover,' she puffed, scrambling behind him, 'that's scrub.'

The Amazon's son grinned over the sack strapped to his shoulder. 'When it's raining arrowheads, you won't be so cynical. Now stop wasting breath and *vlodor* well climb.'

It wasn't so bad. A toehold here, a clump of coarse grass there to hang on to, one yard gained for every two taken, but at least the shore was receding.

'These clothes,' she panted. Obviously not Jason's. The shirt was, if anything, tight over the chest. 'I presume they're a dead man's I'm wearing.'

They'd reached a crack in the rock four feet

wide which, to the men, was no obstacle. 'Oh, please,' Jason protested, swinging her effortlessly over the chasm. 'They most certainly are *not* dead men's clothes.'

'Sorry.'

'So you should be.' He winked as he released her. 'They're women's.'

Better and better. Having a good laugh up there on Olympus, are we?

Below, the *Soskia*'s timbers lay strewn across the sea bed. The corpse of the bow officer lay pinioned beneath the upended cooking brazier, and the square mainsail, bogged down by water, had enveloped the wreckage like a black shroud. But it was the pennants – the red pennants, those ultimate symbols of aggression, which now bobbed so passively – that seemed to sum up the pathos.

Claudia heard a soft, hissing noise coming up from her right.

'DIVE!' Jason yelled.

The clatter was like pebbles being hurled round inside a copper cauldron. 'What the hell was that?' she asked, picking a juniper thorn out of her arm.

'Arrows,' Jason said. 'But then his archers always were crap. He won't waste time or ammunition with that ploy again.'

Good. We can slow down. Claudia adjusted her pace accordingly, but she had barely grabbed hold of the next tuft of grass when a vicelike paw swooped out of nowhere. *'Patoviki,'* Geta growled, hauling her up by her wrist. *'Bastarvac Azan gabanja i patoviki.'*

261

'Shrapnel,' Jason translated. 'He said Azan's loading his ballista.'

'Didn't you miss a word out there?'

'Not one I could repeat to a lady.' To Geta, he pointed at a stand of stunted pines. It seemed a long, long, long way up. 'Two, maybe three volleys,' he told Claudia, 'before we're safe.'

'Tell this flat-faced oaf I've got the message about hurrying, he can let go now,' she shouted.

'I already have,' he said, laughing.

Bumping against Geta's ironclad side, she felt strangely protected when the first shoosh of iron bolts came scything through nothingness. With an unceremonious thud, he slammed her down behind a diminutive cypress and threw his body on top of hers.

'Wide,' Jason yelled, scrambling to his feet. 'Keep climbing, but when I give the word, scrabble as fast as you can to your left.'

'Why not right?' she panted, groping for a handhold.

'Because that's where the volley went wide. Azan will expect us to either continue straight up in a bid to get out of range, or hook right in the hope that his artillery master won't make the same mistake twice.'

'Won't he?'

'He'll broaden his shot to encompass both possibilities. Which means our best tactic is waiting until he's taken aim – then run like blazes.'

Her toe found a slender root to balance on.

'What if the artillery master reckons the same way that you do?'

'You talk too much,' Jason said. 'Now ... *Left!*'

Claudia didn't need any prompting with the second whistle of iron bolts. She was behind a twisted stump before you could blink, but this time the bounce of metal against rock was considerably closer, slamming chunks out of the stone just six feet away. Also, the bolts were much larger. Fifteen inches long, maybe more. The further the range, the heavier the missiles to cover the distance. And thus, of course, the more deadly.

One more. Only one more volley and we're safe.

'This time,' Jason shouted, 'no zigzags. You just keep running.' He hadn't glanced back once, she reflected. He'd just counted, knowing exactly how long it would take to load, take aim and fire.

'Mountain goats will have nothing on me,' she called back, but her limbs betrayed her confidence. Clammy hands made the rocks greasy. Jellified legs could not get a foothold. She was losing more ground than she was gaining, slithering, sliding, slipping inexorably downwards. Come on, come on, don't do this to me, she told her body. But her body refused to listen and, like a teardrop, Claudia Seferius continued to slip down the rockface.

'*Kluv,*' a gruff voice muttered softly and, looping a bearlike arm round her waist, Geta swung her on to his hip.

'NOW!' Jason called, but Geta, too, had been counting, even as he came back for Claudia. Before his captain had opened his mouth, the big ox scuttled across the rocks like a crab, but his burden was hindering him. With Claudia under his arm, he had only one free hand to find a grip on the slippery rocks.

'I can manage,' she said, but he refused to let go, even when the whistling began.

At first it was faint. Faint and oddly comforting. Like a mother's shush when her baby is crying. Then it grew louder. More strident. Geta had barely found a small outcrop of scrub than the ballista's load exploded into the stone. Azan's weapons master had predicted Jason's move. He had fired higher, straight up. Direct hit.

Claudia's breath was expelled as Geta fell on her, and she heard a squeal, as some small, furry mammal caught the blast of a bolt and was sent spinning down the hillside. Metal and rocks rained down over them until finally, mercifully, the last bolt clanged harmlessly down the slope.

'You all right?' Jason called down.

'*Da*,' Geta grunted, hauling himself on to his knees.

'Absolutely bloody *da*!' Claudia shouted.

The pines might be pathetic specimens, stunted and twisted and rooted in gravel, but she had never seen a more beautiful stand. Just as no flat-faced, slant-eyed Scythian ox had ever looked more handsome!

Say what you like, however much blood this

Scythian sun god demanded, the offerings worked. Targitaos certainly protected his own! Dirty, thirsty, white as ghosts from the dust, but by Croesus, the three of them were alive. ALIVE. Claudia felt strangely light-headed as she threw herself into the welcome umbrella of shade. Having survived ship-wreck and shrapnel, how hard could it be to make it a hat-trick and escape from this pair of scalpmongering pirates?

Geta puffed up behind her. *'Litja ba kula!'* He snorted, lumbering on to the soft cush-ioned floor. *'Vlodor bastarvac Azan.'*

'I'll drink to that,' Claudia told him, 'but look on the bright side. We're out of range now.'

'Who told you that?' Jason asked, raising one eyebrow.

'You.' Don't pines smell heavenly? That little murmuring sound they make. So com-forting. And the way the branches creak. Really softly. Like rocking a cradle. 'You said once we reached this stand of trees we'd be safe.'

'That's not the same as out of range,' Jason said dryly, clearing the ground of pine needles with the back of his hand. 'The ballista has a range of over three hundred yards and, as you can see, we're barely a hundred and fifty.'

'Janus! How big will the bolts be at that range?'

'Up to a yard.' He didn't seem remotely fazed by the enormous gap he measured out

265

between his hands. 'Lethal stuff, huh?'

'So what's the plan? Remain here till dark then make a break for it?'

'That's what Azan will be wondering, even as he musters a *mulun*. Er, posse.'

Posse? Claudia flapped the dust off her trousers. 'Call me thick, but am I right in saying we can't stay because we'll be hunted down like stags, but then again we can't go because we'd never make it through another five volleys of shrapnel?'

'A fair assessment.' (And this is what he considers safe.) 'I warned you our chances were slim.'

'Not prone to exaggeration, are you?'

'Ah!' Under the soft layer of leaf litter, Jason seemed to find something of interest. 'Perfect.'

It was, of course, a stone, and Claudia found herself gripped by a sudden urge to hurl herself down the slope and take her chances with Azan.

'You see, it all depends on how accurate an eye his ballistics master has,' Jason said, loading the stone into a small pouch on a string attached to his belt. 'Or not,' he added cheerfully. 'Once I've taken it out with the slingshot.'

The shade was welcome and no mistake. Them pine needles made a comfy soft nest to park his butt and Geta found himself drifting. Aye, and why not? He'd not slept for two moons and he were fair shattered. Especially after rowing all the way to Cressia last night. He wriggled to get comfortable. Worth the effort, though, fetching a woman from the Villa Arcadia for his captain, like what Jason had wanted. And although the tight-lipped bugger didn't say owt, Geta reckoned he'd have been right pleased with that little present! As nice a way of saying thank you for bringing him on this expedition as Geta could think of, particularly after the last bloody fiasco. Kind of balanced things up, like.

Cursing, he shifted position once more, but the rough bark still dug into his back. Bloody land, that's the trouble. Ain't right for a Danubian boatman to be stuck ashore and no ship to go back to. He wriggled again, and decided to put up with the discomfort. What the hell. The rewards were well worth a sore bum, and it weren't for long, after all. Besides. He was that bloody weary. Limbs like sodding anchor stones. Eyelids heavier than the lead markers on the depth lines, making things hard to focus. All the same. Geta sniffed. He'd rather have a ship's wale at his back any day! Planks under his feet, something solid, something reliable, something you know how'll *behave*. Aye, and he ought to have the sky over his head, too. A bloke can't see buggery under this canopy. Stars. That's what a bloke needs to see. Stars to steer by, stars to look up at like the old friends they are, bright shining comforting stars. Not sodding pine cones. This canopy turned the world darker than stormclouds.

Storms. Aye. He'd known storms in the Aegean that had lasted a week and he'd never felt this bloody tired. But it weren't about lack of sleep, were it? Thing is, it just weren't proper, a helmsman having to drive his own ship on to the rocks. Fully manned, too. A fly settled on his cheek and Geta wanted to wipe it away, but his hand was too heavy. The fly flew off anyway. Terrible. Terrible it were, hearing the anguish of men he'd shared suppers and whores with, seeing their blood turn the sea water red. Living through that's bound to catch up with a fellow, and though he'd seen shock affect men in lots of different ways, Geta knew there weren't nowt a good kip couldn't put right.

'Huh?' He forced his drowsy eyes open. 'Oh, it's you, lad.'

'Who were you expecting?' Jason said, settling his tall frame beside him against the pine.

'Did yer get him?'

'Damn right I did.'

'What about them other two ships? They carry ballistas, as well.'

'Them, too,' Jason said. 'First shot every time.'

'Not bad for an Eastern boy, I suppose,' Geta said.

'Reassuring, is it, that I've not lost my touch?' Jason flashed a sideways glance at his friend. 'Rather like someone else I might mention, not a million miles from where I'm

268

sitting. That was fine work back there, Geta.'

'All in a good cause, you crafty bugger.' He were too weary to laugh, and it ended up as a wheeze. 'You're sure Azan don't know?'

'Positive.'

Geta leered. 'Tell me again how much is hidden in that cave over the ridge?'

'More than you can carry, that's for sure, you greedy bastard.'

'All gold?'

'Every last item. Coins, statues, bracelets, pendants—'

'Crowns?' he chuckled. 'I've always fancied a crown, see. Kinda goes with me red hair, don't yer think?'

'Better than a tiara, certainly.' Jason whistled softly under his breath as he adjusted the tension on his bow string, polished the wood with his shirt, ditto the blade on his short sword. It was a tune Geta remembered from way back in his childhood. A Scythian love song about star-crossed young lovers, sung in every house and every felt yurt, over every campfire and in every riverboat from the Caucasus to the Danube and north, over the plains.

'That's all I need, a bloody lullaby,' he muttered.

'So sleep,' Jason said.

'You reckon it's safe?'

'The rest will do you good, you ugly lug. You look knackered.'

'I am knackered.' Geta winced as the bark caught his backbone again. 'Half an hour,

269

then, but no more. Kick me, hard as a mule if you must, but we can't afford to hang about, lad. Not now it's starting to get dark. If Azan sniffs booty up here, he'll be after us faster than a bullet from your bloody slingshot.'

'Azan knows nothing about our private pension fund,' Jason assured him. 'And here's something to cheer you up. He's that pissed off at having all three artillery masters out of action, he's given up. So you rest easy and I'll wake you when it's time to leave.'

'Mind you do, son, because if it gets much darker, we won't be able to see our way up this bloody mountain.' But already his limbs were slack, his head starting to loll.

'Your problem is, you worry too much,' Jason told him with a laugh, patting the solid block that was the helmsman's shoulder.

'Aye, well that's the trouble,' Geta chuckled, his voice slurring as he abandoned himself to the gentle current of sleep, 'when a helmsman has to wreck his own ship, you lousy bastard!'

'By Acca! For a Danube man you don't half nag.' Jason laughed. 'But if it makes you sleep easier, then I promise I won't make you crash any more ships. At least, not this week.' But he was wasting his breath. The current of sleep had already swept Geta up and carried him with it.

'What was that about?' Claudia asked as Jason sauntered across to her. She didn't much trust the chummy way those two had sat conferring and although she'd noticed no

270

sudden change in the pirate captain, it occurred to her that there might not actually *be* any external indicator. In fact, his very charm may well have misled Bulis into trusting him. The same sense of reasonableness that had proved so fatal for Leo and, no doubt, countless others. Claudia Seferius would not make the mistake of trusting him, that's for sure!

'I was putting Geta's mind at rest about the stash of treasure over the ridge,' Jason said, stropping his dagger gently back and forth on a stone. 'Although I may have been a tad economical with the truth in implying that Azan had given up his desire for pursuit.'

Claudia squinted through the branches to what looked suspiciously like a war party making preparations to manoeuvre their rowing boat to the nearest accessible landing point.

'Croesus, Jason, what the hell did you do to piss Azan off so badly?'

Jason tossed her his bow. 'What do you think?' he said, passing his quiver over as well. 'I double-crossed him, of course.'

'About the treasure stashed over this hill?'

'You want the full list? Or would you prefer to get going before they catch up with us? Here.' When the strap of his battle axe landed on her shoulder, her knees nearly buckled with the weight. 'Oh, and you'll have to carry this, too.'

'I am not touching that sack.'

'Yes, you are.'

Scalp hunter or no scalp hunter, there are

271

times when a girl simply has to make a stand. 'Excuse me, but I'm standing here like Diana of the Forests, bow in one hand, quiver on my back and bent double with a bloody battleaxe while you ponce about carrying diddly squat. Why don't *you* carry the damned sack?'

'Because,' he said patiently, 'I shall be carrying Geta. In case you hadn't noticed, he died while I was sitting with him.'

'What?' The great flat-faced, slant-eyed ox was dead? 'How?'

Claudia felt herself swaying. Had he slit Geta's throat back there when she wasn't looking? One more double-cross in a lifetime of double-crosses would hardly notice.

'From the bolt he took saving your life,' Jason said, sheathing his dagger. 'So kindly pick up the sack and get your arse up that hill before I lose my bloody temper.'

Forty

The demon hugged its secret pleasure to its breast. To have a person at one's mercy, to manipulate their fears and terrors and stretch and play with their emotions, was the most powerful feeling on earth.

And now the demon had made another startling discovery. Contrary to all its expectations, men were nowhere near as satisfying as women when it came to the indulgence of torment. Not even close! Too solid and one-dimensional in their thoughts. No imagination to play on. Masculine suggestibility did not have one tenth of the fertile soil that the female mind enjoyed.

The demon turned farmer.

Sowing seeds of terror, watching them sprout and take root in the soul it had chosen. And, like any good landsman, it nurtured its crop, feeding its victim's destruction a bit at a time, just enough to make the crop grow, but not so much that it would bolt.

Because the best time to reap is when the crop is young and at its most tender...

The demon was content to wait.

Time was on its side.

Always had been. Always will.

Forty-One

Sitting beside the fresh-water pond, Clio should have felt elated. She'd beaten off the lynch mob. She was alive, free, the islanders wouldn't touch her now. So why did her legs feel as though they'd been filleted? Why could she not stop shaking? *Why did she not feel triumphant?*

Dragonflies darted back and forth, iridescent rainbows of blue, green and silver in the torrid midday heat. A desultory songbird

273

warbled in the scrub, a goat bleated and the shepherd boy's flute carried from way over the hill on the still island air. But the reflection in the mirror of the pool quaked.

Her ordeal had been abominable, that was true. No human being should be put through that, but she had won, hadn't she? And it wasn't as though she didn't empathize with native superstition. She was Liburnian herself. She understood the minds of the people who made up Illyria – Istrians, Dalmatians, Liburnians, as well as all the islanders – and who so lacked the sense of adventure prevalent among the Greeks and the Romans. To the peaceful and by and large placid Illyrians, travel was anathema, but what they lacked in derring-do they compensated for in other ways. Clio's own people, for instance, had developed into superlative shipbuilders, creating light fast galleys especially suited to these waters, the same type Jason used and which were even called liburnians. The Istrians had honed their hunting skills to procure game from deep in the forests, the Dalmatians had evolved into skilled engravers, exporting their crafts round the Adriatic as far as the Bosphorus, and the islanders rejoiced in their musical skills. But because they rarely travelled beyond their own narrow, self-imposed confines, superstition had become magnified and on Cressia, thanks to the island's dark history, it had a tendency to spiral out of recognition when times were hard, as they were now.

Which was not to excuse lynch-mob mentality. Merely to try and understand where the bastards were coming from. *And use their own superstitions against them.*

With her flawless complexion, proud carriage, magnificent bosom and cape of gleaming black hair, the islanders had mistrusted her from the beginning. For a woman whose childbearing years were almost past to isolate herself from the community seemed unnatural, allowing fertile imaginations to run riot.

A boy runs away from home, as boys do, but they see only the stranger restoring her youth by feasting off his living flesh. The conclusion was hasty, they realized that. Perhaps the boy came home, wrote a letter, who knows? For whatever reason, the *Lamiae* theory quickly died down, but the seeds of sorcery had been sown. Instead of examining their own consciences at how the debilitating illness which claimed the fisherman's wife and the carpenter's son had slipped past their notice, they demanded a scapegoat.

Vampire was the word bruited, but the islanders hadn't actually believed it. Sure, they'd tossed down the odd branch of whitethorn, left piglet intestines, chanted obscenities – but at heart they believed Clio to be human. A witch, who conjured up wickedness.

But suppose Clio really was one of the *Striges*, one of those bloodthirsty birds of the night?

Once she had seen the flip side of the coin, power was hers. She'd spat on a red gown and rubbed the dye round her mouth, trailing lines down her chin as though blood had been dripping. She clawed at her hair, making it wild, covered her face with flour to make it white, stripped herself naked apart from a bright yellow cloak. She had no idea whether the *Striges* were supposed to be winged or otherwise, much less what colour those wings might be, but she'd bet her bottom denarius those murderous bastards outside wouldn't know either!

With her ear to the door, she had waited until footsteps shuffled towards her cottage. Silently lifted the latch. Then, to their total surprise, flung herself into the night.

'Aieeee!'

Screaming at the top of her lungs, she'd lunged headlong into the clearing, yellow wings billowing, the colour of the sulphur of Hades.

'Come to me, my family of gnomes, vampires and witches!'

Thopc, lugats and *shtrigas*. She enunciated the words clearly. It was vital the islanders heard this woman, who they'd believed Roman, speaking their own language fluently.

'Come, wolfman! Come, ye children of the night! Let us dine.'

She began to dance around the rotting intestines, screeching and howling at the top of her voice, calling upon other shapeshifters in her native Liburnian tongue. It was now or

276

never, she calculated. Either they'd rush her, because she was mad or else they'd run screaming down the hillside like the cowards they truly were. Clio was taking no chances. She fell upon one of the stinking piles and pretended to devour it.

'Look, ye harpies and trolls. Someone has spread us a banquet. We will not need to search for food elsewhere tonight!'

She stood up and began to dance again.

'Come to me, my dark friends. Feast upon the blood of the sacrifice, more succulent than a child's I assure you, and let us gain strength.' She made loud smacking noises with her mouth. 'Gather, all you flesh-eating *thropc*. Join me in my banquet, my immortal sisters the *shtrigas*—'

Now, in the pulsing midday heat, Clio's reflection smiled in the fresh-water pool. Of all of them, that runt of a priest was the first to leg it down the hill, and by Croesus, could Llagos's skinny pins shift!

'Couple with me, priest,' she'd called after him. 'Lie with me and my sisters. For I know that in your soul you are one of us.'

A bloody landslide after that! Oh, yes, there'd be no more trouble from the islanders now. The stuff of their nightmares had been proved a reality. Vampires (gasp!) actually exist. Worse. Trolls, werewolves, all the shape-shifting creatures they had feared weren't just real. *They walked among them on Cressia!* From today, the islanders would take pains to appease the vampire's bloodlust with sacrificial offerings and the upsurge in piglet breeding would know no bounds. Yes, well. The sows might be exhausted, but whatever calamity might befall this beleaguered island in the future, one thing was certain. The blame would not be laid on *this* isolated doorstep!

In that respect, Clio had achieved her objective. Total privacy. But now, thanks to Leo, that's all she could expect. Privacy! None of the wealth, the triumphal home-coming, the new life she was expecting. Clio, goddammit, was stuck here on Cressia.

No wonder her reflection still trembled.

Not from fear, or reaction after last night's pantomime.

Her reflection trembled from rage.

Forty-Two

They had been climbing only a few minutes when the last of the scrub petered out. Now it was just bare white karst, slippery and hard to get hold of. Azan's archers might be crap, Claudia thought, as the strap from the quiver grated away at the flesh on her shoulder, but a blindfolded elephant couldn't fail to score a bull's-eye on such a slow-moving target. The only conclusion she could draw was that, in retaliation for disabling his artillery, Azan wanted to take them alive.

'Progress would be a lot faster if I ditched the axe.'

'I'll be needing that,' Jason replied. Geta was strapped across his broad shoulders, and the effects of the additional cargo showed in the lines on his face. Perspiration dripped off him in rivers. Claudia tried not to think about why he might want to lug a corpse around, instead of leaving him back there in the pines.

'Then suppose I dump the sack?' she suggested. Just carrying it made her feel sick. 'Bumping around between the axe and the quiver, it unbalances me.'

He flashed her a dark grin. 'I doubt anything unbalances you,' he said. 'And ask yourself the question, do you really think I've gone to all this trouble to bring along stuff I'm not going to need?'

Which was enough to silence her. If Jason needed an axe plus a sackful of heads plus Claudia Seferius as well as a corpse with a thick thatch of red hair which would look particularly pretty dangling off a war spear, it didn't need Archimedes to work out what he was planning.

Grappling with the slippery handholds, she wondered just how she was going to get out of this. Behind her, the shouts of the posse grew louder by the second. Not for them progress hindered by volleys of shrapnel, impeded by onerous burdens. They were scrambling up the hillside like millipedes. But assuming she escaped her pursuers, what then? Doubling back was out of the question

279

– forget hailing a boat when the coast's in the hands of three pirate warships! While up here, the mountains were a desert. Without food. Without water. Without shelter. Without people. Just vast expanse of bare white rock after vast expanse of bare white rock. Like it or not, Jason was her only chance of survival, but the irony of her situation didn't escape her.

The very man who was keeping her alive was also the man intent on killing her.

Claudia climbed.

The track made in the mountainside by centuries of chamois and mountain goats was a narrow, boulder-strewn death trap, but for Claudia, loaded down by half her own body weight, walking along it was like being fitted with wings. Suddenly the peak was much closer, the pass between the mountains a realistic goal.

'That's far enough for the moment.'

Glancing back, she realized that Jason had eased Geta into a fissure in the rock and was letting the cliff absorb his own weight until his breathing returned to something approaching normal.

'Pass the quiver and bow,' he wheezed. 'High time we shortened some odds.'

Unlike Roman archers, who pulled their bowstrings back to the chest, Jason lifted his bow so his arm was parallel with his shoulder and pulled the string level with his ear. As the first of Azan's men took an arrowhead in the chest, Claudia understood why no Roman archer had beaten a Scythian. Jason's shot was on a par with Parthian bowmen. Accurate. Deadly. Every shot counts. Two more rebels tumbled down the hillside, then, just when things were going well, Jason replaced the lid on his quiver.

'Why don't you finish them off?' she asked, as he heaved Geta's body out of the crevice.

'I got in sufficient shots before they dived for cover. Any more would have been a waste of ammunition, and before you say why don't we stay here and pick them off as they come up the hill, that's simply locking ourselves in a trap.'

Darkness, he explained, would allow Azan's group the opportunity to separate, spread out – and comprehensively seal off the goat track.

'My totem's the bull, not the sitting duck,' he added.

'Strange,' she murmured, 'I could have sworn it was the chameleon.'

If Illyria was one scenic surprise after another, then none was probably more so than the track on the other side of the mountain. Instead of a sea of sparkling turquoise spread out below her, Claudia was plunged into an ocean of dense forest and the first thing that struck her was the birdsong.

'Inverse vegetation,' Jason explained. 'Unlike conventional mountains, where the upper slopes are covered with spruce leading down to rich fir and beechwoods at the bottom, on the karst, in Dalmatia, this is reversed.'

As though to illustrate his point, a squirrel scampered across the track in front of her to shin up an oak tree in a red chattering blur. They paused in the shade to catch their breath, Jason laying Geta reverently against a beech.

'How far to the cave?' she asked. Maybe it wouldn't be so bad, hiding out here for a couple of days, and she pictured Jason's slingshot deer roasting slowly on a spit while Azan's frustrated gorillas gave up their search.

'What cave?'

The hairs on the back of her neck were the first to react. He seemed genuinely confused. Just as he might genuinely not remember how slowly and how painfully he had despatched Bulis and Leo. And suddenly Claudia saw herself roasting over that open fire...

'The one where you've stashed your booty,' she said nonchalantly.

'Oh, that one.' He chuckled as he wiped the sweat from his brow with the back of his hand. 'Well, there *are* caves in these mountains. Hundreds of them, in fact, as Geta knew full well. But as for the gold...' He ruffled the mop of red hair affectionately. 'It was the only story I could think of which would make a plunder-hungry pirate drive his ship at full speed on to the rocks. That, and cutting the rest of the crew out of the deal.'

'What fairy tale were you planning to spin him once he was up here?'

'Hadn't actually thought that far ahead,' he admitted, hefting the helmsman back on to his shoulders. 'But I'd have thought of something.'

And Claudia thought, I'll bet you would. You must have had Bulis and Leo mesmerized, the poor misguided bastards. She caressed the stiletto still strapped to her calf and followed the Scythian deeper into the woods.

Orbilio wasn't sure how he'd get through the day. Time had never stood heavier. What he had wanted to do was jump in the saddle and scour the island for signs that could shed light on Claudia's disappearance, but there it was again. That old patrician millstone...

'You can't go charging off,' Silvia reminded him, tweaking her curls in the mirror. 'You're chief mourner at Leo and Bulis's funeral, and besides, you're Rome's representative on Cressia now. You have an example to set.'

'Bollocks to examples, bollocks to Bulis and bollocks to Cressia, frankly. These people didn't give a toss about Leo when he was alive, the hypocrites can't very well complain when—'

'You'll have to speak up, darling. Your voice is still terribly hungover from last night's binge.'

'That's not the drink,' he said. 'That's the swelling.'

'Good grief!' Big blue eyes jumped out on stalks as they noticed the bruising. 'What happened?'

A Gaul was what happened. Once Orbilio realized Claudia was missing, he'd released Junius and explained the position – only to take the full force of her bodyguard's fist. It was only because he knew how to roll with the punches that his bloody jaw hadn't been broken.

'I tripped down the steps.'

'Then I hope that will teach you a lesson about over-imbibing,' she said tartly. 'But back to this morning, there is no question of escaping your obligations, Marcus. Whether you like it or not, the needs of the many must be balanced against the need of the individual.'

'You're a fine one to dish out lectures on duty,' he snapped. 'Or have you forgotten those three boys of yours?'

'Marcus!'

'Think that's uncalled for, do you? That I shouldn't mention the subject. That you don't deserve it, because it was only the night before last that some bastard left you for dead on the dark shores of Hades and you're frightened, bewildered and pitifully vulnerable? Well, I'm sorry for you, Silvia, truly I am, but that doesn't give you the right to lecture me about marital obligations and denying my children their birthright.'

Silvia laid the mirror down, walked across the room and began to massage the stiffness out of his shoulders. 'You raised those points, darling, not me.'

Shit. 'I'm sorry.' He wiped his hands over

his face. 'My nerves are shot to threads, I'm not thinking straight.'

'Understandable, darling. It's your cousin's funeral and that's a lot of responsibility, but you can't cry off simply because some little wine merchant's widow has taken it upon herself to have an adventure.'

Orbilio resisted the urge to finish the job on Silvia's throat. 'It's a little more serious than that,' he said levelly.

He was wasting his breath.

'It's not just the family who will expect you to fulfil your obligations.' Silvia hesitated. Smoothed the wayward curls at the back of his head. 'The thing is, darling, it wouldn't sit at all well with the Senate should word filter back that you'd turned your back on duty.'

'Hardly turning my back,' he retorted, shrugging her off. 'All I'm suggesting is post-poning the ceremony.'

'Iss too late, I fear,' Llagos said from the doorway. His dainty hands were spread in a gesture of helplessness. 'Things hef not been so good for the islanders lately. Much temp-tation to return to the old ways. So! Thiss morning I gather the people together and tell them –' he coughed apologetically '– I tell them that the death of your cousin iss sacrifice to almighty Neptune.'

'*What?*'

'Iss something they can understand, Marcus. Do not be angry.'

'The hell I—'

'Please listen,' Llagos pleaded. 'Lately there
285

hef been much talk of superstition, bringing big gulf between Roman ways and Cressian traditions. So I use thiss to build bridge. I pretend Leo loved his people so much, he laid down his life for them and that, in return for his sacrifice, Neptune cast his special protection over the island.'

'*Bloody hell, Llagos.*' Orbilio hurled a vase filled with roses against the wall and watched until the last of the petals had cascaded down the plaster to join the glittering shards on the floor. 'Then perhaps you wouldn't mind rushing the service?' he asked levelly.

With a nervous smile, the little priest nodded, but it was Silvia who had the last word. 'One cannot rush a funeral pyre, Marcus, it burns itself out. Now then.' She gave her black skirts a shake. 'How do we look?'

Llagos had not been exaggerating the effect of his pep talk.

'Long live the new governor!'

'Hurrah for Marcus Cornelius Orbilio!'

'Bloody rum way to be sent off, in my opinion,' Volcar grumbled from his litter. 'Anyone would think this was a victory procession, not a bleeding funeral.'

But for the islanders, that's precisely what it was. They hadn't swallowed the priest's story about Leo sacrificing himself on the altar on their behalf, but they had learned their lesson. With Jason on the loose, they needed Rome at their back like no time ever before.

'Long live Orbilio!'

'Long live our new protector!'

Ducking posies and garlands, and politely avoiding the attentions of young girls thrust in his path by their hopeful mamas, Orbilio kept his gaze focused on his cousin's bier. The undertakers had rouged Leo's cheeks, rendered pale through loss of blood, and softened out the rictus, drawing attention away from the face by dressing the corpse in scarlet trimmed with silver, since gold was not permissible on the voyage to the Underworld. Leo's thick dark curls, the family trademark, were coiled artfully between a wreath of shiny laurel leaves. Frankincense, cinnamon and other rich embalming spices wafted in his wake.

Qus was one of the eight pallbearers, the only evidence of emotion being the five parallel scars on his forehead which now shone white in their ebony setting.

The smell of fishing boats hung rank in the air as the procession snaked its way past the harbour. Flax fibre nets had been spread out to dry, willow creels upended, children scrubbed barrels in preparation for preserving oysters and crayfish and squid in brine for the winter. Without a breeze to carry it away, the smoke from the torchbearers' flames rose upwards, like the black feathers of harpies, but Orbilio noticed none of it. It was his cousin's funeral, for gods' sake, he kept reminding himself. You've done enough damage letting him be killed in the way that he had, the least you can do is pay him the courtesy of mourning him properly.

But all he could think of was a girl with flashing eyes and a tongue like a bullwhip who had disappeared off the face of the earth.

Search parties had been sent out and he had placed Junius in charge in his absence, knowing that if anyone was going to find Claudia, it was the Gaul. Orbilio tenderly rubbed at his jaw. He couldn't blame the lad for taking a pop. Or for the threats he had made as he stormed off this morning.

'If she's dead,' Junius had said, wheeling his horse round, 'I will kill you.'

'Long live the governor!'

'Hurrah for Marcus Cornelius!'

A rain of petals showered over his black mourning cloak as he passed the waterside tavern where he had been staying the night Leo was murdered. Would these people still think him a hero if they knew the truth? Dammit, he should never have taken that bloody room. He should have gone straight to the villa, instead of buggering about playing cloak and dagger.

Outside the tavern, the man in his mid-forties, greying at the temple and with the spatulate artistic fingers that Orbilio had envisaged handling fine works of art, watched the first of the two biers pass. Diplomatic, Orbilio decided. And shrewd. Magnus could hardly have joined Leo's cortege with Lydia present; while to pay his respects to Bulis would have been to snub his late patron. He acknowledged the sculptor's tight-lipped nod of sympathy and wondered what exchanges, if any, passed between Magnus and Lydia as she followed her ex-husband's body.

As the procession wound its way to the Temple of Neptune, a woman with malt-brown hair and green eyes sat defiantly on the steps with her arms wrapped round her knees. Nanaï, he concluded. Wondering whether she was here to mourn or to gloat.

It was only once the two biers were laid upon their respective pyres that Orbilio gave his full attention to delivering Leo's ovation, but when he stepped back to allow Saunio to deliver Bulis's, he noticed that the crowd comprised two very different groups. For the majority, this was the first Roman funeral they had witnessed and they were here partly to voice their allegiance to Rome, and partly out of curiosity. Why didn't the Romans simply bury their dead with their hands covering their faces like everybody else? But there was another group, a small minority comprising twelve, maybe thirteen people, who stood out from the crowd. The taverner's son, for example. As white as a barn owl. And the wheelwright, whose hands were shaking. These people, Orbilio realized, were scared. Scared of what? he wondered.

As the funeral attendants set a torch to the pyres, Shamshi rippled his way through to Orbilio's side. 'The organs of the sacrificial beast were sound,' he intoned. 'It augurs well for the souls of the departed.'

'The sun rose thrice more over our heads,'

Orbilio countered, 'but no woman died.'

The smile that hovered at the corner of the Persian's mouth made his blood curdle. 'Did one not?' he asked softly, before drifting back into the throng and for a man who was watching his livelihood literally go up in smoke, he didn't seem unduly troubled, Orbilio reflected.

In front of him, the flames crackled and spat and the only outpouring of grief came from the artists, as Saunio's Beautiful Young Men clustered round to console the maestro as well as each other, ensuring outsiders could not breach their wall of self-contained mourning. At least they mourned. Qus might have been one of Magnus's sculptures. Nikias always looked like he was scowling. Lydia and Silvia were both visions in black, the one petite and fair, the other dark and statuesque, but not a glance had passed between them. And still Shamshi grinned.

Leo, Marcus felt, deserved better. Much, much better. But then we reap what we sow and whatever his intentions, however honourable they might have been, the bottom line was that Leo had not put them into practice. As a result, he'd left an aged uncle too bitter to grieve, plus an ex-wife and sister-in-law who couldn't find a tear to shed between them. His astrologer was indifferent, his bailiff detached, and even Nanaï, for whom he'd provided free housing for many years, felt he'd deserved all he'd got. Siring a son had blinded Leo to everything and everyone else. What made it particularly poignant was that he hadn't seen his motives as selfish. Robbing Petrus to pay Paulus came naturally to him. After all, everyone would be repaid in the end, the Villa Arcadia would be the most splendid palace in the whole of the Adriatic and, to cap it all, the rose-grower's daughter would give him a child every year until he lost count. By Leo's reckoning, this was a win-win situation, what's the problem?

Finally, after an eternity of waiting for messages from search parties that did not come, they approached the final rites of the double cremation. Censers were shaken vigorously, emitting clouds of fragrant grey smoke, handbells rattled, honeycakes thrown on the fire. Once the ashes were purified, a sense of relief fell over the assembly. Nothing stretches time like a body awaiting burial, and now a line had been drawn, allowing people to move on with their lives.

'You will come back to the villa?' Orbilio asked Lydia.

'The hell I will.' Her voice was pitched low and did not carry as far as the crowd. 'I want nothing more to do with that man or, and this is nothing personal Marcus, his kin. Be they related by blood *or by marriage*,' she added, just loud enough for Silvia to hear.

The sun was sinking. Still no news of Claudia. What did Shamshi know, he wondered? He thought about the message that had brought so much trouble to this paradise island. Five words. *Give back what is mine.*

291

If only, if only...

One event sets off another, and so it goes on until a whole train is in motion and becomes unstoppable, out of control. The rage of frustration pulsed through his veins. Impotent. Useless. Hog-tied without any leads. The sun disappeared over the Istrian peaks, and with it withered his hopes.

All he knew for sure was there was a psychopath on the loose with god knows how many victims on his death roll. And that caught up in this whirlwind of evil was a woman with tumbling curls and dark flashing eyes.

Who might already be dead.

Forty-Three

The instant the sun dipped behind the jagged peaks, the beechwoods turned to dark. Shadows appeared, shifting and menacing, and the gorge slipped into silence. These forests were home to all kinds of predator, Claudia reflected: boar, wolf, bear, snake. Just the place to be alone with a cadaver.

'Stay here,' Jason had growled, lowering a stiffening Geta against the bole of a spruce. They had reached the valley bottom, a dried-up river bed which only came to life in spring to drain away the snow melt. 'I need to do some reconnaissance.'

At the time, Claudia was just grateful for the rest. After a night which involved being kidnapped and trussed followed by shipwreck, mountaineering and artillery fire, not even the pack of hounds on her trail could prevent her from sinking into oblivion. A soft scuffle jolted her awake. She couldn't see anything in the blackness, but she sensed movement.

'Jason?' she whispered. 'Is that you?'

Amber eyes flashed in the gloom. There was a flicker of white as it turned, and then it was gone. A lynx, she reflected. After several hours in the heat, Geta was starting to attract attention.

After a while she stopped jumping at every rustle and scratch, each little slither and scrape. Maybe it helped that she was holding the twin-faced battleaxe. Maybe she was just getting used to the wilderness. But next time when she opened her eyes, Jason was stretched out on the ground not four feet away, one knee drawn casually up. She felt the weight of the axe in her hand. With one good swing...

'There's ten, maybe a dozen of them on our tail,' he murmured. He hadn't even opened an eye. 'Four hundred yards behind and closing fast.'

Claudia pushed her hair out of her eyes. 'I'm not surprised. Without the impediments of corpses and heavy weaponry, we could have made better time ourselves.'

White teeth flashed in the dark. 'You

293

wouldn't be criticizing the captain's strategy by any chance, lieutenant?'

'My dear Jason, I would die before I criticized you.' Or if not, shortly afterwards, she suspected. 'I was merely making an observation.'

The flash of white grew larger. Another predator in the forest licking its chops. 'Good,' he said, 'because it's time we got moving.'

'In the *dark*?'

A soft chuckle rang out as he heaved Geta on to his shoulders and set off along the river bed. 'You're forgetting the occupation of the gentlemen behind us, lieutenant. Why do you think merchant ships won't sail at night? Because of a few paltry currents, the odd shallow channel, a couple of treacherous promontories? I think you'll find the threat man-made, rather than natural.'

'Then it can't be because they took place at night, those fires along the Liburnian coast.'

'So you *did* pack the cannabis.'

No, but I could sure use some right now. 'Someone once asked me, didn't I think it odd, those fires along the Liburnian coast,' she explained, trotting along behind. 'I assumed it was because they happened at night.'

'Tut, tut. I would have thought that you, of all people, would have known that darkness is the pirate's friend.' A callused hand patted Geta to illustrate his point. 'Now then. I reckon this is far enough, don't you?'

On the eastern bank he laid Geta flat behind a spruce, placed the axe and bow and quiver alongside and kicked pine needles over the blade.

'No reflection,' he stated quietly.

He is warrior born and bred, he knows what he's doing. He is warrior born and bred, he knows what he's doing. Claudia repeated the phrase another six times and still wasn't convinced. Something just wasn't right here. Her hand slid slowly down her thigh and over her knee.

'Something the matter with your leg?' he asked.

'Itch.'

'Not looking for this, by any chance?' From his belt he drew out a familiar thin blade.

Claudia's fingers flew to the empty strap at her calf. Shit. There was only one moment when he could have removed the stiletto. While she was asleep back there by the stream bed. *And she hadn't felt a bloody thing...*

'I was concerned you might have acquired a certain sentimental attachment to it,' he said, placing it neatly beside the buried axe. Slowly he took off the heavy gold torque round his neck. Unhooked the gold chain link belt. Laid them on the ground.

This is it. This is the moment the sick bastard has chosen. The time and the place.

She should have known.

With Bulis, with Leo, even with Silvia, he hadn't taken his victims away to torment at his leisure. He'd made sure there were plenty

295

of people around when he killed them. Just as there were ten, maybe twelve behind him just now. *The excitement of being caught was as important as the thrill of torture.*

He drew his dagger. Laid that on the ground, too. Along with the scimitar from the belt which tied under his crotch. If he jumped her, she could pull on that belt. Make his eyes water long enough for her to grab hold of a boulder, bring it crashing down on his skull. But she had a horrid feeling jumping wasn't Jason's style.

Suddenly she was cold. Very cold. Paralysed with the cold. 'I don't want to die,' she found herself bleating.

'Nobody wants to die, Claudia.'

A red boot gently covered the metal with a thin layer of pine needles. No reflection, she thought dully. No reflection, because in his warped mind, no one can see what he's doing. Not even him.

'Now then,' he whispered. 'I think it's high time we used our heads, don't you?'

Relief surged through her limbs, making them shake. 'Absolutely,' she said. Silly bitch! Fancy thinking it was some kind of ritual! 'I knew you'd come round to my way of thinking,' she said.

'Excuse me?'

'Ditching Geta and the weapons, and putting our brains into action instead of our muscles.'

'Actually, that's not what I meant.' Jason picked up the sack at Claudia's feet and

296

leisurely began to untie the string. 'I meant, it's time to bring *these* heads into play.'

In the brightly lit courtyard, scented by lavender oil and garlands of roses and herbs, Orbilio stared at the fisherman standing with his thumbs looped into his belt. 'Are you sure?'

Thick, brown and heavily scored, the fisherman's skin was like leather and only the muscles which bulged out of his cheap linen shirt testified to his age being somewhere on the good side of thirty. The fisherman cast a quizzical glance at the priest, who translated.

'He say there iss no mistaking what he hef seen. Three –' he verified the number with the fisherman, who nodded vigorously '– three pirate warships anchored off coast of Dalmatia, also the wreck of the *Soskia*. Many bodies, he say. Not pretty.'

Orbilio made rapid calculations. Half a day to send a message to the garrison on the Istrian mainland at Pula. Half a day for them to send word to the nearest trireme. Half a day before that trireme made it up to Dalmatia. Bugger. 'Does he know what happened?' he asked.

Liagos put the question to the fisherman, but the fisherman shook his head. The first thing he knew of trouble was the stream of flotsam swept down on the current. He had picked up some of the items. Clothing. Rope. A cask of ale. But as soon as he turned the headland and saw Azan's ships, he turned tail and ran.

'What was he doing out there in the first place?' Orbilio asked. It was a long way from Cressia.

'His sister marry a hunter from Dalmatian mainland. He go to trade lobster and crab for boar meat from forest,' the priest explained. 'Iss great delicacy, since no boar left on Cressia now.' He grinned. 'He make much money and much friends when he visit his sister.'

Orbilio didn't smile. 'But the wreck was definitely that of the *Soskia*?'

'*Soskia*, ja,' the fisherman said, and told Llagos how outlines of red painted moths on the galley's splintered oars had testified to the broken vessel's identity.

Marcus began to pace the courtyard, where moths of a different kind were fluttering round the torches set on the walls. 'I don't understand it,' he said. 'Jason?'

'Maybe whirlpool suck her in,' Llagos suggested. 'Many whirlpools in ocean.'

'But not there, or your fishing friend would have known about it.' As would Jason.

'Maybe freak current.'

Maybe, Marcus thought. In which case, the damage would have been severe – but not fatal for a seasoned warship. 'I'd like to see the stuff he picked out of the water,' he said.

The fisherman's face darkened at the priest's translation.

'Tell him,' Orbilio said patiently, 'that he can keep everything he found. I just want
298

to look.'

The leather skin relaxed, and the three men, one tall, one short, one somewhere in between, wound their way down the cliff path. On the jetty, Qus and Junius were already waiting. Their search of the villa, the estate, the town, the island had yielded nothing.

'The only unusual thing,' Qus said, stepping forward and saluting, 'was a goatherd, who claimed he saw a man with red hair in a rowing boat just before sunset. But then –' he shrugged his massive shoulders '– the boy's a musician, a dreamer, a poet who lives in his head.'

Witnesses, as Orbilio knew only too well from experience, could be sublimely imaginative. Nevertheless, he filed this little gem in the ledgers of his mind and ignored Junius's murderous glower as he clambered into the boat. A sad catch, he thought, holding a torch above the sorry assortment. Shirts of a cloth he would not wipe his boots with. Frayed lines. A red painted moth on part of an oar, a souvenir to hang on the wall of the fisherman's cottage. In the stern lay a cask of rough ale, a collection of rings and torques stripped off the corpses. Dead men's boots. Dead men's belts—

Suddenly the boat rocked as Junius jumped down from the jetty. 'Bastard!' he shouted. 'Fucking bastard!'

Fighting to prevent the boat tipping over, at first Orbilio thought the Gaul was swearing at

299

him. Then he realized what had attracted the boy's attention. A swathe of blue cotton. Oh, no. He felt himself reeling and it wasn't from the movement of the boat.

Junius sprang back on to the jetty. 'Where did you find this?' he shouted, waving the cotton in the fisherman's face. Shocked by the ferocity, he took a step back but Junius surged forward. *'Where?'*

'He wants to know,' Orbilio told Llagos with a calmness he did not feel, 'if this gown was taken from someone in the water.'

'But this is a woman's gown!' the fisherman protested through Llagos. 'You think I would stoop to desecrating a woman's corpse?'

Orbilio felt as though he was flying, weightless, high above the jetty. A hundred thoughts whirled in his head.

A red-headed boatman. The *Soskia* wrecked. Her crew dead. Three rebel warships anchored close to the site. And somewhere out there, dead or alive, but indisputably alone was Claudia Seferius. While he, Marcus Cornelius Orbilio, with the whole might of the aristocracy, the force of his wealth and the full authority of the Security Police behind him, stood by, powerless.

Junius had had every right to break his damn jaw.

In the darkness of the perverse, inverse vegetation of the karst, a hand clamped over Claudia's mouth. When he'd said 'heads' she started to run, but he'd caught her before she had covered twenty-five paces.

'Quiet,' he whispered harshly, as she squirmed in his grip. 'Azan's men are only a little way off. One sound, and you'll undo all my good work.'

Bulis might have been fooled, Leo lulled into a false sense of security, but Claudia slammed the heel of her boot directly into his shin.

'*Zlat!*' he hissed. 'Was your mother a mule?'

Her answer was a second kick, which he contrived to outmanoeuvre, so she stamped on his foot. He jerked in pain, grunted; but the arm round her waist and the hand over her mouth didn't budge.

'For gods' sake,' he rasped, 'all I'm asking you to do is run up and down the *vlodor* valley brandishing a few pieces of bronze.'

'Mmm-mm-mm-mmf.'

The hand relaxed slightly. 'What was that?'

'I said you must be the spitting image of your father. By the way, did you ever find out who he was?'

'You Romans,' Jason said, shaking his head, 'have an odd sense of humour.' Slowly he released the hold round her waist. The action didn't fool her. You're playing with me like a cat with a mouse, you sonofabitch. Playing me out, reeling me in. *Giving me hope every time.*

'So then.' He clucked her under the chin. 'Are you going to help, or must I scare the *zlat* out of these bastards all by myself?'

But hope was all she had—

'Old trick,' he said. 'Wouldn't work in the Caucasus, but then –' he shot her his wolfish grin '– this isn't the Caucasus.'

'Are you serious?'

'Oh, yes, I'm pretty sure this is Dalmatia. Aren't you?'

Don't think you can charm me to death, either, you slippery bastard. This might not be the moment you've chosen to kill me, but I'm wise to you, pal. From now on, Claudia Seferius sleeps with her eyes open. 'I meant, are you serious about brandishing a few bits of bronze and expecting it to scare the *zlat* out of a dozen seasoned thugs?'

'Why? What did you think I was going to scare them with?' Grey eyes glittered in the darkness of the forest. 'Listen, lieutenant, while you were catching up on your beauty sleep, I built a fire to make it look like we were camped for a while.' He pointed up the mountain slope.

'Then why this elaborate charade? Why not slip away while they're surrounding the camp.'

She might not have spoken. 'We have to work *tosc*. Before they realize the fire is a ruse and while they're still concentrated in one group.'

'If they split up, surely that makes it easier for you to pick them off one by one?'

'Makes it easier to get an arrow in the back,' Jason said drily. 'Plus it takes time, backtracking, checking, covering our tracks. This way, they'll stay together until morning and we'll

302

have a six-hour start.'

All with a few bits of bronze. 'Good stuff is it, this cannabis?'

'I told you before, you talk too much.'

From the sack he extracted several metal wolf heads and laid them carefully on the bed of pine needles. Precious little moonlight filtered down to the bottom of the gorge, but in any case the heads had been painted black. No reflection, she thought idly. These things were not meant to be seen. But why not? She picked one up. The workmanship was superb. The wolf's mouth was wide open, its jagged teeth sharp as she ran her finger along, and its engraved expression terrifyingly real.

'What's this?' Instead of a mane, a cylinder of black canvas trailed behind the wolf's head. Black canvas. Like the *Soskia*'s sails.

Jason grinned as he impaled each bronze piece on an arrowhead. 'You'll see.'

He placed three arrows in each of Claudia's clenched fists, splayed out the shafts then adjusted the height so that she was holding the wolves in three tiers.

'Whatever you do, don't drop one,' he urged. 'Hold them as if your life depended upon it, because, lieutenant, it does. Azan's men mustn't find out.' Clutching five tiers of bronze heads in each of his own fists, he led her back up the slope. 'When I give the word,' he whispered, 'you let out a scream, then walk – this is important – you *walk* back down to the river bed. Understand? Then you hold up your wolf heads and run like hell until I tell

303

you to stop. Do you understand?'

'Not remotely.'

'That's what I thought. Now scream.'

Claudia screamed. At Jason's nod, she turned and picked her way down the track. Halfway down, her heart lurched. A lone wolf let out a bloodcurdling howl from the hill above. Others joined the ghostly chorus, and by the time she reached the river bed, Claudia didn't need anyone to tell her to run. The canvas tubes billowed out behind the carvings in her hand. Hold them up, he had said. Hold them *up*. She lifted her arms, and amazingly the wolves howled louder. Dozens of them, and suddenly Jason was running beside her, grinning like one of his engraved metal heads, and as they raced up and down the dry river bed, the air howled in through the bronze jaws and out through the black canvas windsocks.

'Simple but effective,' he said, slowing to a halt. 'As I said, Azan's boys won't be keen to separate while *this* pack's on the loose.'

He was right. Claudia's scream would convince Azan's thugs, when they eventually found the camp fire, that their quarry had been scared off by wolves who had scented the helmsman's corpse. Jason quickly dismantled the bronze heads from his arrows while Claudia threw the battleaxe and quiver over her shoulder. This time, he was far too busy to notice the stiletto which slipped silently down the side of her boot.

* * *

The demon was happy. It was an exhilarating experience, knowing a person's life – no, wait, their destiny – lay in your hands.

To tell them? Or to keep them in the dark? That was also part of the thrill. The power of decision-making. Making decisions about their lives.

The demon looked into the future. It saw hundreds of people innocently going about their own business, not knowing there was one who walked among them with the power to break their spirit and condemn their soul to destruction.

Sometimes slowly.

Sometimes not so slowly.

Perhaps, in time, the demon might learn how to juggle several victims at the same time. Like with insects or small, furry mammals. Impale them on a pin or a stake. Pull off a wing or a toe at a time. Watch them squirm, each in different – but distinct – stages of annihilation.

The demon was past pulling wings off butterflies and beetles. Nailing kittens to trees had lost its appeal.

Bigger game was so much more fun.

Forty-Four

'Who's Clio?' Claudia asked.

They were sitting beside a lake whose water was the green of newly sprung grass and whose clarity showed every fin and spot on the fishes and eels. On the rocks by the water's edge, a small fire crackled and spat from the juices dripping off a small deer brought down with one of Jason's lethal arrows, but there was no fear of Azan's men tracing them from its smoke. Twenty-four hours had passed since the wreck of the *Soskia*, and the wolf trick had been sufficient to give them the edge in making good their escape. Azan's thugs would not find them now.

Just as Claudia could not find her way home.

With careful precision, Jason had led her deep into the Illyrian hinterland, to the Land of a Thousand Waterfalls. Lying between high forested mountains, this unique valley comprised a succession of crystal-clear lakes falling one below the other in a series of breathtaking cascades as the valley floor dropped. Awesome, spectacular, inspiring, stunning. These were just some of the words to describe this amazing waterworld. Arguably the most beautiful place in the world. She had never seen scenery to equal it.

But then other words bubbled up to the surface of her brain. Trapped. Isolated. Disorientated. Lost.

She concentrated on the venison and refused to dwell on the fact that the landscape was every bit as forbidding as it was magnificent. With its treacherous chasms, plunging gorges and waterfalls that froze into solid white sheets in the winter, the environment was too harsh for man to colonize. This

306

was the domain of the predators. Wolves, bears and lynx were the masters here.

That summed up the valley. Beautiful but deadly – like Jason. From the corner of her eye, she observed the solid musculature straining the thighs of his trousers. How many women had fallen for his dashing good looks? Been swept off their feet by his dazzling smile, easy manner and lilting Scythian brogue? How many women had thrashed beneath that burnished body in the throes of passion? Or simply in their death throes? The venison was succulent and sweet, but it could have been ash. Like the Scythian's gold belt, this ten-mile chain of green lakes was neither separate nor apart, but linked inextricably one to the other. *Just as she was with Jason.*

'Clio?' He sliced another chunk off the roast. 'I told you, she's a vampire. At least, that was the latest theory, but then, a few days earlier they had her pegged as a flesh-eating monster, which means by now they'll probably have her turned into a harpy.' He chewed without looking up. 'Why do you ask?'

Shortly after daybreak, the name had come back to her. Overtaken by kidnap, the shipwreck, Geta's death and an artillery attack followed by a frantic chase for her life, events at the Villa Arcadia had blurred into insignificance. Now they had clarified once again. Clio was the weapon with which Silvia had tried to blackmail Leo. Clio was the woman Leo had denied knowing. And Clio was the name which had tripped so lightly off

Jason's tongue outside the abandoned shepherd's hut.

'Just curious at how you came to know her, that's all.'

'Me?' he seemed surprised. 'I introduced her to Leo. What's the matter? Something go down the wrong way?'

You bet it did, pal. Claudia waited until her choking fit subsided. 'She was your moll, presumably?'

'My...?' He tipped his handsome head back and laughed until tears filled his eyes. 'I must remember that. My –' he rolled the word around on his tongue '– my moll. She'll *love* that.'

Claudia wondered why Clio might find that amusing, but noted he didn't deny it. Hmm. No wonder Leo was so keen to put Silvia on the first boat out of Cressia, if she was threatening to blow the whistle on his relationship with a pirate's floozy. Gossip like that could ruin a man. Hundreds of miles away in Rome, where they understood nothing of the situation out here, Leo's behaviour could easily be construed as being in league with the rebels, effectively branding him a traitor – wait! *Give back what is mine.*

Very deliberately, Claudia sipped at the cool, mountain water. 'Was Clio the cause of the vendetta between you and Leo?' she asked casually.

Jason pulled off his boots, stretched himself out on the bank and closed his eyes. 'Now what vendetta might that be?'

Still playing games. Cat and mouse. She said nothing, glad beyond words of the knife down her boot. High in the whispering branches, green warblers sang their little hearts out. She nibbled at the wild raspberries she had collected. She could not kill him, of course. The paradox of her situation lay in that her very survival depended on the man who was intent on destroying her. But there would come a time, and probably soon, when paradox became confrontation. She was ready.

'Why did you leave the wolf heads behind?' she asked. About an hour after pulling their stunt, Jason had hurriedly stuffed the sack inside the bole of a dead beech tree. 'You didn't know at that stage we weren't being followed. We could have used them again to frighten them off.'

'Hardly.' He reached for a grass of blade and chewed lazily. 'If Azan's little playmates were still on our trail, there was no way they'd fall for that old chestnut twice. We'd only have wasted precious time trying, so I dumped them in the first dead tree we came across.'

'They were valuable.'

'No point in lugging around stuff we have no use for.'

Claudia thought of Geta, lying several hundred yards away and not a pretty sight any more. And she thought about the axe, whose vicious blade was right now embedded in a silver birch, glinting like a malevolent eye in the sun.

309

'You used those wolf heads on the *Soskia*, didn't you?'

Volcar talked about the pirate ship howling like banshees after blood. The sound would have been made by the bronze sculptures impaled upon the same spikes that held the torches the night the little *Moth* anchored off the villa when she was lit up brighter than a midsummer noon.

'I presume the objective was to drown the screams of the women and children you'd captured.'

The Scythian groaned and covered his face with his hands. 'Good god, woman, your husband must have gone to his grave with his ears plugged. Don't you *ever* let up?'

In the calm reflection of the lake, she watched two swans flap lazily across the canyon. Swoosh, swoosh, swoosh. Like the oars of the warship. The swans were long out of sight before she asked, 'How did you know my husband was dead?'

'Same as I know everything else that happens at the Villa Arcadia. I make it my business. Now for heaven's sake, will you let a man sleep.'

Claudia pictured the battleaxe embedded in his heart, instead of the birch. But the forest was dark and she would never find her way back to the coast. 'Why?' she asked. 'Why is the Villa Arcadia so important to you?' What's the link?

Faster than a cobra strike, Jason was on top of her, pinning her down. A hundred and eighty pounds of immovable muscle smelling of cinnamon and raw masculinity.

'I have a cure for women who talk too much,' he rasped, drawing his lips down on hers.

A girl doesn't dance for her supper in a rough tough naval tavern in just a bangle and some skimpy bits of cotton without learning the odd trick or two. Jason might be strong and athletic, but compared to a drunken sailor who hasn't had a woman in weeks, he was a baby.

'There go my chances of fathering children,' he wheezed.

'I don't kiss killers.'

'So I noticed.' Eyes watering, he tried to unbend and found being doubled up much more comfortable. After a few minutes in which his face eventually lost its green tinge, he said, 'I make no apologies for what I've done.'

'That's a coincidence, because neither do I.'

He hobbled on to all fours, then hauled himself upright with the help of a stripling. 'They need to change the name of this valley,' he said, wiping the cataract of sweat off his forehead with the back of his hand. 'Call it the Land of a Thousand and *One* Waterfalls.' He staggered into the lake up to his groin. 'Is it my imagination or is there steam rising off the surface?' he asked.

Still trying to charm me, eh? Even when you've admitted the atrocities, you're still trying to charm me. Cat and mouse. The old I-know-that-you-know-and-you-know-that-I-know-that-you-know routine. Bluff and double bluff. *How can I possibly be the monster you think I am? Do I look like a sick, depraved killer?* No, you don't, Jason, and that's your camouflage. Just like the mild little man back in Rome who went around strangling women for kicks. So meek, so well mannered, so utterly trustworthy that his victims literally invited him into their homes. But you, Jason. You're a wolf in wolf's clothing, and that's the genius of your disguise. No one suspects you to be worse than you are. Except me. I know what you are.

Yet she could still taste the mint on his breath and feel the imprint of his lips on her own, and the lips were not rough or chapped, and his breath had been warm, and the place where his hands had gripped her shoulders tingled and burned, and ... and the sensation was far from unpleasant.

He waded out of the shallows and hauled on his red leather boots. 'Nothing quite like having your nuts twisted then marinated in ice-cold water to put a chap off his post-prandial nap,' he said, tweaking the axe out of the birch. 'So I suggest we knuckle down to the real business we came to this place for. Sorting out Geta.'

Claudia gulped. 'Define "we".'

'Straight choice,' he said. 'Either come with me and help. Or I tie you up and leave you here until I've finished.'

Tied up at the mercy of a playful psychopath like Bulis? I'd rather drink poison. On the other hand ... 'What exactly are you proposing to do to him?' she asked.

'Why the hell do you *think* I've carried Geta on my shoulders all this way?' For twenty long seconds, hard grey eyes bored into hers. 'I'm going to bury the poor bugger, of course.'

The demon yawned, stretched, then settled back to sleep.
It had its victim exactly where it wanted it.
On the end of a string.
No hurry.
None at all.

When Jason said bury, of course, he meant it in the broadest sense of the word. As in 'disposal of body'. He did not mean inter, neither did he mean cremate. Fire, he explained, stripping the helmsman of his clothes, was Targitaos the sun god's holy gift. To defile this gift with human flesh would be an abomination and an outrage, so Scythian custom decreed that corpses be exposed.

'*Exposed?*' Different cultures, different customs, fair enough. The Egyptians embalmed. Britons interred. The Gallic and Nordic tribes favoured cremation. In parts of the land of Kush they were even rumoured to bury their dead upright in pits. But no civilized society, repeat none, left their loved ones to be picked clean by carrion!

313

'Has to be a willow,' he said, hacking away at the canopy with his battleaxe. He had stripped off his white shirt, revealing not only the bull, but tattoos of wryneck birds and cranes. As he chopped, the lynx on his back bared its fangs in a snarl as his muscles expanded. 'Willow is our sacred tree.'

Claudia thought of the leaf pattern engraved on the gold torque which glittered round his neck. Everything was symbolism with this race. The ritual every bit as important as the act. A point to bear in mind when Jason felt the bloodlust come upon him.

'The body has to be wrapped in an untanned skin.' His mouth twisted at one corner as he held up the velvety hide of the deer they had just eaten. 'Although I'd like to think there is a certain flexibility in the definition of "wrap".'

Either that or slaughter half the herd. Geta was a big man.

'According to legend,' Jason said, binding the hide tight, 'Geta's homeland was settled when two brothers followed a white stag to a beautiful and bountiful land. Hence the sacred deer skin.'

'You've gone to a lot of trouble,' Claudia said. 'You must have been fond of him.'

'Geta?' Jason gave the red mop one last affectionate pat. 'Not particularly, but he served me well and we are, after all, brothers in blood and Scythians take care of their own. It is our code, and since Geta came from the Danube delta, it is to freshwater that he

314

must return.'

'What about you?' Claudia asked quietly. 'Where will you return to?'

Jason stopped what he was doing and looked at her. For the first time, she saw a flicker of raw emotion behind those grey eyes. 'Without sons to carry the bull on their chests, my spirit will have nowhere to go.' Then he brightened. 'But if the bull is stamped on the chests of my sons? Then so long as my corpse lies where the sun and the moon can shine down on it, I'll be happy. Now then.' He hefted Geta over his shoulder and began to heave it up through the branches. 'Let's get this ugly lug settled once and for all.'

With Jason, of course, mere exposure wasn't enough. Having wrestled his compatriot up to his leafy bier, he insisted on adorning it with sacred insignia. Preferably, it would have been a crane, like the ones which migrate from the Danube delta in autumn to overwinter in Egypt, returning again in the spring to breed. Geta had to make do with a widgeon laid in his lap. But Jason's deadly arrow did manage to find a water serpent, the helmsman's clan totem, to place on his chest. And finally, in lieu of a reaping hook, he left the axe.

'Since we have no more use for it,' he added with a natty smile.

Clambering up the rocks between one of the hundreds of waterfalls, Claudia paused to look back down the valley. As the lakes fell

315

away, to become pools of liquid emerald dwarfed by vertical walls of white rock, she had a bird's eye view of Geta's final resting place. A bizarre eagle's eyrie, flat on the tree tops, where his bones would eventually fall through the branches, back to the earth, the battleaxe along with them. Macabre, but then we all have rituals, she thought, remembering the sacrificial haunch of venison she had left under the willow, covered with spikes of lilac-blue vervain, when Jason hadn't been looking.

Geta might have kidnapped her twice – once on the night of the fire, and once again as she was leaving Nanaï – and he might have been a pirate without conscience who had willingly crashed his own ship and let the crew drown rather than share the treasure he believed hidden by his captain in the cave, but the great flat-faced, slant-eyed ox had died saving her life.

Vervain was sacred to Venus, and although Venus could not possibly be the same goddess of love that the red-headed barbarian claimed as his clan protectress, maybe – just maybe – this Argimpasa of his, whose symbol was the serpent, might recognize the sanctity of the offering. For good measure, Claudia had strewn marigold petals, as well. Flowering all year round, they symbolized everlasting life and Geta would appreciate that, because, she suspected, he would already be at the helm of some celestial warship raiding the dark shores of Hades!

But a few flowers are one thing. Jason's determination was quite another.

He had carried the corpse for twenty-four hours simply to reach a place where willows and water combined. Altruistic? To give a fellow countryman the send-off he felt he owed him? Or a determination to follow the ritual, no matter what obstacles stood in his path? She considered the way he had worked. Not just with Geta's funeral rites, but in every detail from the low, insolent bow on the prow of his warship to the slow, mimed handclap. From the casual way he took out the eye of his opponents with the slingshot to the planning well in advance of the wolf howls. He would undoubtedly argue his was a methodical nature, others might call it controlling.

To a killer, control is everything. Control empowers him. Lifts him above the material plane to a metaphysical level.

The key to her survival was to deny him that chance.

At the top of the last cascade, Jason pointed. 'Smoke,' he said. He was carrying his own quiver and bow now, and without encumbrances they were able to travel much faster. 'Too much for a single house, it looks like there's a settlement over the ridge. With luck, we can buy horses from them.'

'To strangle or ride?'

He flashed her his wolfish grin. 'I'll let you know when we get there.'

Terrific. An adventuring psychopath who knows that I'm wise to him and doesn't care.

317

He's played on my fear of his headhunting tendencies, not just with the wolf heads but by deliberately keeping me in the dark about Geta, and he's keeping the pressure up still. Same old game he'd played with Leo when he delivered the war spears. First in the boat shed, then in the stables, then in the bath-house door: creeping that little bit closer each time, making Leo aware of what he was doing, taunting him, even. But still Leo fell into the trap. And why? Because Jason had taken care to coat it with his special honey.

'But I don't have a sweet tooth,' she whispered to the forest.

For now, though, she was safe. Jason the pirate moved under cover of darkness, sneaking in, sneaking out, leaving no trace. Jason the butcher liked to take risks. He preferred to operate when people were buzzing around, because the fear of discovery was every bit as thrilling as the agony of his helpless victim. It underscored his superiority over the rest of the human race. Highlighted his supremacy over mere mortals. Allowed him to rise above them.

Claudia's instincts had been right on target when, with Azan's thugs crowding in, she had believed that was the moment Jason had chosen to kill her. Her error lay not in the timing ... but in the location.

'You're going back to the Villa Arcadia, aren't you?'

'What makes you think that, lieutenant?'

318

'Because you have unfinished business there,' she replied. Me.

The demon laughed.

Far from subsiding, Clio's anger had bloated into a great balloon of outrage. Like a cripple's hunch, it sat on her back, throbbing with fury, ugly and violent, and screaming for justice.

This wasn't fair.

This was not how it was supposed to be.

She should have been rich by now. Returning home to her hilltop village in fine clothes and foolish shoes, riding in a litter, *her* litter, carried shoulder high through the streets by slaves, *her* slaves, tossing alms to street beggars like petals.

Instead, she was stuck in this hell-hole with no food and no means to earn food and she had certainly left it too late to start socializing with the townspeople now! Tolerating a vampire on the outskirts of their community was one thing. The bastards probably even bragged about it to their neighbours. But that wasn't to say they'd countenance one in their midst.

'This isn't my fault!' she yelled at the sky. 'I've done nothing wrong!'

Her fists tore up tussocks of grass, pummelled chunks out of the drystone walls, hurled rocks at the carrion birds pecking at the piles of rotting intestines.

'Bastards!' she screamed. 'Bastards, the lot

319

of you!'

Jason. Leo. Every man, woman and child in the town, including that runt of a priest. *Especially* that runt of a priest.

'I hope your soul burns in the Lake of Fire for eternity!'

Llagos could have spared her this, the dirty, sneaking, peeking bastard pervert. As the most respected priest on the island, his voice carried influence. They would have listened to him. Now they shunned her. As a result, Clio was destined to starve slowly to death, unable to get off the island because even if she could pay, no one would take her.

'Damn you all,' she shouted. 'Damn you and your ludicrous superstitions!'

That little Persian creep didn't help. Muttering to himself in his own unintelligible language as he pored over livers and entrails, finding portents in everything from clouds to wave formations to lizard prints in the dust. And the silly sods drank in every one of Shamshi's dire warnings!

'When the moon wears a halo and little lambs bleat, so Cressian cradles will rock.'

That, apparently had been his first pronouncement upon arrival at the Villa Arcadia two years ago, a prediction any fool could have made. After the midsummer revelries, there was *always* a rash of new-born babies in spring. But Shamshi had banked on the islanders' innate apprehension of foreigners. His ways could not possibly be their ways, they reasoned, so his predictions must truly

320

be a gift from the gods. And when he said that before the sun rises thrice more over their heads, a woman shall die, they knew it to be true. At first they had tried to make Clio herself the victim. Nudge the prophecy along a bit. Help the cause. But they hadn't needed to. From her hilltop eyrie, Clio had watched another solemn funeral procession wind its way out of town, where a woman in traditional dress was buried with her hands folded over her breast. An old woman, by the size of her. Probably the cobbler's ancient mother, which meant Shamshi had seen the old crone and recognized that she'd been near to death.

Yet the islanders *still* believed that every word which dripped off that miserable fraud's tongue was a result of his divinations!

'It's not fair!' she screamed. 'It's not bloody fair, I've done nothing wrong!'

She hadn't harmed these people. Why did they hate her so much that they would let her starve to death rather than help her?

'May your souls shrivel in the Lake of Ice,' she cried. 'May your children and your children's children be cursed!'

Bastards.

She could not turn to Silvia, because Silvia knew why she was here, and Silvia would be looking after Number One. In any case, Leo's cousin from the Security Police was ensconced at the Villa Arcadia now, and that would make things doubly difficult. Stealing food would be well nigh impossible, there were just too many people around, sooner or later Clio would be caught, which would be worse than throwing herself on Silvia's mercy in the first place.

But she had to do something. She couldn't just sit up here and waste quietly away. Leo owed her. Clio smashed a stone against the side of her cottage. Croesus, how Leo owed her.

Which meant someone, somewhere had to pay.

Fast.

Forty-Five

'You're not seriously inviting him to stay *here*?'

Was Silvia out of her mind? Offering those same seafaring hands which had squeezed her windpipe like a grape the luxury of a guest bedroom?

'What were we supposed to do?' Silvia retorted. Two high spots of colour stood out on her perfect cheeks. 'He returns you safe and sound, we can hardly throw him out, can we? Anyway.' She tossed her head in a haze of golden ringlets. 'He has nowhere to go.'

Only to hell, Claudia reflected, and there was no great rush to send Jason there. With a contented sigh, she sank below the warm, scented waters of her sunken, tiled bath and recalled how easy it would have been to slip her stiletto into the heart of the blue bull as he slept last night. Too easy! She exhaled in a series of satisfied bubbles. If the murdering bastard expected to escape that lightly, he had another think coming. It was a parade through the streets of Rome in chains for him. Followed by a slow, painful and humiliating death in the arena. She surfaced among the heliotrope and hibiscus petals bobbing on the bathwater and felt better already.

She would have felt a whole lot better, of course, had the Security Police been around to do the job they were trained for. Namely, clapping psychopaths in irons. But, as Silvia was particularly quick to point out, Orbilio *wasn't* here.

'So conscientious in his official duties,' she'd gushed, perching daintily on a footstool as Claudia was enveloped in coils of fragrant steam. 'He'll make a splendid Senator, don't you think? So handsome, too, in full insignia.'

The big blue eyes took on a misty glaze.

'I can see us now – fêted by the cream of society, invited to the very best dinner parties. And if his career in law shines like his military career in the past, maybe we shall even attend imperial banquets one day!'

'Remind me again how long I've been gone?' Claudia murmured. 'Only when I left, I could have sworn he was an investigator in the Security Police.'

Silvia dismissed Orbilio's position with a wrinkling of her pretty nose. 'Sordid, sordid, can't have that. Best to play up his stint as a young tribune, concentrate on that, because really, Claudia, and apart from the ignominy of it all, a family man can't afford to risk his neck on the mean streets at night. Advocacy is Marcus's future, trust me.'

Claudia thought about the chestnut gelding which Jason had procured from that village in the wilds of Illyria and which had been her transport home, and saw the same gelding knife glistening in Silvia's hand.

'Does Marcus know he's about to become a lawyer any minute?' she asked sweetly.

'All in good time.' Immaculate lips parted in a slight smile, which widened and became more catlike, as her gaze fixed on a point in the middle distance. 'With a husband serving in the Senate, society won't dare to cut me. It will,' she sighed, 'be just like the old days.'

Then, as fast as a tallow being snuffed, Silvia's expression returned to glacial normality.

'You *will* come and visit us one afternoon, won't you, dear? I'm sure my husband wouldn't want us to abandon his old friend's quirky widow, simply because she's not patrician.'

But when those big blue eyes refocused on the warm, fragrant waters, all that remained of Claudia Seferius was a trail of wet footprints fading their way out of the bath house.

'Claudia.' The whisper echoed like a kiss

along the gallery which enclosed the gymnasium yard and she wondered how long the Persian had been waiting. How much naked flesh he had been hoping to see. 'I am glad to see you returned safely.'

'I'd have expected your entrails and livers to have seen that, Shamshi. Not your eyes.'

The only object to emerge from the shadow was one shoe, tied in a bow and partially covered by the hem of his kaftan. 'Dear child, I am but the guardian of the prophecies, not their originator.'

'Well, considering the sun rose above our heads far more than thrice and no woman died, I suggest you stick your prophecies where it doesn't rise and fall, and guard *that*.'

'Ah, but a woman did die. On the very morning I predicted, the cobbler's mother commenced her long and arduous journey across the River Styx.' Enough oil came from his smile to drain a whole olive tree. 'The gods never lie to me, Claudia.'

'I could ask you nicely to get out of my way, Shamshi. Then again, I could just kick you in the balls.'

The Persian twisted his thin hands together and stood his ground. 'I fetched a clay beaker as commanded last night in my dream. I filled it with milk mixed with honey, then added the blood of a jet-black ram and drank it down as the gods instructed.'

'You might try prunes for breakfast next time.'

'The warning that came through was as

clear as the crystal Qus keeps in his room,' Shamshi persisted, and she didn't like the way he pushed his hooked nose into her face as he lowered his voice to a whisper. 'Beware, Claudia.' His breath was still as sweet as an overripe melon. *'Beware the Trojan horse.'*

Which just goes to prove, she supposed, the dangers of mixing your drinks. Milk, blood and honey in the same bowl can seriously damage a man's mental health.

The boat carrying Orbilio back to Cressia needed no pilot to guide her into the harbour. Her captain was a local skipper from the Istrian mainland, who knew the rocks and the currents like the back of his hand, navigating his way through the channels with confidence. As terns wheeled and dived into the limpid sea and the plunging cliffs loomed closer, Orbilio could see brown and naked children splashing on the white rocks and squealing with pleasure. As the boat approached the shelter of the harbour, his gaze fixed on the quayside, quiet this time of day. Only a handful of fishermen braved the scorch of the midday sun, and they were engaged in a game of knucklebones with a young woman in a flame-coloured gown. Something inside constricted as he took in the dark, tumbling curls, the curve of her breasts as she pocketed her winnings and slipped the loaded dice back into the folds of her gown. As mooring ropes were thrown over the side, Orbilio rubbed a slow hand over his jaw, still swollen from where her bodyguard's fist had connected, and the vice tightened.

'Straightforward quid pro quo,' she announced, marching up the gangplank. 'I deliver you a pirate on a silver platter. In return, you drop the doping charge. What's so funny? Orbilio, would you please explain why you're laughing? I mean, for a start you might have been just a tad relieved to know I'm safe.'

Mother of Tarquin, she had no idea what he had experienced when he discovered she'd escaped the shipwreck. 'Once reports came in of your survival,' he said, 'I stopped worrying about you and began to worry for Jason.'

'Bastard.'

'But a self-made man.'

'Don't let the conceit go to your head, Orbilio. Just agree to my terms.' There was a splash, as a porter discharging sacks was knocked off the gangplank by an accidental female elbow.

Marcus licked the salt off his lips and knew he was going to enjoy himself here. She didn't know. Goddammit, Claudia Seferius and she still didn't realize! 'Azan's mistake,' he said, tipping the floundering porter a silver sesterces, 'wasn't mustering his three ships together. It was dallying far too long waiting for his men to bring Jason back. I imagine our trusty marines are blasting him out of the water even as we speak.'

'Bugger Azan. I'm talking about me. And

cutting a deal.'

'Those Liburnian galleys are all very well in and around the islands, but once they're out in open water, they're no match for Roman triremes. Outmanned, outnumbered, outgunned, they'll be at the bottom of the ocean before the navy's within their range.'

'For gods' sake, Orbilio, insurrection isn't the issue here. Yes, yes, it's wonderful that you've scotched it; I'm sure they'll write you up in dispatches or whatever they write people up in, and the islanders will doubtless praise your name for ever for delivering them from Azan the Butcher. But there's a psychopath wandering around the Villa Arcadia who's in desperate need of locking up, and in return there's me, waiting for your word that you'll drop all charges against me.'

He kept his eyes on the top of the mast, where a seagull had perched and was preening its wings, and tried to compose his features. 'This may come as a shock to you, Mistress Seferius, but one of the first things we're taught at Security Police School is: catch the bad guys.'

'Then what are you waiting for?'

Marcus stuck out his lower lip as though deep in thought. 'Well...' He spread his hands. 'I guess it's the second thing they teach us at Security Police School.' He was enjoying this. 'Identify the bad guys first.'

'You don't think Jason's tattooed arms tied Bulis to the pillar in the grain store, stuffed a gag in his mouth, then set the granary alight?'

'No,' he said, keeping his gaze on the sea-gull, 'I don't.'

'Like those aren't the imprints of Jason's thumbs in Silvia's neck?'

'Oh, he's a lady-killer. Just not in the sense that you mean.'

'So it was pure coincidence that his war spear just happened to skewer Leo to the atrium door, leaving him to die in unspeakable agony?'

The laughter died from Orbilio's eyes, but he kept them fixed on the ratlines. 'Have I ever given the impression, even once, that I believed in coincidence?' he asked, meeting Claudia's eyes at long last. But as he opened his mouth to speak, a statuesque female came striding across the cobbled quayside, and suddenly all the noise and hubbub of the wharfside stopped. The crowd parted, their heads turned away and their hands rapidly making the sign of the horns.

'You must be Leo's cousin,' Clio said without preamble. Her voice was low and husky, with a hint of Liburnian brogue. 'I'm very pleased to meet you.'

He took in the cloak of black shining hair shimmering down to her waist when no respectable woman would dare be seen with her hair loose, much less that long. It wasn't the only area in which Clio defied convention, of course. He took the back of her hand and kissed it. 'The pleasure's all mine, I assure you.'

'Then I won't beat about the bush.' When

she placed her hands on her hips, the action caused her breasts to thrust forward and for a moment he feared he'd lost his eyeballs down her cleavage for ever. There were worse places to spend eternity, he thought happily, ignoring the roll of Claudia's eyes. 'Your cousin owed me money, Marcus. A lot of money, in fact.'

'I know.'

Surprise widened her eyes, but she quickly recovered. 'I'm not asking you to cover his entire debt, that wouldn't be fair. But I need to get away from this island, so I'm prepared to settle for five thousand gold pieces.'

'That's very generous of you,' he said. Almost as generous as her bosom. 'But I have a better idea, Clio.' He opened the bronze purse round his wrist and emptied its contents into his hand. 'It's not five thousand. Less than forty, I should imagine, but it's all I have on me, and then you stay on this boat.'

'What kind of insult is that? Leo owed me *fifteen* thousand, you penny-pinching bastard—'

'It's this boat, Clio.' There was an edge to his voice that drained every drop of colour from her cheeks. 'Or court.'

Ten seconds passed in which her gaze locked with his, then long fingernails raked up the coins and she was striding up the gangplank in search of the captain.

Claudia's breath came out in a whistle. 'So *that* was the vampire.'

'No,' Marcus corrected. 'That was Leo's accomplice.'

That was what brought him to Cressia. Leo and his voluptuous partner in crime. Twenty-eight aristocrats had held banquets in the eight months since Saturnalia, only to find that they'd been relieved of their jewellery and fine arts in the process. Inexplicably, however, none of the articles had appeared on Rome's black market, suggesting the gems were being prised out and reset, the metals melted down and the ivory recarved. Such a sophisticated operation could only be run by an educated mind, and when Marcus heard about Leo's extensive restoration programme, far in excess of his income, he began to wonder. After all, if the robberies included several of his own relatives, it stood to reason they were Leo's relatives as well.

'The renovations worked out more costly than he planned,' Marcus said. His stomach rumbled and now he wished he had retained a few coppers to buy one of the juicy lamb pies whose tantalizing aroma wafted over the quayside. 'So he started on places closer to home. Such as the Senator's summer house in Pula, where it looked as though Margarita wouldn't get her cameo back after all.'

'Where did Clio fit in?'

'By all accounts, she is an extremely talented harpist. Leo simply recommended her to his friends and relations.' Orbilio pictured Clio, scooping up coins and accolades after a virtuoso solo; leaving the hall to cool down, so she said, but instead gathering up jewellery and other precious items using the inside information passed on by her aristocratic accomplice.

'You travelled four hundred miles to arrest a bloody harpist?'

'In an ideal world, I'd have caught them red-handed, but I'd assembled enough of a case to at least prevent Leo's marriage to the rose-grower's daughter going ahead.' Life and death break contracts, as Lydia had taken such pains to point out. But so, too, do slave chains.

'No wonder your family want you out of the Security Police,' Claudia said. 'If you continue to arrest them at this rate, the line will die out in ten years.' She turned to look up at him and the laughter had died from her eyes. 'But of course, he didn't live long enough for you to arrest him, did he?'

A picture flashed up, gut-wrenchingly recurrent, of Leo slumped over the spear which had fastened him to the atrium door. If only he'd confronted his cousin when he arrived. 'No,' he said thickly. 'He didn't.'

'Then tell me why you don't believe Jason killed Bulis and Leo, then nearly made it a hat-trick with the human glacier.'

Marcus's thoughts spun back to the moment, just minutes ago, when a certain young widow had marched up the gangplank wanting to trade a pirate for criminal immunity. He had been set to enjoy himself teasing her, but there was no sport to be found now. 'Why wasn't it Jason?' He drew a deep breath and let it out slowly. 'Show me one self-respecting Scythian who'd leave without taking a war scalp,' he replied, 'and I'll show you Hades admitting day-trippers.' Not a hair on Leo's head had been touched.

The demon smiled to itself.
Sometimes human beings could be such fools.

There is a moment when you're rattling along at full speed and the wheel of your chariot comes off. You know what's happened because you can see the bloody thing rolling into the gutter. But the thing is, *you don't actually believe it.* That's because, for one brief fraction of a second, nothing changes. Momentum keeps the chariot on course. Momentum keeps it upright. And momentum means the horses haven't skipped a beat. Claudia was suddenly propelled into that same frozen momentary limbo. She understood the logic of what Orbilio was saying. She just couldn't accept it. 'If it wasn't Jason, then who?' Had he been drinking?

'Consider Homer's Odyssey,' Marcus said, steering her through the tangle of hawsers and rings littering the quayside. 'The Cyclops, for one. That one-eyed giant, who'd dined off several of Odysseus's crew before our hero blinded him with a spear and made good his escape.'

Strange. He didn't smell of booze. 'Odysseus battled the sea monsters Scylla and Charybdis. He navigated the Clashing Rocks and survived. He also met his ancestors in the Underworld. But *you* should see a doctor.'

Sunstroke is a terrible thing.

'Then there was his yearning to hear the song of the Sirens,' Orbilio persisted. 'Voices so haunting that anyone who heard them was drawn to their doom, their flesh devoured by the virgins who made their homes of the bones of their victims. No man had ever listened to their song and lived, but Odysseus, determined to be the first, plugged the ears of his crew with wax that they might not hear—'

'And ordered them to bind him fast to the mast that he might not yield to temptation. Yes, I know, and the physician's house is there, on the left.'

'Odysseus's travels took him to lots of places, as you pointed out. He came to Cressia, of course, just as he visited the island where the world's winds were kept.'

STOP PRESS. ICEBERGS INVADE LIBURNIAN GULF.

Claudia felt the full blast of the chill as her mind jerked back. To Llagos conducting the purification ceremony at the atrium door the morning after Leo's murder. Orbilio had been standing alone in the portico, staring up at the frieze of the Sirens. Not to admire Magnus's skill, as she'd imagined. He had been putting the pieces of the puzzle together, and the puzzle was there for all to see. Homer's epic. Of course!

334

Odysseus tied to the mast: *Bulis tied to the pillar*. The Cyclops blinded in his single eye by a war spear: *Leo impaled on the same weapon*. Odysseus struggling to contain the escaping winds by clutching the neck of the sack which contained them: *Just like someone had squeezed Silvia's throat*.

Everything that had happened, every killing, every attempted killing, had been a bizarre recreation of Odysseus's adventures. There was a strange rattle on the quayside, which could have been a wagon rumbling over the cobbles. Then again it might be the chattering of her own teeth. 'You think there's a lunatic out there who believes he's Odysseus reborn?'

'If only,' Marcus said quietly. 'I think we're dealing with an even grimmer possibility.' He led her into the cool shade of Neptune's temple, where the sea god's grove of sacred rowan trees cast their feathery reflections in his hallowed pool and small birds twittered in the branches. 'I believe Bulis and Silvia were a smokescreen.'

The chill went into her marrow. 'You are joking?'

'Am I? Suppose Bulis was tied up and gagged and the grain store set alight with the intention of the alarm being raised *before* tragedy struck?'

'But it wasn't.'

'No. But suppose that had been the plan? Just like Silvia was never meant to die, either?'

335

'And Leo was?'

'Exactly.' Marcus buried his face in his hands. 'Leo made a lot of enemies before he died. How better to cover up revenge than to make it appear that Bulis and Silvia were victims of a deranged mind, whereas the real motive was to kill Leo.'

Claudia watched the frogs in the margins of the pool. Dammit, this was the grief talking. Orbilio believed he had failed his cousin by spending the night in the tavern instead of heading straight for the villa. Now, that guilt was set to haunt him for the rest of his life if he cocked up on bringing his killer to justice. But the reasoning was utterly irrational. *Wasn't it?*

'Of them all – Qus, Silvia, Volcar, Jason, Nanaï, Nikias, Clio—'

'Clio?'

'She had fifteen thousand good reasons to kill him, remember. But Lydia has the strongest motive. Archetypal wronged wife, dismissed like a housekeeper after eighteen years of marriage, cheated out of her divorce dowry then expected to live within sight of her own fabulously refurbished house while her husband impregnates his new and incidentally much younger bride. I'd call that a motive.'

When Claudia dabbled her fingers in the pool, several small fishes came to the surface. *I'm not quite the bastard you think I am, Claudia.* Leo's voice echoed in her memory and she smiled. No, Leo, you weren't. Despite your obsession for sons, you still retained some vestige of honour, even though your pride refused to let others see it. Would things have been different, I wonder, had Lydia been privy to your master plan? That you were merely using the rose-grower's daughter as a means to an end, because once she had given you your precious heirs, you intended to remarry her? *Magnus is out of her class, Claudia, in more ways than one.* Dammit, Leo, I should have guessed then how much you cared! That the renovations in which you sank so much of other people's money weren't intended to impress some stranger of a child bride. They weren't even a monument for your future sons. Leoville was built as a tribute to Lydia! The woman you continued to refer to as your *wife*. The woman you never stopped loving...

'Life and death break contracts,' Orbilio quoted.

'Don't they just.' Claudia didn't wait to see whether he followed her out of the temple compound. He caught up with her at the door of the tavern. 'You knew a man of Magnus's skill and stature wouldn't doss in cheap taverns without good reason, so you assumed he was behind the robberies.'

'I didn't assume anything,' he murmured. 'I just *hoped* he might be.' His face took on a tight smile. 'How much simpler, if Magnus had been the mastermind and not Leo and I'd got it all wrong. Anyway.' His expression brightened. 'I'll have you know, Mistress Seferius, I'm not the type of chap to go

337

upstairs with girls in strange taverns. If you want my favours, I insist you ply me with silver, like everyone else.'

'Stick to the Security Police, Orbilio. The pay might be poor, but if you tried earning your keep as a gigolo, you'd starve within a week.'

'I hate it when you couch your words. Why don't you just give it to me straight? And you might like to tell me what we're doing here,' he added as Claudia flounced along the narrow walkway, trying the rooms as she went.

No doors in this place. Just tatty woollen drapes for privacy and she didn't understand why her stomach should flip at picturing Orbilio in one of these rat holes. Not at the thought of him, a nobleman, roughing it with straw mattresses in place of swandown and enough fleas to make the bedstead rattle, more that, once Silvia got her claws into him, such adventures would be strictly off limits.

'Silvia knew, of course.' Sisters are still sisters no matter how sour the relationship, and the Immaculate One understood only too well why, after being dumped, diddled and seemingly dumped again, Lydia looked happy. More than happy, in fact. She looked bloody marvellous. 'Skin blooming, hair glossy, there's only one explanation,' Claudia said.

Turning in the hallway, her shoulder brushed with Orbilio's. Electricity jarred her bones as the heat from his body transferred

338

itself to hers. Distracted by the scent of sandalwood, the pulse that beat at the side of his neck, the dark hairs on the back of his wrist, she almost forgot the danger he posed.

'Leo could warn Magnus off all he liked,' she said, 'but you only have to look at his statues to understand the soul of their creator and know that it would be water off a duck's back if he had truly fallen in love.'

No way would Magnus sail off and leave Lydia. He had merely backed off and given her space. Space in which she could make her own mind up about her future, without outside influence or prompting.

'Explains a lot,' Orbilio said, making no move to back away in the narrow corridor. His pupils had darkened to pools of liquid jet, and his breath was warm on her face. 'The other day,' he said, 'I followed Magnus down to the point. Lydia was holding the tunics of two little girls, waving to the kids splashing around with the dolphin, and he stood there, perhaps for half an hour, just watching, before going down to speak with her.' He swallowed. 'I'm glad she's found true love,' he said. 'Everyone should have that.'

'Oh, she's found more than love,' Claudia said. Life and death break contracts, as Lydia took such pains to point out at that dinner party. Death certainly. But so, equally, does a new life. 'Lydia is pregnant.' She threw open a threadbare blue curtain. 'Aren't you, Lydia?'

Forty-Six

Tact and diplomacy were a patrician's stock in trade, as Claudia well knew. But it was going to take every drop of Orbilio's blue blood to persuade Lydia to return to the Villa Arcadia.

'Comfort be buggered,' she snapped. 'My little house on the point is more than adequate.'

It was anything but, of course, but Marcus Cornelius was far too polite to mention the fact. Instead he turned to the subject of Leo's will, which he had deposited in the Treasury of the Temple of Neptune in the town. In it, Orbilio explained, Leo had left Lydia everything.

'Including his debts!' she snorted. 'I hope the dirty bastard rots in hell.'

Intractable pregnant widows would be no match for Orbilio's charm, but these things took time. Claudia took the shortcut. 'For gods' sake, Magnus, tell the silly bitch it's in her baby's interest.'

The sculptor laughed. 'I'm not sure whether to cast you as Venus or Medusa.'

'Not Medusa,' Orbilio pleaded. 'She'd frighten the snakes. Now Lydia, are you coming back voluntarily, or do I have to put you over my shoulder?'

Lydia grunted. 'Might as well enjoy my own bloody investments,' she muttered, but it was a different story when she saw just how sumptuous the renovations had been. 'Leo had taste, I'll give him that,' she said, running her fingertip over the painted feathers of a dove in the master bedroom. 'Although I have to say Nikias doesn't seem to be much of a portrait painter. The rose-grower's daughter looks more like me at that age.'

'That's why you told Leo that his marriage contract was invalid,' Marcus cut in, before Claudia and Magnus burst out laughing. 'If no child had come along during eighteen years of trying and suddenly you're pregnant, it wouldn't take the rose-grower long to figure out that it was Leo who was sterile, not you.'

'I was tempted not to tell the selfish bastard,' Lydia admitted. 'Let him find out after he'd wed the little bitch, but it wouldn't have been fair on the rose-grower's daughter. She's only a child herself, after all.' She rubbed her still-flat stomach. 'A baby was all I ever wanted,' she said, flashing a tender glance at the sculptor, 'and a husband who adores me will be the icing on the cake.'

'You'll wait until you're asked, woman,' Magnus said, but their laughter was interrupted by a lilac tornado.

'So it's true!' Silvia's eyes were bulging with horror. 'My own sister found fornicating in a fleapit with a – *commoner!*'

341

'That's what she can't tolerate,' Lydia said to the ceiling. 'That I'm not coercing some poor patrician into marriage for social status.' Lydia shot a sharp glance at Orbilio. 'Like she can talk,' she added nastily.

'How dare you,' Silvia hissed. 'I'm only concerned with your welfare, Lydia. I can't stand idly by while my older sister sacrifices the birthright of her unborn child for something she thinks is love but which we all know will wear off the minute her belly grows large.'

'Is that what happened to you?' Lydia snapped. 'Did Loverboy tire of you once you lost *your* perfect figure?'

'It was nothing of the sort and you know it,' Silvia snarled. 'I just don't want to see your life ruined the way mine has been.' She drew herself up to her full height and tilted her chin in the air. 'I'm young,' she said. 'I have time on my side.'

'And I haven't?' The slap that rang out left a wheal on Silvia's cheek. 'You really are a spiteful bitch.'

'Just because I'm giving you a taste of reality? Listen to me, you selfish cow, your child won't only be born a bastard, you're forfeiting its claim to the nobility and all the privileges that go with it. *That's* spiteful. Condemning a wean to that!' She pursed his lips until they were white. 'Look, it's not too late. Pretend this is Leo's child, and I promise you no one will contradict the story. We'll soon spread the rumours about a reconciliation—'

'Fuck you, Silvia. I love Magnus, and the

gods know why, but he loves me. This baby doesn't need nobility, when it has so much love.' Except the tears in her eyes betrayed her words. Her sister's caution had hit home. 'Marcus.' Lydia looked straight at her ex-husband's cousin. 'I've known you for so long, you're like a baby brother. What do you say? Should I follow my heart? Or—' She gulped back the tears. 'Or should I do right by my child?'

The silence that followed was anything but golden.

'Funny you should ask,' he said eventually, and his voice was barely audible. 'I bumped into an old friend recently. Margarita. That same issue arose then.' His face took on an expression bordering pain. 'With my ancestors tracing their lineage back to Apollo, the question was: could I honestly deny my children the inheritance they were entitled to by marrying a woman who wasn't patrician?'

'And?'

The question came from Lydia's lips, but it was strung tight across Claudia's brain. *And...?* She couldn't breathe, and the silence stretched to infinity.

'The answer, I'm very much ashamed to say,' he said, pausing to glance at Silvia's immaculate poise and couture, 'is yes. For the right woman, Lydia, I would sacrifice everything. For her,' and this time his eyes bored straight into Claudia's, 'for her, I would lay down my life.'

★ ★ ★

343

You couldn't make this up, Claudia thought, you really couldn't. Darkness had enveloped the island and a constant procession of liveried slaves now ferried tray after tray of spiced delicacies across the outdoor dining terrace. Cooled by the portico, scented by garlands and soothed by the babble of a gentle fountain, this might have been any dinner party, anywhere. Relaxed, amusing conversation, music, juggling, dancers – you'd think murder, kidnap, arson and shipwreck were parts of other people's tragedies, not theirs.

'I tell you, the way Claudia's horse was dragging its hooves home from Dalmatia,' Jason quipped, 'it would have been quicker for her to carry the gelding, not the other way round.'

That's it. Laugh. Everyone forget they're sharing a meal with a pirate. The whole thing was beyond Claudia's comprehension: why Silvia had invited Jason to stay; why Orbilio hadn't locked him up; why everyone was so bloody polite. Even if he wasn't responsible for Leo's murder, he was a self-confessed killer with enough crimes to warrant arrest twelve times over. Yet he had the aristocracy eating out of his tattooed hand! Dammit, even Silvia seemed almost human under Jason's charm – but then the sand in that woman's timer was running out fast. To catch her prey, The Glacier had to move quickly and if that meant coping with the most perverse of social dilemmas to impress her future husband, so be it. How long she'd continue taking her cue from Orbilio, Claudia would not like to guess. Immaculate and unruffled on the outside, there was steel in Silvia's belly. (Maybe once, long ago, even fire.) But that glance in Lydia's room had shaken her, as had the huskiness in Orbilio's voice.

Claudia popped a stuffed date in her mouth. What the Ice Queen didn't know, of course, was the history between Claudia and the Security Police. That his emotional declaration was nothing more than an act. Another of his weasel ploys to win her trust – and, thus, her confession. Marcus Cornelius Orbilio marry out of his class? Ha! Rain would fall upwards first. Claudia raised her glass in a silent toast to him and smiled broadly. It was a smile he mistrusted with every fibre of his body. Good. Things were starting to perk up at long last.

'They say you've sailed the whole world,' Nanaï said gushingly, and Jason laughed as he drained his silver goblet of wine.

'Hardly the whole world, Nanaï, but there aren't many ports between Lusitania and the Black Sea that I haven't seen.'

'Amazing,' Nanaï sighed, 'and so dangerous, too.'

'Jason or his voyages?' Claudia asked sweetly.

She wasn't remotely surprised that Silvia had invited Nanaï tonight. The Ice Queen saw this as full dress rehearsal for senatorial dinner parties of the future, juggling every conceivable political adversity. Oh, and she'd stepped up her game in the looks department, as well. No ringlet was ever tighter. No jewels gleamed brighter. No pleat could be sharper without drawing blood. Like a swan, she glided gracefully back and forth across the terrace to supervise the crab, the lobsters, the oysters, scallops and milk-fed snails, ensuring they were all washed down with the very finest vintage wines from Leo's cellar. Bitch.

'Sorry I iss late, everyones.' Breathless, Llagos slipped out of his sandals and took a place beside Lydia and Magnus. 'My littlest one would not let me leave until I rescues her kitten from top of tree.' He flapped the neck of his robe to cool himself. 'I do not minds, but by the time I iss halfway up ladder in dark, the kitten, she runs down by herself! Do I miss much gossip, please?'

'Bugger all,' Volcar growled. 'Mistress High-and-Mighty's lording it over us like she'd inherited the bloody villa, instead of her sister. The Orphan Bitch has been boring us rigid about the progress of her bastard brood. And all art's twin leading lights can manage,' he snorted disdainfully at Nikias and the maestro, 'is a lecture on spatial recession and miniaturist precision, whatever the hell those might be.'

'As long as everyones iss enjoying themselves.' Llagos laughed, and even Silvia's lips almost succumbed to a smile.

346

Impossible to give credence to Orbilio's theory, Claudia mused, as the sound of banter filled the night air. Impossible to believe that one of these people is a vicious, cold-blooded killer. I mean who – *who?* – milling around helping themselves from this platter or that and drifting from couch to couch to follow the wit and conversation, could *possibly* be capable of running Leo through with a spear and leaving him to (maybe even watching him?) die.

'Don't forget,' a voice whispered in her ear. The voice was soft and sibilant and made goosebumps rise on her skin. *'Beware the Trojan Horse.'*

All right, who apart from Shamshi?

But come on. Shamshi might be many things. A fraud, who made a living from listening at keyholes and using whatever he picked up to utter prophecies which were then almost guaranteed to come true. A crank, who genuinely believed what some dead animal's dripping liver told him. Hell, he might even have a gift! Sure, it would be a gift, which he played for all it was worth with his creepy demeanour and obscenely glinting bands of gold at his ears. But what would have been the advantage in killing his meal ticket?

Motive. That was the thing. Nobody kills without motive.

Nanaï was a strange and unlikeable woman with the narrowest of vision, who would have no qualms in killing to protect Snowdrop and the others, but Nanaï's blood ran hot.

With a longed-for baby on the way and a man who adored her, Lydia had no reason to kill her ex-husband, Magnus even less! His skills as a sculptor had made him wealthy, far richer than the debt-ridden Leo, and to suggest Magnus would go to the trouble of staging two other murderous attempts to cover up his crime was risible in the extreme.

The Ice Queen? She had motive enough, Claudia supposed. Disgraced from society and with Leo squandering what little money she had left, Silvia had tried to blackmail him into marriage and had been soundly thrashed. Who knows what steps a scorned and bitter woman might take? But if Silvia killed Leo, who tried to strangle her in her sleep?

Volcar couldn't run a fork into Leo, much less a spear, and surely Qus would have contrived for his master to meet with an accident when they were alone on the estate, if the issue over the crystal had become non-negotiable.

Like snowflakes in a blizzard, problems kept swirling around in Claudia's head. Passions ran high at the Villa Arcadia, higher than most, and in an isolated island community they were bound to be hotter, wilder, more likely to run out of control. Was that what happened? Had Little Things become Big Things until eventually they became Insurmountable Things? Could something which started out as nothing more than a slight *really* mutate into a grievance which could only be assuaged by full-blown tragedy?

Was the sad truth of it that Leo had died for the simple lack of a release valve?

Nowhere else in the world would Corinth's most famous son pick a fight with his patron over a dolphin. Then again, nowhere else would a crystal be considered capable of scaring a woman into miscarriage! But those were hardly motives for murder.

Yes, Nikias was Corinthian and Corinthians worship Apollo in the form of a dolphin and, yes, Leo intended to spear the poor devil because the locals churned up his land. But for gods' sake, no one commits murder over a dolphin! Yet how adamant Nikias had been, she reflected, that Leo should not destroy the creature, which brought such healing and happiness to the island. How far would the taciturn artist go to protect his god? Claudia looked at him, engaged in debate with Saunio over whether the best celadonite to create pale green came from the hills of northern Italy or from the island of Cyprus, and realized that if he had killed Leo, then Bulis's death must have also been deliberate. (The young apprentice would hardly have allowed the Empire's finest portrait painter to tie him up and half kill him and then fail to mention it.) Dolphins might be divine, but dammit, even the most devoted of Apollo's followers would not sacrifice two innocent lives along the way!

In any case, there was no point to killing Leo. He hadn't had a chance to spear the

349

wretched dolphin; Claudia had sabotaged the *Medea* to make sure of that. Which reminded her. In Leo's office when he was talking to Qus, hadn't he mentioned renaming his ship? What were the odds that she had previously been called the *Lydia*, but that wasn't the point. Leo said that someone had talked him into calling her the *Medea*, but why *Medea*? Medea was a murderess without conscience or compassion, who planned her crimes to the last meticulous detail, even down to the dismembering of her own brother and children. Who in their right mind would suggest naming a ship after that treacherous bitch?

'Would someone mind giving me a hand getting this old buzzard to bed?' Magnus asked, indicating Volcar, who had fallen asleep on his shoulder.

'Here, I'll take him.' When Jason scooped the frail old frame into his arms, Volcar didn't even stir.

Sipping her fine, vintage red, Claudia watched Jason convey his burden along the marble portico. No directions required. The crafty sonofabitch knew exactly which was Volcar's bedroom. *Just like he'd known which was Claudia's on the night of the fire*. It had been too dark and too smoky to identify the tussling figures on the granary steps, but it was Geta who had locked her in the bear hug, and Jason who had carried her back to bed. Cinnamon. She had smelled it just before Geta knocked her senseless. *Not you again,* Jason had said when he found her locked and

350

tied in the shepherd's hut. *Not you again.*

Leo might not have been Mr Popular when he died, but it takes a certain mentality to kill so barbarically. Hatred on an unimaginable scale, for instance. *Or the warrior son of an Amazon, for whom human suffering has a different meaning?*

As the Scythian returned and topped up his goblet, she thought, why the Odyssey? Why hadn't the killer recreated scenes from Jason and the Argonauts, which Magnus had also depicted in graphic detail on the frieze? Jason. The single thread running through.

Jason and the *Argo*.

Jason and the *Moth*.

Jason and his lover, Medea.

Medea. Like a pall of smoke above a forest fire, Medea's legacy clung to this island. Stifling, claustrophobic, malignant, it impregnated every stone and rock face. There was no other word for it, she thought. Pure, unadulterated evil. And maybe that was the connection? Both Odysseus and Jason called in at Cressia. The Argonaut had simply been passing through with his treacherous lover, but Odysseus made this paradise island his home. For seven summers he shared the bed of Circe the enchantress, and nuts to the idea that he got lost on his way home from the Trojan War. Circe had supplied him with a navigational chart, for gods' sake! No, no, no. Homer might be happy to portray him as a swashbuckling adventurer, but popular opinion had always had Odysseus pegged as a pirate.

All of which leads back to this Jason.

The chive bread in Claudia's mouth turned to bile. Leo didn't die for the simple lack of a release valve, any more than Bulis's death was an accident and Silvia's narrow escape had been planned. The Odyssey had been recreated, because someone – someone here now – believes ancient heroic blood runs in their veins. Odysseus sired several sons with Circe, but let's not forget that Medea was Circe's niece. Medea. That was the key.

Jason, goddammit, hadn't collected his war scalp for one simple reason. In his twisted recreation of his ancestor's adventures, there was no room for Scythian customs. The Jason who killed Bulis, Leo and then tried for Silvia was living an Odyssean fantasy. What Claudia needed to establish, and fast, was Jason's connection with the Villa Arcadia.

Before the sonofabitch struck again.

Forty-Seven

Lying on his blanket in the alcove of his master's bedroom, Ajax snored. His ancient, callused paws twitched with pleasure as he raced once more across the open plains of his youth in pursuit of bristly boar and panting stags, bounding over streams and hurdling obstacles, leading the pack by a mile.

In his dreams, his keen nose scented spoor, but in Volcar's bedroom, he didn't even pick up the draught when the door swung quietly open on its hinges. Deaf old ears failed to catch the sound of conversation and laughter out on the terrace, much less soft footfalls on the newly laid mosaic.

Ears flapping in the wind of his dreams, Ajax closed the distance on his quarry, unaware of the pillow being slid from underneath his master's head. So close, so close, Ajax could smell the stag's fear now and, whimpering with pleasure in his sleep, knew nothing of the pillow pressed down on the wizened walnut face.

Of the moment when the thin chest ceased to heave.

Of the pillow replaced under the lolling head.

Of the door closing quietly once again.

The demon rubbed its hands. How exciting, how thrilling, to be in a position where it could exert this amazing power over human life. To slip away in full view of everyone. To stand over someone while they sleep. To then decide whether that person should rise to greet another dawn – or be sent to meet his ancestors in the Kingdom of Decay. Inspirational. Truly inspirational. Resuming its place at the dinner table, the demon rejoiced. Who among these people had even the faintest inkling that one old man had begun his watery journey across the River of Lamentation? Hell, it

353

wouldn't mind betting that even old Volcar wasn't yet aware of what had happened to him!

Oh, yes, truly inspirational, this power to decide who should live and who should die. But Volcar had been merely a diversion. A small sport taken on the spur of the moment, one which could be repeated, admittedly, but then forgotten. For memories that lingered, however, the demon had planned an entertainment which would make Leo's torment look as quick as a throat being slit. As the candied fruits were brought out, along with nuts and sweet honey cakes laced with wine, the demon set its mind to imagining the torture and agony to be faced by its next victim. Genius. Sheer bloody genius! Medea and her aunt would be so proud of the way their skills had been honed. Indeed, as a celebration of its illustrious female ancestry, the demon decided there and then to bring its schedule forward.

What a thoroughly enjoyable party this was turning out to be!

Forty-Eight

With Qus keeping a watchful eye on Lydia, the mistress he'd never stopped serving in his heart, Claudia felt there was no better time to investigate the crystal which had been such a bone of contention between the big Ethiopian and his master.

354

'Curiosity killed the cat,' she whispered to Drusilla as she slipped behind the laurels, but the blue-eyed, cross-eyed, dark Egyptian feline had no interest in proverbs. Now that the mice had been driven from their nests beneath the grain store by the fire, Drusilla felt it incumbent upon her to make their short lives even more miserable. With one fluid movement, she slipped between Claudia's ankles to fuse with the shadows.

There was no sound from the slave quarters save that of creaking bedsteads, breaking wind and snoring. Hardly surprising. Those who weren't required in the kitchens tonight would be rising at the first hint of dawn. On the mainland, farmhands would be busy turning straw into haystacks and bringing in the end of the harvest. Cressian soil was too thin for wheat, but there were still thistles and goose grass to weed out of the vegetable crops, vines to be watered, animals tended and figs to be pollinated. Claudia tiptoed silently past the snoozing porter to the bailiff's quarters, plucking a torch from the wall along the way. I ask you. What could possibly be so sinister about a bit of glass that it's considered capable of bringing on a miscarriage in a healthy young wom—

'Janus bloody Croesus!'

The torch fell from her hand. Holy Mother of Mars, the Fiend must stand six feet eight! Black like Qus, the same five parallel tribal lines stood out bone-white on its forehead. The Fiend was leaning against the wall before

355

a meal of apples, wine and honey-roasted crispy duck. Its blue eyes bulged in delight at its glamorous midnight caller, and its teeth bared in a bloodcurdling smile.

'Don't move,' Claudia said. At least, she hoped she said. Her teeth seemed to have a mind of their own. 'You just stay where the hell you are. Don't come any closer.'

'Speak to him firmly enough,' an amused baritone suggested in her ear, 'and he does exactly what you tell him.'

Orbilio. Thank Jupiter! Because if Qus has been hiding this ... this *thing* in his quarters, there had to be a bloody good reason. 'This must be the man who killed Leo,' she hissed under her breath.

'Who? Qus's brother?'

'I don't care if he's the bloody Emperor. He found out that Leo wanted him out and he killed him out of revenge. Now if I'm wrong,' she said, 'I'll be the first to make it up to the boy, I swear. But to be on the safe side, Orbilio, I suggest you clap him in irons.'

'You don't mind if I put the fire out first?' Orbilio picked up the fallen torch and proceeded to stamp out the flames, which were now licking their way up the cotton coverlet on the bed. And still the Fiend kept on grinning.

'Orbilio!'

'Don't worry. You're safe enough with Qus's brother,' he said, and it was impossible for him to contain his laughter any longer. 'He's dead.' He crossed the room and held up the

356

torch. 'In fact, he's been that way for over three months.'

'D-dead?' She peered at the creature standing against the far wall. *Dead?*

Under the light, she could see that the smile was a death rictus, drawing his lips back over his brilliant white teeth, and that the eyes, those bulging delighted eyes, were coloured glass inlaid in empty sockets.

'The rest of him, though.' I mean, those *hands*.

'The muscular demeanour is down to padding inside his clothes,' Orbilio explained. 'And the lifelike appearance owes much to skilful body paint, but much of it's due to Ethiopian embalming techniques.'

The Egyptians didn't have the monopoly on corpse preservation, then. 'What about the meal?'

'I rather suspect that's Qus's supper,' he said, helping himself to a sliver of duck. 'The custom, you see, is for the next of kin to keep the body in their house for a year before it can be buried, head facing east.'

All right, all right, body paint, glass, and padding I understand. But — 'What's keeping him upright?'

'This.' Orbilio's knuckles rapped against something Claudia could not see.

She peered closer, and as she did so, she realized that there was a sheen around Qus's brother. Glass? Surely not? Glass is too opaque, too reflective. Then, of course, she understood. 'Crystal!'

The body had been sealed inside a tube of hollowed out crystal from the Ethiopian mines. Which, when placed against a white wall, became ... invisible! Leo had been taking no chances when he insisted on a no-shock rule for his new bride. The question was, did this change one damn thing?

Saunio was standing in the doorway of the atrium gazing into space as flutes and lyres made sweet music on the terrace. Grey faced and hollow-eyed, the maestro had pushed himself to the edge of his physical limits, and even though he had still managed to create the definitive Judgement of Paris, it was about time, Claudia thought, that someone told him that grief cannot be expunged in work. That he can run all he likes, but he can't hide, that fate catches up with everyone in the end.

Silently, she mounted the steps. Carefully positioned oil lamps illuminated the gold leaf coating the capitals of the soaring marble columns. Sweet resins burning in wall-mounted bronze braziers filled the air with mysterious, exotic scent, and a fountain splashed and chattered, its silvery arc reflected a thousand flickering times in the mirrors.

'You must have loved Bulis very much,' she said quietly.

Surprised, Saunio spun round to face her. 'You have no idea.'

Oh, but I do, maestro, I do. *If the eye can be led, so can the mind.* The art of illusion is

358

everything, and that was what he had been trying to tell her, both here in the atrium and the following night in the garden, the night the *Soskia* dropped anchor below the cliffs. It had struck a chord with her then that, of all people, it was Saunio who had concerned himself with the welfare of the rose-grower's daughter. *Emotions are not an architect's plans on a page. They are not lines to be rubbed out, edited, and redrawn.* Of course not. He worried for a thirteen-year-old girl in the way only a parent can worry. Hence his raising the question of heirs. Do you agree, he had asked, that a man is entitled to take whatever action he deems necessary when it comes to the question of sons?

'You wanted people to think he was your lover, when in fact Bulis was your own son.'

Saunio wouldn't compromise his monumental reputation by leaving behind a trail of gossip about bloodthirsty rituals and unnatural practices, so why hadn't he quashed it? Why travel with an inflated entourage? Why this dogged insistence that the artists kept themselves to themselves? *Do you agree a man is entitled to take whatever action he deems necessary when it comes to the question of sons?* That had sod all to do with Leo's obsession for heirs. Saunio couldn't give a toss about Leo. No, there was only one reason why a man of his standing would allow the rumours to persist. He was covering up. And who but a son was precious enough for him to lay his international reputation on the line? Bereft and bereaved, he had been on the brink of confiding the long line of pay-offs and compensation packages that night in the garden.

'No young boy was safe,' Saunio said sadly. 'The scandal made my wife kill herself from the shame. But,' he let out a shuddering sigh, 'Bulis was my son, my own flesh and blood, he was all I had left in the world. Better, I think, that I was around to control him than let him run wild.'

Claudia swallowed. Suddenly Saunio was no longer such a repulsive little worm. Not such a pretentious bore who shaved his lips, dyed his hair and curled his silly beard. He was just one more lost and lonely father. In an effort to control a corrupt, debauched son, Saunio had created a package – an illusion – of pompous homosexuality combined with an inflated artistic temperament. Bulis might have suffered horribly, Claudia thought sadly, but the truth was, he was no loss to the world.

'You knew straight away that he'd died chained, like Odysseus, to the mast, didn't you?'

That was where he had been standing that night in the portico. Not eavesdropping on her conversation with Volcar. Lost in his grief over his only son's murder.

Saunio nodded. 'Somebody killed my boy, because he had listened to the call of the Sirens and followed his bestial nature as a result. But that doesn't make it right, my lovely. It doesn't make it right at all.'

'Bulis wasn't killed out of revenge,' Claudia

360

told him, and goddammit there was a lump in her throat. 'Neither was Leo.'

How wide were the ripples from death. Bulis's light might have been snuffed, but the real victim of the tragedy that night had been Saunio, just as Silvia's children would have suffered had her throat been crushed as had been intended. Ditto, Leo. Think of all those people whose debts could no longer be repaid. Men such as Volcar, who had been left destitute in his old age. And not simply material deprivation. Lydia might be pregnant, but she would never know how much Leo, in his silly distorted vision, had loved her. As a result of his murder, his legacy to her was the coldness inside her heart, but worse was to come. In killing Leo, the lives of hundreds of slaves had been thrown into jeopardy. Lydia would not be remaining here on Cressia. When the estate was sold, the chances were, and whatever undertaking they might give, that the new owners were more likely to bring their own people in, selling the existing slaves on for profit. Severing hundreds of men, women and children not just from their family and friends, but from the land they'd grown up in.

Jason must not get away with this. He must be stopped before any more lives could be destroyed. Which meant she had to devise a trap.

How?

Claudia's life had not been in danger away from this island. It was here, on the paradise

361

island of Cressia, that the Odyssey had to be recreated in its heroic splendour. This wasn't a killer who disassociated himself from his crimes. He *revelled* in them. Think slow hand-clap. Think bow. Think howling wolf heads. Bottom line, Jason was a compulsive show-man. He thrived on an audience. He needed people to know that his ancestral blood had empowered him, how superior he was to the human race. With the palace of the Enchant-tress long fallen into the ground, the Villa Arcadia had become his amphitheatre. This was where his drama had to be enacted. This was where the trap had to be set. All that needed to be established was what – or who – should be the bait. Why did Claudia think it would be her?

The steward called the second hour, but there was no indication of the party breaking up. People came, people went, drifting back and forth, laughing, joking, their spirits as high as the star-studded night sky as they applauded the dancing girls and acrobats, the singers and the jugglers. Claudia had been gone longer than most, Orbilio noticed, but he wasn't remotely worried. Now that he'd proved conclusively to her that their home-grown psychopath wasn't Jason, she wouldn't be so stupid as to wander far, especially without her diligent Gaul. In fact, he imagined her right now beating old Volcar hands down at dice in his bedroom, or slipping titbits to Drusilla down in the kitchens.

'Nikias,' he said cheerfully. 'Why don't you give us another Corinthian love song?'

Apart from a clutch of playful kittens, the stables were utterly silent. No flies buzzed round the dungheap. None of the horses had so much as snickered when Claudia eased open the heavy, wide door. She had desperately needed a place where objectivity could function away from the intoxicating drag of the villa. Somewhere quiet, and nothing fitted the bill like the stables. The estate dogs had been rounded up and kennelled long ago, and if the nightwatchmen had been making their rounds, Claudia hadn't seen them. The perfect place to be alone with one's thoughts. Settling herself on a hay bale, she'd drawn her knees up to her chin and watched dust motes dance in the moonbeams as she considered various traps and vicarious baits. With a soft whoosh, a bat darted between the thick wooden beams in search of moths and, three stalls along, a sleeping hoof gently nudged the partition.

Horses.

All this started with horses. Right from the moment on the Field of Mars in Rome, when Claudia Seferius fed a sedative to a four-year-old mare belonging to a certain Hylas the Greek. That one simple action had set a trail in motion. First, it brought her into contact with a member of the Security Police, who in turn talked his cousin into suckering her out here to Cressia.

Bloody nags. Can't get away from them. Even Jason chose the stables to deliver his second war spear. Now Shamshi's lisping whisper echoed in her head. *Beware the Trojan Horse.* Bloody stinking rotten nags.

Like a shattered urn, the pieces were there, Claudia thought. They just weren't in the right shape and goddammit she wished she hadn't partaken so freely of Leo's cellar tonight! Sitting on the hay bale, her eyelids grew heavy. Pictures and sounds merged together. *Give back what is mine.* Silvia's three small boys. Geta and his Scythian tattoos. In a haze of wine, the blue menagerie swam before her: bulls, water snakes, lynx. Then there was the Amazon priestess who served the moon. The sun god who demanded human sacrifice. Gilded skulls. Wolf heads. Breasts. Something to do with big breasts.

Claudia jerked awake. Of course. Breasts. Clio could never have fitted into that tight, white shirt on board the *Soskia*. Her curvaceous hips could never have squeezed into those pantaloons, which meant Clio was no pirate's moll. Jason might have introduced her to Leo, but it must have been purely as a recommendation. No, wait. Claudia tried to rub the sleep out of her eyes and failed miserably. Her throat was too dry to swallow and she knew she should be in bed, but dammit, the game had to stop now. She tried to concentrate. Why should Jason go around recommending harpists to Leo? Why, for that matter, would Jason have *any* contact with

Leo? Shoot, that vintage was strong. Exhausted from play, the stable kittens had fallen asleep in a furry, communal heap. A rat scuttled across the open doorway.

What she needed to clear the cobwebs from her head was a good walk. The moon was waning but it was still full, the sky clear, she should have no trouble locating the hilltop cottage in the dark. Leaving in a hurry as she had, Clio would have had no time to pack. Maybe the answer lay there? *Give back what is mine.* Because what did Leo owe Jason, if not money?

But the vintage was strong and Claudia's feet felt like they'd been strapped into lead, instead of light, leather sandals. Her gown weighed a ton; every bone resisted the orders despatched from her brain. *As though Medea's evil was crushing her spirit as well as her movements ...* What a mix, island superstition and drink! But as she approached the tiny stone cottage, with its piles of whitethorn and heaps of slimy innards being pulled apart by scavengers scuffling away at the sound of her footsteps, the hairs on the back of her neck started to prickle.

The door creaked as she pushed it open, flooding the single room with silvery moonlight. She sniffed. The cottage smelled of burning. Roast meat. Recently, too. From the corner she heard the whimpering of some poor injured animal. It was too dark to make out what kind of creature or where it was hiding, but if the animal was in pain, it would show no mercy to anyone it perceived as a threat. The stiletto slipped from the strap on her calf as she stepped across the stone threshold. The whimpering grew louder.

'Help,' it rasped. 'Please.'

The knife clenched in Claudia's hand. 'Who's there?'

'Help ... me.'

As her eyes adjusted to the darkness, they made out a bed, and on the bed something which had once been human. Except now there was not a shred of skin left which wasn't blackened or raw.

'*Clio.*' The long black hair was burned away. What few wisps remained were welded to the remnants of her skin in treacly strands. 'Clio, listen to me. Don't be frightened.' Sweet Janus, there was nothing left of her. 'I'm going for help.'

'Don't ... leave.'

'I won't be gone long.' Her head was spinning with the shock. She wondered whether she would make it out of the cottage before she was sick. 'You'll be fine, Clio, I promise.'

As she backed away from the twitching creature on the bed, the moon slipped behind a cloud, plunging the cottage into blackness.

'You are foolish to make such a promise,' a husky voice whispered. What cloud? The night was clear. 'Clio is dying.'

Oh, shit. Moonlight had been blocked by the closing of the door.

'You'll be in Hades before her.' Claudia reached for the stiletto. Then remembered she'd dropped it when she ran to help Clio. 'Three days and three nights will pass before she succumbs to her injuries.' The voice purred. 'Without balm to soothe the burns. Without poppy juice to ease the pain.'

Clio, Clio, why did you have to come back? Claudia inched backwards. Why the hell hadn't she rammed that stiletto into his chest when she had the chance? 'You sick bastard.'

'Delirious only with pleasure. Talking Clio into disembarking was a master stroke, don't you think?'

Claudia's toe probed the floor. With the door shut, everything was fuzzy and the steel cast no reflection in the dark. She knew she had just one chance before he jumped her. She had to make it first time.

'As I explained to Clio, although I'm not sure she could hear me through her screams, when Odysseus visited his ancestors in the Kingdom of Decay, he had to first navigate the River of Flaming Fire.'

Stall. Stall for time, while her feet located their deadly steel target. 'Kill me if you must, but for heaven's sake do it quickly, don't bore me to death.'

Yet even as he laughed in the darkness, a jolt of terror shot through her. This wasn't wine making her head thick. This wasn't shock making her limbs leaden and disorientating her co-ordination. *Sweet Jupiter, she had been drugged.* You bastard, Jason. You dirty, rotten conniving sonofabitch, I even took the goblet from your hand while you continued to charm the pants off us as we debated the Quest for the Golden Fleece. Nikias's opinion was that it would have been a raid along the Black Sea to break the Scythian monopoly on trade. Llagos, of course, being local born and bred insisted it was a delegation of amber merchants. But you. You insisted, it was the stolen death cloak of a Scythian king, without which his soul was unable to rest. In other words, a quest to return the embodiment of the king's spirit, the way your own soul would be doomed without sons to carry the bull tattoo on their chests.

And I fell for it. Even though I had Junius standing closer than your own shadow, to ensure you could cause no more harm!

'Your knees are buckling, Claudia. You cannot stand up, no matter how hard you try.'

I can! I can stand up. And when I do, I'll kill you, you bastard. *If only I could find that bloody knife.*

'Circe plied her victims with moly. It made them forget, but that is not what I have planned for you, Claudia. Your fate is to remember.'

'Go to hell,' she said, but her voice was slurred.

'I've been there,' he said. 'It's a grey place, without power, without control, without domination. Hell is a place to which I can no longer return.'

But Claudia could no longer hear the boasts of the demon. The drug had sucked her too deep into oblivion. Although in the moment before it claimed her totally, she recalled the doctored goblet of wine being passed to Jason by a thinner, much smaller hand.

Forty-Nine

Life for the demon had never been sweeter. For several days now, it had been hard at work constructing a box. Not personally constructing, of course. This was the product of a master carpenter's skill, but the design had been the demon's, and tell me, who could deny the box was beautiful?

It had been planed until it was silky soft to the touch and a glass panel had been set into the lid. The glass was so thick as to be almost obscure, but it was adequate for the purpose intended.

'Looks more like a blooming coffin,' the carpenter had joked when he and his boy had delivered it.

The demon had forced a smile, but the box was no laughing matter. The approximate height, depth and breadth of a woman, there were a few modifications to be made before it could be put into use. The demon hadn't completed them all, but, inspired by Clio and Volcar, it had decided to bring its schedule forward. This would be a day to remember, would it not!

'Beware of Greeks bearing gifts,' the demon whispered.

As it closed the lid over Claudia.

Fifty

Claudia's eyelids fluttered open. Everything was dark, pitch black, and she smelled wood. Croesus, where was she? Who was she? What was she doing? More importantly, how much had she drunk? She tried to think back, but memory was a blank, as dark as the void she was trapped in, and when she tried to move, it was as though Medusa had turned her body to stone. After a few minutes, she gave up the unequal struggle and listened. The only sound she could hear was the hammering inside her skull. Oh, lord. That much wine. Her mouth was dry, her tongue way too big, furred, and there was a tickle of sawdust at the back of her throat. She lay helpless, motionless, unable to swallow and too damn weary to care. Hangovers are hangovers. They wear off eventually. Go to sleep.

But as pictures and sounds had swirled through her brain as the narcotic had begun to take effect, so they did as the drug wore off. The illustrations were graphic. Shipwreck. Bodies in the water. Parts of bodies. Blood.

370

She heard screaming, pleading, bubbles from the lips of drowning men, saw Geta's stiffening, discoloured corpse bloating up on Jason's broad shoulders, smelled decay...

When she came to the next time, the hangover was no less of a fog, but at least the visions were less of a nightmare. Through the mist, familiar shapes twisted and formed. Nanaï appeared, barefoot in a threadbare cotton tunic, singing a lullaby to the latest addition to the clan. Then rags metamorphosed into red leather boots into which pantaloons had been tucked, and there was gold glittering at his waist and from the willow-leaf torque round his neck. Like a spectator at the arena, Claudia watched the replay of Jason's slow handclap on the prow of his warship, his long, low, insolent bow. Then *pooof!* Snowdrop's rabbit eyes took his place. *Kids, who'd have 'em?* Matted curls shook sadly, and in her grubby fist she clutched a bunch of wilting marigolds. *Thirteen or fourteen, you lose count.* But before Claudia could reach out to the knobby little scrap, the kaleidoscope turned and her thoughts cartwheeled helplessly with it. To rebel fires along the Liburnian coast, dolphins playing, children squealing, and Silvia's immaculate honey-coloured ringlets. *You have heard about the pirate down in the cove?* Of course the Ice Queen had heard. *He's just taunting us.* Goats clip-clopped through Claudia's confused brain, their bells tinkling on the dry, stony, thyme-scented hills, while white-headed vultures wheeled above cliffs which plunged hundreds of feet into a turquoise blue ocean. How she longed to swim in its warm, limpid waters, but the vision distorted again, and plunging cliffs became soaring columns in an atrium of marble and gold. *The future lies in illusion*. Illusion. Yes. Saunio had been talking about art and how he'd tried to hide his son's depravity. But just as Leo's atrium was an illusion of space, so was the man who had commissioned it. A face swam before her. It had a cleft in its chin and a spear in its gut, and it was calling out something she couldn't hear. A younger face pushed it aside. Same dark, wavy hair as his cousin, the face smelled of sandalwood, but before she could ask the new face why it mattered a damn to her who the hell Orbilio married, the kaleidoscope swirled again and she was swept with it. Trying to make sense of a mishmash of bronze wolf heads and bull tattoos, a cloak of long, black hair and voluptuous breasts. And in her hungover hell, Claudia thought, dammit, whichever way you look at it, there's no escaping the breasts.

When she awoke next time, much of the fog had cleared, although the night had turned hotter, because she was sweating and the air seemed a lot thinner. Where was she? But memory had become sludge in a ditch. When stirred, things you'd rather not see come to the surface. Things such as those fires along the Liburnian coast. Now she realized what was so odd. It's because that's all they were.

Fires. A timber yard up in smoke here, a warehouse there, but where was the bloodfest when the *Soskia* came to town? When the little *Moth* fluttered off, how many homes had been ransacked and looted? How many women raped, how much livestock carried off, how many poor unfortunates rounded up to be sold on as slaves? All that had taken place further south – on the islands and around the coast of Dalmatia. Not up round the Liburnian Gulf.

Jason had been merely playing at pirate. As a means of providing himself with a ship and a crew, he'd convinced Azan of his devotion to the cause, losing no sleep when the *Moth* was dashed to a pulp. Rapists, butchers, slave-traders, looters, her crew got what they deserved. But why should Jason have needed a ship in the first place? Come along now, pay attention! How else would a seafaring captain pass the time until he got back what was his?

'He's just taunting us,' Silvia had said. Us. Us. As in that pretentious royal "we" and Claudia would have smiled, if only her body would have allowed it. The breasts gave it away, of course. Tiny, perfect breasts that would be an ideal fit inside a crisp, white, cotton shirt tucked into black pantaloons. No wonder Jason had roared with laughter at the idea of the Immaculate One being labelled a pirate's moll. Ice might turn to fire then freeze again, but Silvia's sense of humour would never stretch that far! *Not you again*. It was Silvia he'd been wanting. Both times.

Give back what is mine.

Beads of sweat trickled down Claudia's neck and pooled in the hollow of her collarbones, and she found herself almost gasping for air in the darkness. But her thoughts were stuck on the treadmill. *Give back what is mine.* Silvia didn't know, of course. She wouldn't have had a clue that Jason had even made his demands, much less at the point of a war spear. That was Leo's secret weapon in his search for glory. He knew Jason was no more a pirate than he was! Same as he knew that, sooner or later, Jason would stop buggering around with notes impaled on pieces of parchment and tackle Silvia direct. In the meantime, however, he would milk the situation for all it was worth by creating the illusion that Jason was a dangerous adversary.

Was Jason really the type to piss about with coded warnings creeping closer every time, or (and Claudia would bet money on this) were there three splintered gouges in the atrium door where he'd delivered his message for everybody to see? It was Leo who'd planted the spears, first in the boat shed, then in the stables and finally in the bath-house door. Leo who set fire to his own grain store then despatched his trusted lieutenant for water in the sure and certain knowledge that Qus would find the evidence to bolster his master's claim that Jason was the arsonist.

Quite what went through Leo's mind when he discovered Bulis's body chained to the pillar, Claudia had no idea. That it came as a shock showed clearly, and maybe he had seen Jason at the villa that night and suspected that he was indeed responsible for the boy's murder. That would explain why he was so keen to get shot of Silvia. Her blowing the gaff on his felonious dealings with Clio would undoubtedly have helped book her passage on that merchantman, but Leo was more than capable of swatting problems like that aside. But by forcing his sister-in-law to leave, then Jason, by default, would have to follow. Pirate, murderer, marauder, call him what you will, but Leo was the chap who'd seen the dog off. The glory was his for the taking.

If he could, of course, Leo would have removed Jason's impaled message. Only since Silvia would have found out eventually, he'd probably planned to cover himself by telling her, with Qus as his witness, that he had only been trying to protect her. At the time of the fire, Claudia had thought it suspicious that he'd appeared on the scene fully dressed. The whole operation had smacked of a badly rehearsed theatrical drama, which is precisely what it had been. A cheap melodrama, staged for an audience of one.

His ex-wife.

With sisterly communication thin on the ground, why should Lydia question the character of the man Silvia had run off? All she'd know was the evidence laid before her ... so: cue the hero. Chasing after the *Soskia* in a blatantly unequal battle, what woman could fail to be impressed? Unfortunately, Leo had been too engrossed in his own self-importance and locked too deeply in his spiral of plans to notice that Lydia had slipped away from him. Even as he was drugging his own nightwatchmen and sacrificing the estate corn supply, he was creating an illusion out of another illusion. For had he but looked, he would have realized that Lydia didn't give an Arcadian fig for his safety. Her sole concern lay in the health and well-being of the treasure inside her womb.

How much of his grand scheme had Leo been about to confide that day in his office when Silvia walked in and interrupted what she thought was a kiss? How much history would have been rewritten, with Claudia in on the secret? Would she have allowed Leo to continue using Jason's children as pawns? Would she have allowed Silvia, for that matter, to persist in the same spiteful game? Would it have made one iota of difference?

Because *had* Orbilio come to the villa, instead of remaining in town, Leo *would* still be alive. It would just mean that, with his cousin under arrest, some other poor sod would have been skewered on the atrium door in his place – and who's to say one life is more important than another?

That was the enormity of the guilt Orbilio carried.

And the knowledge was like a vice round her heart.

But that was another time, another place. First, she must tackle this godawful hangover, and then she must find a way of extricating herself from that ridiculous doping fiasco. No wonder Orbilio scoffed at her offer of trading a pardon for a pirate! Since he knew exactly what Jason was about – wait. *How* did he know? How could Marcus Cornelius have had any idea about the man his cousin's sister-in-law had run off with? A couple of fires burning along the Liburnian coast was too much of a leap of faith to...

Well, I'll be damned. The answer had been staring her in the face all the time. With its big blue eyes and honey-coloured ringlets! Silvia had been ostracized from society because of a scandal, but who else had caused aristocratic sparks to fly when she eloped with a sea captain from Lusitania? *From* was the key. Marcus Cornelius never said he was born there. Just *from* Lusitania. The scandal would be seismic enough without adding a skull-guzzling, hide-stripping, scalp-mongering Scythian to the equation. Claudia realized there was something between Sylvia and Orbilio when he'd found her half-strangled on the bed: the tenderness with which he pulled up the sheet, the look on her face when it registered who had saved her. But calculation was Silvia's middle name. She might have been close to death, but she'd recognized the emotion in his face and stored it for later use. *There was a child, you know.* All other doors had closed in her face. She was desperate. *A boy.* Yes, indeed, Claudia thought. Except it wasn't Orbilio's.

For a moment, she felt again the crush of Jason's lips on hers beside the lake. Smelled cinnamon. *I don't kiss killers.* Oh, but he wasn't the only man who'd ever sent another soul to the land of his ancestors, was he? The Empire, especially Rome, was a dangerous place. Men were often required to kill in the course of their duties, so it wasn't that she didn't kiss killers. *It was that Jason's weren't the right lips.* The realization struck home like a slap. Because the right lips, she was certain, would taste, ever so faintly, of sandalwood – Shit! She really must give up the booze, if it put ideas like that in her head! It was making her sweat, too. You could wring this gown out, and the hot sultry air didn't help either. She could hardly breathe. O Bacchus, your servant quits.

Dreamlike, her thoughts drifted back to Jason. *Give back what is mine.* Bull tattoos. Spirits condemned to wander the earth for eternity, unless the clan emblem was carried forward on the chests of his heirs. How could she have been so blind, not to have put the pieces together before? What else would he have come all this way for – if not his sons? That was Jason's quest. To take the three boys he'd had by the Ice Queen to Scythia, where they could be raised in the place that was their spiritual home and receive guidance in their Scythian heritage. Wide awake now, Claudia struggled to sit up, but her muscles would still not obey her. Vaguely she remembered the party, the music, the dancing, with everyone coming and going, and vaguely she remembered the wine flowing freely. But come on, she'd drunk more than this in the past and not felt so ghastly. If only she could remember what had happened afterwards ... where she was now ... Oh, lord, if only her head would stop throbbing!

But lethargy, however luxurious, would not acquaint Jason with what Silvia had done with his sons. Only Claudia could do that. And she must tell Orbilio that the child wasn't his. Because she had seen him. The Little Bustard, bruising her foot with his imaginary chariot. Right age, right colour hair, right colour grey eyes. A miniature version of his father. She'd seen the twins, too. In the one place no one would think of looking, among thirteen or fourteen others. *You lose count.* Don't you just! Nanaï was no spectre at tonight's feast. No social outcast being given patronage by the self-appointed patrician hostess. Nanaï had been invited so that Silvia might receive a progress report on her boys without arousing Jason's suspicion.

Leo had known, of course. That was why he'd been so desperate to throw Nanaï out. Yes, he'd wanted to terminate his association. Handouts had been fine at the beginning, only Nanaï abused his charity to the point where the forge had become dirty, unhygienic, in a bad state of repair and she blamed him for being a bad landlord. But then Nanaï wanted everyone to do everything for her.

379

She had no interest in maintenance, budgeting, management, abdicating responsibility for the older children to Snowdrop, because all she wanted was to wallow in the unconditional love of the babies. Let's face it, who else could love a woman who was waspish, self-centred and deeply embittered? True, her selfishness helped Snowdrop and her rag-tag siblings along the way, but what future did they have now that orphan numbers had passed the point where Nanaï's budget could cope?

Even without knowing the reason for his shortfall in grapes, Leo was wise to be shot of her. The sooner she faced reality and stood on her own two feet, the better for all concerned, but there was no great hurry. Leo disapproved of Lydia's association with the woman, of course. The constant dripping of poison into her ear. And it wouldn't suit his new order, Leoville, to have a slum on his doorstep. But it was the arrival of Silvia's sons that had prompted drastic action. If Nanaï knew who the father was, as she surely must, then it was only a question of time before she confided in Lydia. Exit the hero, before he'd even stepped on to the stage!

So it was only right that Jason should be told where to find his sons. He had been separated from them for long enough and god knows, so had his mother. Claudia struggled to sit up. It had to end, this game of using her children as pawns. Silvia could bloody well negotiate like everyone else!

Except Claudia's body still wouldn't respond and dammit it was getting too bloody hot, her clothes were drenched, and she was sucking in air in bloody great gulps.

Then she realized.

Her arms and legs weren't prisoner to some terrible hangover. These were ropes binding her tight, and the reason it was so dark was terrifying simple. Claudia Seferius had been locked in a coffin and buried alive.

The air was running out fast.

The demon yawned. The hour was late and sufficient energy had been invested in witticisms and observations at this excellent party to substantiate an alibi.

Drugs were notoriously difficult to judge, of course, but the demon had calculated the dosage carefully and gauged at least an hour's worth of air inside the box. By its reckoning, the full effects of the soporific would have worn off around two quarters of the hour ago, leaving two quarters of unendurable torture.

Medea's blood ran strong in the demon's veins, and it had vowed to give her as much homage as it possibly could. Talking Leo into changing the name of his boat had been a good start. Which was why Leo had had to die before he could besmirch the memory of the demon's illustrious ancestor by changing it back.

The demon made its excuses and slipped silently into the night.

My, my. It rubbed its hands. With Volcar safely across the River Styx, Clio another three days in

381

agonizing limbo and *an occupant for the box, what a marvellous day this had been.*

There was no air left. Only an immense pressure inside her lungs, bursting, heaving, choking, implacable. Darkness turned to red. It tore at her eyeballs. Ripped at her heart. Clawed her liver. Claudia prayed. She prayed to live, to die, no, to live. Please Jupiter, don't let it end like this, I'm not ready. Her throat arched backwards, gurgling frantically to catch the last few drops of air that remained in the coffin.

Not yet. Not yet. Dear Juno, I've hardly lived. Please, not yet.

But the pressure grew stronger, and in a relentless volley of blistering gasps, Claudia's lungs expelled her life force. You don't understand. I'm not ready to meet my mother. I don't want to see her. I don't want to know why she slit her wrists without leaving a note for her only child. I don't want to hear why she could not say goodbye, or that she was sorry. Or that she had never loved me.

The light told Claudia she had no choice in the matter. Give up the fight, said the light. Come with me. And the light was faint, a dull yellow glow, but then it grew brighter and brighter, until— Fresh air blasted her face. Thank you, thank you, you gods on Olympus. Thank you so much. The light was not that of the Ferryman rowing across, but that of a common or garden oil lamp. She was saved.

Greedily, Claudia sucked in the clean, wholesome air. And with it the scent of the demon.

Fifty-One

Lamp held high, the demon gazed down on its handiwork. Perfect. The ligatures around the victim's neck, wrists and ankles had chafed the skin raw. Blood oozed in thick red dribbles from the leather straps that bound her and dreamily the demon wondered what it would be like to lick one. To taste her blood on the tip of its tongue. The demon recoiled. Disgusting idea! Ugh! Ghoulish. Vile. Worse than necrophilia!

It watched, fascinated, as its victim's wheezing lungs gasped to fill up with air. It reminded the demon of a salmon thrashing and writhing on the river bank. Drowning in air. At first, the gasps came in short, shallow bursts. Then they juddered and shuddered as they returned to normality, and the salmon's hair was wringing with sweat. Her eyes, unfocused still, were bloodshot. The demon hadn't expected that. An unexpected bonus, if ever there was one. Just like with Clio. Some of the effects there had been particularly stimulating in their unexpectedness and their—

'Thought – no one would – come.' Claudia's strangled voice startled the demon out of its reverie. 'Thought – I'd been – buried alive.'

Buried alive? Good gracious, where was the pleasure in that? Actually, there was quite a lot of pleasure in that – but there was even more pleasure in watching them suffer. Bringing them to the brink again and again and again. And, thanks to the genius touch of the glass panel, this was a show the demon could follow at the closest of quarters.

'Untie me.' Good. Her senses were slowly returning. 'I'm strapped in.'

'The best thing about this piece of equipment,' the demon crooned, 'is its capacity for multiple usage.'

It leaned forward to drink in her terror as understanding finally dawned. Fear, the demon decided, made her even more beautiful.

'I plan to visit in Medea's footsteps,' it confided. Claudia's eyes were bulging with horror. Beautiful eyes, terrified eyes, with long, sweat-soaked lashes. 'Corinth, for example. A wonderful city, full of excitement.' A veritable mine waiting to be tapped. 'Athens, perhaps. Ithaca, definitely. Rome, though, is where I shall settle.'

Home to the homeless, succour to the sick, comfort to the companionless, this was a city where the demon could live out its ancestral fantasies without arousing suspicion. It laughed softly. Everyone trusts a priest!

'Leo trusted me,' Llagos whispered. 'Enough to show me the Scythian war spear. Enough to explain the significance of its feathers and carvings. Enough, even, to let me hold it.'

'Enough to play act with him.'

Llagos was surprised by her perceptiveness. This

*would be more satisfying than he had imagined.
A woman who* **understands**. *Days could pass, he
mused, maybe weeks, bringing her to the brink
and throwing her back. He could toy with her like
a ball.*

*'Yes, indeed,' he said. 'Dear Leo. He was
laughing, even as the bronze point buried itself in
his flesh.* Squelch.*'*

*The demon delighted at the heave of Claudia's
stomach. Should he elaborate on Leo's agonizing
linger in full consciousness, the pattern the blood
made on the threshold, the things he'd told Leo
about his whoring ex-wife? There was no hurry.
Maybe tomorrow, maybe the next day he could
share his reminiscences over that delicious
brutality.*

*'Bulis trusted me, too, but in a rather different
way.'*

*One more perversion in which to experiment,
and that had been some erection the boy had had,
Llagos thought enviously, as he'd fastened the
chains. He'd learned a lot from Bulis, however.
He'd learned that killing wasn't the food that
sustained his inner self, it was power and control
that kept it alive. A trick he had been employing
for some time with Clio. Clio had trusted him, too,
his being a priest. Short, thin and clumsy, with his
sticky-out teeth, no one took Llagos seriously. It
was an image he'd cultivated over the years, until
he had been spinning Clio's trust like wool on a
spindle. Reducing her to caressing her own naked
body for the sake of a few silver coins had been
just the start. Llagos had planned a lengthy
process of further physical degradations, until the*

385

moment he saw her talking to Marcus. Disaster!
Clio was his own special toy, a pet to push and
pull at his whim. He could not let her sail away.
Not after he had invested so much.

'I created the vampire myth,' he told Claudia. 'It
was me, *who kept the old traditions alive on this*
island. Me, *who told the islanders not to follow*
false Roman gods.'

'Because you want them to serve the old ways
like you do, you deviant sonofabitch.'

'Claudia, Claudia, calm yourself.' He stroked
her cheek with his thumb. 'I told you before.
Bindus, Poseidon, Neptune, it doesn't matter by
what name one invokes the God of the Sea, or
any of the gods for that matter. It merely suits my
purpose to divide the islanders from their
overlords.'

Dissent, anarchy and bloodthirsty legends were
all weapons in Llagos's armoury. He alone had
whipped up suspicions of Clio's lifestyle and
voluptuous beauty. Through their priest, the
islanders had been drip-fed tales of flesh-eating
monsters preying on their community, and he had
played his part to perfection the night he ran,
scared shitless as they believed, from the scream-
ing banshee.

'But you're married,' Claudia said. 'You have
children.'

'Four,' the priest nodded. 'Who will travel with
me. Perfect cover, you see.'

'Like your pidgin Latin.'

Better and better, Llagos thought. She was on
the same wavelength, this woman. He adjusted
his shoulders to their accustomed public droop, let

386

his chin hang a little. 'Iss better if everyones laugh at me,' he said, lapsing into his act. 'Thiss way I can moves around freely, and everyones trust me, you see.'

Thin fingers closed the lid once more over Claudia Seferius.

Outside, the first blackbird of the morning broke into song.

Fifty-Two

The stiletto hadn't fallen on to the floor as the woman Clio had seen with Leo's cousin on the gangplank had thought. When she'd realized the raw, twitching lump in the stone cottage on the hill had been human, the knife *had* fallen from her hand, but it landed on the mattress beside Clio.

Then Llagos arrived. Clio fought back the surge of terror, which gripped her now as violently as it had when his silhouette had first blocked out the sun as the woman went to fetch help. Through waves of pain and fear, Clio had been able to see what the woman could not, that Llagos had drugged her and followed her here. Two for the price of one, she'd thought bitterly. To her credit, the woman had wanted to fight. She'd backed up, inch by inch, towards the bed, feeling with her toe for the knife.

'Here,' Clio had rasped, but either the drug was too strong or her voice was too weak, because the woman didn't heed her. Then it was too late. The woman's legs had given way; she had collapsed in a heap. Stronger than he appeared, the priest had scooped her up and carried her out of the cottage, leaving his River of Fire victim screaming with pain and frustration.

How could the gods do this to her?

Llagos hadn't noticed the knife … but it didn't matter, because the knife was beyond her reach.

Or was it? Perhaps there was another way. Every time Clio strained against the chains, lightning bolts of agony wracked her body as the flesh from her wrist fell away. The bastard had burned her hands and feet first. Tied her down at the elbows and knees, then burned the flesh off her extremities before chaining those same terrible injuries to the bed. He wanted her to die in as much pain as he could possibly inflict, but just as a wild animal will gnaw off its own leg to free itself from a trap so Clio pulled at the irons now.

Twice she passed out from the pain, saw the white of her own bone through the blood. But each time she came to, she was an infinitesimal fraction closer to wriggling one apology for a hand free of its shackle.

Let me reach the knife before he returns.

Let me end this unendurable suffering.

With the woman in his arms, Llagos hadn't thought to close the door and now the light of a new dawn was flooding the cottage. Clio

388

could hear whitethroats and warblers, the croak of a sea raven, the mewing of squirrels, and tears pricked her eyes. The pond – the pond she had hated – would be a silver mirror by now, reflecting another perfect and cloudless sky. Frogs would croak in its margins. Deer would come down to drink, bringing their spindly, spotted fawns with them, just as deer would be drinking at the stream which fed her Liburnian village. Whitethroats and warblers would be singing there, too, and a lump formed in Clio's throat. They had laughed at her, the villagers, because she had been drawn to the harp. Even her own family had ridiculed the waste of a fine, strong, Liburnian wife. A waste of good childbearing hips.

'If you must play an instrument,' her father had growled, 'why does it have to be something so bloody highfalutin?'

How could you explain to a woodsman that, in the beauty of the strings, Clio had discovered her soul? The harp freed her spirit, left it unburdened by dependence or convention. She became one with her music. Equally, though, it left her with a sense of being apart, of not belonging. As the years passed and her success grew, so the urge to return to Liburnia had grown stronger. What stopped her was pride; the prospect of going home poor. Told you the harp were kind of no bleeding instrument, her father would snarl. Poor *and* barren, the women would sneer. Clio would be a pariah in her own village.

Unless, of course, she returned in style. The buggers would see her differently, then! Respect her for what she was, not what they thought she should be! The thread of fate began to unravel.

Men. All bloody bastards. They had put her in this position, the motherfuckers. Her father. Her brothers. Leo. Especially Leo, who'd cheated her out of her share, even though she'd taken the risks. The anger drained out of her, sucking self-pity with it. Because finally, of course, there was Llagos. The biggest bastard of all. Far from the buck-toothed, spitting buffoon he made out, Llagos had systematically stripped her of clothes, her dignity and her flesh. But there was one thing no man, even Llagos, could defile. Clio's spirit.

Outside, the first spear of sunlight pierced the sky, sending a shaft of brilliance across the earth floor like a gold fissure. Redstarts and chaffinches, she noticed, had joined the avian chorus.

Finally, the footsteps she had been waiting for. Only once before in her life had Clio prayed. It had been in this same cottage, when the islanders had crowded around and she had prayed to her falcon god to give her strength. She had felt the brush of his wings against her cheek then. Just as she felt them now.

Clio blocked her mind against the approaching footfalls, the shadow that blocked out the gold, the fingernails that raked her blistered skin.

Instead she drank in the song of the warblers, the gentle rasp of the crickets and imagined the vivid blue of the sea, the liquid eyes of the deer, the soft touch of her mother's hand on her hair. From somewhere else, far away, she heard the gentle plucking of strings on a harp.

'I am coming,' she said.

Fifty-Three

Sunshine was reflecting off the cloud concealing the peak of Sorcerer's Mountain on the Istrian mainland, turning it into a soft cap of baby hair. Fine and golden, wispy and innocent, it belied a horror, which had not been played out on the Isle of the Dawn in three and a half centuries.

Orbilio was the first across the threshold of Clio's hilltop cottage, Jason and the others hot on his heels. He hadn't slept. For the second time in less than a week, he had been scouring the villa and its outbuildings for a woman with more courage than sense, and this time it was he who turned on Junius, not the other way round. Why had he left her? he'd demanded to know. He was her bodyguard, it was his bloody job to watch over her! White-faced and stiff with shame the young

391

Gaul explained his orders. Goddammit, did that woman never listen to a damn word he said? Orbilio's fist punched into his open palm. He'd bloody told her it wasn't Jason behind the killings, proved the point several times over, but what does she do? Tells Junius to stick closer than a bud graft, because she's too damn stubborn to admit she was wrong!

Mother of Tarquin, if he's killed her.

Orbilio tore up every room, every shed, every store, but nothing. No sign of her anywhere. Someone had seen her near the stables, Qus said, and sure enough, there was an ivory hairpin stuck in a hay bale, but an ivory pin, goddammit, meant nothing. Orbilio clenched it in his fist until the blood oozed through his fingers and someone prised it out of his hand.

If she's dead.

Then one of the slaves said rumours were going round that the vampire had returned. Lights had been seen in the middle of the night in the stone cottage up on the hill. Orbilio's ears pricked up. Clio? Or did the answer lie in something more sinister?

The answer, it transpired, was both.

The pitiful creature that had once been a vibrant young woman with a cloak of black hair lay in a pool of blood on the mattress. The blood wasn't all hers. In his neck, where it had been twisted with a savagery which Marcus had rarely seen, even in battle, protruded the hilt of a thin-bladed stiletto. The neck into which it had been plunged belonged to the priest. His eyes and his mouth were open, as though caught by surprise, and he had been dead barely a few minutes. The blood hadn't even congealed. But the effort of stabbing him, of not letting go of the knife, had been too much for Clio. It had, Marcus thought as he closed her staring eyes, been a merciful release. His body started to tremble.

'Where's Claudia,' he rasped, grabbing Llagos by his thin shoulders. 'What have you done with her, you bastard?'

It was Jason who pulled him off. 'He's dead, Marcus. The priest can't give you answers.'

He knew that, of course. But if Llagos couldn't, who the hell could?

Strapped into her blackened oaken hell, Claudia experienced the first small fluttering of panic.

Once she realized that Llagos intended to torture her by suffocating her almost to, but not beyond, the point of death, she began to plan. In the hourly intervals during which she was trapped in the box, she could niggle away at the ligatures round her arms in the hope that she might be able to pull at least one hand free. One hand meant the other hand, meant the neck, meant the feet. It would take time, of course, but time was all she had. In fact, it was the only thing on her side.

Slowly, as it climbed above the hills, sunlight began to stream in through the glass panel in the lid. If only she could be sure that was responsible for the increase in temperature in here. She breathed slowly to conserve air, bracing herself for the moment when the gloating apparition appeared at the window, loathing herself for wanting to see it, but praying all the same, because with it came release, however short.

He was going to pay a call on Clio, he'd said, but Claudia knew that control was Llagos's stock in trade and that he would not submerse himself in one victim's torment at the expense of losing another. She waited, forcing herself to be calm. He would be back.

Her mind wandered. To a different place. A different time. Still black. The fire in the granary was raging. Two figures tussling on the stone steps leading up to it.

Act I. The stage props were already set in place. When the pirate ship dropped anchor, that was Leo's cue to drug his own nightwatchmen and pour oil around the grain store. Like any theatrical production, the principal character wouldn't know that the villain had seen him lugging jars of oil up from the cellar. Or that he intended to use those same props to his own unspeakable end by luring Bulis to the building while the soporific took effect.

Act II. Leo sets the first flame to the oil. The fire quickly takes a hold. The corn crackles. Bulis, gagged in all probability, struggles helplessly against his shackles.

Act III. Llagos enters, villain disguised as priest. 'Please let me pass,' he pleads, as the flames lick ever higher. 'I muss try put fire out.' Knowing damn well Leo would not allow him to enter the burning building, it was too dangerous, and besides, it was only grain.

Another badly scripted, badly acted drama.

Except it wasn't a theatrical production, was it? It was every bit as real as the coffin which held her prisoner.

Still no face appeared. No smirk to block the sunlight from the panel in the lid, and all the while the air grew thinner, the heat intensified, and the blood thundered in her ears. At this point, Claudia realized something had gone badly wrong.

Llagos wasn't coming back.

He had killed her, and buried her, and now he would never know where.
Spewing his fear over the path outside the cottage, a nightmare vision swam before Marcus of Claudia's body being dug up by foxes. It was the rasp of the crickets in the coarse grass, of course, but equally, it might have been the sound of their teeth crunching into her bones.

Death was too good for him. Clio meant well, but in killing Llagos she had denied Orbilio that most primeval right, the right of revenge.
All he could do was hope, and pray, that somewhere in the middle of this theatre of horrors, Claudia was still alive.

★ ★ ★

She was.

Just.

But the red mist was forming, and her throat had arched back, and her breath was shallow and rapid.

'Beware the Trojan Horse,' a voice lisped in the stillness of the dawn light outside Clio's cottage.

Orbilio wiped the bile from his mouth. 'Excuse me?'

In the early morning sunshine, the gold bands in Shamshi's ears glinted obscenely. 'It was the warning I gave to Claudia,' he said smugly. 'Beware the Trojan Horse.'

'So?' Orbilio had no time for the Persian's oily bragging.

'So.' Shamshi tapped the side of his hooked nose with a long, skinny finger. 'I think I might know where she is.'

Sandalwood. She could smell it. No, wait. She could taste it. On her lips, on her tongue, on every part of her, inside and out.

This is it, then. I'm dying.

I know this, because I feel I'm returning to consciousness, but I still can't breathe. And what does it feel like? Dear Diana, it feels wonderful! No longer afraid of the dark, of dying, of being alone, Claudia succumbed to the kiss of the Ferryman.

Except Charon didn't kiss his passengers.

She opened her eyes and found another pair staring straight into hers. Dark eyes. Misted

396

with something that couldn't possibly be tears. *I don't kiss killers*. But other men kill in the course of their duties. Just that Jason's were the wrong lips. The right lips, as she'd known all along, would taste ever so faintly of sandal—

'Wood.'

'The wooden horse. Yes.' Orbilio had turned into a frog. He was croaking. 'Odysseus broke the siege of Troy by smuggling men inside a horse fashioned from wood.'

'How...' long I have waited for this.

'How did we find you?' The lips drew slowly away from hers and she felt cheated. 'That was Shamshi. He noticed the box in the olive-oil cellar and put two and two together.' Orbilio knuckled something away from the corner of each eye. 'So I fancy you have Shamshi to thank for saving your life.'

Her? Fancy Shamshi? 'You,' she corrected.

Strong arms hoisted her out of the coffin. 'Don't try to talk, you're still very weak.'

No, you don't understand. I'm talking about you, you — 'Dope.'

Incredibly, he began to laugh. 'You're not still on about that, are you?'

What? She'd been paddling in the shallows of the River Styx, and he thinks all she was worried about was that business on the Field of Mars? But he was right. She was too weak to argue, and his arms around her felt good, and the sunshine was warm on her hair.

'You didn't honestly think you were in trouble?' He chuckled. His boots echoed on the stone cellar floor.

'Course not.' Orbilio, I will kill you for this.

'The thing is, until then, I'd had no angle with which to get at Hylas the Greek. You thoughtfully provided me with the ticket to nail the cheating bastard.'

Were her ears still in a coma? *Hylas?*

'Contrary to popular opinion, his winners owe less to training or breeding and more to the stimulants he slips his horses.' He navigated a careful path through the terracotta forest, the tangy smell of olives warm and familiar. 'Thanks to the mix you used to sedate White Star, your trusty Security Policeman can now go undercover, worming his way into Hylas's organization and get him bang to rights, as my boss likes to say.'

Then – this made less and less sense. 'Why did you get Leo to invite me to Cressia?'

Her human carriage faltered imperceptibly. Must be the stairs, she thought. Difficult to manoeuvre.

'Well?'

Orbilio blinked. Truth or dare? He pretended that negotiating the door to the cellar was more difficult than it actually was. Should he tell? Dare he tell? The violence of the moment when he knew for sure that his life had restored hers would remain with him for ever. Then, when she clasped her hands round his neck, so close that he inhaled her fear as well as her relief, he feared he would explode.

For the right woman, I would lay down my life.

Truth or dare.

'Don't you know?' A pain like none he had ever known shot through him.

How could she not realize? That the prospect of spending weeks on end tying up his cousin's felonious affairs on the paradise island of Cressia with her four hundred miles away was too bleak to contemplate. There had, whether she admitted it or not, always been this raw energy between them. Who knows how it might have been harnessed if they spent the summer together under the shimmering sky as terns dived among violet-blue coral and a thousand herbs on the hillside wafted out their enticing scents?

Truth or dare?

He looked down at her in his arms as he carried her along the marble portico. At the hair plastered flat to her face. At the gown so wet it looked like paint on her body.

Truth or dare.

He lowered her gently on to the damask counterpane in her bedroom. Felt a rush of tenderness that threatened to choke him.

'The honest answer—' He cleared his throat, flexed his shoulders, spiked his fringe out of his face with his fingers. 'The honest answer, Mistress Seferius, is that I knew you'd want to check out Leo's revolutionary method of training the vines.'

Deftly, he ducked the green, narrow-necked vase that whizzed past his ear, but was too slow for the jug and the bolster.

And Claudia thought, I could get used to paradise.